WORLDS OF EXILE
AND ILLUSION

ursula k. le guin

A TOM DOHERTY
ASSOCIATES BOOK
NEW YORK

TOR ESSENTIALS

worlds of exile and illusion

WORLDS OF EXILE AND ILLUSION

Rocannon's World copyright © 1964, 1994 by Ursula K. Le Guin.
Planet of Exile copyright © 1966, 1994 by Ursula K. Le Guin.
City of Illusions copyright © 1967, 1995 by Ursula K. Le Guin.

Introduction copyright © 2021 by Amal El-Mohtar

A Tor Essentials Book
Published by Tom Doherty Associates
120 Broadway
New York, NY 10271

www.tor-forge.com

Tor® is a registered trademark of Macmillan Publishing Group, LLC.

The Library of Congress has cataloged the Orb edition as follows:

Le Guin, Ursula K., 1929–2018, author.
Worlds of exile and illusion / Ursula K. Le Guin.—First Orb edition.
    p. cm.
"A Tom Doherty Associates book."
ISBN 978-0-312-86211-4 (trade paperback)
1. Science fiction, American.
I. Title.
PS3562.E42 A6 1996
813'.54—dc23
96026194

ISBN 978-1-250-78126-0 (trade paperback)
ISBN 978-0-7653-9766-9 (ebook)

Our books may be purchased in bulk for promotional, educational, or business use. Please contact your local bookseller or the Macmillan Corporate and Premium Sales Department at 1-800-221-7945, extension 5442, or by email at MacmillanSpecialMarkets@macmillan.com.

First Edition: 1996
First Tor Essentials Edition: 2022

Printed in the United States of America

0 9 8 7 6 5 4

CONTENTS

INTRODUCTION

by Amal El-Mohtar

Ursula K. Le Guin's 2004 collection of nonfiction, *The Wave in the Mind,* contains a curious, two-page essay titled "Being Taken for Granite"; punning on "granted," she declares that she isn't granite, she's mud:

> I am not granite and should not be taken for it. . . . Granite does not accept footprints. It refuses them. Granite makes pinnacles, and then people rope themselves together and put pins on their shoes and climb the pinnacles at great trouble, expense, and risk, and maybe they experience a great thrill, but the granite does not. Nothing whatever results and nothing whatever is changed. . . . I have been changed. You change me. Do not take me for granite.[1]

I took Le Guin for granted. When she died in 2018, I could have fit the span of my life inside hers almost three times. She had always been there, like a mountain, or the sun, and it was easy to fall into the certainty that she always would be. I was unfamiliar with her most celebrated works—*The Left Hand of Darkness, The Dispossessed,* books by which she became the first woman to win a Hugo Award for Best Novel, and then, five years later, the first woman to have won it twice. I had assumed, with all the oblivious confidence of youth, that I'd get to read them while she was still with us and talk to her about them. I imagined that I would meet her one day, under ideal conditions that would make me seem interesting enough for conversation, and ask her about poetry, about being a middle-aged woman in the 1970s, and about science fiction. Her passing hit me harder than I expected, considering my slender acquaintance with her work, but that was the thing about Le Guin: to have lost her was to have lost a world I longed to visit.

I came to Le Guin's work both early and late. On the one hand she introduced

---

[1] Ursula K. Le Guin, "Being Taken for Granite," in *The Wave in the Mind: Talks and Essays on the Writer, the Reader, and the Imagination* (Boston: Shambhala Publications, 2004).

me to science fiction literature: I read "The Ones Who Walk Away from Omelas"—Le Guin's famous story about a wonderful city whose existence depends on the torture of a single miserable child—when I was perhaps eight or nine and far too young for it, in a neighbor's ragged old edition of *Literature and the Writing Process*. I remember feeling keenly the difference between "Omelas" and everything else I read in the anthology: the colors brighter, the voice clearer, the ending a quiet explosion in the mind. I would return to "Omelas" every few years and find a different story there, and admire its capacity to unmoor my certainties and launch them in new, questing directions.

On the other hand, I wouldn't read anything else of Le Guin's until about a decade later, and I would read it badly, indifferently. I was introduced to *A Wizard of Earthsea* when I was eighteen, feeling like I was getting away with something by taking a contemporary fantasy literature course for which I could have written the syllabus. But in the late 1990s and early 2000s, wizard schools and Jungian shadows were all the rage, saturating all the comics and novels I was enjoying. In the cacophony of sorting hats and color-coded Houses, *A Wizard of Earthsea* seemed drab, boring—and I mistook as derivative work that was foundational. It would be still further years before I revisited *Earthsea* and found treasure in it.

But shortly after Le Guin's passing I read "The Day Before the Revolution"—a short-story prequel to *The Dispossessed*—and it shattered me. It's the story of an old woman's last day, trembling on the cusp of her life's work bearing fruit while looking back at everything she denied herself to get there. I still can't think of the ending without tearing up: "On ahead, on there, the dry white flowers nodded and whispered in the open fields of evening. Seventy-two years and she had never had time to learn what they were called."[2]

In one sense, I read this too late—too late to write to Le Guin and tell her everything it had made me feel, how much it made me want to live my life by its light. But in another, I felt as if I was at last coming into alignment with Le Guin—that I was reading the right thing of hers at the right time to fall completely in love. It was almost like a meeting: hearing her voice clear and true, speaking through an old woman's mouth and ringing in my heart like a bell.

[2] Ursula K. Le Guin, "The Day Before the Revolution," *Galaxy*, August 1974.

The Books

All roads lead to Le Guin's accomplishments, and whatever age you are, however familiar or unfamiliar with Le Guin you may be, this book is as good a place as any to begin or renew an acquaintance with her work. Collected in this edition are Le Guin's first three published novels: *Rocannon's World*, *Planet of Exile*, and *City of Illusions*. Each one is set on a different planet, and only thin filaments of continuity bind them to one another. The books don't form a trilogy; no circle closes between the first novel and the last, and they can only loosely be called a cycle, or a series. Voices, histories, and themes echo and repeat: the importance of names, the gift of mindspeech, the enormity of the universe and the resilient smallness of human life within it. Animated by the same spirit, these books are variations more than movements, improvisations on an aeolian harp, sounding again and again the importance of names, and journeys, and time.

In "Semley's Necklace"—initially a standalone short story, which now functions as a prologue—a woman seeks a fabled inheritance without knowing what it will ultimately cost her. In *Rocannon's World*, a spacefaring traveler becomes stranded on a Bronze Age planet and struggles to reach an ansible—a technology that will allow him to speak instantly with people light-years away. In *Planet of Exile*, human settlers struggle to adjust to life on a planet that takes sixty Earth years to complete a circuit around its sun. In *City of Illusions*, a man is robbed of his name and his memories, and must begin again from scratch on an Earth that has, like him, been forced to forget its past and forfeit its future.

In each of these, the heroes experience time's relativity in moments of shocking dislocation. Nine years will pass in a single night; winter can last the whole of a man's youth; a voyage through the stars will feel a few years long while over a hundred years pass on the planet left behind. Le Guin observes the nature of lineage and community by this uncanny, implacable light, never forgetting the human scale of a lifetime before obliterating it.

There is a common line that critics sometimes adopt when looking at an author's early writing, appreciating it only insofar as it heralds or presents in miniature later themes and accomplishments, as if the arc of the author's life bends inevitably towards the work you're more likely to have heard of or enjoyed. This baffles me; there is so much in these novels to be dazzled and moved by, so much to admire and marvel at. I'm awed by the stately grace of Le Guin's prose, that feels both spoken from a great height and rumbled up through the earth; the physicality of her writing, the weight and dance of it, sounding a deep, pure love for the human body in a landscape.

"Most of my stories," Le Guin writes in her own introduction to *City of Illusions,* "are excuses for a journey. I never did care much about plots, all I want is to go from A to B—or, more often, from A to A—by the most difficult and circuitous route." She says this somewhat self-deprecatingly, while her work demonstrates the multitudes a journey contains: movement, and friction, and transformation. Two of these novels feature long, difficult walks, punctuated by the rhythm of setting up and breaking down camp, of asking for hospitality and either receiving it or being violently, horribly denied it; one of them features a reversal of those dynamics, the heroes besieged, holding their city against a march of invaders. If there is a slowness here, there is a richness too—a propagation of sound through water, an immersion in the confident, clarion voice of a storyteller.

I read all of Le Guin's introductions to these works in preparation for writing my own, much as one might consult a guidebook before setting out on one's own journey. But guidebooks have a very short shelf life; it isn't long before signposts become curious artifacts themselves, describing in intimate detail a long-vanished restaurant or hotel, or more generally suggesting the shape of a bygone culture's interests and concerns.

Le Guin wrote her introduction to *Rocannon's World* thirteen years after the book's initial release. In it, she regrets what she calls "the promiscuous mixing" of fantasy and science fiction, of putting flying cats and impermasuits in the same story—placing her novel in a conversation about genre that is always exhausting but never exhausted. Reading that introduction almost fifty years after its appearance, I found that what embarrassed her had thrilled me, and couldn't have failed to thrill every generation that found something to love in *Star Wars*'s battling space wizards—who, incidentally, would make their first appearance on cinema screens a single year after Le Guin's introduction was published. What she named "promiscuous mixing" was, to me, generative and delightful originality, proof that genres can and should be bent and twisted into new shapes, new meanings. Each of these books strikes genre conventions together like pieces of flint, and kindles new flame from the sparks that result.

It wasn't all apologia, though; Le Guin also wrote that she could see in *Rocannon's World* "the timidity, and the rashness, and the beginner's luck, of the apprentice demiurge . . . I certainly couldn't write it now, but I can read it; and the thirteen-year distance lets me see, peacefully, what isn't very good in it, and what is. . . . And it has a good shape." Were I equipped with an ansible I would reach across the decades to those words and engage them, say that genre rigidity will soon be as unfashionable as shoulder pads and plucked eyebrows (all the while casting an eye over my shoulder to future readers living at a time when those things will have again come into vogue). But while one needs an ansible to speak to the vanishing past, books are the technology we have to speak to the future, collapsing space and time into the simple honesty of an aging woman's voice, telling the story of her earliest stories.

I'm now the age Le Guin was when she wrote *Rocannon's World,* and I'm perversely glad that I still haven't read her more famous novels. I intend to, of course—but I'm grateful to have now the opportunity of keeping pace with Le Guin's books as she wrote them, to follow the path she blazed without knowing what comes next. To treat her, and her work, not as a mountain to scale or a sun to see by, but as a journey to begin; to take her, not for granite or granted, but as a cheerfully muddy road, fragrant and yielding and winding through the ferny brae, over the hills and far away, beyond the worlds we know and through those we mistakenly think we know well. To have come to her work, not early or late, but in my own time—and to greet you here, fellow traveler, on the cusp of new adventure, whether or not you've passed through this work before, and to say to you, as we set out together:

> *Return with us, return to us,*
> *be always coming home.*[3]

Ottawa, Canada
August 2021

[3] Ursula K. Le Guin, "Initiation Song from the Finders' Lodge," in *Always Coming Home* (New York: Harper and Row, 1985).

This book is gratefully dedicated
to the memory of Cele Lalli,
Don Wollheim, and Terry Carr.

rocannon's world

PROLOGUE
The Necklace

How can you tell the legend from the fact on these worlds that lie so many years away?—planets without names, called by their people simply The World, planets without history, where the past is the matter of myth, and a returning explorer finds his own doings of a few years back have become the gestures of a god. Unreason darkens that gap of time bridged by our lightspeed ships, and in the darkness uncertainty and disproportion grow like weeds.

In trying to tell the story of a man, an ordinary League scientist, who went to such a nameless half-known world not many years ago, one feels like an archeologist amid millennial ruins, now struggling through choked tangles of leaf, flower, branch and vine to the sudden bright geometry of a wheel or a polished cornerstone, and now entering some commonplace, sunlit doorway to find inside it the darkness, the impossible flicker of a flame, the glitter of a jewel, the half-glimpsed movement of a woman's arm.

How can you tell fact from legend, truth from truth?

Through Rocannon's story the jewel, the blue glitter seen briefly, returns. With it let us begin, here:

Galactic Area 8, No. 62: FOMALHAUT II.
High-Intelligence Life Forms: Species Contacted:

Species I.
   A) Gdemiar (singular Gdem): Highly intelligent, fully hominoid noc-turnal troglodytes, 120–135 cm. in height, light skin, dark head-hair. When contacted these cave-dwellers possessed a rigidly stratified oligarchic ur-ban society modified by partial colonial telepathy, and a technologically oriented Early Steel culture. Technology enhanced to Industrial, Point C, during League Mission of 252–254. In 254 an Automatic Drive ship (to-from New South Georgia) was presented to oligarchs of the Kiriensea Area community. Status C-Prime.

B) Fiia (singular Fian): Highly intelligent, fully hominoid, diurnal, av. ca. 130 cm. in height, observed individuals generally light in skin and hair. Brief contacts indicated village and nomadic communal societies, partial colonial telepathy, also some indication of short-range TK. The race appears a-technological and evasive, with minimal and fluid culture-patterns. Currently untaxable. Status E-Query.

Species II.

Liuar (singular Liu): Highly intelligent, fully hominoid, diurnal, av. height above 170 cm., this species possesses a fortress/village, clan-descent society, a blocked technology (Bronze), and feudal-heroic culture. Note horizontal social cleavage into 2 pseudo-races: (a: Olgyior, "midmen," light-skinned and dark-haired; (b: Angyar, "lords," very tall, dark-skinned, yellow-haired—

"That's her," said Rocannon, looking up from the *Abridged Handy Pocket Guide to Intelligent Life-forms* at the very tall, dark-skinned, yellow-haired woman who stood halfway down the long museum hall. She stood still and erect, crowned with bright hair, gazing at something in a display case. Around her fidgeted four uneasy and unattractive dwarves.

"I didn't know Fomalhaut II had all those people besides the trogs," said Ketho, the curator.

"I didn't either. There are even some 'Unconfirmed' species listed here, that they never contacted. Sounds like time for a more thorough survey mission to the place. Well, now at least we know what she is."

"I wish there were some way of knowing *who* she is. . . ."

She was of an ancient family, a descendant of the first kings of the Angyar, and for all her poverty her hair shone with the pure, steadfast gold of her inheritance. The little people, the Fiia, bowed when she passed them, even when she was a barefoot child running in the fields, the light and fiery comet of her hair brightening the troubled winds of Kirien.

She was still very young when Durhal of Hallan saw her, courted her, and carried her away from the ruined towers and windy halls of her childhood to his own high home. In Hallan on the mountainside there was no comfort either, though splendor endured. The windows were unglassed, the stone floors bare; in coldyear one might wake to see the night's snow in long, low drifts beneath each window. Durhal's bride stood with narrow bare feet on the snowy floor, braiding up the fire of her hair and laughing at her young husband in the silver mirror that hung in their room. That mirror, and his mother's bridal-gown sewn with a thousand tiny crystals, were all his wealth. Some of his lesser kinfolk of Hallan still possessed wardrobes of brocaded clothing, furniture of gilded wood, silver harness for their steeds, armor and silver-mounted swords, jewels and jewelry—and on these last Durhal's bride looked enviously, glancing back at a gemmed coronet or a golden brooch even when the wearer of the ornament stood aside to let her pass, deferent to her birth and marriage-rank.

Fourth from the High Seat of Hallan Revel sat Durhal and his bride Semley, so close to Hallanlord that the old man often poured wine for Semley with his own hand, and spoke of hunting with his nephew and heir Durhal, looking on the young pair with a grim, unhopeful love. Hope came hard to the Angyar of Hallan and all the Western Lands, since the Starlords had appeared with their houses that leaped about on pillars of fire and their awful weapons that could level hills. They had interfered with all the old ways and wars, and though the sums were small there was terrible shame to the Angyar in having to pay a tax to them, a tribute for the Starlords' war that was to be fought with some strange enemy, somewhere in the hollow places between the stars, at the end of years. "It will be your war too," they said, but for a generation now the Angyar had sat in idle shame in their revelhalls, watching their double swords rust, their sons grow up without ever striking a blow in battle, their daughters marry poor men, even midmen, having no dowry of heroic loot to bring a noble husband. Hallanlord's face was bleak when he watched the fair-haired couple and heard their laughter as they drank bitter wine and joked together in the cold, ruinous, resplendent fortress of their race.

Semley's own face hardened when she looked down the hall and saw, in seats far below hers, even down among the halfbreeds and the midmen, against white skins and black hair, the gleam and flash of precious stones. She herself had brought nothing in dowry to her husband, not even a silver hairpin. The dress of a thousand crystals she had put away in a chest for the wedding-day of her daughter, if daughter it was to be.

It was, and they called her Haldre, and when the fuzz on her little brown skull grew longer it shone with steadfast gold, the inheritance of the lordly generations, the only gold she would ever possess. . . .

Semley did not speak to her husband of her discontent. For all his gentleness to her, Durhal in his hard lordly pride had only contempt for envy, for vain wishing, and she dreaded his contempt. But she spoke to Durhal's sister Durossa.

"My family had a great treasure once," she said. "It was a necklace all of gold, with the blue jewel set in the center—sapphire?"

Durossa shook her head, smiling, not sure of the name either. It was late in warmyear, as these Northern Angyar called the summer of the eight-hundred-day year, beginning the cycle of months anew at each equinox; to Semley it seemed an outlandish calendar, a midmannish reckoning. Her family was at an end, but it had been older and purer than the race of any of these northwestern marchlanders, who mixed too freely with the Olgyior. She sat with Durossa in the sunlight on a stone windowseat high up in the Great Tower, where the older woman's apartment was. Widowed young, childless, Durossa had been given in second marriage to Hallanlord, who was her father's brother. Since it was a kinmarriage and a second marriage on both sides she had not taken the title of Hallanlady, which Semley would some day bear; but she sat with the old lord in the High Seat and ruled with him his domains. Older than her brother Durhal, she was fond of his young wife, and delighted in the bright-haired baby Haldre.

"It was bought," Semley went on, "with all the money my forebear Leynen got when he conquered the Southern Fiefs—all the money from a whole king-dom, think of it, for one jewel! Oh, it would outshine anything here in Hal-lan, surely, even those crystals like koob-eggs your cousin Issar wears. It was so beautiful they gave it a name of its own; they called it the Eye of the Sea. My great-grandmother wore it."

"You never saw it?" the older woman asked lazily, gazing down at the green mountainslopes where long, long summer sent its hot and restless winds straying among the forests and whirling down white roads to the seacoast far away.

"It was lost before I was born."

"The Starlords took it for tribute?"

"No, my father said it was stolen before the Starlords ever came to our realm. He wouldn't talk of it, but there was an old midwoman full of tales who always told me the Fiia would know where it was."

"Ah, the Fiia I should like to see!" said Durossa. "They're in so many songs and tales; why do they never come to the Western Lands?"

"Too high, too cold in winter, I think. They like the sunlight of the valleys of the south."

"Are they like the Clayfolk?"

"Those I've never seen; they keep away from us in the south. Aren't they white like midmen, and misformed? The Fiia are fair; they look like children, only thinner, and wiser. Oh, I wonder if they know where the necklace is, who stole it and where he hid it! Think, Durossa—if I could come into Hallan Revel and sit down by my husband with the wealth of a kingdom round my neck, and outshine the other women as he outshines all men!"

Durossa bent her head above the baby, who sat studying her own brown toes on a fur rug between her mother and aunt. "Semley is foolish," she murmured to the baby. "Semley who shines like a falling star, Semley whose husband loves no gold but the gold of her hair. . . ."

And Semley, looking out over the green slopes of summer toward the distant sea, was silent.

But when another coldyear had passed, and the Starlords had come again to collect their taxes for the war against the world's end—this time using a couple of dwarvish Clayfolk as interpreters, and so leaving all the Angyar humiliated to the point of rebellion—and another warmyear too was gone, and Haldre had grown into a lovely, chattering child, Semley brought her one morning to Durossa's sunlit room in the tower. Semley wore an old cloak of blue, and the hood covered her hair.

"Keep Haldre for me these few days, Durossa," she said, quick and calm. "I'm going south to Kirien."

"To see your father?"

"To find my inheritance. Your cousins of Harget Fief have been taunting Durhal. Even that halfbreed Parna can torment him, because Parna's wife has a satin coverlet for her bed, and a diamond earring, and three gowns, the dough-faced black-haired trollop! while Durhal's wife must patch her gown—"

"Is Durhal's pride in his wife, or what she wears?"

But Semley was not to be moved. "The Lords of Hallan are becoming poor men in their own hall. I am going to bring my dowry to my lord, as one of my lineage should."

"Semley! Does Durhal know you're going?"

"My return will be a happy one—that much let him know," said young Semley, breaking for a moment into her joyful laugh; then she bent to kiss her daughter, turned and before Durossa could speak, was gone like a quick wind over the floors of sunlit stone.

Married women of the Angyar never rode for sport, and Semley had not been from Hallan since her marriage; so now, mounting the high saddle of a windsteed, she felt like a girl again, like the wild maiden she had been, riding half-broken steeds on the north wind over the fields of Kirien. The beast that bore her now down from the hills of Hallan was of finer breed, striped coat fitting sleek over hollow, buoyant bones, green eyes slitted against the wind, light and mighty wings sweeping up and down to either side of Semley, revealing and hiding, revealing and hiding the clouds above her and the hills below.

On the third morning she came to Kirien and stood again in the ruined courts. Her father had been drinking all night, and, just as in the old days, the morning sunlight poking through his fallen ceilings annoyed him, and the sight of his daughter only increased his annoyance. "What are you back for?" he growled, his swollen eyes glancing at her and away. The fiery hair of his youth was quenched, gray strands tangled on his skull. "Did the young Halla not marry you, and you've come sneaking home?"

"I am Durhal's wife. I came to get my dowry, father."

The drunkard growled in disgust; but she laughed at him so gently that he had to look at her again, wincing.

"Is it true, father, that the Fiia stole the necklace Eye of the Sea?"

"How do I know? Old tales. The thing was lost before I was born, I think. I wish I never had been. Ask the Fiia if you want to know. Go to them, go back to your husband. Leave me alone here. There's no room at Kirien for girls and gold and all the rest of the story. The story's over here; this is the fallen place, this is the empty hall. The sons of Leynen all are dead, their treasures are all lost. Go on your way, girl."

Gray and swollen as the web-spinner of ruined houses, he turned and went blundering toward the cellars where he hid from daylight.

Leading the striped windsteed of Hallan, Semley left her old home and walked down the steep hill, past the village of the midmen, who greeted her with sullen respect, on over fields and pastures where the great, wing-clipped, half-wild herilor grazed, to a valley that was green as a painted bowl and full to the brim with sunlight. In the deep of the valley lay the village of the Fiia, and as she descended leading her steed the little, slight people ran up toward her from their huts and gardens, laughing, calling out in faint, thin voices.

"Hail Halla's bride, Kirienlady, Windborne, Semley the Fair!"

They gave her lovely names and she liked to hear them, minding not at all their laughter, for they laughed at all they said. That was her own way, to speak and laugh. She stood tall in her long blue cloak among their swirling welcome.

"Hail Lightfolk, Sundwellers, Fiia friends of men!"

They took her down into the village and brought her into one of their airy houses, the tiny children chasing along behind. There was no telling the age of a Fian once he was grown; it was hard even to tell one from another and be sure, as they moved about quick as moths around a candle, that she spoke always to the same one. But it seemed that one of them talked with her for a while, as the others fed and petted her steed, and brought water for her to drink, and bowls of fruit from their gardens of little trees. "It was never the Fiia that stole the necklace of the Lords of Kirien!" cried the little man. "What would the Fiia do with gold, Lady? For us there is sunlight in warmyear, and in coldyear the remembrance of sunlight; the yellow fruit, the yellow leaves in end-season, the yellow hair of our lady of Kirien; no other gold."

"Then it was some midman stole the thing?"

Laughter rang long and faint about her. "How would a midman dare? O Lady of Kirien, how the great jewel was stolen no mortal knows, not man nor midman nor Fian nor any among the Seven Folk. Only dead minds know how it was lost, long ago when Kireley the Proud whose great-granddaughter is Semley walked alone by the caves of the sea. But it may be found perhaps among the Sunhaters."

"The Clayfolk?"

A louder burst of laughter, nervous.

"Sit with us, Semley, sunhaired, returned to us from the north." She sat with them to eat, and they were as pleased with her graciousness as she with theirs. But when they heard her repeat that she would go to the Clayfolk to find her inheritance, if it was there, they began not to laugh; and little by little there were fewer of them around her. She was alone at last with perhaps the one she had spoken with before the meal. "Do not go among the Clayfolk, Semley," he said, and for a moment her heart failed her. The Fian, drawing his hand down slowly over his eyes, had darkened all the air about them. Fruit lay ash-white on the plate; all the bowls of clear water were empty.

"In the mountains of the far land the Fiia and the Gdemiar parted. Long ago we parted," said the slight, still man of the Fiia. "Longer ago we were one. What we are not, they are. What we are, they are not. Think of the sunlight and the grass and the trees that bear fruit, Semley; think that not all roads that lead down lead up as well."

"Mine leads neither down nor up, kind host, but only straight on to my inheritance. I will go to it where it is, and return with it."

The Fian bowed, laughing a little.

Outside the village she mounted her striped windsteed, and, calling farewell in answer to their calling, rose up into the wind of afternoon and flew southwestward toward the caves down by the rocky shores of Kiriensea.

She feared she might have to walk far into those tunnel-caves to find the people she sought, for it was said the Clayfolk never came out of their caves into the light of the sun, and feared even the Greatstar and the moons. It was a long ride; she landed once to let her steed hunt tree-rats while she ate a little bread from her saddle-bag. The bread was hard and dry by now and tasted of leather, yet kept a faint savor of its making, so that for a moment, eating it alone in a glade of the southern forests, she heard the quiet tone of a voice and saw Durhal's face turned to her in the light of the candles of Hallan. For a while she sat daydreaming of that stern and vivid young face, and of what she would say to him when she came home with a kingdom's ransom around her neck: "I wanted a gift worthy of my husband, Lord . . ." Then she pressed on, but when she reached the coast the sun had set, with the Greatstar sinking behind it. A mean wind had come up from the west, starting and gusting and veering, and her windsteed was weary fighting it. She let him glide down on the sand. At once he folded his wings and curled his thick, light limbs under him with a thrum of purring. Semley stood holding her cloak close at her throat, stroking the steed's neck so that he flicked his ears and purred again. The warm fur comforted her hand, but all that met her eyes was gray sky full of smears of cloud, gray sea, dark sand. And then running over the sand a low, dark creature—another—a group of them, squatting and running and stopping.

She called aloud to them. Though they had not seemed to see her, now in a moment they were all around her. They kept a distance from her windsteed; he had stopped purring, and his fur rose a little under Semley's hand. She took up the reins, glad of his protection but afraid of the nervous ferocity he might display. The strange folk stood silent, staring, their thick bare feet planted in the sand. There was no mistaking them: they were the height of the Fiia and in all else a shadow, a black image of those laughing people. Naked, squat, stiff, with lank black hair and gray-white skins, dampish looking like the skins of grubs; eyes like rocks.

"You are the Clayfolk?"

"Gdemiar are we, people of the Lords of the Realms of Night." The voice was unexpectedly loud and deep, and rang out pompous through the salt, blowing dusk; but, as with the Fiia, Semley was not sure which one had spoken.

"I greet you, Nightlords. I am Semley of Kirien, Durhal's wife of Hallan. I come to you seeking my inheritance, the necklace called Eye of the Sea, lost long ago."

"Why do you seek it here, Angya? Here is only sand and salt and night."

"Because lost things are known of in deep places," said Semley, quite ready for a play of wits, "and gold that came from earth has a way of going back to the earth. And sometimes the made, they say, returns to the maker." This last was a guess; it hit the mark.

"It is true the necklace Eye of the Sea is known to us by name. It was made in our caves long ago, and sold by us to the Angyar. And the blue stone came from the Clayfields of our kin to the east. But these are very old tales, Angya."

"May I listen to them in the places where they are told?"

The squat people were silent a while, as if in doubt. The gray wind blew by over the sand, darkening as the Greatstar set; the sound of the sea loudened and lessened. The deep voice spoke again: "Yes, lady of the Angyar. You may enter the Deep Halls. Come with us now." There was a changed note in his voice, wheedling. Semley would not hear it. She followed the Claymen over the sand, leading on a short rein her sharp-taloned steed.

At the cave-mouth, a toothless, yawning mouth from which a stinking warmth sighed out, one of the Claymen said, "The air-beast cannot come in."

"Yes," said Semley.

"No," said the squat people.

"Yes, I will not leave him here. He is not mine to leave. He will not harm you, so long as I hold his reins."

"No," deep voices repeated; but others broke in, "As you will," and after a moment of hesitation they went on. The cave-mouth seemed to snap shut behind them, so dark was it under the stone. They went in single file, Semley last.

The darkness of the tunnel lightened, and they came under a ball of weak white fire hanging from the roof. Farther on was another, and another; between them long black worms hung in festoons from the rock. As they went on these fire-globes were set closer, so that all the tunnel was lit with a bright, cold light.

Semley's guides stopped at a parting of three tunnels, all blocked by doors that looked to be of iron. "We shall wait, Angya," they said, and eight of them stayed with her, while three others unlocked one of the doors and passed through. It fell to behind them with a clash.

Straight and still stood the daughter of the Angyar in the white, blank light of the lamps; her windsteed crouched beside her, flicking the tip of his striped tail, his great folded wings stirring again and again with the checked impulse to fly. In the tunnel behind Semley the eight Claymen squatted on their hams, muttering to one another in their deep voices, in their own tongue.

The central door swung clanging open. "Let the Angya enter the Realm of Night!" cried a new voice, booming and boastful. A Clayman who wore some clothing on his thick gray body stood in the doorway beckoning to her. "Enter and behold the wonders of our lands, the marvels made by hands, the works of the Nightlords!"

Silent, with a tug at her steed's reins, Semley bowed her head and followed him under the low doorway made for dwarfish folk. Another glaring tunnel stretched ahead, dank walls dazzling in the white light, but, instead of a way to walk upon, its floor carried two bars of polished iron stretching off side as far as she could see. On the bars rested some kind of cart with metal wheels. Obeying her new guide's gestures, with no hesitation and no trace of wonder on her face, Semley stepped into the cart and made the wind-steed crouch beside her. The Clayman got in and sat down in front of her, moving bars and wheels about. A loud grinding noise arose, and a screaming of metal on metal, and then the walls of the tunnel began to jerk by. Faster and faster the walls slid past, till the fire-globes overhead ran into a blur, and the stale warm air became a foul wind blowing the hood back off her hair.

The cart stopped. Semley followed the guide up basalt steps into a vast anteroom and then a still vaster hall, carved by ancient waters or by the burrowing Clayfolk out of the rock, its darkness that had never known sunlight lit with the uncanny cold brilliance of the globes. In grilles cut in the walls huge blades turned and turned, changing the stale air. The great closed space hummed and boomed with noise, the loud voices of the Clayfolk, the grinding and shrill buzzing and vibration of turning blades and wheels, the echoes and re-echoes of all this from the rock. Here all the stumpy figures of the Claymen were clothed in garments imitating those of the Starlords—divided trousers, soft boots, and hooded tunics—though the few women to be seen, hurrying servile dwarves, were naked. Of the males many were soldiers, bearing at their sides weapons shaped like the terrible light-throwers of the Starlords, though even Semley could see these were merely shaped iron clubs. What she saw, she saw without looking. She followed where she was led, turning her head neither to left nor right. When she came before a group of Claymen who wore iron circlets on their black hair her guide halted, bowed, boomed out, "The High Lords of the Gdemiar!"

There were seven of them, and all looked up at her with such arrogance on their lumpy gray faces that she wanted to laugh.

"I come among you seeking the lost treasure of my family, O Lords of the Dark Realm," she said gravely to them. "I seek Leynen's prize, the Eye of the Sea." Her voice was faint in the racket of the huge vault.

"So said our messengers, Lady Semley." This time she could pick out the one who spoke, one even shorter than the others, hardly reaching Semley's breast, with a white, powerful, fierce face. "We do not have this thing you seek."

"Once you had it, it is said."

"Much is said, up there where the sun blinks."

"And words are borne off by the winds, where there are winds to blow. I do not ask how the necklace was lost to us and returned to you, its makers of old. Those are old tales, old grudges. I only seek to find it now. You do not have it now; but it may be you know where it is."

"It is not here."

"Then it is elsewhere."

"It is where you cannot come to it. Never, unless we help you."

"Then help me. I ask this as your guest."

"It is said, *The Angyar take; the Fiia give; the Gdemiar give and take.* If we do this for you, what will you give us?"

"My thanks, Nightlord."

She stood tall and bright among them, smiling. They all stared at her with a heavy, grudging wonder, a sullen yearning.

"Listen, Angya, this is a great favor you ask of us. You do not know how great a favor. You cannot understand. You are of a race that will not understand, that cares for nothing but windriding and crop-raising and sword-fighting and shouting together. But who made your swords of the right steel? We, the Gdemiar! Your lords come to us here and in Clayfields and buy their swords and go away, not looking, not understanding. But you are here now, you will look, you can see a few of our endless marvels, the lights that burn forever, the car that pulls itself, the machines that make our clothes and cook our food and sweeten our air and serve us in all things. Know that all these things are beyond your understanding. And know this: we, the Gdemiar, are the friends of those you call the Starlords! We came with them to Hallan, to Reohan, to Hul-Orren, to all your castles, to help them speak to you. The lords to whom you, the proud Angyar, pay tribute, are our friends. They do us favors as we do them favors! Now, what do your thanks mean to us?"

"That is your question to answer," said Semley, "not mine. I have asked my question. Answer it, Lord."

For a while the seven conferred together, by word and silence. They would glance at her and look away, and mutter and be still. A crowd grew around them, drawn slowly and silently, one after another till Semley was encircled by hundreds of the matted black heads, and all the great booming cavern floor was covered with people, except a little space directly around her. Her wind-steed was quivering with fear and irritation too long controlled, and his eyes had gone very wide and pale, like the eyes of a steed forced to fly at night. She stroked the warm fur of his head, whispering, "Quietly now, brave one, bright one, windlord. . . ."

"Angya, we will take you to the place where the treasure lies." The Clayman with the white face and iron crown had turned to her once more. "More than that we cannot do. You must come with us to claim the necklace where it lies, from those who keep it. The air-beast cannot come with you. You must come alone."

"How far a journey, Lord?"

His lips drew back and back. "A very far journey, Lady. Yet it will last only one long night."

"I thank you for your courtesy. Will my steed be well cared for this night? No ill must come to him."

"He will sleep till you return. A greater windsteed you will have ridden, when you see that beast again! Will you not ask where we take you?"

"Can we go soon on this journey? I would not stay long away from my home."

"Yes. Soon." Again the gray lips widened as he stared up into her face.

What was done in those next hours Semley could not have retold; it was all haste, jumble, noise, strangeness. While she held her steed's head a Clay-man stuck a long needle into the golden-striped haunch. She nearly cried out at the sight, but her steed merely twitched and then, purring, fell asleep. He was carried off by a group of Clayfolk who clearly had to summon up their courage to touch his warm fur. Later on she had to see a needle driven into her own arm—perhaps to test her courage, she thought, for it did not seem to make her sleep; though she was not quite sure. There were times she had to travel in the rail-carts, passing iron doors and vaulted caverns by the hundred and hundred; once the rail-cart ran through a cavern that stretched off on either hand measureless into the dark, and all that darkness was full of great flocks of herilor. She could hear their cooing, husky calls, and glimpse the flocks in the front-lights of the cart; then she saw some more clearly in the white light, and saw that they were all wingless, and all blind. At that she shut her eyes. But there were more tunnels to go through, and always more caverns, more gray lumpy bodies and fierce faces and booming boasting voices, until at last they led her suddenly out into the open air. It was full night; she raised her eyes joyfully to the stars and the single moon shining, little Heliki brightening in the west. But the Clayfolk were all about her still, making her climb now into some new kind of cart or cave, she did not know which. It was small, full of little blinking lights like rushlights, very narrow and shining after the great dank caverns and the starlit night. Now another needle was stuck in her, and they told her she would have to be tied down in a sort of flat chair, tied down head and hand and foot.

"I will not," said Semley.

But when she saw that the four Claymen who were to be her guides let themselves be tied down first, she submitted. The others left. There was a roaring sound, and a long silence; a great weight that could not be seen pressed upon her. Then there was no weight; no sound; nothing at all.

"Am I dead?" asked Semley.

"Oh no, Lady," said a voice she did not like.

Opening her eyes, she saw the white face bent over her, the wide lips pulled back, the eyes like little stones. Her bonds had fallen away from her, and she leaped up. She was weightless, bodiless; she felt herself only a gust of terror on the wind.

"We will not hurt you," said the sullen voice or voices. "Only let us touch you, Lady. We would like to touch your hair. Let us touch your hair. . . ."

The round cart they were in trembled a little. Outside its one window lay blank night, or was it mist, or nothing at all? One long night, they had said. Very long. She sat motionless and endured the touch of their heavy gray hands on her hair. Later they would touch her hands and feet and arms, and one her throat: at that she set her teeth and stood up, and they drew back.

"We have not hurt you, Lady," they said. She shook her head.

When they bade her, she lay down again in the chair that bound her down; and when light flashed golden, at the window, she would have wept at the sight, but fainted first.

"Well," said Rocannon, "now at least we know what she is."

"I wish there were some way of knowing *who* she is," the curator mumbled. "She wants something we've got here in the Museum, is that what the trogs say?"

"Now, don't call 'em trogs," Rocannon said conscientiously; as a hilfer, an ethnologist of the High-Intelligence Life Forms, he was supposed to resist such words. "They're not pretty, but they're Status C Allies . . . I wonder why the Commission picked them to develop? Before even contacting all the HILF species? I'll bet the survey was from Centaurus—Centaurans always like nocturnals and cave-dwellers. I'd have backed Species II, here, I think."

"The troglodytes seem to be rather in awe of her."

"Aren't you?"

Ketho glanced at the tall woman again, then reddened and laughed. "Well, in a way. I never saw such a beautiful alien type in eighteen years here on New South Georgia. I never saw such a beautiful woman anywhere, in fact. She looks like a goddess." The red now reached the top of his bald head, for Ketho was a shy curator, not given to hyperbole. But Rocannon nodded soberly, agreeing.

"I wish we could talk to her without those tr—Gdemiar as interpreters. But there's no help for it." Rocannon went toward their visitor, and when she turned her splendid face to him he bowed down very deeply, going right down to the floor on one knee, his head bowed and his eyes shut. This was what he called his All-purpose Intercultural Curtsey, and he performed if with some grace. When he came erect again the beautiful woman smiled and spoke.

"She say, Hail, Lord of Stars," growled one of her squat escorts in Pidgin-Galactic.

"Hail, Lady of the Angyar," Rocannon replied. "In what way can we of the Museum serve the lady?"

Across the troglodytes' growling her voice ran like a brief silver wind.

"She say, Please give her necklace which treasure her blood-kin-forebears long long."

"Which necklace?" he asked, and understanding him, she pointed to the central display of the case before them, a magnificent thing, a chain of yellow gold, massive but very delicate in workmanship, set with one big hot-blue sapphire. Rocannon's eyebrows went up, and Ketho at his shoulder murmured, "She's got good taste. That's the Fomalhaut Necklace—famous bit of work."

She smiled at the two men, and again spoke to them over the heads of the troglodytes.

"She say, O Starlords, Elder and Younger Dwellers in House of Treasures, this treasure her one. Long long time. Thank you."

"How did we get the thing, Ketho?"

"Wait; let me look it up in the catalogue. I've got it here. Here. It came from these trogs—trolls—whatever they are: Gdemiar. They have a bargain-obsession, it says; we had to let 'em buy the ship they came here on, an AD-4. This was part payment. It's their own handiwork."

"And I'll bet they can't do this kind of work anymore, since they've been steered to Industrial."

"But they seem to feel the thing is hers, not theirs or ours. It must be important, Rocannon, or they wouldn't have given up this time-span to her errand. Why, the objective lapse between here and Fomalhaut must be considerable!"

"Several years, no doubt," said the hilfer, who was used to star-jumping. "Not very far. Well, neither the *Handbook* nor the *Guide* gives me enough data to base a decent guess on. These species obviously haven't been properly studied at all. The little fellows may be showing her simple courtesy. Or an interspecies war may depend on this damn sapphire. Perhaps her desire rules them, because they consider themselves totally inferior to her. Or despite appearances she may be their prisoner, their decoy. How can we tell? . . . Can you give the thing away, Ketho?"

"Oh yes. All the Exotica are technically on loan, not our property, since these claims come up now and then. We seldom argue. Peace above all, until the War comes. . . ."

"Then I'd say give it to her."

Ketho smiled. "It's a privilege," he said. Unlocking the case, he lifted out the great golden chain; then, in his shyness, he held it out to Rocannon, saying, "You give it to her."

So the blue jewel first lay, for a moment, in Rocannon's hand.

His mind was not on it; he turned straight to the beautiful, alien woman, with his handful of blue fire and gold. She did not raise her hands to take it, but bent her head, and he slipped the necklace over her hair. It lay like a burning fuse along her golden-brown throat. She looked up from it with such pride, delight, and gratitude in her face that Rocannon stood wordless, and the little curator murmured hurriedly in his own language, "You're welcome, you're very welcome." She bowed her golden head to him and to Rocannon. Then, turning, she nodded to her squat guards—or captors?—and, drawing her worn blue cloak about her, paced down the long hall and was gone. Ketho and Rocannon stood looking after her.

"What I feel . . ." Rocannon began.

"Well?" Ketho inquired hoarsely, after a long pause.

"What I feel sometimes is that I . . . meeting these people from worlds we know so little of, you know, sometimes . . . that I have as it were blundered through the corner of a legend, of a tragic myth, maybe, which I do not understand. . . ."

"Yes," said the curator, clearing his throat. "I wonder . . . I wonder what her name is."

Semley the Fair, Semley the Golden, Semley of the Necklace. The Clayfolk had bent to her will, and so had even the Starlords in that terrible place where the Clayfolk had taken her, the city at the end of the night. They had bowed to her, and given her gladly her treasure from amongst their own.

But she could not yet shake off the feeling of those caverns about her where rock lowered overhead, where you could not tell who spoke or what they did, where voices boomed and gray hands reached out—Enough of that. She had paid for the necklace; very well. Now it was hers. The price was paid, the past was the past.

Her windsteed had crept out of some kind of box, with his eyes filmy and his fur rimed with ice, and at first when they had left the caves of the Gdemiar he would not fly. Now he seemed all right again, riding a smooth south wind through the bright sky toward Hallan. "Go quick, go quick," she told him, beginning to laugh as the wind cleared away her mind's darkness. "I want to see Durhal soon, soon. . . ."

And swiftly they flew, coming to Hallan by dusk of the second day. Now the caves of the Clayfolk seemed no more than last year's nightmare, as the steed swooped with her up the thousand steps of Hallan and across the Chasmbridge where the forests fell away for a thousand feet. In the gold light of evening in the flightcourt she dismounted and walked up the last steps between the stiff carven figures of heroes and the two gatewards, who bowed to her, staring at the beautiful, fiery thing around her neck.

In the Forehall she stopped a passing girl, a very pretty girl, by her looks one of Durhal's close kin, though Semley could not call to mind her name. "Do you know me, maiden? I am Semley Durhal's wife. Will you go tell the Lady Durossa that I have come back?"

For she was afraid to go on in and perhaps face Durhal at once, alone; she wanted Durossa's support.

The girl was gazing at her, her face very strange. But she murmured, "Yes, Lady," and darted off toward the Tower.

Semley stood waiting in the gilt, ruinous hall. No one came by; were they all at table in the Revelhall? The silence was uneasy. After a minute Semley started toward the stairs to the Tower. But an old woman was coming to her across the stone floor, holding her arms out, weeping.

"Oh Semley, Semley!"

She had never seen the gray-haired woman, and shrank back.

"But Lady, who are you?"

"I am Durossa, Semley."

She was quiet and still, all the time that Durossa embraced her and wept, and asked if it were true the Clayfolk had captured her and kept her under a spell all these long years, or had it been the Fiia with their strange arts? Then, drawing back a little, Durossa ceased to weep.

"You're still young, Semley. Young as the day you left here. And you wear round your neck the necklace. . . ."

"I have brought my gift to my husband Durhal. Where is he?"

"Durhal is dead."

Semley stood unmoving.

"Your husband, my brother, Durhal Hallanlord was killed seven years ago in battle. Nine years you had been gone. The Starlords came no more. We fell to warring with the Eastern Halls, with the Angyar of Log and Hul-Orren. Durhal, fighting, was killed by a midman's spear, for he had little armor for his body, and none at all for his spirit. He lies buried in the fields above Orren Marsh."

Semley turned away. "I will go to him, then," she said, putting her hand on the gold chain that weighed down her neck. "I will give him my gift."

"Wait, Semley! Durhal's daughter, your daughter, see her now, Haldre the Beautiful!"

It was the girl she had first spoken to and sent to Durossa, a girl of nineteen or so, with eyes like Durhal's eyes, dark blue. She stood beside Durossa, gazing with those steady eyes at this woman Semley who was her mother and was her own age. Their age was the same, and their gold hair, and their beauty. Only Semley was a little taller, and wore the blue stone on her breast.

"Take it, take it. It was for Durhal and Haldre that I brought it from the end of the long night!" Semley cried this aloud, twisting and bowing her head to get the heavy chain off, dropping the necklace so it fell on the stones with a cold, liquid clash. "O take it, Haldre!" she cried again, and then, weeping aloud, turned and ran from Hallan, over the bridge and down the long, broad steps, and, darting off eastward into the forest of the mountainside like some wild thing escaping, was gone.

PART ONE

The Starlord

I

So ends the first part of the legend; and all of it is true. Now for some facts, which are equally true, from the League *Handbook for Galactic Area Eight*.

Number 62: FOMALHAUT II.

Type AE—Carbon Life. An iron-core planet, diameter 6600 miles, with heavy oxygen-rich atmosphere. Revolution: 800 Earthdays 8 hrs. 11 min. 42 sec. Rotation: 29 hrs. 51 min. 02 sec. Mean distance from sun 3.2 AU, orbital eccentricity slight. Obliquity of ecliptic 27° 20' 20" causing marked seasonal change. Gravity .86 Standard.

Four major landmasses, Northwest, Southwest, East and Antarctic Continents, occupy 38% of planetary surface.

Four satellites (types Perner, Loklik, R-2 and Phobos). The Companion of Fomalhaut is visible as a superbright star.

Nearest League World: New South Georgia, capital Kerguelen (7.88 lt. yrs.).

History: The planet was charted by the Elieson Expedition in 202, robot-probed in 218.

First Geographical Survey, 235-6. Director: J. Kiolaf. The major land-masses were surveyed by air (see maps 3114-a, b, c, 3115-a, b). Landings, geological and biological studies and HILF contacts were made only on East and Northwest Continents (see description of intelligent species below).

Technological Enhancement Mission to Species I-A, 252-4. Director: J. Kiolaf (Northwest Continent only).

Control and Taxation Missions to Species I-A and II were carried out under auspices of the Area Foundation in Kerguelen, N.S.Ga., in 254, 258, 262, 266, 270; in 275 the planet was placed under Interdict by the Allworld HILF Authority, pending more adequate study of its intelligent species.

First Ethnographic Survey, 321. Director: G. Rocannon.

A high tree of blinding white grew quickly, soundlessly up the sky from behind South Ridge. Guards on the towers of Hallan Castle cried out, striking bronze on bronze. Their small voices and clangor of warning were swallowed by the roar of sound, the hammerstroke of wind, the staggering of the forest.

Mogien of Hallan met his guest the Starlord on the run, heading for the flightcourt of the castle. "Was your ship behind South Ridge, Starlord?"

Very white in the face, but quiet-voiced as usual, the other said, "It was."

"Come with me." Mogien took his guest on the postillion saddle of the windsteed that waited ready saddled in the flightcourt. Down the thousand steps, across the Chasmbridge, off over the sloping forests of the domain of Hallan the steed flew like a gray leaf on the wind.

As it crossed over South Ridge the riders saw smoke rise blue through the level gold lances of the first sunlight. A forest fire was fizzling out among damp, cool thickets in the streambed of the mountainside.

Suddenly beneath them a hole dropped away in the side of the hills, a black pit filled with smoking black dust. At the edge of the wide circle of annihilation lay trees burnt to long smears of charcoal, all pointing their fallen tops away from the pit of blackness.

The young Lord of Hallan held his gray steed steady on the updraft from the wrecked valley and stared down, saying nothing. There were old tales from his grandfather's and great-grandfather's time of the first coming of the Starlords, how they had burnt away hills and made the sea boil with their terrible weapons, and with the threat of those weapons had forced all the Lords of Angien to pledge them fealty and tribute. For the first time now Mogien believed those tales. His breath was stuck in his throat for a second. "Your ship was . . ."

"The ship was here. I was to meet the others here, today. Lord Mogien, tell your people to avoid this place. For a while. Till after the rains, next coldyear."

"A spell?"

"A poison. Rain will rid the land of it." The Starlord's voice was still quiet, but he was looking down, and all at once he began to speak again, not to Mogien but to that black pit beneath them, now striped with the bright early sunlight. Mogien understood no word he said, for he spoke in his own tongue, the speech of the Starlords; and there was no man now in Angien or all the world who spoke that tongue.

The young Angya checked his nervous mount. Behind him the Starlord drew a deep breath and said, "Let's go back to Hallan. There is nothing here. . . ."

The steed wheeled over the smoking slopes. "Lord Rokanan, if your people are at war now among the stars, I pledge in your defense the swords of Hallan!"

"I thank you, Lord Mogien," said the Starlord, clinging to the saddle, the wind of their flight whipping at his bowed graying head.

The long day passed. The night wind gusted at the casements of his room in the tower of Hallan Castle, making the fire in the wide hearth flicker. Cold-year was nearly over; the restlessness of spring was in the wind. When he raised his head he smelled the sweet musty fragrance of grass tapestries hung on the walls and the sweet fresh fragrance of night in the forests outside. He spoke into his transmitter once more: "Rocannon here. This is Rocannon. Can you answer?" He listened to the silence of the receiver a long time, then once more tried ship frequency: "Rocannon here . . ." When he noticed how low he was speaking, almost whispering, he stopped and cut off the set. They were dead, all fourteen of them, his companions and his friends. They had all been on Fomalhaut II for half one of the planet's long years, and it had been time for them to confer and compare notes. So Smate and his crew had come around from East Continent, and picked up the Antarctic crew on the way, and ended up back here to meet with Rocannon, the Director of the First Ethnographic Survey, the man who had brought them all here. And now they were dead.

And their work—all their notes, pictures, tapes, all that would have justified their death to them—that was all gone too, blown to dust with them, wasted with them.

Rocannon turned on his radio again to Emergency frequency; but he did not pick up the transmitter. To call was only to tell the enemy that there was a survivor. He sat still. When a resounding knock came at his door he said in the strange tongue he would have to speak from now on, "Come in!"

In strode the young Lord of Hallan, Mogien, who had been his best informant for the culture and mores of Species II, and who now controlled his fate. Mogien was very tall, like all his people, bright-haired and dark-skinned, his handsome face schooled to a stern calm through which sometimes broke the lightning of powerful emotions: anger, ambition, joy. He was followed by his Olgyior servant Raho, who set down a yellow flask and two cups on a chest, poured the cups full, and withdrew. The heir of Hallan spoke: "I would drink with you, Starlord."

"And my kin with yours and our sons together, Lord," replied the ethnologist, who had not lived on nine different exotic planets without learning the value of good manners. He and Mogien raised their wooden cups bound with silver and drank.

"The wordbox," Mogien said, looking at the radio, "it will not speak again?"

"Not with my friends' voices."

Mogien's walnut-dark face showed no feeling, but he said, "Lord Rokanan, the weapon that killed them, this is beyond all imagining."

"The League of All Worlds keeps such weapons for use in the War To Come. Not against our own worlds."

"Is this the War, then?"

"I think not. Yaddam, whom you knew, was staying with the ship; he would have heard news of that on the ansible in the ship, and radioed me at once. There would have been warning. This must be a rebellion against the League. There was rebellion brewing on a world called Faraday when I left Kerguelen, and by sun's time that was nine years ago."

"This little wordbox cannot speak to the City Kerguelen?"

"No; and even if it did, it would take the words eight years to go there, and the answer eight years to come back to me." Rocannon spoke with his usual grave and simple politeness, but his voice was a little dull as he explained his exile. "You remember the ansible, the machine I showed you in the ship, which can speak instantly to other worlds, with no loss of years—it was that that they were after, I expect. It was only bad luck that my friends were all at the ship with it. Without it I can do nothing."

"But if your kinfolk, your friends, in the City Kerguelen, call you on the ansible, and there is no answer, will they not come to see—" Mogien saw the answer as Rocannon said it:

"In eight years. . . ."

When he had shown Mogien over the Survey ship, and shown him the instantaneous transmitter, the ansible, Rocannon had told him also about the new kind of ship that could go from one star to another in no time at all.

"Was the ship that killed your friends an FTL?" inquired the Angyar warlord.

"No. It was manned. There are enemies here, on this world, now."

This became clear to Mogien when he recalled that Rocannon had told him that living creatures could not ride the FTL ships and live; they were used only as robot-bombers, weapons that could appear and strike and vanish all within a moment. It was a queer story, but no queerer than the story Mogien knew to be true: that, though the kind of ship Rocannon had come here on took years and years to ride the night between the worlds, those years to the men in the ship seemed only a few hours. In the City Kerguelen on the star Forrosul this man Rocannon had spoken to Semley of Hallan and given her the jewel Eye of the Sea, nearly half a hundred years ago. Semley who had lived sixteen years in one night was long dead, her daughter Haldre was an old woman, her grandson Mogien a grown man; yet here sat Rocannon, who was not old. Those years had passed, for him, in riding between the stars. It was very strange, but there were other tales stranger yet.

"When my mother's mother Semley rode across the night . . ." Mogien began, and paused.

"There was never so fair a lady in all the worlds," said the Starlord, his face less sorrowful for a moment.

"The lord who befriended her is welcome among her kinfolk," said Mogien. "But I meant to ask, Lord, what ship she rode. Was it ever taken from the Clayfolk? Does it have the ansible on it, so you could tell your kinfolk of this enemy?"

For a second Rocannon looked thunderstruck, then he calmed down. "No," he said, "it doesn't. It was given to the Clayfolk seventy years ago; there was no instantaneous transmission then. And it would not have been installed recently, because the planet's been under Interdict for forty-five years now. Due to me. Because I interfered. Because, after I met Lady Semley, I went to my people and said, what are we doing on this world we don't know anything about? Why are we taking their money and pushing them about? What right have we? But if I'd left the situation alone at least there'd be someone coming here every couple of years; you wouldn't be completely at the mercy of this invader—"

"What does an invader want with us?" Mogien inquired, not modestly, but curiously.

"He wants your planet, I suppose. Your world. Your earth. Perhaps yourselves as slaves. I don't know."

"If the Clayfolk still have that ship, Rokanan, and if the ship goes to the City, you could go, and rejoin your people."

The Starlord looked at him a minute. "I suppose I could," he said. His tone was dull again. There was silence between them for a minute longer, and then Rocannon spoke with passion: "I left you people open to this. I brought my own people into it and they're dead. I'm not going to run off eight years into the future and find out what happened next! Listen, Lord Mogien, if you could help me get south to the Clayfolk, I might get the ship and use it here on the planet, scout about with it. At least, if I can't change its automatic drive, I can send it off to Kerguelen with a message. But I'll stay here."

"Semley found it, the tale tells, in the caves of the Gdemiar near the Kirien-sea."

"Will you lend me a windsteed, Lord Mogien?"

"And my company, if you will."

"With thanks!"

"The Clayfolk are bad hosts to lone guests," said Mogien, looking pleased. Not even the thought of that ghastly black hole blown in the mountainside could quell the itch in the two long swords hitched to Mogien's belt. It had been a long time since the last foray.

"May our enemy die without sons," the Angya said gravely, raising his re-filled cup.

Rocannon, whose friends had been killed without warning in an unarmed ship, did not hesitate. "May they die without sons," he said, and drank with Mogien, there in the yellow light of rushlights and double moon, in the High Tower of Hallan.

II

By evening of the second day Rocannon was stiff and wind-burned, but had learned to sit easy in the high saddle and to guide with some skill the great flying beast from Hallan stables. Now the pink air of the long, slow sunset stretched above and beneath him, levels of rose-crystal light. The windsteeds were flying high to stay as long as they could in sunlight, for like great cats they loved warmth. Mogien on his black hunter—a stallion, would you call it, Rocannon wondered, or a tom?—was looking down, seeking a camping place, for windsteeds would not fly in darkness. Two midmen soared behind on smaller white mounts, pink-winged in the after-glow of the great sun Fomalhaut.

"Look there, Starlord!"

Rocannon's steed checked and snarled, seeing what Mogien was pointing to: a little black object moving low across the sky ahead of them, dragging behind it through the evening quiet a faint rattling noise. Rocannon gestured that they land at once. In the forest glade where they alighted, Mogien asked, "Was that a ship like yours, Starlord?"

"No. It was a planet-bound ship, a helicopter. It could only have been brought here on a ship much larger than mine was, a starfrigate or a trans-port. They must be coming here in force. And they must have started out before I did. What are they doing here anyhow, with bombers and helicopters? . . . They could shoot us right out of the sky from a long way off. We'll have to watch out for them, Lord Mogien."

"The thing was flying up from the Clayfields. I hope they were not there before us."

Rocannon only nodded, heavy with anger at the sight of that black spot on the sunset, that roach on a clean world. Whoever these people were that had bombed an unarmed Survey ship at sight, they evidently meant to survey this planet and take it over for colonization or for some military use. The High-Intelligence Life Forms of the planet, of which there were at least three species, all of low technological achievement, they would ignore or enslave or extirpate, whichever was most convenient. For to an aggressive people only technology mattered.

And there, Rocannon said to himself as he watched the midmen unsaddle the windsteeds and loose them for their night's hunting, right there perhaps was the League's own weak spot. Only technology mattered. The two missions to this world in the last century had started pushing one of the species toward a pre-atomic technology before they had even explored the other continents or contacted all intelligent races. He had called a halt to that, and had finally managed to bring his own Ethnographic Survey here to learn something about the planet; but he did not fool himself. Even his work here would finally have served only as an informational basis for encouraging technological advance in the most likely species or culture. This was how the League of All Worlds prepared to meet its ultimate enemy. A hundred worlds had been trained and armed, a thousand more were being schooled in the uses of steel and wheel and tractor and reactor. But Rocannon the hilfer, whose job was learning, not teaching, and who had lived on quite a few backward worlds, doubted the wisdom of staking everything on weapons and the uses of machines. Dominated by the aggressive, tool-making humanoid species of Centaurus, Earth, and the Cetians, the League had slighted certain skills and powers and potentialities of intelligent life, and judged by too narrow a standard.

This world, which did not even have a name yet beyond Fomalhaut II, would probably never get much attention paid to it, for before the League's arrival none of its species seemed to have got beyond the lever and the forge. Other races on other worlds could be pushed ahead faster, to help when the extragalactic enemy returned at last. No doubt this was inevitable. He thought of Mogien offering to fight a fleet of lightspeed bombers with the swords of Hallan. But what if lightspeed or even FTL bombers were very much like bronze swords, compared to the weapons of the Enemy? What if the weapons of the Enemy were things of the mind? Would it not be well to learn a little of the different shapes minds come in, and their powers? The League's policy was too narrow; it led to too much waste, and now evidently it had led to rebellion. If the storm brewing on Faraday ten years ago had broken, it meant that a young League world, having learned war promptly and been armed, was now out to carve its own empire from the stars.

He and Mogien and the two dark-haired servants gnawed hunks of good hard bread from the kitchens of Hallan, drank yellow *vaskan* from a skin flask, and soon settled to sleep. Very high all around their small fire stood the trees, dark branches laden with sharp, dark, closed cones. In the night a cold, fine rain whispered through the forest. Rocannon pulled the feathery herilo-fur bedroll up over his head and slept all the long night in the whisper of the rain. The windsteeds came back at daybreak, and before sunrise they were aloft again, windriding toward the pale lands near the gulf where the Clay-folk dwelt.

Landing about noon in a field of raw clay, Rocannon and the two servants, Raho and Yahan, looked about blankly, seeing no sign of life. Mogien said with the absolute confidence of his caste, "They'll come."

And they came: the squat hominoids Rocannon had seen in the museum years ago, six of them, not much taller than Rocannon's chest or Mogien's belt. They were naked, a whitish-gray color like their clay-fields, a singularly earthy-looking lot. When they spoke, they were uncanny; for there was no telling which one spoke; it seemed they all did, but with one harsh voice. *Partial colonial telepathy,* Rocannon recalled from the *Handbook,* and looked with increased respect at the ugly little men with their rare gift. His three tall companions evinced no such feeling. They looked grim.

"What do the Angyar and the servants of the Angyar wish in the field of the Lords of Night?" one of the Claymen, or all of them, was or were asking in the Common Tongue, an Angyar dialect used by all species.

"I am the Lord of Hallan," said Mogien, looking gigantic. "With me stands Rokanan, master of stars and the ways between the night, servant of the League of All Worlds, guest and friend of the Kinfolk of Hallan. High honor is due him! Take us to those fit to parley with us. There are words to be spoken, for soon there will be snow in warmyear and winds blowing backward and trees growing upside down!" The way the Angyar talked was a real pleasure, Rocannon thought, though its tact was not what struck you.

The Claymen stood about in dubious silence. "Truly this is so?" they or one of them asked at last.

"Yes, and the sea will turn to wood, and stones will grow toes! Take us to your chiefs, who know what a Starlord is, and waste no time!"

More silence. Standing among the little troglodytes, Rocannon had an uneasy sense as of mothwings brushing past his ears. A decision was being reached.

"Come," said the Claymen aloud, and led off across the sticky field. They gathered hurriedly around a patch of earth, stooped, then stood aside, revealing a hole in the ground and a ladder sticking out of it: the entrance to the Domain of Night.

While the midmen waited aboveground with the steeds, Mogien and Rocannon climbed down the ladder into a cave-world of crossing, branching tunnels cut in the clay and lined with coarse cement, electric-lighted, smelling of sweat and stale food. Padding on flat gray feet behind them, the guards took them to a half-lit, round chamber like a bubble in a great rock stratum, and left them there alone.

They waited. They waited longer.

Why the devil had the first surveys picked these people to encourage for League membership? Rocannon had a perhaps unworthy explanation: those first surveys had been from cold Centaurus, and the explorers had dived rejoicing into the caves of the Gdemiar, escaping the blinding floods of light and heat from the great A-3 sun. To them, sensible people lived underground on a world like this. To Rocannon, the hot white sun and the bright nights of quadruple moonlight, the intense weather-changes and ceaseless winds, the rich air and light gravity that permitted so many airborne species, were all not only compatible but enjoyable. But, he reminded himself, just by that he was less well qualified than the Centaurans to judge these cave-folk. They were certainly clever. They were also telepathic—a power much rarer and much less well understood than electricity—but the first surveys had not made anything of that. They had given the Gdemiar a generator and a lock-drive ship and some math and some pats on the back, and left them. What had the little men done since? He asked a question along this line of Mogien.

The young lord, who had certainly never see anything but a candle or a resin-torch in his life, glanced without the least interest at the electric light-bulb over his head. "They have always been good at making things," he said, with his extraordinary, straightforward arrogance.

"Have they made new sorts of things lately?"

"We buy our steel swords from the Clayfolk; they had smiths who could work steel in my grandfather's time; but before that I don't know. My people have lived a long time with Clayfolk, suffering them to tunnel beneath our border-lands, trading them silver for their swords. They are said to be rich, but forays on them are tabu. Wars between two breeds are evil matters—as you know. Even when my grandfather Durhal sought his wife here, thinking they had stolen her, he would not break the tabu to force them to speak. They will neither lie nor speak truth if they can help it. We do not love them, and they do not love us; I think they remember old days before the tabu. They are not brave."

A mighty voice boomed out behind their backs: "Bow down before the presence of the Lords of Night!" Rocannon had his hand on his laser-gun and Mogien both hands on his sword-hilts as they turned; but Rocannon immediately spotted the speaker set in the curving wall, and murmured to Mogien, "Don't answer."

"Speak, O strangers in the Caverns of the Nightlords!" The sheer blare of sound was intimidating, but Mogien stood there without a blink, his high-arching eyebrows indolently raised. Presently he said, "Now you've windridden three days, Lord Rokanan, do you begin to see the pleasure of it?"

"Speak and you shall be heard!"

"I do. And the striped steed goes light as the west wind in warmyear," Rocannon said, quoting a compliment overheard at table in the Revelhall.

"He's of very good stock."

"Speak! You are heard!"

They discussed windsteed-breeding while the wall bellowed at them. Eventually two Claymen appeared in the tunnel. "Come," they said stolidly. They led the strangers through further mazes to a very neat little electric-train system, like a giant but effective toy, on which they rode several miles more at a good clip, leaving the clay tunnels for what appeared to be a limestone-cave area. The last station was at the mouth of a fiercely-lighted hall, at the far end of which three troglodytes stood waiting on a dais. At first, to Rocannon's shame as an ethnologist, they all looked alike. As Chinamen had to the Dutch, as Russians had to the Centaurans. . . . Then he picked out the individuality of the central Clayman, whose face was lined, white, and powerful under an iron crown.

"What does the Starlord seek in the Caverns of the Mighty?"

The formality of the Common Tongue suited Rocannon's need precisely as he answered, "I had hoped to come as a guest to these caverns, to learn the ways of the Nightlords and see the wonders of their making. I hope yet to do so. But ill doings are afoot and I come now in haste and need. I am an officer of the League of All Worlds. I ask you to bring me to the starship which you keep as a pledge of the League's confidence in you."

The three stared impassively. The dais put them on a level with Rocannon; seen thus on a level, their broad, ageless faces and rock-hard eyes were impressive. Then, grotesquely, the left-hand one spoke in Pidgin-Galactic: "No ship," he said.

"There is a ship."

After a minute the one repeated ambiguously, "No ship."

"Speak the Common Tongue. I ask your help. There is an enemy to the League on this world. It will be your world no longer if you admit that enemy."

"No ship," said the left-hand Clayman. The other two stood like stalagmites.

"Then must I tell the other Lords of the League that the Clayfolk have betrayed their trust, and are unworthy to fight in the War To Come?"

Silence.

"Trust is on both sides, or neither," the iron-crowned Clayman in the center said in the Common Tongue.

"Would I ask your help if I did not trust you? Will you do this at least for me: send the ship with a message to Kerguelen? No one need ride it and lose the years; it will go itself."

Silence again.

"No ship," said the left-hand one in his gravel voice.

"Come, Lord Mogien," said Rocannon, and turned his back on them.

"Those who betray the Starlords," said Mogien in his clear arrogant voice, "betray older pacts. You made our swords of old, Clayfolk. They have not got rusty." And he strode out beside Rocannon, following the stumpy gray guides who led them in silence back to the railway, and through the maze of dank, glaring corridors, and up at last into the light of day.

They windrode a few miles west to get clear of Clayfolk territory, and landed on the bank of a forest river to take counsel.

Mogien felt he had let his guest down; he was not used to being thwarted in his generosity, and his self-possession was a little shaken. "Cave-grubs," he said. "Cowardly vermin! They will never say straight out what they have done or will do. All the Small Folk are like that, even the Fiia. But the Fiia can be trusted. Do you think the Clayfolk gave the ship to the enemy?"

"How can we tell?"

"I know this: they would give it to no one unless they were paid its price twice over. Things, things—they think of nothing but heaping up things. What did the old one mean, trust must be on both sides?"

"I think he meant that his people feel that we—the League—betrayed them. First we encourage them, then suddenly for forty-five years we drop them, send them no messages, discourage their coming, tell them to look after themselves. And that was my doing, though they don't know it. Why should they do me a favor, after all? I doubt they've talked with the enemy yet. But it would make no difference if they did bargain away the ship. The enemy could do even less with it than I could have done." Rocannon stood looking down at the bright river, his shoulders stooped.

"Rokanan," said Mogien, for the first time speaking to him as to a kinsman, "near this forest live my cousins of Kyodor, a strong castle, thirty Angyar swordsmen and three villages of midmen. They will help us punish the Clayfolk for their insolence—"

"No." Rocannon spoke heavily. "Tell your people to keep an eye on the Clayfolk, yes; they might be bought over by this enemy. But there will be no tabus broken or wars fought on my account. There is no point to it. In times like this, Mogien, one man's fate is not important."

"If it is not," said Mogien, raising his dark face, "what is?"

"Lords," said the slender young midman Yahan, "someone's over there among the trees." He pointed across the river to a flicker of color among the dark conifers.

"Fiia!" said Mogien. "Look at the windsteeds." All four of the big beasts were looking across the river, ears pricked.

"Mogien Hallanlord walks the Fiia's ways in friendship!" Mogien's voice rang over the broad, shallow, clattering water, and presently in mixed light and shadow under the trees on the other shore a small figure appeared. It seemed to dance a little as spots of sunlight played over it making it flicker and change, hard to keep the eyes on. When it moved, Rocannon thought it was walking on the surface of the river, so lightly it came, not stirring the sunlit shallows. The striped windsteed rose and stalked softly on thick, hollow-boned legs to the water's edge. As the Fian waded out of the water the big beast bowed its head, and the Fian reached up and scratched the striped, furry ears. Then he came toward them.

"Hail Mogien Halla's heir, sunhaired, swordbearer!" The voice was thin and sweet as a child's, the figure short and light as a child's, but it was no child's face. "Hail Hallan-guest, Starlord, Wanderer!" Strange, large, light eyes turned for a moment full on Rocannon.

"The Fiia know all names and news," said Mogien, smiling; but the little Fian did not smile in response. Even to Rocannon, who had only briefly visited one village of the species with the Survey team, this was startling.

"O Starlord," said the sweet, shaking voice, "who rides the windships that come and kill?"

"Kill—your people?"

"All my village," the little man said. "I was with the flocks out on the hills. I mindheard my people call, and I came, and they were in the flames burning and crying out. There were two ships with turning wings. They spat out fire. Now I am alone and must speak aloud. Where my people were in my mind there is only fire and silence. Why was this done, Lords?"

He looked from Rocannon to Mogien. Both were silent. He bent over like a man mortally hurt, crouching, and hid his face.

Mogien stood over him, his hands on the hilts of his swords, shaking with anger. "Now I swear vengeance on those who harmed the Fiia! Rokanan, how can this be? The Fiia have no swords, they have no riches, they have no enemy! Look, his people are all dead, those he speaks to without words, his tribesmen. No Fian lives alone. He will die alone. Why would they harm his people?"

"To make their power known," Rocannon said harshly. "Let us bring him to Hallan, Mogien."

The tall lord knelt down by the little crouching figure. "Fian, man's-friend, ride with me. I cannot speak in your mind as your kinsmen spoke, but airborne words are not all hollow."

In silence they mounted, the Fian riding the high saddle in front of Mogien like a child, and the four steeds rose up again on the air. A rainy south wind favored their flight, and late the next day under the beating of his steed's wing Rocannon saw the marble stairway up through the forest, the Chasmbridge across the green abyss, and the towers of Hallan in the long western light.

The people of the castle, blond lords and dark-haired servants, gathered around them in the flightcourt, full of the news of the burning of the castle nearest them to the east, Reohan, and the murder of all its people. Again it had been a couple of helicopters and a few men armed with laser-guns; the warriors and farmers of Reohan had been slaughtered without giving one stroke in return. The people of Hallan were half berserk with anger and defiance, into which came an element of awe when they saw the Fian riding with their young lord and heard why he was there. Many of them, dwellers in this northernmost fortress of Angien, had never seen one of the Fiia before, but all knew them as the stuff of legends and the subject of a powerful tabu. An attack, however bloody, on one of their own castles fit into their warrior outlook; but an attack on the Fiia was desecration. Awe and rage worked together in them. Late that evening in his tower room Rocannon heard the tumult from the Revelhall below, where the Angyar of Hallan all were gathered swearing destruction and extinction to the enemy in a torrent of metaphor and a thunder of hyperbole. They were a boastful race, the Angyar: vengeful, overweening, obstinate, illiterate, and lacking any first-person forms for the verb "to be unable." There were no gods in their legends, only heroes.

Through their distant racket a near voice broke in, startling Rocannon so his hand jumped on the radio tuner. He had at last found the enemy's communication band. A voice rattled on, speaking a language Rocannon did not know. Luck would have been too good if the enemy had spoken Galactic; there were hundreds of thousands of languages among the Worlds of the League, let alone the recognized planets such as this one and the planets still unknown. The voice began reading a list of numbers, which Rocannon understood, for they were in Cetian, the language of a race whose mathematical attainments had led to the general use throughout the League of Cetian mathematics and therefore Cetian numerals. He listened with strained attention, but it was no good, a mere string of numbers.

The voice stopped suddenly, leaving only the hiss of static.

Rocannon looked across the room to the little Fian, who had asked to stay with him, and now sat cross-legged and silent on the floor near the casement window.

"That was the enemy, Kyo."

The Fian's face was very still.

"Kyo," said Rocannon—it was the custom to address a Fian by the Angyar name of his village, since individuals of the species perhaps did and perhaps did not have individual names—"Kyo, if you tried, could you mindhear the enemies?"

In the brief notes from his one visit to a Fian village Rocannon had commented that Species 1-B seldom answered direct questions directly; and he well remembered their smiling elusiveness. But Kyo, left desolate in the alien country of speech, answered what Rocannon asked him. "No, Lord," he said submissively.

"Can you mindhear others of your own kind, in other villages?"

"A little. If I lived among them, perhaps . . . Fiia go sometimes to live in other villages than their own. It is said even that once the Fiia and the Gdemiar mindspoke together as one people, but that was very long ago. It is said . . ." He stopped.

"Your people and the Clayfolk are indeed one race, though you follow very different ways now. What more, Kyo?"

"It is said that very long ago, in the south, in the high places, the gray places, lived those who mindspoke with all creatures. All thoughts they could hear, the Old Ones, the Most Ancient. . . . But we came down from the mountains, and lived in the valleys and the caves, and have forgotten the harder way."

Rocannon pondered a moment. There were no mountains on the continent south of Hallan. He rose to get his *Handbook for Galactic Area Eight,* with its maps, when the radio, still hissing on the same band, stopped him short. A voice was coming through, much fainter, remote, rising and falling on billows of static, but speaking in Galactic. "Number Six, come in. Number Six, come in. This is Foyer. Come in, Number Six." After endless repetitions and pauses it continued: "This is Friday. No, this is Friday.... This is Foyer; are you there, Number Six? The FTLs are due tomorrow and I want a full report on the Seven Six sidings and the nets. Leave the staggering plan to the Eastern Detachment. Are you getting me, Number Six? We are going to be in ansible communication with Base tomorrow. Will you get me that information on the sidings at once. Seven Six sidings. Unnecessary—" A surge of starnoise swallowed the voice, and when it re-emerged it was audible only in snatches. Ten long minutes went by in static, silence, and snatches of speech, then a nearer voice cut in, speaking quickly in the unknown language used before. It went on and on; moveless, minute after minute, his hand still on the cover of his *Handbook,* Rocannon listened. As moveless, the Fian sat in the shadows across the room. A double pair of numbers was spoken, then repeated; the second time Rocannon caught the Cetian word for "degrees." He flipped his notebook open and scribbled the numbers down; then at last, though he still listened, he opened the *Handbook* to the maps of Fomalhaut II.

The numbers he had noted were 28° 28—121° 40. If they were coordinates of latitude and longitude . . . He brooded over the maps a while, setting the point of his pencil down a couple of times on blank open sea. Then, trying 121 West with 28 North, he came down just south of a range of mountains, halfway down the Southwest Continent. He sat gazing at the map. The radio voice had fallen silent.

"Starlord?"

"I think they told me where they are. Maybe. And they've got an ansible there." He looked up at Kyo unseeingly, then back at the map. "If they're down there—if I could get there and wreck their game, if I could get just one message out on their ansible to the League, if I could . . ."

Southwest Continent had been mapped only from the air, and nothing but the mountains and major rivers were sketched inside the coastlines: hundreds of kilometers of blank, of unknown. And a goal merely guessed at.

"But I can't just sit here," Rocannon said. He looked up again, and met the little man's clear, uncomprehending gaze.

He paced down the stone-floored room and back. The radio hissed and whispered.

There was one thing in his favor: the fact that the enemy would not be expecting him. They thought they had the planet all to themselves. But it was the only thing in his favor.

"I'd like to use their weapons against them," he said. "I think I'll try to find them. In the land to the south. . . . My people were killed by these strangers, like yours, Kyo. You and I are both alone, speaking a language not our own. I would rejoice in your companionship."

He hardly knew what moved him to the suggestion.

The shadow of a smile went across the Fian's face. He raised his hands, parallel and apart. Rushlight in sconces on the walls bowed and flickered and changed. "It was foretold that the Wanderer would choose companions," he said. "For a while."

"The Wanderer?" Rocannon asked, but this time the Fian did not answer.

III

The Lady of the Castle crossed the high hall slowly, skirts rustling over stone. Her dark skin was deepened with age to the black of an ikon; her fair hair was white. Still she kept the beauty of her lineage. Rocannon bowed and spoke a greeting in the fashion of her people: "Hail Hallanlady, Durhal's daughter, Haldre the Fair!"

"Hail Rokanan, my guest," she said, looking calmly down at him. Like most Angyar women and all Angyar men she was considerably taller than he. "Tell me why you go south." She continued to pace slowly across the hall, and Rocannon walked beside her. Around them was dark air and stone, dark tapestry hung on high walls, the cool light of morning from clerestory windows slanting across the black of rafters overhead.

"I go to find my enemy, Lady."

"And when you have found them?"

"I hope to enter their . . . their castle, and make use of their . . . message-sender, to tell the League they are here, on this world. They are hiding here, and there is very little chance of their being found: the worlds are thick as sand on the sea-beach. But they must be found. They have done harm here, and they would do much worse on other worlds."

Haldre nodded her head once. "Is it true you wish to go lightly, with few men?"

"Yes, Lady. It is a long way, and the sea must be crossed. And craft, not strength, is my only hope against their strength."

"You will need more than craft, Starlord," said the old woman. "Well, I'll send with you four loyal midmen, if that suffices you, and two windsteeds laden and six saddled, and a piece or two of silver in case barbarians in the foreign lands want payment for lodging you, and my son Mogien."

"Mogien will come with me? These are great gifts, Lady, but that is the greatest!"

She looked at him a minute with her clear, sad, inexorable gaze. "I am glad it pleases you, Starlord." She resumed her slow walking, and he beside her. "Mogien desires to go, for love of you and for adventure; and you, a great lord on a very perilous mission, desire his company. So I think it is surely his way to follow. But I tell you now, this morning in the Long Hall, so that you may remember and not fear my blame if you return: I do not think he will come back with you."

"But Lady, he is the heir of Hallan."

She went in silence a while, turned at the end of the room under a time-darkened tapestry of winged giants fighting fair-haired men, and finally spoke again. "Hallan will find other heirs." Her voice was calm and bitter cold. "You Starlords are among us again, bringing new ways and wars. Reohan is dust; how long will Hallan stand? The world itself has become a grain of sand on the shore of night. All things change now. But I am certain still of one thing: that there is darkness over my lineage. My mother, whom you knew, was lost in the forests in her madness; my father was killed in battle, my husband by treachery; and when I bore a son my spirit grieved amid my joy, foreseeing his life would be short. That is no grief to him; he is an Angya, he wears the double swords. But my part of the darkness is to rule a failing domain alone, to live and live and outlive them all. . . ."

She was silent again a minute. "You may need more treasure than I can give you, to buy your life or your way. Take this. To you I give it, Rokanan, not to Mogien. There is no darkness on it to you. Was it not yours once, in the city across the night? To us it has been only a burden and a shadow. Take it back, Starlord; use it for a ransom or a gift." She unclasped from her neck the gold and the great blue stone of the necklace that had cost her mother's life, and held it out in her hand to Rocannon. He took it, hearing almost with terror the soft, cold clash of the golden links, and lifted his eyes to Haldre. She faced him, very tall, her blue eyes dark in the dark clear air of the hall.

"Now take my son with you, Starlord, and follow your way. May your enemy die without sons."

Torchlight and smoke and hurrying shadows in the castle flightcourt, voices of beasts and men, racket and confusion, all dropped away in a few wingbeats of the striped steed Rocannon rode. Behind them now Hallan lay, a faint spot of light on the dark sweep of the hills, and there was no sound but a rushing of air as the wide half-seen wings lifted and beat down. The east was pale behind them, and the Greatstar burned like a bright crystal, herald-ing the sun, but it was long before daybreak. Day and night and the twilights were stately and unhurried on this planet that took thirty hours to turn. And the pace of the seasons also was large; this was the dawn of the vernal equi-nox, and four hundred days of spring and summer lay ahead.

"They'll sing songs of us in the high castles," said Kyo, riding postillion behind Rocannon. "They'll sing how the Wanderer and his companions rode south across the sky in the darkness before the spring. . . ." He laughed a little. Beneath them the hills and rich plains of Angien unfolded like a land-scape painted on gray silk, brightening little by little, at last glowing vivid with colors and shadows as the lordly sun rose behind them.

At noon they rested a couple of hours by the river whose southwest course they were following to the sea; at dusk they flew down to a little castle, on a hilltop like all Angyar castles, near a bend of the same river. There they were made welcome by the lord of the place and his household. Curiosity obvi-ously itched in him at the sight of a Fian traveling by windsteed, along with the Lord of Hallan, four midmen, and one who spoke with a queer accent, dressed like a lord, but wore no swords and was white-faced like a midman. To be sure, there was more intermingling between the two castes, the Angyar and Olgyior, than most Angyar like to admit; there were light-skinned warriors, and gold-haired servants; but this "Wanderer" was altogether too anoma-lous. Wanting no further rumor of his presence on the planet, Rocannon said nothing, and their host dared ask no questions of the heir of Hallan; so if he ever found out who his strange guests had been, it was from minstrels sing-ing the tale, years later.

The next day passed the same for the seven travelers, riding the wind above the lovely land. They spent that night in an Olgyior village by the river, and on the third day came over country new even to Mogien. The river, curving away to the south, lay in loops and oxbows, the hills ran out into long plains, and far ahead was a mirrored pale brightness in the sky. Late in the day they came to a castle set alone on a white bluff, beyond which lay a long reach of lagoons and gray sand, and the open sea.

Dismounting, stiff and tired and his head ringing from wind and motion, Rocannon thought it the sorriest Angyar stronghold he had yet seen: a cluster of huts like wet chickens bunched under the wings of a squat, seedy-looking fort. Midmen, pale and short-bodied, peered at them from the straggling lanes. "They look as if they'd bred with Clayfolk," said Mogien. "This is the gate, and the place is called Tolen, if the wind hasn't carried us astray. Ho! Lords of Tolen, the guest is at your gate!"

There was no sound within the castle.

"The gate of Tolen swings in the wind," said Kyo, and they saw that indeed the portal of bronze-bound wood sagged on its hinges, knocking in the cold sea-wind that blew up through the town. Mogien pushed it open with his sword-point. Inside was darkness, a scuttering rustle of wings, and a dank smell.

"The Lords of Tolen did not wait for their guests," said Mogien. "Well, Yahan, talk to these ugly fellows and find us lodging for the night."

The young midman turned to speak to the townsfolk who had gathered at the far end of the castle forecourt to stare. One of them got up the courage to hitch himself forward, bowing and going sideways like some seaweedy beach-creature, and spoke humbly to Yahan. Rocannon could partly follow the Olgyior dialect, and gathered that the old man was pleading that the village had no proper housing for *pedanar,* whatever they were. The tall midman Raho joined Yahan and spoke fiercely, but the old man only hitched and bowed and mumbled, till at last Mogien strode forward. He could not by the Angyar code speak to the serfs of a strange domain, but he unsheathed one of his swords and held it up shining in the cold sea-light. The old man spread out his hands and with a wail turned and shuffled down into the darkening alleys of the village. The travelers followed, the furled wings of their steeds brushing the low reed roofs on both sides.

"Kyo, what are pedanar?"

The little man smiled.

"Yahan, what is that word, pedanar?"

The young midman, a goodnatured, candid fellow, looked uneasy. "Well, Lord, a pedan is . . . one who walks among men . . ."

Rocannon nodded, snapping up even this scrap. While he had been a student of the species instead of its ally, he had kept seeking for their religion; they seemed to have no creeds at all. Yet they were quite credulous. They took spells, curses, and strange powers as matter of fact, and their relation to nature was intensely animistic; but they had no gods. This word, at last, smelled of the supernatural. It did not occur to him at the time that the word had been applied to himself.

It took three of the sorry huts to lodge the seven of them, and the wind-steeds, too big to fit any house of the village, had to be tied outside. The beasts huddled together, ruffling their fur against the sharp sea-wind. Rocannon's striped steed scratched at the wall and complained in a mewing snarl till Kyo went out and scratched its ears. "Worse awaits him soon, poor beast," said Mogien, sitting beside Rocannon by the stove-pit that warmed the hut. "They hate water."

"You said at Hallan that they wouldn't fly over the sea, and these villagers surely have no ships that would carry them. How are we going to cross the channel?"

"Have you your picture of the land?" Mogien inquired. The Angyar had no maps, and Mogien was fascinated by the Geographic Survey's maps in the *Handbook*. Rocannon got the book out of the old leather pouch he had carried from world to world, and which contained the little equipment he had had with him in Hallan when the ship had been bombed—*Handbook* and notebooks, suit and gun, medical kit and radio, a Terran chess-set and a battered volume of Hainish poetry. At first he had kept the necklace with its sapphire in with this stuff, but last night, oppressed by the value of the thing, he had sewn the sapphire pendant up in a little bag of soft barilo-hide and strung the necklace around his own neck, under his shirt and cloak, so that it looked like an amulet and could not be lost unless his head was too.

Mogien followed with a long, hard forefinger the contours of the two Western Continents where they faced each other: the far south of Angien, with its two deep gulfs and a fat promontory between them reaching south; and across the channel, the northernmost cape of the Southwest Continent, which Mogien called Fiern. "Here we are," Rocannon said, setting a fish vertebra from their supper on the tip of the promontory.

"And here, if these cringing fish-eating yokels speak truth, is a castle called Plenot." Mogien put a second vertebra a half-inch east of the first one, and admired it. "A tower looks very like that from above. When I get back to Hallan, I'll send out a hundred men on steeds to look down on the land, and from their pictures we'll carve in stone a great picture of all Angien. Now at Plenot there will be ships—probably the ships of this place, Tolen, as well as their own. There was a feud between these two poor lords, and that's why Tolen stands now full of wind and night. So the old man told Yahan."

"Will Plenot lend us ships?"

"Plenot will *lend* us nothing. The lord of Plenot is an Errant." This meant, in the complex code of relationships among Angyar domains, a lord banned

by the rest, an outlaw, not bound by the rules of hospitality, reprisal, or res-
titution.

"He has only two windsteeds," said Mogien, unbuckling his swordbelt for
the night. "And his castle, they say, is built of wood."

Next morning as they flew down the wind to that wooden castle a guard
spotted them almost as they spotted the tower. The two steeds of the castle
were soon aloft, circling the tower; presently they could make out little figures with bows leaning from window-slits. Clearly an Errant Lord expected
no friends. Rocannon also realized now why Angyar castles were roofed over,
making them cavernous and dark inside, but protecting them from an airborne enemy. Plenot was a little place, ruder even than Tolen, lacking a village
of midmen, perched out on a spit of black boulders above the sea; but poor
as it was, Mogien's confidence that six men could subdue it seemed excessive.
Rocannon checked the thighstraps of his saddle, shifted his grip on the long
air-combat lance Mogien had given him, and cursed his luck and himself.
This was no place for an ethnologist of forty-three.

Mogien, flying well ahead on his black steed, raised his lance and yelled.
Rocannon's mount put down its head and beat into full flight. The black-and-
gray wings flashed up and down like vanes; the long, thick, light body was
tense, thrumming with the powerful heartbeat. As the wind whistled past,
the thatched tower of Plenot seemed to hurtle toward them, circled by two
rearing gryphons. Rocannon crouched down on the windsteed's back, his
long lance couched ready. A happiness, an old delight was swelling in him; he
laughed a little, riding the wind. Closer and closer came the rocking tower
and its two winged guards, and suddenly with a piercing falsetto shout Mogien hurled his lance, a bolt of silver through the air. It hit one rider square in
the chest, breaking his thighstraps with the force of the blow, and hurled him
over his steed's haunches in a clear, seemingly slow arc three hundred feet
down to the breakers creaming quietly on the rocks. Mogien shot straight
on past the riderless steed and opened combat with the other guard, fighting in close, trying to get a swordstroke past the lance which his opponent
did not throw but used for jabbing and parrying. The four midmen on their
white and gray mounts hovered nearby like terrible pigeons, ready to help but
not interfering with their lord's duel, circling just high enough that the archers below could not pierce the steeds' leathern bellymail. But all at once all
four of them, with that nerve-rending falsetto yell, closed in on the duel. For
a moment there was a knot of white wings and glittering steel hanging in
midair. From the knot dropped a figure that seemed to be trying to lie down

on the air, turning this way and that with loose limbs seeking comfort, till it struck the castle roof and slid to a hard bed of rock below.

Now Rocannon saw why they had joined in the duel: the guard had broken its rules and struck at the steed instead of the rider. Mogien's mount, purple blood staining one black wing, was straining inland to the dunes. Ahead of him shot the midmen, chasing the two riderless steeds, which kept circling back, trying to get to their safe stables in the castle. Rocannon headed them off, driving his steed right at them over the castle roofs. He saw Raho catch one with a long cast of his rope, and at the same moment felt something sting his leg. His jump startled his excited steed; he reined in too hard, and the steed arched up its back and for the first time since he had ridden it began to buck, dancing and prancing all over the wind above the castle. Arrows played around him like reversed rain. The midmen and Mogien mounted on a wild-eyed yellow steed shot past him, yelling and laughing. His mount straightened out and followed them. "Catch, Starlord!" Yahan yelled, and a comet with a black tail came arching at him. He caught it in self-defense, found it a lighted resin-torch, and joined the others in circling the tower at close range, trying to set its thatch roof and wooden beams alight.

"You've got an arrow in your left leg," Mogien called as he passed Rocannon, who laughed hilariously and hurled his torch straight into a window-slit from which an archer leaned. "Good shot!" cried Mogien, and came plummeting down onto the tower roof, re-arising from it in a rush of flame.

Yahan and Raho were back with more sheaves of smoking torches they had set alight on the dunes, and were dropping these wherever they saw reed or wood to set afire. The tower was going up now in a roaring fountain of sparks, and the windsteeds, infuriated by constant reining-in and by the sparks stinging their coats, kept plunging down toward the roofs of the castle, making a coughing roar very horrible to hear. The upward rain of arrows had ceased, and now a man scurried out into the forecourt, wearing what looked like a wooden salad bowl on his head, and holding up in his hands what Rocannon first took for a mirror, then saw was a bowl full of water. Jerking at the reins of the yellow beast, which was still trying to get back down to its stable, Mogien rode over the man and called, "Speak quick! My men are lighting new torches!"

"Of what domain, Lord?"

"Hallan!"

"The Lord-Errant of Plenot craves time to put out the fires, Hallanlord!"

"In return for the lives and treasures of the men of Tolen, I grant it."

"So be it," cried the man, and, still holding up the full bowl of water, he trotted back into the castle. The attackers withdrew to the dunes and watched the Plenot folk rush out to man their pump and set up a bucket-brigade from the sea. The tower burned out, but they kept the walls and hall standing. There were only a couple of dozen of them, counting some women. When the fires were out, a group of them came on foot from the gate, over the rocky spit and up the dunes. In front walked a tall, thin man with the walnut skin and fiery hair of the Angyar; behind him came two soldiers still wearing their salad-bowl helmets, and behind them six ragged men and women staring about sheepishly. The tall man raised in his two hands the clay bowl filled with water. "I am Ogoren of Plenot, Lord-Errant of this domain."

"I am Mogien Halla's heir."

"The lives of the Tolenfolk are yours, Lord." He nodded to the ragged group behind him. "No treasure was in Tolen."

"There were two longships, Errant."

"From the north the dragon flies, seeing all things," Ogoren said rather sourly. "The ships of Tolen are yours."

"And you will have your windsteeds back, when the ships are at Tolen wharf," said Mogien, magnanimous.

"By what other lord had I the honor to be defeated?" Ogoren asked with a glance at Rocannon, who wore all the gear and bronze armor of an Angyar warrior, but no swords. Mogien too looked at his friend, and Rocannon responded with the first alias that came to mind, the name Kyo called him by—"Olhor," the Wanderer.

Ogoren gazed at him curiously, then bowed to both and said, "The bowl is full, Lords."

"Let the water not be spilled and the pact not be broken!"

Ogoren turned and strode with his two men back to his smouldering fort, not giving a glance to the freed prisoners huddled on the dune. To these Mogien said only, "Lead home my windsteed; his wing was hurt," and, remounting the yellow beast from Plenot, he took off. Rocannon followed, looking back at the sad little group as they began their trudge home to their own ruinous domain.

By the time he reached Tolen his battle-spirits had flagged and he was cursing himself again. There had in fact been an arrow sticking out of his left calf when he dismounted on the dune, painless till he had pulled it out without stopping to see if the point were barbed, which it was. The Angyar certainly did not use poison; but there was always blood poisoning. Swayed by his companions' genuine courage, he had been ashamed to wear his protective and

almost invisible impermasuit for this foray. Owning armor that could withstand a laser-gun, he might die in this damned hovel from the scratch of a
bronze-headed arrow. And he had set off to save a planet, when he could not
even save his own skin.

The oldest midman from Hallan, a quiet stocky fellow named Iot, came
in and almost wordlessly, gentle-mannered, knelt and washed and bandaged
Rocannon's hurt. Mogien followed, still in battle dress, looking ten feet tall
with his crested helmet, and five feet wide across the shoulders exaggerated by
the stiff winglike shoulderboard of his cape. Behind him came Kyo, silent as
a child among the warriors of a stronger race. Then Yahan came in, and Raho,
and young Bien, so that the hut creaked at the seams when they all squatted
around the stove-pit. Yahan filled seven silver-bound cups, which Mogien
gravely passed around. They drank. Rocannon began to feel better. Mogien
inquired of his wound, and Rocannon felt much better. They drank more vaskan, while scared and admiring faces of villagers peered momentarily in the
doorway from the twilit lane outside. Rocannon felt benevolent and heroic.
They ate, and drank more, and then in the airless hut reeking with smoke and
fried fish and harness-grease and sweat, Yahan stood up with a lyre of bronze
with silver strings, and sang. He sang of Durholde of Hallan who set free the
prisoners of Korhalt, in the days of the Red Lord, by the marshes of Born; and
when he had sung the lineage of every warrior in that battle and every stroke
he struck, he sang straight on the freeing of the Tolenfolk and the burning of
Plenot Tower, of the Wanderer's torch blazing through a rain of arrows, of the
great stroke struck by Mogien Halla's heir, the lance cast across the wind finding its mark like the unerring lance of Hendin in the days of old. Rocannon
sat drunk and contented, riding the river of song, feeling himself now wholly
committed, sealed by his shed blood to this world to which he had come a
stranger across the gulfs of night. Only beside him now and then he sensed
the presence of the little Fian, smiling, alien, serene.

IV

The sea stretched in long misty swells under a smoking rain. No color was
left in the world. Two windsteeds, wingbound and chained in the stern of the
boat, lamented and yowled, and over the swells through rain and mist came
a doleful echo from the other boat.

They had spent many days at Tolen, waiting till Rocannon's leg healed, and till the black windsteed could fly again. Though these were reasons to wait, the truth was that Mogien was reluctant to leave, to cross the sea they must cross. He roamed the gray sands among the lagoons below Tolen all alone, struggling perhaps with the premonition that had visited his mother Haldre. All he could say to Rocannon was that the sound and sight of the sea made his heart heavy. When at last the black steed was fully cured, he abruptly decided to send it back to Hallan in Bien's care, as if saving one valuable thing from peril. They had also agreed to leave the two packsteeds and most of their load to the old Lord of Tolen and his nephews, who were still creeping about trying to patch their drafty castle. So now in the two dragon-headed boats on the rainy sea were only six travelers and five steeds, all of them wet and most of them complaining.

Two morose fishermen of Tolen sailed the boat. Yahan was trying to comfort the chained steeds with a long and monotonous lament for a long-dead lord; Rocannon and the Fian, cloaked and with hoods pulled over their heads, were in the bow. "Kyo, once you spoke of mountains to the south."

"Oh yes," said the little man, looking quickly northward, at the lost coast of Angien.

"Do you know anything of the people that live in the southern land—in Fiern?"

His *Handbook* was not much help; after all, it was to fill the vast gaps in the *Handbook* that he had brought his Survey here. It postulated five High-Intelligence Life Forms for the planet, but described only three: the Angyar/Olgyior; the Fiia and Gdemiar; and a non-humanoid species found on the great Eastern Continent on the other side of the planet. The geographers' notes on Southwest Continent were mere hearsay: *Unconfirmed species ?4: Large humanoids said to inhabit extensive towns* (?). *Unconfirmed Species ?5: Winged marsupials.* All in all, it was about as helpful as Kyo, who often seemed to believe that Rocannon knew the answers to all the questions he asked, and now replied like a schoolchild, "In Fiern live the Old Races, is it not so?" Rocannon had to content himself with gazing southward into the mist that hid the questionable land, while the great bound beasts howled and the rain crept chilly down his neck.

Once during the crossing he thought he heard the racket of a helicopter overhead, and was glad the fog hid them; then he shrugged. Why hide? The army using this planet as their base for interstellar warfare were not going to be very badly scared by the sight of ten men and five overgrown housecats bobbing in the rain in a pair of leaky boats. . . .

They sailed on in a changeless circle of rain and waves. Misty darkness rose from the water. A long, cold night went by. Gray light grew, showing mist, and rain, and waves. Then suddenly the two glum sailors in each boat came alive, steering and staring anxiously ahead. A cliff loomed all at once above the boats, fragmentary in the writhing fog. As they skirted its base, boulders and wind-dwarfed trees hung high over their sails.

Yahan had been questioning one of the sailors. "He says we'll sail past the mouth of a big river here, and on the other side is the only landingplace for a long way." Even as he spoke the overhanging rocks dropped back into mist and a thicker fog swirled over the boat, which creaked as a new current struck her keel. The grinning dragonhead at the bow rocked and turned. The air was white and opaque; the water breaking and boiling at the sides was opaque and red. The sailors yelled to each other and to the other boat. "The river's in flood," Yahan said. "They're trying to turn— Hang on!" Rocannon caught Kyo's arm as the boat yawed and then pitched and spun on crosscurrents, doing a kind of crazy dance while the sailors fought to hold her steady, and blind mist hid the water, and the windsteeds struggled to free their wings, snarling with terror.

The dragonhead seemed to be going forward steady again, when in a gust of fog-laden wind the unhandy boat jibbed and heeled over. The sail hit water with a slap, caught as if in glue, and pulled the boat right over on her side. Red, warm water quietly came up to Rocannon's face, filled his mouth, filled his eyes. He held on to whatever he was holding and struggled to find the air again. It was Kyo's arm he had hold of, and the two of them floundered in the wild sea warm as blood that swung them and rolled them and tugged them farther from the capsized boat. Rocannon yelled for help, and his voice fell dead in the blank silence of fog over the waters. Was there a shore—which way, how far? He swam after the dimming hulk of the boat, Kyo dragging on his arm.

"Rokanan!"

The dragonhead prow of the other boat loomed grinning out of the white chaos. Mogien was overboard, fighting the current beside him, getting a rope into his hands and around Kyo's chest. Rocannon saw Mogien's face vividly, the arched eyebrows and yellow hair dark with water. They were hauled up into the boat, Mogien last.

Yahan and one of the fishermen from Tolen had been picked up right away. The other sailor and the two windsteeds were drowned, caught under the boat. They were far enough out in the bay now that the flood-currents and winds from the river-gorge were weaker. Crowded with soaked, silent men, the boat rocked on through the red water and the wreathing fog.

"Rokanan, how comes it you're not wet?"

Still dazed, Rocannon looked down at his sodden clothing and did not understand. Kyo, smiling, shaking with cold, answered for him: "The Wanderer wears a second skin." Then Rocannon understood and showed Mogien the "skin" of his impermasuit, which he had put on for warmth in the damp cold last night, leaving only head and hands bare. So he still had it, and the Eye of the Sea still lay hidden on his breast; but his radio, his maps, his gun, all other links with his own civilization, were gone.

"Yahan, you will go back to Hallan."

The servant and his master stood face to face on the shore of the southern land, in the fog, surf hissing at their feet. Yahan did not reply.

They were six riders now, with three windsteeds. Kyo could ride with one midman and Rocannon with another, but Mogien was too heavy a man to ride double for long distances; to spare the windsteeds, the third midman must go back with the boat to Tolen. Mogien had decided Yahan, the youngest, should go.

"I do not send you back for anything ill done or undone, Yahan. Now go— the sailors are waiting."

The servant did not move. Behind him the sailors were kicking apart the fire they had eaten by. Pale sparks flew up briefly in the fog.

"Lord Mogien," Yahan whispered, "send Iot back."

Mogien's face got dark, and he put a hand on his swordhilt.

"Go, Yahan!"

"I will not go, Lord."

The sword came hissing out of its sheath, and Yahan with a cry of despair dodged backward, turned, and disappeared into the fog.

"Wait for him a while," Mogien said to the sailors, his face impassive. "Then go on your way. We must seek our way now. Small Lord, will you ride my steed while he walks?" Kyo sat huddled up as if very cold; he had not eaten, and had not spoken a word since they landed on the coast of Fiern. Mogien set him on the gray steed's saddle and walked at the beast's head, leading them up the beach away from the sea. Rocannon followed glancing back after Yahan and ahead at Mogien, wondering at the strange being, his friend, who one moment would have killed a man in cold wrath and the next moment spoke with simple kindness. Arrogant and loyal, ruthless and kind, in his very disharmony Mogien was lordly.

The fisherman had said there was a settlement east of this cove, so they went east now in the pallid fog that surrounded them in a soft dome of blindness. On windsteeds they might have got above the fog-blanket, but the big animals, worn out and sullen after being tied two days in the boat, would not fly. Mogien, Iot and Raho led them, and Rocannon followed behind, keeping a surreptitious lookout for Yahan, of whom he was fond. He had kept on his impermasuit for warmth, though not the headpiece, which insulated him entirely from the world. Even so, he felt uneasy in the blind mist walking an unknown shore, and he searched the sand as he went for any kind of staff or stick. Between the grooves of the windsteeds' dragging wings and ribbons of seaweed and dried salt scum he saw a long white stick of driftwood; he worked it free of the sand and felt easier, armed. But by stopping he had fallen far behind. He hurried after companions' tracks through the fog. A figure loomed up to his right. He knew at once it was none of his companions, and brought his stick up like a quarterstaff, but was grabbed from behind and pulled down backwards. Something like wet leather was slapped across his mouth. He wrestled free and was rewarded with a blow on his head that drove him into unconsciousness.

When sensation returned, painfully and a little at a time, he was lying on his back in the sand. High up above him two vast foggy figures were ponderously arguing. He understood only part of their Olgyior dialect. "Leave it here," one said, and the other said something like, "Kill it here, it hasn't got anything." At this Rocannon rolled on his side and pulled the headmask of his suit up over his head and face and sealed it. One of the giants turned to peer down at him and he saw it was only a burly midman bundled in furs. "Take it to Zgama, maybe Zgama wants it," the other one said. After more discussion Rocannon was hauled up by the arms and dragged along at a jogging run. He struggled, but his head swam and the fog had got into his brain. He had some consciousness of the mist growing darker, of voices, of a wall of sticks and clay and interwoven reeds, and a torch flaring in a sconce. Then a roof overhead, and more voices, and the dark. And finally, face down on a stone floor, he came to and raised his head.

Near him a long fire blazed in a hearth the size of a hut. Bare legs and hems of ragged pelts made a fence in front of it. He raised his head farther and saw a man's face: a midman, white-skinned, black-haired, heavily bearded, clothed in green and black striped furs, a square fur hat on his head. "What are you?" he demanded in a harsh bass, glaring down at Rocannon.

"I . . . I ask the hospitality of this hall," Rocannon said when he had got himself onto his knees. He could not at the moment get any farther.

"You've had some of it," said the bearded man, watching him feel the lump on his occiput. "Want more?" The muddy legs and fur rags around him jigged, dark eyes peered, white faces grinned.

Rocannon got to his feet and straightened up. He stood silent and motionless till his balance was steady and the hammering of pain in his skull had lessened. Then he lifted his head and gazed into the bright black eyes of his captor. "You are Zgama," he said.

The bearded man stepped backwards, looking scared. Rocannon, who had been in trying situations on several worlds, followed up his advantage as well as he could. "I am Olhor, the Wanderer. I come from the north and from the sea; from the land behind the sun. I come in peace and I go in peace. Passing by the Hall of Zgama, I go south. Let no man stop me!"

"Ahh," said all the open mouths in the white faces, gazing at him. He kept his own eyes unwavering on Zgama.

"I am master here," the big man said, his voice rough and uneasy. "None pass by me!"

Rocannon did not speak, or blink.

Zgama saw that in this battle of eyes he was losing: all his people still gazed with round eyes at the stranger. "Leave off your staring!" he bellowed. Rocannon did not move. He realized he was up against a defiant nature, but it was too late to change his tactics now. "Stop staring!" Zgama roared again, then whipped a sword from under his fur cloak, whirled it, and with a tremendous blow sheered off the stranger's head.

But the stranger's head did not come off. He staggered, but Zgama's swordstroke had rebounded as from rock. All the people around the fire whispered, "Ahhh!" The stranger steadied himself and stood unmoving, his eyes fixed on Zgama.

Zgama wavered; almost he stood back to let this weird prisoner go. But the obstinacy of his race won out over his bafflement and fear. "Catch him—grab his arms!" he roared, and when his men did not move he grabbed Rocannon's shoulders and spun him around. At that his men moved in, and Rocannon made no resistance. His suit protected him from foreign elements, extreme temperatures, radioactivity, shocks, and blows of moderate velocity and weight such as swordstrokes or bullets; but it could not get him out of the grasp of ten or fifteen strong men.

"No man passes by the Hall of Zgama, Master of the Long Bay!" The big man gave his rage full vent when his braver bullies had got Rocannon pinioned. "You're a spy for the Yellowheads of Angien. I know you! You come with your Angyar talk and spells and tricks, and dragonboats will follow you out of the north. Not to this place! I am the master of the masterless. Let the Yellowheads and their lickspittle slaves come here—we'll give 'em a taste of bronze! You crawl up out of the sea asking a place by my fire, do you? I'll get you warm, spy. I'll give you roast meat, spy. Tie him to the post there!" His brutal bluster had heartened his people, and they jostled to help lash the stranger to one of the hearth-posts that supported a great spit over the fire, and to pile up wood around his legs.

Then they fell silent. Zgama strode up, grim and massive in his furs, took up a burning branch from the hearth and shook it in Rocannon's eyes, then set the pyre aflame. It blazed up hot. In a moment Rocannon's clothing, the brown cloak and tunic of Hallan, took fire and flamed up around his head, at his face.

"Ahhh," all the watchers whispered once more, but one of them cried, "Look!" As the blaze died down they saw through the smoke the figure stand motionless, flames licking up its legs, gazing straight at Zgama. On the naked breast, dropping from a chain of gold, shone a great jewel like an open eye.

"Pedan, pedan," whimpered the women, cowering in dark corners.

Zgama broke the hush of panic with his bellowing voice. "He'll burn! Let him burn! Deho, throw on more wood, the spy's not roasting quick enough!" He dragged a little boy out into the leaping, restless firelight and forced him to add wood to the pyre. "Is there nothing to eat? Get food, you women! You see our hospitality, you Olhor, see how we eat?" He grabbed a joint of meat off the trencher a woman offered him, and stood in front of Rocannon tearing at it and letting the juice run down his beard. A couple of his bullies imitated him, keeping a little farther away. Most of them did not come anywhere near that end of the hearth; but Zgama got them to eat and drink and shout, and some of the boys dared one another to come up close enough to add a stick to the pyre where the mute, calm man stood with flames playing along his red-lit, strangely shining skin.

Fire and noise died down at last. Men and women slept curled up in their fur rags on the floor, in corners, in the warm ashes. A couple of men watched, sword on knees and flask in hand.

Rocannon let his eyes close. By crossing two fingers he unsealed the headzone of his suit, and breathed fresh air again. The long night wore along and slowly the long dawn lightened. In gray daylight, through fog wreathing in the windowholes, Zgama came sliding on greasy spots on the floor and stepping over snoring bodies, and peered at his captive. The captive's gaze was grave and steady, the captor's impotently defiant. "Burn, burn!" Zgama growled, and went off.

Outside the rude hall Rocannon heard the cooing mutter of herilor, the fat and feathery domesticated meat-animals of the Angyar, kept wing-clipped and here pastured probably on the sea-cliffs. The hall emptied out except for a few babies and women, who kept well away from him even when it came time to roast the evening meat.

By then Rocannon had stood bound for thirty hours, and was suffering both pain and thirst. That was his deadline, thirst. He could go without eating for a long time, and supposed he could stand in chains at least as long, though his head was already light; but without water he could get through only one more of these long days.

Powerless as he was, there was nothing he could say to Zgama, threat or bribe, that would not simply increase the barbarian's obduracy.

That night as the fire danced in front of his eyes and through it he watched Zgama's bearded, heavy, white face, he kept seeing in his mind's eye a different face, bright-haired and dark: Mogien, whom he had come to love as a friend and somewhat as a son. As the night and the fire went on and on he thought also of the little Fian Kyo, childlike and uncanny, bound to him in a way he had not tried to understand; he saw Yahan singing of heroes; and Iot and Raho grumbling and laughing together as they curried the great-winged steeds; and Haldre unclasping the gold chain from her neck. Nothing came to him from all his earlier life, though he had lived many years on many worlds, learned much, done much. It was all burnt away. He thought he stood in Hallan, in the long hall hung with tapestries of men fighting giants, and that Yahan was offering him a bowl of water.

"Drink it, Starlord. Drink."

And he drank.

V

Feni and Feli, the two largest moons, danced in white reflections on the water as Yahan held a second bowlful for him to drink. The hearthfire glimmered only in a few coals. The hall was dark picked out with flecks and shafts of moonlight, silent except for the breathing and shifting of many sleepers.

As Yahan cautiously loosed the chains Rocannon leaned his full weight back against the post, for his legs were numb and he could not stand unsupported.

"They guard the outer gate all night," Yahan was whispering in his ear, "and those guards keep awake. Tomorrow when they take the flocks out—"

"Tomorrow night. I can't run. I'll have to bluff out. Hook the chain so I can lean my weight on it, Yahan. Get the hook here, by my hand." A sleeper nearby sat up yawning, and with a grin that flashed a moment in the moonlight Yahan sank down and seemed to melt in shadows.

Rocannon saw him at dawn going out with the other men to take the herilor to pasture, wearing a muddy pelt like the others, his black hair sticking out like a broom. Once again Zgama came up and scowled at his captive. Rocannon knew the man would have given half his flocks and wives to be rid of his unearthly guest, but was trapped in his own cruelty: the jailer is the prisoner's prisoner. Zgama had slept in the warm ashes and his hair was smeared with ash, so that he looked more the burned man than Rocannon, whose naked skin shone white. He stamped off, and again the hall was empty most of the day, though guards stayed at the door. Rocannon improved his time with surreptitious isometric exercises. When a passing woman caught him stretching, he stretched on, swaying and emitting a low, weird croon. She dropped to all fours and scuttled out, whimpering.

Twilit fog blew in the windows, sullen womenfolk boiled a stew of meat and seaweed, returning flocks cooed in hundreds outside, and Zgama and his men came in, fog-droplets glittering in their beards and furs. They sat on the floor to eat. The place rang and reeked and steamed. The strain of returning each night to the uncanny was showing; faces were grim, voices quarrelsome. "Build up the fire—he'll roast yet!" shouted Zgama, jumping up to push a burning log over onto the pyre. None of his men moved.

"I'll eat your heart, Olhor, when it fries out between your ribs! I'll wear that blue stone for a nosering!" Zgama was shaking with rage, frenzied by the silent steady gaze he had endured for two nights. "I'll make you shut your eyes!" he screamed, and snatching up a heavy stick from the floor he brought it down with a whistling crack on Rocannon's head, jumping back at the same moment as if afraid of what he handled. The stick fell among the burning logs and stuck up at an angle.

Slowly, Rocannon reached out his right hand, closed his fist about the stick and drew it out of the fire. Its end was ablaze. He raised it till it pointed at Zgama's eyes, and then, as slowly, he stepped forward. The chains fell away from him. The fire leaped up and broke apart in sparks and coals about his bare feet.

"Out!" he said, coming straight at Zgama, who fell back one step and then another. "You're not master here. The lawless man is a slave, and the cruel man is a slave, and the stupid man is a slave. You are my slave, and I drive you like a beast. Out!" Zgama caught both sides of the doorframe, but the blazing staff came at his eyes, and he cringed back into the courtyard. The guards crouched down, motionless. Resin-torches flaring beside the outer gate brightened the fog; there was no noise but the murmur of the herds in their byres and the hissing of the sea below the cliffs. Step by step Zgama went backward till he reached the outer gate between the torches. His black-and-white face stared masklike as the fiery staff came closer. Dumb with fear, he clung to the log doorpost, filling the gateway with his bulky body. Rocannon, exhausted and vindictive, drove the flaming point hard against his chest, pushed him down, and strode over his body into the blackness and blowing fog outside the gate. He went about fifty paces into the dark, then stumbled, and could not get up.

No one pursued. No one came out of the compound behind him. He lay half-conscious in the dune-grass. After a long time the gate torches died out or were extinguished, and there was only darkness. Wind blew with voices in the grass, and the sea hissed down below.

As the fog thinned, letting the moons shine through, Yahan found him there near the cliff's edge. With his help, Rocannon got up and walked. Feeling their way, stumbling, crawling on hands and knees where the going was rough and dark, they worked eastward and southward away from the coast. A couple of times they stopped to get their breath and bearings, and Rocannon fell asleep almost as soon as they stopped. Yahan woke him and kept him going until, some time before dawn, they came down a valley under the eaves of a steep forest. The domain of trees was black in the misty dark. Yahan and Rocannon entered it along the streambed they had been following, but did not go far. Rocannon stopped and said in his own language, "I can't go any farther." Yahan found a sandy strip under the streambank where they could lie hidden at least from above; Rocannon crawled into it like an animal into its den, and slept.

When he woke fifteen hours later at dusk, Yahan was there with a small collection of green shoots and roots to eat. "It's too early in warmyear for fruit," he explained ruefully, "and the oafs in Oafscastle took my bow. I made some snares but they won't catch anything till tonight."

Rocannon consumed the salad avidly, and when he had drunk from the stream and stretched and could think again, he asked, "Yahan, how did you happen to be there—in Oafscastle?"

The young midman looked down and buried a few inedible root-tips neatly in the sand. "Well, Lord, you know that I . . . defied my Lord Mogien. So after that, I thought I might join the Masterless."

"You'd heard of them before?"

"There are tales at home of places where we Olgyior are both lords and servants. It's even said that in old days only we midmen lived in Angien, and were hunters in the forests and had no masters; and the Angyar came from the south in dragonboats. . . . Well, I found the fort, and Zgama's fellows took me for a runaway from some other place down the coast. They grabbed my bow and put me to work and asked no questions. So I found you. Even if you hadn't been there I would have escaped. I would not be a lord among such oafs!"

"Do you know where our companions are?"

"No. Will you seek for them, Lord?"

"Call me by my name, Yahan. Yes, if there's any chance of finding them I'll seek them. We can't cross a continent alone, on foot, without clothes or weapons."

Yahan said nothing, smoothing the sand, watching the stream that ran dark and clear beneath the heavy branches of the conifers.

"You disagree?"

"If my Lord Mogien finds me he'll kill me. It is his right."

By the Angyar code, this was true; and if anyone would keep the code, it was Mogien.

"If you find a new master, the old one may not touch you: is that not true, Yahan?"

The boy nodded. "But a rebellious man finds no new master."

"That depends. Pledge your service to me, and I'll answer for you to Mogien—if we find him. I don't know what words you use."

"We say"—Yahan spoke very low—"*to my Lord I give the hours of my life and the use of my death.*"

"I accept them. And with them my own life which you gave back to me."

The little river ran noisily from the ridge above them, and the sky darkened solemnly. In late dusk Rocannon slipped off his impermasuit and, stretching out in the stream, let the cold water running all along his body wash away sweat and weariness and fear and the memory of the fire licking at his eyes. Off, the suit was a handful of transparent stuff and semivisible, hairthin tubes and wires and a couple of translucent cubes the size of a fingernail. Yahan watched him with an uncomfortable look as he put the suit on again (since he had no clothes, and Yahan had been forced to trade his

Angyar clothing for a couple of dirty herilo fleeces). "Lord Olhor," he said at last, "it was . . . was it that skin that kept the fire from burning you? Or the . . . the jewel?"

The necklace was hidden now in Yahan's own amulet-bag, around Rocannon's neck. Rocannon answered gently, "The skin. No spells. It's a very strong kind of armor."

"And the white staff?"

He looked down at the driftwood stick, one end of it heavily charred; Yahan had picked it up from the grass of the sea-cliff, last night, just as Zgama's men had brought it along to the fort with him; they had seemed determined he should keep it. What was a wizard without his staff? "Well," he said, "it's a good walking-stick, if we've got to walk." He stretched again, and for want of more supper before they slept, drank once more from the dark, cold, noisy stream.

Late next morning when he woke, he was recovered, and ravenous. Yahan had gone off at dawn, to check his snares and because he was too cold to lie longer in their damp den. He returned with only a handful of herbs, and a piece of bad news. He had crossed over the forested ridge which they were on the seaward side of, and from its top had seen to the south another broad reach of the sea.

"Did those misbegotten fish-eaters from Tolen leave us on an island?" he growled, his usual optimism subverted by cold, hunger, and doubt.

Rocannon tried to recall the coastline on his drowned maps. A river running in from the west emptied on the north of a long tongue of land, itself part of a coastwise mountainchain running west to east; between that tongue and the mainland was a sound, long and wide enough to show up very clear on the maps and in his memory. A hundred, two hundred kilometers long? "How wide?" he asked Yahan, who answered glumly, "Very wide. I can't swim, Lord."

"We can walk. This ridge joins the mainland, west of here. Mogien will be looking for us along that way, probably." It was up to him to provide leadership—Yahan had certainly done more than his share—but his heart was low in him at the thought of that long detour through unknown and hostile country. Yahan had seen no one, but had crossed paths, and there must be men in these woods to make the game so scarce and shy.

But for there to be any hope of Mogien's finding them—if Mogien was alive, and free, and still had the windsteeds—they would have to work southward, and if possible out into open country. He would look for them going south, for that was all the goal of their journey. "Let's go," Rocannon said, and they went.

A little after midday they looked down from the ridge across a broad inlet running east and west as far as eye could see, lead-gray under a low sky. Nothing of the southern shore could be made out but a line of low, dark, dim hills. The wind that blew up the sound was bitter cold at their backs as they worked down to the shore and started westward along it. Yahan looked up at the clouds, hunched his head down between his shoulders and said mournfully, "It's going to snow."

And presently the snow began, a wet windblown snow of spring, vanishing on the wet ground as quickly as on the dark water of the sound. Rocannon's suit kept the cold from him, but strain and hunger made him very weary; Yahan was also weary, and very cold. They slogged along, for there was nothing else to do. They forded a creek, plugged up the bank through coarse grass and blowing snow, and at the top came face to face with a man.

"Houf!" he said staring in surprise and then in wonder. For what he saw was two men walking in a snowstorm, one blue-lipped and shivering in ragged furs, the other one stark naked. "Ha, houf!" he said again. He was a tall, bony, bowed, bearded man with a wild look in his dark eyes. "Ha you, there!" he said in the Olgyior speech, "you'll freeze to death!"

"We had to swim—our boat sank," Yahan improvised promptly. "Have you a house with a fire in it, hunter of pelliunur?"

"You were crossing the sound from the south?"

The man looked troubled, and Yahan replied with a vague gesture, "We're from the east—we came to buy pelliun-furs, but all our tradegoods went down in the water."

"Hanh, hanh," the wild man went, still troubled, but a genial streak in him seemed to win out over his fears. "Come on; I have fire and food," he said, and turning, he jigged off into the thin, gusting snow. Following, they came soon to his hut perched on a slope between the forested ridge and the sound. Inside and out it was like any winter hut of the midmen of the forests and hills of Angien, and Yahan squatted down before the fire with a sigh of frank relief, as if at home. That reassured their host better than any ingenious explanations. "Build up the fire, lad," he said, and he gave Rocannon a homespun cloak to wrap himself in.

Throwing off his own cloak, he set a clay bowl of stew in the ashes to warm, and hunkered down companionably with them, rolling his eyes at one and then the other. "Always snows this time of year, and it'll snow harder soon.

Plenty of room for you; there's three of us winter here. The others will be in tonight or tomorrow or soon enough; they'll be staying out this snowfall up on the ridge where they were hunting. Pelliun hunters we are, as you saw by my whistles, eh lad?" He touched the set of heavy wooden panpipes dangling at his belt, and grinned. He had a wild, fierce, foolish look to him, but his hospitality was tangible. He gave them their fill of meat stew, and when the evening darkened, told them to get their rest. Rocannon lost no time. He rolled himself up in the stinking furs of the bed-niche, and slept like a baby.

In the morning snow still fell, and the ground now was white and featureless. Their host's companions had not come back. "They'll have spent the night over across the Spine, in Timash village. They'll come along when it clears."

"The Spine—that's the arm of the sea there?"

"No, that's the sound—no villages across it! The Spine's the ridge, the hills up above us here. Where do you come from, anyhow? You talk like us here, mostly, but your uncle don't."

Yahan glanced apologetically at Rocannon, who had been asleep while acquiring a nephew. "Oh—he's from the Backlands; they talk differently. We call that water the sound, too. I wish I knew a fellow with a boat to bring us across it."

"You want to go south?"

"Well, now that all our goods are gone, we're nothing here but beggars. We'd better try to get home."

"There's a boat down on the shore, a ways from here. We'll see about that when the weather clears. I'll tell you, lad, when you talk so cool about going south my blood gets cold. There's no man dwelling between the sound and the great mountains, that ever I heard of, unless it's the Ones not talked of. And that's all old stories, and who's to say if there's any mountains even? I've been over on the other side of the sound—there's not many men can tell you that. Been there myself, hunting, in the hills. There's plenty of pelliunur there, near the water. But no villages. No men. None. And I wouldn't stay the night."

"We'll just follow the southern shore eastward," Yahan said indifferently, but with a perplexed look; his inventions were forced into further complexity with every question.

But his instinct to lie had been correct—"At least you didn't sail from the north!" their host, Piai, rambled on, sharpening his long, leaf-bladed knife on a whetstone as he talked. "No men at all across the sound, and across the sea only mangy fellows that serve as slaves to the Yellowheads. Don't your people know about them? In the north country over the sea there's a race of men with yellow heads. It's true. They say that they live in houses high as trees, and carry silver swords, and ride between the wings of windsteeds! I'll believe that when I see it. Windsteed fur brings a good price over on the coast, but the beasts are dangerous to hunt, let alone taming one and riding it. You can't believe all people tell in tales. I make a good enough living out of pelliun furs. I can bring the beasts from a day's flight around. Listen!" He put his panpipes to his hairy lips and blew, very faintly at first, a half-heard, halting plaint that swelled and changed, throbbing and breaking between notes, rising into an almost-melody that was a wild beast's cry. The chill went up Rocannon's back; he had heard that tune in the forests of Hallan. Yahan, who had been trained as a huntsman, grinned with excitement and cried out as if on the hunt and sighting the quarry, "Sing! sing! she rises there!" He and Piai spent the rest of the afternoon swapping hunting-stories, while outside the snow still fell, windless now and steady.

The next day dawned clear. As on a morning of coldyear, the sun's ruddy-white brilliance was blinding on the snow-whitened hills. Before midday Piai's two companions arrived with a few of the downy gray pelliun-furs. Black-browed, strapping men like all those southern Olgyior, they seemed still wilder than Piai, wary as animals of the strangers, avoiding them, glancing at them only sideways.

"They call my people slaves," Yahan said to Rocannon when the others were outside the hut for a minute. "But I'd rather be a man serving men than a beast hunting beasts, like these." Rocannon raised his hand, and Yahan was silent as one of the Southerners came in, glancing sidelong at them, unspeaking.

"Let's go," Rocannon muttered in the Olgyior tongue, which he had mastered a little more of these last two days. He wished they had not waited till Piai's companions had come, and Yahan also was uneasy. He spoke to Piai, who had just come in:

"We'll be going now—this fair weather should hold till we get around the inlet. If you hadn't sheltered us we'd never have lived through these two nights of cold. And I never would have heard the pelliun-song so played. May all your hunting be fortunate!"

But Piai stood still and said nothing. Finally he hawked, spat on the fire, rolled his eyes, and growled, "Around the inlet? Didn't you want to cross by boat? There's a boat. It's mine. Anyhow, I can use it. We'll take you over the water."

"Six days walking that'll save you," the shorter newcomer, Karmik, put in.

"It'll save you six days walking," Piai repeated. "We'll take you across in the boat. We can go now."

"All right," Yahan replied after glancing at Rocannon; there was nothing they could do.

"Then let's go," Piai grunted, and so abruptly, with no offer of provision for the way, they left the hut, Piai in the lead and his friends bringing up the rear. The wind was keen, the sun bright; though snow remained in sheltered places, the rest of the ground ran and squelched and glittered with the thaw. They followed the shore westward for a long way, and the sun was set when they reached a little cove where a rowboat lay among rocks and reeds out on the water. Red of sunset flushed the water and the western sky; above the red glow the little moon Heliki gleamed waxing, and in the darkening east the Greatstar, Fomalhaut's distant companion, shone like an opal. Under the brilliant sky, over the brilliant water, the long hilly shores ran featureless and dark.

"There's the boat," said Piai, stopping and facing them, his face red with the western light. The other two came and stood in silence beside Rocannon and Yahan.

"You'll be rowing back in darkness," Yahan said.

"Greatstar shines; it'll be a light night. Now, lad, there's the matter of paying us for our rowing you."

"Ah," said Yahan.

"Piai knows—we have nothing. This cloak is his gift," said Rocannon, who, seeing how the wind blew, did not care if his accent gave them away.

"We are poor hunters. We can't give gifts," said Karmik, who had a softer voice and a saner, meaner look than Piai and the other one.

"We have nothing," Rocannon repeated. "Nothing to pay for the rowing. Leave us here."

Yahan joined in, saying the same thing more fluently, but Karmik interrupted: "You're wearing a bag around your neck, stranger. What's in it?"

"My soul," said Rocannon promptly.

They all stared at him, even Yahan. But he was in a poor position to bluff, and the pause did not last. Karmik put his hand on his leaf-bladed hunting knife, and moved closer; Piai and the other imitated him. "You were in Zgama's fort," he said. "They told a long tale about it in Timash village. How a naked man stood in a burning fire, and burned Zgama with a white stick, and walked out of the fort wearing a great jewel on a gold chain around his neck. They said it was magic and spells. I think they are all fools. Maybe you can't be hurt. But this one—" He grabbed Yahan lightning-quick by his long hair, twisted his head back and sideways, and brought the knife up against his throat. "Boy, you tell this stranger you travel with to pay for your lodging—eh?"

They all stood still. The red dimmed on the water, the Greatstar brightened in the east, the cold wind blew past them down the shore.

"We won't hurt the lad," Piai growled, his fierce face twisted and frowning. "We'll do what I said, we'll row you over the sound—only pay us. You didn't say you had gold to pay with. You said you'd lost all your gold. You slept under my roof. Give us the thing and we'll row you across."

"I will give it—over there," Rocannon said, pointing across the sound.

"No," Karmik said.

Yahan, helpless in his hands, had not moved a muscle; Rocannon could see the beating of the artery in his throat, against which the knife-blade lay.

"Over there," he repeated grimly, and tilted his driftwood walking stick forward a little in case the sight of it might impress them. "Row us across; I give you the thing. This I tell you. But hurt him and you die here, now. This I tell you!"

"Karmik, he's a pedan," Piai muttered. "Do what he says. They were under the roof with me, two nights. Let the boy go. He promises the thing you want."

Karmik looked scowling from him to Rocannon and said at last, "Throw that white stick away. Then we'll take you across."

"First let the boy go," said Rocannon, and when Karmik released Yahan, he laughed in his face and tossed the stick high, end over end, out into the water.

Knives drawn, the three huntsmen herded him and Yahan to the boat; they had to wade out and climb in her from the slippery rocks on which dull-red ripples broke. Piai and the third man rowed, Karmik sat knife in hand behind the passengers.

"Will you give him the jewel?" Yahan whispered in the Common Tongue, which these Olgyior of the peninsula did not use.

Rocannon nodded.

Yahan's whisper was very hoarse and shaky. "You jump and swim with it, Lord. Near the south shore. They'll let me go, when it's gone—"

"They'd slit your throat. Shh."

"They're casting spells, Karmik," the third man was saying. "They're going to sink the boat—"

"Row, you rotten fish-spawn. You, be still, or I'll cut the boy's neck."

Rocannon sat patiently on the thwart, watching the water turn misty gray as the shores behind and before them receded into night. Their knives could not hurt him, but they could kill Yahan before he could do much to them. He could have swum for it easy enough, but Yahan could not swim. There was no choice. At least they were getting the ride they were paying for.

Slowly the dim hills of the southern shore rose and took on substance. Faint gray shadows dropped westward and few stars came out in the gray sky; the remote solar brilliance of the Greatstar dominated even the moon Heliki, now in its waning cycle. They could hear the sough of waves against the shore. "Quit rowing," Karmik ordered, and to Rocannon: "Give me the thing now."

"Closer to shore," Rocannon said impassively.

"I can make it from here, Lord," Yahan muttered shakily. "There are reeds sticking up ahead there—"

The boat moved a few oarstrokes ahead and halted again.

"Jump when I do," Rocannon said to Yahan, and then slowly rose and stood up on the thwart. He unsealed the neck of the suit he had worn so long now, broke the leather cord around his neck with a jerk, tossed the bag that held the sapphire and its chain into the bottom of the boat, resealed the suit and in the same instant dived.

He stood with Yahan a couple of minutes later among the rocks of the shore, watching the boat, a blackish blur in the gray quarter-light on the water, shrinking.

"Oh may they rot, may they have worms in their bowels and their bones turn to slime," Yahan said, and began to cry. He had been badly scared, but more than the reaction from fear broke down his self-control. To see a "lord" toss away a jewel worth a kingdom's ransom to save a midman's life, his life, was to see all order subverted, admitting unbearable responsibility. "It was wrong, Lord!" he cried out. "It was wrong!"

"To buy your life with a rock? Come on, Yahan, get a hold of yourself. You'll freeze if we don't get a fire going. Have you got your drill? There's a lot of brushwood up this way. Get a move on!"

They managed to get a fire going there on the shore, and built it up till it drove back the night and the still, keen cold. Rocannon had given Yahan the huntsman's fur cape, and huddling in it the young man finally went to sleep. Rocannon sat keeping the fire burning, uneasy and with no wish to sleep. His own heart was heavy that he had had to throw away the neck-lace, not because it was valuable, but because once he had given it to Semley, whose remembered beauty had brought him, over all the years, to this world; because Haldre had given it to him, hoping, he knew, thus to buy off the shadow, the early death she feared for her son. Maybe it was as well the thing was gone, the weight, the danger of its beauty. And maybe, if worst came to worst, Mogien would never know that it was gone; because Mogien would not find him, or was already dead. . . . He put that thought aside. Mogien was looking for him and Yahan—that must be his assumption. He would look for them going south. For what plan had they ever had, except to go south— there to find the enemy, or, if all his guesses had been wrong, not to find the enemy? But with or without Mogien, he would go south.

They set out at dawn, climbing the shoreline hills in the twilight, reaching the top of them as the rising sun revealed a high, empty plain running sheer to the horizon, streaked with the long shadows of bushes. Piai had been right, apparently, when he said nobody lived south of the sound. At least Mogien would be able to see them from miles off. They started south.

It was cold, but mostly clear. Yahan wore what clothes they had, Rocannon his suit. They crossed creeks angling down toward the sound now and then, often enough to keep them from thirst. That day and next day they went on, living on the roots of a plant called peya and on a couple of stump-winged, hop-flying, coney-like creatures that Yahan knocked out of the air with a stick and cooked on a fire of twigs lit with his firedrill. They saw no other living thing. Clear to the sky the high grasslands stretched, level, treeless, roadless, silent.

Oppressed by immensity, the two men sat by their tiny fire in the vast dusk, saying nothing. Overhead at long intervals, like the beat of a pulse in the night, came a soft cry very high in the air. They were barilor, wild cousins of the tamed herilor, making their northward spring migration. The stars for a hand's breadth would be blotted out by the great flocks, but never more than a single voice called, brief, a pulse on the wind.

"Which of the stars do you come from, Olhor?" Yahan asked softly, gazing up.

"I was born on a world called Hain by my mother's people, and Davenant by my father's. You call its sun the Winter Crown. But I left it long ago. . . ."

"You're not all one people, then, the Starfolk?"

"Many hundred peoples. By blood I'm entirely of my mother's race; my father, who was a Terran, adopted me. This is the custom when people of different species, who cannot conceive children, marry. As if one of your kin should marry a Fian woman."

"This does not happen," Yahan said stiffly.

"I know. But Terran and Davenanter are as alike as you and I. Few worlds have so many different races as this one. Most often there is one, much like us, and the rest are beasts without speech."

"You've seen many worlds," the young man said dreamily, trying to conceive of it.

"Too many," said the older man. "I'm forty, by your years; but I was born a hundred and forty years ago. A hundred years I've lost without living them, between the worlds. If I went back to Davenant or Earth, the men and women I knew would be a hundred years dead. I can only go on; or stop, somewhere— What's that?" The sense of some presence seemed to silence even the hissing of wind through grass. Something moved at the edge of the firelight—a great shadow, a darkness. Rocannon knelt tensely; Yahan sprang away from the fire.

Nothing moved. Wind hissed in the grass in the gray starlight. Clear around the horizon the stars shone, unbroken by any shadow.

The two rejoined at the fire. "What was it?" Rocannon asked.

Yahan shook his head. "Piai talked of . . . something . . ."

They slept patchily, trying to spell each other keeping watch. When the slow dawn came they were very tired. They sought tracks or marks where the shadow had seemed to stand, but the young grass showed nothing. They stamped out their fire and went on, heading southward by the sun.

They had thought to cross a stream soon, but they did not. Either the stream-courses now were running north-south, or there simply were no more. The plain or pampas that seemed never to change as they walked had been becoming always a little dryer, a little grayer. This morning they saw none of the peya bushes, only the coarse gray-green grass going on and on.

At noon Rocannon stopped.

"It's no good, Yahan," he said.

Yahan rubbed his neck, looking around, then turned his gaunt, tired young face to Rocannon. "If you want to go on, Lord, I will."

"We can't make it without water or food. We'll steal a boat on the coast and go back to Hallan. This is no good. Come on."

Rocannon turned and walked northward. Yahan came along beside him. The high spring sky burned blue, the wind hissed endlessly in the endless grass. Rocannon went along steadily, his shoulders a little bent, going step by step into permanent exile and defeat. He did not turn when Yahan stopped.

"Windsteeds!"

Then he looked up and saw them, three great gryphoncats circling down upon them, claws outstretched, wings black against the hot blue sky.

PART TWO

The Wanderer

VI

Mogien leaped off his steed before it had its feet on the ground, ran to Rocannon and hugged him like a brother. His voice rang with delight and relief. "By Hendin's lance, Starlord! why are you marching stark naked across this desert? How did you get so far south by walking north? Are you—" Mogien met Yahan's gaze, and stopped short.

Rocannon said, "Yahan is my bondsman."

Mogien said nothing. After a certain struggle with himself he began to grin, then he laughed out loud. "Did you learn our customs in order to steal my servants, Rokanan? But who stole your clothes?"

"Olhor wears more skins than one," said Kyo, coming with his light step over the grass. "Hail, Firelord! Last night I heard you in my mind."

"Kyo led us to you," Mogien confirmed. "Since we set foot on Fiern's shore ten days ago he never spoke a word, but last night, on the bank of the sound, when Lioka rose, he listened to the moonlight and said, 'There!' Come daylight we flew where he had pointed, and so found you."

"Where is Iot?" Rocannon asked, seeing only Raho stand holding the windsteeds' reins. Mogien with unchanging face replied, "Dead. The Olgyior came on us in the fog on the beach. They had only stones for weapons, but they were many. Iot was killed, and you were lost. We hid in a cave in the seacliffs till the steeds would fly again. Raho went forth and heard tales of a stranger who stood in a burning fire unburnt, and wore a blue jewel. So when the steeds would fly we went to Zgama's fort, and not finding you we dropped fire on his wretched roofs and drove his herds into the forests, and then began to look for you along the banks of the sound."

"The jewel, Mogien," Rocannon interrupted; "the Eye of the Sea—I had to buy our lives with it. I gave it away."

"The jewel?" said Mogien, staring. "Semley's jewel—you gave it away? Not to buy your life—who can harm you? To buy that worthless life, that disobedient halfman? You hold my heritage cheap! Here, take the thing; it's not so easily lost!" He spun something up in the air with a laugh, caught it, and tossed it glittering to Rocannon, who stood and gaped at it, the blue stone burning in his hand, the golden chain.

"Yesterday we met two Olgyior, and one dead one, on the other shore of the sound, and we stopped to ask about a naked traveler they might have seen going by with his worthless servant. One of them groveled on his face and told us the story, and so I took the jewel from the other one. And his life along with it, because he fought. Then we knew you had crossed the sound; and Kyo brought us straight to you. But why were you going northward, Rokanan?"

"To—to find water."

"There's a stream to the west," Raho put in. "I saw it just before we saw you."

"Let's go to it. Yahan and I haven't drunk since last night."

They mounted the windsteeds, Yahan with Raho, Kyo in his old place behind Rocannon. The wind-bowed grass dropped away beneath them, and they skimmed southwestward between the vast plain and the sun.

They camped by the stream that wound clear and slow among flowerless grasses. Rocannon could at last take off the impermasuit, and dressed in Mogien's spare shirt and cloak. They ate hard bread brought from Tolen, peya roots, and four of the stump-winged coneys shot by Raho and by Yahan, who was full of joy when he got his hands on a bow again. The creatures out here on the plain almost flew upon the arrows, and let the windsteeds snap them up in flight, having no fear. Even the tiny green and violet and yellow creatures called kilar, insect-like with transparent buzzing wings, though they were actually tiny marsupials, here were fearless and curious, hovering about one's head, peering with round gold eyes, lighting on one's hand or knee a moment and skimming distractingly off again. It looked as if all this immense grassland were void of intelligent life. Mogien said they had seen no sign of men or other beings as they had flown above the plain.

"We thought we saw some creature last night, near the fire," Rocannon said hesitantly, for what had they seen? Kyo looked around at him from the cooking-fire; Mogien, unbuckling his belt that held the double swords, said nothing.

They broke camp at first light and all day rode the wind between plain and sun. Flying above the plain was as pleasant as walking across it had been hard. So passed the following day, and just before evening, as they looked out for one of the small streams that rarely broke the expanse of grass, Yahan turned in his saddle and called across the wind, "Olhor! See ahead!" Very far ahead, due south, a faint ruffling or crimping of gray broke the smooth horizon.

"The mountains!" Rocannon said, and as he spoke he heard Kyo behind him draw breath sharply, as if in fear.

During the next day's flight the flat pampas gradually rose into low swells and rolls of land, vast waves on a quiet sea. High-piled clouds drifted northward above them now and then, and far ahead they could see the land tilting upward, growing dark and broken. By evening the mountains were clear; when the plain was dark the remote, tiny peaks in the south still shone bright gold for a long time. From those far peaks as they faded, the moon Lioka rose and sailed up like a great, hurrying, yellow star. Feni and Feli were already shining, moving in more stately fashion from east to west. Last of the four rose Heliki and pursued the others, brightening and dimming in a half-hour cycle, brightening and dimming. Rocannon lay on his back and watched, through the high black stems of grass, the slow and radiant complexity of the lunar dance.

Next morning when he and Kyo went to mount the gray-striped windsteed Yahan cautioned him, standing at the beast's head: "Ride him with care today, Olhor." The windsteed agreed with a cough and a long snarl, echoed by Mogien's gray.

"What ails them?"

"Hunger!" said Raho, reining in his white steed hard. "They got their fill of Zgama's herilor, but since we started across this plain there's been no big game, and these hop-flyers are only a mouthful to 'em. Belt in your cloak, Lord Olhor—if it blows within reach of your steed's jaws you'll be his dinner." Raho, whose brown hair and skin testified to the attraction one of his grandmothers had exerted on some Angyar nobleman, was more brusque and mocking than most midmen. Mogien never rebuked him, and Raho's harshness did not hide his passionate loyalty to his lord. A man near middle age, he plainly thought this journey a fool's errand, and as plainly had never thought to do anything but go with his young lord into any peril.

Yahan handed up the reins and dodged back from Rocannon's steed, which leaped like a released spring into the air. All that day the three steeds flew wildly, tirelessly, toward the hunting-grounds they sensed or scented to the south, and a north wind hastened them on. Forested foothills rose always darker and clearer under the floating barrier of mountains. Now there were trees on the plain, clumps and groves like islands in the swelling sea of grass. The groves thickened into forests broken by green parkland. Before dusk they came down by a little sedgy lake among wooded hills. Working fast and gingerly, the two midmen stripped all packs and harness off the steeds, stood back and let them go. Up they shot, bellowing, wide wings beating, flew off in three different directions over the hills, and were gone.

"They'll come back when they've fed," Yahan told Rocannon, "or when Lord Mogien blows his still whistle."

"Sometimes they bring mates back with them—wild ones," Raho added, baiting the tenderfoot.

Mogien and the midmen scattered, hunting hop-flyers or whatever else turned up; Rocannon pulled some fat peya roots and put them to roast wrapped in their leaves in the ashes of the campfire. He was expert at making do with what any land offered, and enjoyed it; and these days of great flights between dusk and dusk, of constant barely-assuaged hunger, of sleep on the bare ground in the wind of spring, had left him very fine-drawn, tuned and open to every sensation and impression. Rising, he saw that Kyo had wandered down to the lake-edge and was standing there, a slight figure no taller than the reeds that grew far out into the water. He was looking up at the mountains that towered gray across the south, gathering around their high heads all the clouds and silence of the sky. Rocannon, coming up beside him, saw in his face a look both desolate and eager. He said without turning, in his light hesitant voice, "Olhor, you have again the jewel."

"I keep trying to give it away," Rocannon said, grinning.

"Up there," the Fian said, "you must give more than gold and stones. . . . What will you give, Olhor, there in the cold, in the high place, the gray place? From the fire to the cold. . . ." Rocannon heard him, and watched him, yet did not see his lips move. A chill went through him and he closed his mind, retreating from the touch of a strange sense into his own humanity, his own identity. After a minute Kyo turned, calm and smiling as usual, and spoke in his usual voice. "There are Fiia beyond these foothills, beyond the forests, in green valleys. My people like the valleys, even here, the sunlight and the low places. We may find their villages in a few days' flight."

This was good news to the others when Rocannon reported it. "I thought we were going to find no speaking beings here. A fine, rich land to be so empty," Raho said.

Watching a pair of the dragonfly-like kilar dancing like winged amethysts above the lake, Mogien said, "It was not always empty. My people crossed it long ago, in the years before the heroes, before Hallan was built or high Oynhall, before Hendin struck the great stroke or Kirfiel died on Orren Hill. We came in boats with dragonheads from the south, and found in Angien a wild folk hiding in woods and sea-caves, a white-faced folk. You know the song, Yahan, the Lay of Orhogien—

Riding the wind,
walking the grass,
skimming the sea,
toward the star Brehen
on Lioka's path . . .

Lioka's path is from the south to the north. And the battles in the song tell how we Angyar fought and conquered the wild hunters, the Olgyior, the only ones of our race in Angien; for we're all one race, the Liuar. But the song tells nothing of those mountains. It's an old song, perhaps the beginning is lost. Or perhaps my people came from these foothills. This is a fair country—woods for hunting and hills for herds and heights for fortresses. Yet no men seem to live here now. . . ."

Yahan did not play his silver-strung lyre that night; and they all slept uneasily, maybe because the windsteeds were gone, and the hills were so deathly still, as if no creature dared move at all by night.

Agreeing that their camp by the lake was too boggy, they moved on next day, taking it easy and stopping often to hunt and gather fresh herbs. At dusk they came to a hill the top of which was humped and dented, as if under the grass lay the foundations of a fallen building. Nothing was left, yet they could trace or guess where the flightcourt of a little fortress had been, in years so long gone no legend told of it. They camped there, where the windsteeds would find them readily when they returned.

Late in the long night Rocannon woke and sat up. No moon but little Lioka shone, and the fire was out. They had set no watch. Mogien was standing about fifteen feet away, motionless, a tall vague form in the starlight. Rocannon sleepily watched him, wondering why his cloak made him look so tall and narrow-shouldered. That was not right. The Angyar cloak flared out at the shoulders like a pagoda-roof, and even without his cloak Mogien was notably broad across the chest. Why was he standing there so tall and stooped and lean?

The face turned slowly, and it was not Mogien's face.

"Who's that?" Rocannon asked, starting up, his voice thick in the dead silence. Beside him Raho sat up, looked around, grabbed his bow and scrambled to his feet. Behind the tall figure something moved slightly—another like it. All around them, all over the grass-grown ruins in the starlight, stood tall, lean, silent forms, heavily cloaked, with bowed heads. By the cold fire only he and Raho stood.

"Lord Mogien!" Raho shouted.

No answer.

"Where is Mogien? What people are you? Speak—"

They made no answer, but they began slowly to move forward. Raho nocked an arrow. Still they said nothing, but all at once they expanded weirdly, their cloaks sweeping out on both sides, and attacked from all directions at once, coming in slow, high leaps. As Rocannon fought them he fought to waken from the dream—it must be a dream; their slowness, their silence, it was all unreal, and he could not feel them strike him. But he was wearing his suit. He heard Raho cry out desperately, "Mogien!" The attackers had forced Rocannon down by sheer weight and numbers, and then before he could struggle free again he was lifted up head downward, with a sweeping, sickening movement. As he writhed, trying to get loose from the many hands holding him, he saw starlit hills and woods swinging and rocking beneath him—far beneath. His head swam and he gripped with both hands onto the thin limbs of the creatures that had lifted him. They were all about him, their hands holding him, the air full of black wings beating.

It went on and on, and still sometimes he struggled to wake up from this monotony of fear, the soft hissing voices about him, the multiple laboring wing-beats jolting him endlessly on. Then all at once the flight changed to a long slanting glide. The brightening east slid horribly by him, the ground tilted up at him, the many soft, strong hands holding him let go, and he fell. Unhurt, but too sick and dizzy to sit up, he lay sprawling and stared about him.

Under him was a pavement of level, polished tile. To left and right above him rose a wall, silvery in the early light, high and straight and clean as if cut of steel. Behind him rose the huge dome of a building, and ahead, through a topless gateway, he saw a street of windowless silvery houses, perfectly aligned, all alike, a pure geometric perspective in the unshadowed clarity of dawn. It was a city, not a stone-age village or a bronze-age fortress but a great city, severe and grandiose, powerful and exact, the product of a high technology. Rocannon sat up, his head still swimming.

As the light grew he made out certain shapes in the dimness of the court, bundles of something; the end of one gleamed yellow. With a shock that broke his trance he saw the dark face under the shock of yellow hair. Mogien's eyes were open, staring at the sky, and did not blink.

All four of his companions lay the same, rigid, eyes open. Raho's face was hideously convulsed. Even Kyo, who had seemed invulnerable in his very fragility, lay still with his great eyes reflecting the pale sky.

Yet they breathed, in long, quiet breaths seconds apart; he put his ear to Mogien's chest and heard the heartbeat very faint and slow, as if from far away.

A sibilance in the air behind him made him cower down instinctively and hold as still as the paralyzed bodies around him. Hands tugged at his shoulders and legs. He was turned over, and lay looking up into a face; a large, long face, somber and beautiful. The dark head was hairless, lacking even eyebrows. Eyes of clear gold looked out between wide, lashless lids. The mouth, small and delicately carved, was closed. The soft, strong hands were at his jaw, forcing his own mouth open. Another tall form bent over him, and he coughed and choked as something was poured down his throat—warm water, sickly and stale. The two great beings let him go. He got to his feet, spitting, and said, "I'm all right, let me be!" But their backs were already turned. They were stooping over Yahan, one forcing open his jaws, the other pouring in a mouthful of water from a long, silvery vase.

They were very tall, very thin, semi-humanoid; hard and delicate, moving rather awkwardly and slowly on the ground, which was not their element. Narrow chests projected between the shoulder-muscles of long, soft wings that fell curving down their backs like gray capes. The legs were thin and short, and the dark, noble heads seemed stooped forward by the upward jut of the wingblades.

Rocannon's *Handbook* lay under the fog-bound waters of the channel, but his memory shouted at him: *High-Intelligence Life Forms, Unconfirmed Species ?4: Large humanoids said to inhabit extensive towns (?).* And he had the luck to confirm it, to get the first sight of a new species, a new high culture, a new member for the League. The clean, precise beauty of the buildings, the impersonal charity of the two great angelic figures who brought water, their kingly silence, it all awed him. He had never seen a race like this on any world. He came to the pair, who were giving Kyo water, and asked with diffident courtesy, "Do you speak the Common Tongue, winged lords?"

They did not heed him. They went quietly with their soft, slightly crippled ground-gait to Raho and forced water into his contorted mouth. It ran out again and down his cheeks. They moved on to Mogien, and Rocannon followed them. "Hear me!" he said, getting in front of them, but stopped: it came on him sickeningly that the wide golden eyes were blind, that they were blind and deaf. For they did not answer or glance at him, but walked away, tall, aerial, the soft wings cloaking them from neck to heel. And the door fell softly to behind them.

Pulling himself together, Rocannon went to each of his companions, hoping an antidote to the paralysis might be working. There was no change. In each he confirmed the slow breath and faint heartbeat—in each except one.

Raho's chest was still and his pitifully contorted face was cold. The water they had given him was still wet on his cheeks.

Anger broke through Rocannon's awed wonder. Why did the angel-men treat him and his friends like captured wild animals? He left his companions and strode across the courtyard, out the topless gate into the street of the incredible city.

Nothing moved. All doors were shut. Tall and windowless, one after another, the silvery facades stood silent in the first light of the sun.

Rocannon counted six crossings before he came to the street's end: a wall. Five meters high it ran in both directions without a break; he did not follow the circumferential street to seek a gate, guessing there was none. What need had winged beings for city gates? He returned up the radial street to the central building from which he had come, the only building in the city different from and higher than the high silvery houses in their geometric rows. He reëntered the courtyard. The houses were all shut, the streets clean and empty, the sky empty, and there was no noise but that of his steps.

He hammered on the door at the inner end of the court. No response. He pushed, and it swung open.

Within was a warm darkness, a soft hissing and stirring, a sense of height and vastness. A tall form lurched past him, stopped and stood still. In the shaft of low early sunlight he had let in the door, Rocannon saw the winged being's yellow eyes close and reopen slowly. It was the sunlight that blinded them. They must fly abroad, and walk their silver streets, only in the dark.

Facing that unfathomable gaze, Rocannon took the attitude that hilfers called "GCO" for Generalised Communications Opener, a dramatic, receptive pose, and asked in Galactic, "Who is your leader?" Spoken impressively, the question usually got some response. None this time. The Winged One gazed straight at Rocannon, blinked once with an impassivity beyond disdain, shut his eyes, and stood there to all appearances sound asleep.

Rocannon's eyes had eased to the near-darkness, and he now saw, stretching off into the warm gloom under the vaults, rows and clumps and knots of the winged figures, hundreds of them, all unmoving, eyes shut.

He walked among them and they did not move.

Long ago, on Davenant, the planet of his birth, he had walked through a museum full of statues, a child looking up into the unmoving faces of the ancient Hainish gods.

Summoning his courage, he went up to one and touched him—her? they could as well be females—on the arm. The golden eyes opened, and the beautiful face turned to him, dark above him in the gloom. "Hassa!" said the

Winged One, and, stooping quickly, kissed his shoulder, then took three steps away, refolded its cape of wings and stood still, eyes shut.

Rocannon gave them up and went on, groping his way through the peaceful, honeyed dusk of the huge room till he found a farther doorway, open from floor to lofty ceiling. The area beyond it was a little brighter, tiny roof holes allowing a dust of golden light to sift down. The walls curved away on either hand, rising to a narrow arched vault. It seemed to be a circular passage-room surrounding the central dome, the heart of the radial city. The inner wall was wonderfully decorated with a pattern of intricately linked triangles and hexagons repeated clear up to the vault. Rocannon's puzzled ethnological enthusiasm revived. These people were master builders. Every surface in the vast building was smooth and every joint precise; the conception was splendid and the execution faultless. Only a high culture could have achieved this. But never had he met a highly-cultured race so unresponsive. After all, why had they brought him and the others here? Had they, in their silent angelic arrogance, saved the wanderers from some danger of the night? Or did they use other species as slaves? If so, it was queer how they had ignored his apparent immunity to their paralyzing agent. Perhaps they communicated entirely without words; but he inclined to believe, in this unbelievable palace, that the explanations might lie in the fact of an intelligence that was simply outside human scope. He went on, finding in the inner wall of the torus-passage a third door, this time very low, so that he had to stoop, and a Winged One must have to crawl.

Inside was the same warm, yellowish, sweet-smelling gloom, but here stirring, muttering, susurrating with a steady soft murmur of voices and slight motions of innumerable bodies and dragging wings. The eye of the dome, far up, was golden. A long ramp spiraled at a gentle slant around the wall clear up to the drum of the dome. Here and there on the ramp movement was visible, and twice a figure, tiny from below, spread its wings and flew soundlessly across the great cylinder of dusty golden air. As he started across the hall to the foot of the ramp, something fell from midway up the spiral, landing with a hard dry crack. He passed close by it. It was the corpse of one of the Winged Ones. Though the impact had smashed the skull, no blood was to be seen. The body was small, the wings apparently not fully formed.

He went doggedly on and started up the ramp.

Ten meters or so above the floor he came to a triangular niche in the wall in which Winged Ones crouched, again short and small ones, with wrinkled wings. There were nine of them, grouped regularly, three and three and three at even intervals, around a large pale bulk that Rocannon peered at a while before he made out the muzzle and the open, empty eyes. It was a windsteed, alive, paralyzed. The little delicately carved mouths of nine Winged Ones bent to it again and again, kissing it, kissing it.

Another crash on the floor across the hall. This Rocannon glanced at as he passed at a quiet run. It was the drained withered body of a barilo.

He crossed the high ornate torus-passage and threaded his way as quickly and softly as he could among the sleep-standing figures in the hall. He came out into the courtyard. It was empty. Slanting white sunlight shone on the pavement. His companions were gone. They had been dragged away for the larvae, there in the domed hall, to suck dry.

VII

Rocannon's knees gave way. He sat down on the polished red pavement, and tried to repress his sick fear enough to think what to do. What to do. He must go back into the dome and try to bring out Mogien and Yahan and Kyo. At the thought of going back in there among the tall angelic figures whose noble heads held brains degenerated or specialized to the level of insects, he felt a cold prickling at the back of his neck; but he had to do it. His friends were in there and he had to get them out. Were the larvae and their nurses in the dome sleepy enough to let him? He quit asking himself questions. But first he must check the outer wall all the way around, for if there was no gate, there was no use. He could not carry his friends over a fifteen-foot wall.

There were probably three castes, he thought as he went down the silent perfect street: nurses for the larvae in the dome, builders and hunters in the outer rooms, and in these houses perhaps the fertile ones, the egglayers and hatchers. The two that had given water would be nurses, keeping the paralyzed prey alive till the larvae sucked it dry. They had given water to dead Raho. How could he not have seen that they were mindless? He had wanted to think them intelligent because they looked so angelically human. *Strike Species* ?4, he told his drowned *Handbook,* savagely. Just then, something dashed across the street at the next crossing—a low, brown creature, whether large or small he could not tell in the unreal perspective of identical housefronts. It clearly was no part of the city. At least the angel-insects had vermin infesting their fine hive. He went on quickly and steadily through the utter silence, reached the outer wall, and turned left along it.

A little way ahead of him, close to the jointless silvery base of the wall, crouched one of the brown animals. On all fours it came no higher than his knee. Unlike most low-intelligence animals on this planet, it was wingless. It crouched there looking terrified, and he simply detoured around it, trying not to frighten it into defiance, and went on. As far as he could see ahead there was no gate in the curving wall.

"Lord," cried a faint voice from nowhere. "Lord!"

"Kyo!" he shouted, turning, his voice clapping off the walls. Nothing moved. White walls, black shadows, straight lines, silence.

The little brown animal came hopping toward him. "Lord," it cried thinly, "Lord, O come, come. O come, Lord!"

Rocannon stood staring. The little creature sat down on its strong haunches in front of him. It panted, and its heartbeat shook its furry chest, against which tiny black hands were folded. Black, terrified eyes looked up at him. It repeated in quavering Common Speech, "Lord . . ."

Rocannon knelt. His thoughts raced as he regarded the creature; at last he said very gently, "I do not know what to call you."

"O come," said the little creature, quavering. "Lords—lords. Come!"

"The other lords—my friends?"

"Friends," said the brown creature. "Friends. Castle. Lords, castle, fire, windsteed, day, night, fire. O come!"

"I'll come," said Rocannon.

It hopped off at once, and he followed. Back down the radial street it went, then one side-street to the north, and in one of the twelve gates of the dome. There in the red-paved court lay his four companions as he had left them. Later on, when he had time to think, he realized that he had come out from the dome into a different courtyard and so missed them.

Five more of the brown creatures waited there, in a rather ceremonious group near Yahan. Rocannon knelt again to minimize his height and made as good a bow as he could. "Hail, small lords," he said.

"Hail, hail," said all the furry little people. Then one, whose fur was black around the muzzle, said, "Kiemhrir."

"You are the Kiemhrir?" They bowed in quick imitation of his bow. "I am Rokanan Olhor. We come from the north, from Angien, from Hallan Castle."

"Castle," said Blackface. His tiny piping voice trembled with earnestness. He pondered, scratched his head. "Days, night, years, years," he said. "Lords go. Years, years, years . . . Kiemhrir ungo." He looked hopefully at Rocannon.

"The Kiemhrir . . . stayed here?" Rocannon asked.

"Stay!" cried Blackface with surprising volume. "Stay! Stay!" And the others all murmured as if in delight, "Stay . . ."

"Day," Blackface said decisively, pointing up at this day's sun, "lords come. Go?"

"Yes, we would go. Can you help us?"

"Help!" said the Kiemher, latching onto the word in the same delighted, avid way. "Help go. Lord, stay!"

So Rocannon stayed: sat and watched the Kiemhrir go to work. Blackface whistled, and soon about a dozen more came cautiously hopping in. Rocannon wondered where in the mathematical neatness of the hive-city they found places to hide and live; but plainly they did, and had storerooms too, for one came carrying in its little black hands a white spheroid that looked very like an egg. It was an eggshell used as a vial; Blackface took it and carefully loosened its top. In it was a thick, clear fluid. He spread a little of this on the puncture-wounds in the shoulders of the unconscious men; then, while others tenderly and fearfully lifted the men's heads, he poured a little of the fluid in their mouths. Raho he did not touch. The Kiemhrir did not speak among themselves, using only whistles and gestures, very quiet and with a touching air of courtesy.

Blackface came over to Rocannon and said reassuringly, "Lord, stay."

"Wait? Surely."

"Lord," said the Kiemher with a gesture towards Raho's body, and then stopped.

"Dead," Rocannon said.

"Dead, dead," said the little creature. He touched the base of his neck, and Rocannon nodded.

The silver-walled court brimmed with hot light. Yahan, lying near Rocannon, drew a long breath.

The Kiemhrir sat on their haunches in a half-circle behind their leader. To him Rocannon said, "Small lord, may I know your name?"

"Name," the black-faced one whispered. The others all were very still. "Liuar," he said, the old word Mogien had used to mean both nobles and midmen, or what the *Handbook* called Species II. "Liuar, Fiia, Gdemiar: names. Kiemhrir: unname."

Rocannon nodded, wondering what might be implied here. The word "kiemher, kiemhrir" was in fact, he realized, only an adjective, meaning lithe or swift.

Behind him Kyo caught his breath, stirred, sat up. Rocannon went to him. The little nameless people watched with their black eyes, attentive and quiet. Yahan roused, then finally Mogien, who must have got a heavy dose of the paralytic agent, for he could not even lift his hand at first. One of the

Kiemhrir shyly showed Rocannon that he could do good by rubbing Mogien's arms and legs, which he did, meanwhile explaining what had happened and where they were.

"The tapestry," Mogien whispered.

"What's that?" Rocannon asked him gently, thinking he was still confused, and the young man whispered, "The tapestry, at home—the winged giants."

Then Rocannon remembered how he had stood with Haldre beneath a woven picture of fair-haired warriors fighting winged figures, in the Long Hall of Hallan.

Kyo, who had been watching the Kiemhrir, held out his hand. Blackface hopped up to him and put his tiny, black, thumbless hand on Kyo's long, slender palm.

"Wordmasters," said the Fian softly. "Wordlovers, the eaters of words, the nameless ones, the lithe ones, long remembering. Still you remember the words of the Tall People, O Kiemhrir?"

"Still," said Blackface.

With Rocannon's help Mogien got to his feet, looking gaunt and stern. He stood a while beside Raho, whose face was terrible in the strong white sunlight. Then he greeted the Kiemhrir, and said, answering Rocannon, that he was all right again.

"If there are no gates, we can cut footholds and climb," Rocannon said.

"Whistle for the steeds, Lord," mumbled Yahan.

The question whether the whistle might wake the creatures in the dome was too complex to put across to the Kiemhrir. Since the Winged Ones seemed entirely nocturnal, they opted to take the chance. Mogien drew a little pipe on a chain from under his cloak, and blew a blast on it that Rocannon could not hear, but that made the Kiemhrir flinch. Within twenty minutes a great shadow shot over the dome, wheeled, darted off north, and before long returned with a companion. Both dropped with a mighty fanning of wings into the courtyard: the striped windsteed and Mogien's gray. The white one they never saw again. It might have been the one Rocannon had seen on the ramp in the musty, golden dusk of the dome, food for the larvae of the angels.

The Kiemhrir were afraid of the steeds. Blackface's gentle miniature courtesy was almost lost in barely controlled panic when Rocannon tried to thank him and bid him farewell. "O fly, Lord!" he said piteously, edging away from the great, taloned feet of the windsteeds; so they lost no time in going.

An hour's windride from the hive-city their packs and saddles, and the spare cloaks and furs they used for bedding, lay untouched beside the ashes of last night's fire. Partway down the hill lay three Winged Ones dead, and near them both Mogien's swords, one of them snapped off near the hilt. Mogien had waked to see the Winged Ones stooping over Yahan and Kyo. One of them had bitten him, "and I could not speak," he said. But he had fought and killed three before the paralysis brought him down. "I heard Raho call. He called to me three times, and I could not help him." He sat among the grassgrown ruins that had outlived all names and legends, his broken sword on his knees, and said nothing else.

They built up a pyre of branches and brushwood, and on it laid Raho, whom they had borne from the city, and beside him his hunting-bow and arrows. Yahan made a new fire, and Mogien set the wood alight. They mounted the windsteeds, Kyo behind Mogien and Yahan behind Rocannon, and rose spiraling around the smoke and heat of the fire that blazed in the sunlight of noon on a hilltop in the strange land.

For a long time they could see the thin pillar of smoke behind them as they flew.

The Kiemhrir had made it clear that they must move on, and keep under cover at night, or the Winged Ones would be after them again in the dark. So toward evening they came down to a stream in a deep, wooded gorge, making camp within earshot of a waterfall. It was damp, but the air was fragrant and musical, relaxing their spirits. They found a delicacy for dinner, a certain shelly, slow-moving water animal very good to eat; but Rocannon could not eat them. There was vestigial fur between the joints and on the tail; they were ovipoid mammals, like many animals here, like the Kiemhrir probably. "You eat them, Yahan. I can't shell something that might speak to me," he said, wrathful with hunger, and came to sit beside Kyo.

Kyo smiled, rubbing his sore shoulder. "If all things could be heard speaking . . ."

"I for one would starve."

"Well, the green creatures are silent," said the Fian, patting a rough-trunked tree that leaned across the stream. Here in the south the trees, all conifers, were coming into bloom, and the forests were dusty and sweet with drifting pollen. All flowers here gave their pollen to the wind, grasses and conifers: there were no insects, no petaled flowers. Spring on the unnamed world was all in green, dark green and pale green, with great drifts of golden pollen.

Mogien and Yahan went to sleep as it grew dark, stretched out by the warm ashes; they kept no fire lest it draw the Winged Ones. As Rocannon had guessed, Kyo was tougher than the men when it came to poisons; he sat and talked with Rocannon, down on the streambank in the dark.

"You greeted the Kiemhrir as if you knew of them," Rocannon observed, and the Fian answered:

"What one of us in my village remembered, all remembered, Olhor. So many tales and whispers and lies and truths are known to us, and who knows how old some are. . . ."

"Yet you knew nothing of the Winged Ones?"

It looked as if Kyo would pass this one, but at last he said, "The Fiia have no memory for fear, Olhor. How should we? We chose. Night and caves and swords of metal we left to the Clayfolk, when our way parted from theirs, and we chose the green valleys, the sunlight, the bowl of wood. And therefore we are the Half-People. And we have forgotten, we have forgotten much!" His light voice was more decisive, more urgent this night than ever before, sounding clear through the noise of the stream below them and the noise of the falls at the head of the gorge. "Each day as we travel southward I ride into the tales that my people learn as little children, in the valleys of Angien. And all the tales I find true. But half of them all we have forgotten. The little Name-Eaters, the Kiemhrir, these are in old songs we sing from mind to mind; but not the Winged Ones. The friends, but not the enemies. The sunlight, not the dark. And I am the companion of Olhor who goes southward into the legends, bearing no sword. I ride with Olhor, who seeks to hear his enemy's voice, who has traveled through the great dark, who has seen the World hang like a blue jewel in the darkness. I am only a half-person. I cannot go farther than the hills. I cannot go into the high places with you, Olhor!"

Rocannon put his hand very lightly on Kyo's shoulder. At once the Fian fell still. They sat hearing the sound of the stream, of the falls in the night, and watching starlight gleam gray on water that ran, under drifts and whorls of blown pollen, icy cold from the mountains to the south.

Twice during the next day's flight they saw far to the east the domes and spoked streets of hive-cities. That night they kept double watch. By the next night they were high up in the hills, and a lashing cold rain beat at them all night long and all the next day as they flew. When the rain-clouds parted a little there were mountains looming over the hills now on both sides. One more rain-sodden, watch-broken night went by on the hilltops under the ruin of an ancient tower, and then in early afternoon of the next day they came down the far side of the pass into sunlight and a broad valley leading off southward into misty, mountain-fringed distances.

To their right now while they flew down the valley as if it were a great green roadway, the white peaks stood serried, remote and huge. The wind was keen and golden, and the windsteeds raced down it like blown leaves in the sunlight. Over the soft green concave below them, on which darker clumps of shrubs and trees seemed enameled, drifted a narrow veil of gray. Mogien's mount came circling back, Kyo pointing down, and they rode down the golden wind to the village that lay between hill and stream, sunlit, its small chimneys smoking. A herd of herilor grazed the slopes above it. In the center of the scattered circle of little houses, all stilts and screens and sunny porches, towered five great trees. By these the travelers landed, and the Fiia came to meet them, shy and laughing.

These villagers spoke little of the Common Tongue, and were unused to speaking aloud at all. Yet it was like a homecoming to enter their airy houses, to eat from bowls of polished wood, to take refuge from wilderness and weather for one evening in their blithe hospitality. A strange little people, tangential, gracious, elusive: the Half-People, Kyo had called his own kind. Yet Kyo himself was no longer quite one of them. Though in the fresh clothing they gave him he looked like them, moved and gestured like them, in the group of them he stood out absolutely. Was it because as a stranger he could not freely mindspeak with them, or was it because he had, in his friendship with Rocannon, changed, having become another sort of being, more solitary, more sorrowful, more complete?

They could describe the lay of this land. Across the great range west of their valley was desert, they said; to continue south the travelers should follow the valley, keeping east of the mountains, a long way, until the range itself turned east. "Can we find passes across?" Mogien asked, and the little people smiled and said, "Surely, surely."

"And beyond the passes do you know what lies?"

"The passes are very high, very cold," said the Fiia, politely.

The travelers stayed two nights in the village to rest, and left with packs filled with waybread and dried meat given by the Fiia, who delighted in giving. After two days' flight they came to another village of the little folk, where they were again received with such friendliness that it might have been not a strangers' arrival, but a long-awaited return. As the steeds landed a group of Fian men and women came to meet them, greeting Rocannon, who was first to dismount, "Hail, Olhor!" It startled him, and still puzzled him a little after he thought that the word of course meant "wanderer," which he obviously was. Still, it was Kyo the Fian who had given him the name.

Later, farther down the valley after another long, calm day's flight, he said to Kyo, "Among your people, Kyo, did you bear no name of your own?"

"They call me 'herdsman,' or 'younger brother,' or 'runner.' I was quick in our racing."

"But those are nicknames, descriptions—like Olhor or Kiemhrir. You're great namegivers, you Fiia. You greet each comer with a nickname, Starlord, Swordbearer, Sunhaired, Wordmaster—I think the Angyar learned their love of such nicknaming from you. And yet you have no names."

"Starlord, far-traveled, ashen-haired, jewel-bearer," said Kyo, smiling;— "what then is a name?"

"Ashen-haired? Have I turned gray?—I'm not sure what a name is. My name given me at birth was Gaverel Rocannon. When I've said that, I've described nothing, yet I've named myself. And when I see a new kind of tree in this land I ask you—or Yahan and Mogien, since you seldom answer—what its name is. It troubles me, until I know its name."

"Well, it is a tree; as I am a Fian; as you are a . . . what?"

"But there are distinctions, Kyo! At each village here I ask what are those western mountains called, the range that towers over their lives from birth to death, and they say, 'Those are mountains, Olhor.'"

"So they are," said Kyo.

"But there are other mountains—the lower range to the east, along this same valley! How do you know one range from another, one being from another, without names?"

Clasping his knees, the Fian gazed at the sunset peaks burning high in the west. After a while Rocannon realized that he was not going to answer.

The winds grew warmer and the long days longer as warmyear advanced and they went each day farther south. As the windsteeds were double-loaded they did not push on fast, stopping often for a day or two to hunt and to let the steeds hunt; but at last they saw the mountains curving around in front of them to meet the coastal range to the east, barring their way. The green of the valley ran up the knees of huge hills, and ceased. Much higher lay patches of green and brown-green, alpine valleys; then the gray of rock and talus; and finally, halfway up the sky, the luminous storm-ridden white of the peaks.

They came, high up in the hills, to a Fian village. Wind blew chill from the peaks across frail roofs, scattering blue smoke among the long evening light and shadows. As ever they were received with cheerful grace, given water and fresh meat and herbs in bowls of wood, in the warmth of a house, while their dusty clothes were cleaned, and their windsteeds fed and petted by tiny, quicksilver children. After supper four girls of the village danced for them, without music, their movements and footfalls so light and swift that they seemed bodiless, a play of light and dark in the glow of the fire, elusive, fleeting. Rocannon glanced with a smile of pleasure at Kyo, who as usual sat beside him. The Fian returned his look gravely and spoke: "I shall stay here, Olhor."

Rocannon checked his startled reply and for a while longer watched the dancers, the changing unsubstantial patterns of firelit forms in motion. They wove a music from silence, and a strangeness in the mind. The firelight on the wooden walls bowed and flickered and changed.

"It was foretold that the Wanderer would choose companions. For a while."

He did not know if he had spoken, or Kyo, or his memory. The words were in his mind and in Kyo's. The dancers broke apart, their shadows running quickly up the walls, the loosened hair of one swinging bright for a moment. The dance that had no music was ended, the dancers that had no more name than light and shadow were still. So between him and Kyo a pattern had come to its end, leaving quietness.

VIII

Below his windsteed's heavily beating wings Rocannon saw a slope of broken rock, a slanting chaos of boulders running down behind, tilted up ahead so that the steed's left wingtip almost brushed the rocks as it labored up and forward towards the col. He wore the battle-straps over his thighs, for updrafts and gusts sometimes blew the steeds off balance, and he wore his impermasuit for warmth. Riding behind him, wrapped in all the cloaks and furs the two of them had, Yahan was still so cold that he had strapped his wrists to the saddle, unable to trust his grip. Mogien, riding well ahead on his less burdened steed, bore the cold and altitude much better than Yahan, and met their battle with the heights with a harsh joy.

Fifteen days ago they had left the last Fian village, bidding farewell to Kyo, and set out over the foothills and lower ranges for what looked like the widest pass. The Fiia could give them no directions; at any mention of crossing the mountains they had fallen silent, with a cowering look.

The first days had gone well, but as they got high up the windsteeds began to tire quickly, the thinner air not supplying them with the rich oxygen intake they burned while flying. Higher still they met the cold and the treacherous weather of high altitudes. In the last three days they had covered perhaps fifteen kilometers, most of that distance on a blind lead. The men went hungry to give the steeds an extra ration of dried meat; this morning Rocannon had let them finish what was left in the sack, for if they did not get across the pass today they would have to drop back down to woodlands where they could hunt and rest, and start all over. They seemed now on the right way toward a pass, but from the peaks to the east a terrible thin wind blew, and the sky was getting white and heavy. Still Mogien flew ahead, and Rocannon forced his mount to follow; for in this endless cruel passage of the great heights, Mogien was his leader and he followed. He had forgotten why he wanted to cross these mountains, remembering only that he had to, that he must go south. But for the courage to do it, he depended on Mogien. "I think this is your domain," he had said to the young man last evening when they had discussed their present course; and, looking out over the great, cold view of peak and abyss, rock and snow and sky, Mogien had answered with his quick lordly certainty, "This is my domain."

He was calling now, and Rocannon tried to encourage his steed, while he peered ahead through frozen lashes seeking a break in the endless slanting chaos. There it was, an angle, a jutting roofbeam of the planet: the slope of rock fell suddenly away and under them lay a waste of white, the pass. On either side wind-scoured peaks reared on up into the thickening snowclouds. Rocannon was close enough to see Mogien's untroubled face and hear his shout, the falsetto battle-yell of the victorious warrior. He kept following Mogien over the white valley under the white clouds. Snow began to dance about them, not falling, only dancing here in its habitat, its birthplace, a dry flickering dance. Half-starved and overladen, the windsteed gasped at each lift and downbeat of its great barred wings. Mogien had dropped back so they would not lose him in the snowclouds, but still kept on, and they followed.

There was a glow in the flickering mist of snowflakes, and gradually there dawned a thin, clear radiance of gold. Pale gold, the sheer fields of snow reached downward. Then abruptly the world fell away, and the windsteeds floundered in a vast gulf of air. Far beneath, very far, clear and small, lay valleys, lakes, the glittering tongue of a glacier, green patches of forest. Rocannon's mount floundered and dropped, its wings raised, dropped like a stone so that Yahan cried out in terror and Rocannon shut his eyes and held on.

The wings beat and thundered, beat again; the falling slowed, became again a laboring glide, and halted. The steed crouched trembling in a rocky valley. Nearby Mogien's gray beast was trying to lie down while Mogien, laughing, jumped off its back and called, "We're over, we did it!" He came up to them, his dark, vivid face bright with triumph. "Now both sides of the mountains are my domain, Rokanan! . . . This will do for our camp tonight. Tomorrow the steeds can hunt, farther down where trees grow, and we'll work down on foot. Come, Yahan."

Yahan crouched in the postillion-saddle, unable to move. Mogien lifted him from the saddle and helped him lie down in the shelter of a jutting boulder; for though the late afternoon sun shone here, it gave little more warmth than did the Greatstar, a tiny crumb of crystal in the southwestern sky; and the wind still blew bitter cold. While Rocannon unharnessed the steeds, the Angyar lord tried to help his servant, doing what he could to get him warm. There was nothing to build a fire with—they were still far above timberline. Rocannon stripped off the impermasuit and made Yahan put it on, ignoring the midman's weak and scared protests, then wrapped himself up in furs. The windsteeds and the men huddled together for mutual warmth, and shared a little water and Fian waybread. Night rose up from the vague lands below. Stars leaped out, released by darkness, and the two brighter moons shone within hand's reach.

Deep in the night Rocannon roused from blank sleep. Everything was star-lit, silent, deathly cold. Yahan had hold of his arm and was whispering feverishly, shaking his arm and whispering. Rocannon looked where he pointed and saw standing on the boulder above them a shadow, an interruption in the stars.

Like the shadow he and Yahan had seen on the pampas, far back to north-ward, it was large and strangely vague. Even as he watched it the stars began to glimmer faintly through the dark shape, and then there was no shadow, only black transparent air. To the left of where it had been Heliki shone, faint in its waning cycle.

"It was a trick of moonlight, Yahan," he whispered. "Go back to sleep, you've got a fever."

"No," said Mogien's quiet voice beside him. "It wasn't a trick, Rokanan. It was my death."

Yahan sat up, shaking with fever. "No, Lord! not yours; it couldn't be! I saw it before, on the plains when you weren't with us—so did Olhor!"

Summoning to his aid the last shreds of common sense, of scientific moderation, of the old life's rules, Rocannon tried to speak authoritatively: "Don't be absurd," he said.

Mogien paid no attention to him. "I saw it on the plains, where it was seeking me. And twice in the hills while we sought the pass. Whose death would it be if not mine? Yours, Yahan? Are you a lord, an Angya, do you wear the second sword?"

Sick and despairing, Yahan tried to plead with him, but Mogien went on, "It's not Rokanan's, for he still follows his way. A man can die anywhere, but his own death, his true death, a lord meets only in his domain. It waits for him in the place which is his, a battlefield or a hall or a road's end. And this is my place. From these mountains my people came, and I have come back. My second sword was broken, fighting. But listen, my death: I am Halla's heir Mogien—do you know me now?"

The thin, frozen wind blew over the rocks. Stones loomed about them, stars glittering out beyond them. One of the windsteeds stirred and snarled.

"Be still," Rocannon said. "This is all foolishness. Be still and sleep. . . ."

But he could not sleep soundly after that, and whenever he roused he saw Mogien sitting by his steed's great flank, quiet and ready, watching over the night-darkened lands.

Come daylight they let the windsteeds free to hunt in the forests below, and started to work their way down on foot. They were still very high, far above timberline, and safe only so long as the weather held clear. But before they had gone an hour they saw Yahan could not make it; it was not a hard descent, but exposure and exhaustion had taken too much out of him and he could not keep walking, let alone scramble and cling as they sometimes must. Another day's rest in the protection of Rocannon's suit might give him the strength to go on; but that would mean another night up here without fire or shelter or enough food. Mogien weighed the risks without seeming to consider them at all, and suggested that Rocannon stay with Yahan on a sheltered and sunny ledge, while he sought a descent easy enough that they might carry Yahan down, or, failing that, a shelter that might keep off snow.

After he had gone, Yahan, lying in a half stupor, asked for water. Their flask was empty. Rocannon told him to lie still, and climbed up the slanting rock-face to a boulder-shadowed ledge fifteen meters or so above, where he saw some packed snow glittering. The climb was rougher than he had judged, and he lay on the ledge gasping the bright, thin air, his heart going hard.

There was a noise in his ears which at first he took to be the singing of his own blood; then near his hand he saw water running. He sat up. A tiny stream, smoking as it ran, wound along the base of a drift of hard, shadowed snow. He looked for the stream's source and saw a dark gap under the overhanging cliff: a cave. A cave was their best hope of shelter, said his rational mind, but it spoke only on the very fringe of a dark non-rational rush of feeling—of panic. He sat there unmoving in the grip of the worst fear he had ever known.

All about him the unavailing sunlight shone on gray rock. The mountain peaks were hidden by the nearer cliffs, and the lands below to the south were hidden by unbroken cloud. There was nothing at all here on this bare gray ridgepole of the world but himself, and a dark opening between boulders.

After a long time he got to his feet, went forward stepping across the steaming rivulet, and spoke to the presence which he knew waited inside that shadowy gap. "I have come," he said.

The darkness moved a little, and the dweller in the cave stood at its mouth. It was like the Clayfolk, dwarfish and pale; like the Fiia, frail and clear-eyed; like both, like neither. The hair was white. The voice was no voice, for it sounded within Rocannon's mind while all his ears heard was the faint whistle of the wind; and there were no words. Yet it asked him what he wished.

"I do not know," the man said aloud in terror, but his set will answered silently for him: *I will go south and find my enemy and destroy him.*

The wind blew whistling; the warm stream chuckled at his feet. Moving slowly and lightly, the dweller in the cave stood aside, and Rocannon, stooping down, entered the dark place.

What do you give for what I have given you?

 What must I give, Ancient One?

 That which you hold dearest and would least willingly give.

 I have nothing of my own on this world. What thing can I give?

 A thing, a life, a chance; an eye, a hope, a return: the name need not be known. But you will cry its name aloud when it is gone. Do you give it freely?

 Freely, Ancient One.

Silence and the blowing of wind. Rocannon bowed his head and came out of the darkness. As he straightened up red light struck full in his eyes, a cold red sunrise over a gray-and-scarlet sea of cloud.

Yahan and Mogien slept huddled together on the lower ledge, a heap of furs and cloaks, unstirring as Rocannon climbed down to them. "Wake up," he said softly. Yahan sat up, his face pinched and childish in the hard red dawn. "Olhor! We thought—you were gone—we thought you had fallen—"

Mogien shook his yellow-maned head to clear it of sleep, and looked up a minute at Rocannon. Then he said hoarsely and gently, "Welcome back, Star-lord, companion. We waited here for you."

"I met . . . I spoke with . . ."

Mogien raised his hand. "You have come back; I rejoice in your return. Do we go south?"

"Yes."

"Good," said Mogien. In that moment it was not strange to Rocannon that

Mogien, who for so long had seemed his leader, now spoke to him as a lesser to a greater lord.

Mogien blew his whistle, but though they waited long the windsteeds did not come. They finished the last of the hard, nourishing Fian bread, and set off once more on foot. The warmth of the impermasuit had done Yahan good, and Rocannon insisted he keep it on. The young midman needed food and real rest to get his strength back, but he could get on now, and they had to get on; behind that red sunrise would come heavy weather. It was not dangerous going, but slow and wearisome. Midway in the morning one of the steeds appeared: Mogien's gray, flitting up from the forests far below. They loaded it with the saddles and harness and furs—all they carried now—and it flew along above or below or beside them as it pleased, sometimes letting out a ringing yowl as if to call its striped mate, still hunting or feasting down in the forests.

About noon they came to a hard stretch: a cliff-face sticking out like a shield, over which they would have to crawl roped together. "From the air you might see a better path for us to follow, Mogien," Rocannon suggested. "I wish the other steed would come." He had a sense of urgency; he wanted to be off this bare gray mountainside and be hidden down among trees.

"The beast was tired out when we let it go; it may not have made a kill yet. This one carried less weight over the pass. I'll see how wide this cliff is. Perhaps my steed can carry all three of us for a few bowshots." He whistled and the gray steed, with the loyal obedience that still amazed Rocannon in a beast so large and so carnivorous, wheeled around in the air and came looping gracefully up to the cliffside where they waited. Mogien swung up on it and with a shout sailed off, his bright hair catching the last shaft of sunlight that broke through thickening banks of cloud.

Still the thin, cold wind blew. Yahan crouched back in an angle of rock, his eyes closed. Rocannon sat looking out into the distance at the remotest edge of which could be sensed the fading brightness of the sea. He did not scan the immense, vague landscape that came and went between drifting clouds, but gazed at one point, south and a little east, one place. He shut his eyes. He listened, and heard.

It was a strange gift he had got from the dweller in the cave, the guardian of the warm well in the unnamed mountains; a gift that went all against his grain to ask. There in the dark by the deep warm spring he had been taught a skill of the senses that his race and the men of Earth had witnessed and studied in other races, but to which they were deaf and blind, save for brief glimpses and rare exceptions. Clinging to his humanity, he had drawn back from the totality of the power that the guardian of the well possessed and offered. He had learned to listen to the minds of one race, one kind of creature, among all the voices of all the worlds one voice: that of his enemy.

With Kyo he had had some beginnings of mindspeech; but he did not want to know his companions' minds when they were ignorant of his. Understanding must be mutual, when loyalty was, and love.

But those who had killed his friends and broken the bond of peace he spied upon, he overheard. He sat on the granite spur of a trackless mountain-peak and listened to the thoughts of men in buildings among rolling hills thousands of meters below and a hundred kilometers away. A dim chatter, a buzz and babble and confusion, a remote roil and storming of sensations and emotions. He did not know how to select voice from voice, and was dizzy among a hundred different places and positions; he listened as a young infant listens, undiscriminating. Those born with eyes and ears must learn to see and hear, to pick out a face from a double eyeful of upside-down world, to select meaning from a welter of noise. The guardian of the well had the gift, which Rocannon had only heard rumor of on one other planet, of unsealing the telepathic sense; and he had taught Rocannon how to limit and direct it, but there had been no time to learn its use, its practice. Rocannon's head spun with the impingement of alien thoughts and feelings, a thousand strangers crowded in his skull. No words came through. Mindhearing was the word the Angyar, the outsiders, used for the sense. What he "heard" was not speech but intentions, desires, emotions, the physical locations and sensual-mental directions of many different men jumbling and overlapping through his own nervous system, terrible gusts of fear and jealousy, drifts of contentment, abysses of sleep, a wild racking vertigo of half-understanding, half-sensation. And all at once out of the chaos something stood absolutely clear, a contact more definite than a hand laid on his naked flesh. Someone was coming toward him: a man whose mind had sensed his own. With this certainty came lesser impressions of speed, of confinement; of curiosity and fear.

Rocannon opened his eyes, staring ahead as if he would see before him the face of that man whose being he had sensed. He was close; Rocannon was sure he was close, and coming closer. But there was nothing to see but air and lowering clouds. A few dry, small flakes of snow whirled in the wind. To his left bulked the great bosse of rock that blocked their way. Yahan had come out beside him and was watching him, with a scared look. But he could not reassure Yahan, for that presence tugged at him and he could not break the contact. "There is ... there is a ... an airship," he muttered thickly, like a sleeptalker. "There!"

There was nothing where he pointed; air, cloud.

"There," Rocannon whispered.

Yahan, looking again where he pointed, gave a cry. Mogien on the gray steed was riding the wind well out from the cliff; and beyond him, far out in a scud of cloud, a larger black shape had suddenly appeared, seeming to hover or to move very slowly. Mogien flashed on downwind without seeing it, his face turned to the mountain wall looking for his companions, two tiny figures on a tiny ledge in the sweep of rock and cloud.

The black shape grew larger, moving in, its vanes clacking and hammering in the silence of the heights. Rocannon saw it less clearly than he sensed the man inside it, the uncomprehending touch of mind on mind, the intense defiant fear. He whispered to Yahan, "Take cover!" but could not move himself. The helicopter nosed in unsteadily, rags of cloud catching in its whirring vanes. Even as he watched it approach, Rocannon watched from inside it, not knowing what he looked for, seeing two small figures on the mountainside, afraid, afraid—A flash of light, a hot shock of pain, pain in his own flesh, intolerable. The mind-contact was broken, blown clean away. He was himself, standing on the ledge pressing his right hand against his chest and gasping, seeing the helicopter creep still closer, its vanes whirring with a dry loud rattle, its laser-mounted nose pointing at him.

From the right, from the chasm of air and cloud, shot a gray winged beast ridden by a man who shouted in a voice like a high, triumphant laugh. One beat of the wide gray wings drove steed and rider forward straight against the hovering machine, full speed, head on. There was a tearing sound like the edge of a great scream, and then the air was empty.

The two on the cliff crouched staring. No sound came up from below. Clouds wreathed and drifted across the abyss.

"Mogien!"

Rocannon cried the name aloud. There was no answer. There was only pain, and fear, and silence.

IX

Rain pattered hard on a raftered roof. The air of the room was dark and clear.

Near his couch stood a woman whose face he knew, a proud, gentle, dark face crowned with gold.

He wanted to tell her that Mogien was dead, but he could not say the words.

He lay there sorely puzzled, for now he recalled that Haldre of Hallan was an old woman, white-haired; and the golden-haired woman he had known was long dead; and anyway he had seen her only once, on a planet eight lightyears away, a long time ago when he had been a man named Rocannon.

He tried again to speak. She hushed him, saying in the Common Tongue though with some difference in sounds, "Be still, my lord." She stayed beside him, and presently told him in her soft voice, "This is Breygna Castle. You came here with another man, in the snow, from the heights of the mountains. You were near death and still are hurt. There will be time. . . ."

There was much time, and it slipped by vaguely, peacefully in the sound of the rain.

The next day or perhaps the next, Yahan came in to him, Yahan very thin, a little lame, his face scarred with frostbite. But a less understandable change in him was his manner, subdued and submissive. After they had talked a while Rocannon asked uncomfortably, "Are you afraid of me, Yahan?"

"I will try not to be, Lord," the young man stammered.

When he was able to go down to the Revelhall of the castle, the same awe or dread was in all faces that turned to him, though they were brave and genial faces. Gold-haired, dark-skinned, a tall people, the old stock of which the Angyar were only a tribe that long ago had wandered north by sea: these were the Liuar, the Earthlords, living since before the memory of any race here in the foothills of the mountains and the rolling plains to the south.

At first he thought that they were unnerved simply by his difference in looks, his dark hair and pale skin; but Yahan was colored like him, and they had no dread of Yahan. They treated him as a lord among lords, which was a joy and a bewilderment to the ex-serf of Hallan. But Rocannon they treated as a lord above lords, one set apart.

There was one who spoke to him as to a man. The Lady Ganye, daughter-in-law and heiress of the castle's old lord, had been a widow for some months; her bright-haired little son was with her most of the day. Though shy, the child had no fear of Rocannon, but was rather drawn to him, and liked to ask him questions about the mountains and the northern lands and the sea. Rocannon answered whatever he asked. The mother would listen, serene and gentle as the sunlight, sometimes turning smiling to Rocannon her face that he had remembered even as he had seen it for the first time.

He asked her at last what it was they thought of him in Breygna Castle, and she answered candidly, "They think you are a god."

It was the word he had noted long since in Tolen village, *pedan*.

"I'm not," he said, dour.

She laughed a little.

"Why do they think so?" he demanded. "Do the gods of the Liuar come with gray hair and crippled hands?" The laserbeam from the helicopter had caught him in the right wrist, and he had lost the use of his right hand almost entirely.

"Why not?" said Ganye with her proud, candid smile. "But the reason is that you came *down* the mountain."

He absorbed this a while. "Tell me, Lady Ganye, do you know of . . . the guardian of the well?"

At this her face was grave. "We know tales of that people only. It is very long, nine generations of the Lords of Breygna, since Iollt the Tall went up into the high places and came down changed. We knew you had met with them, with the Most Ancient."

"How do you know?"

"In your sleep in fever you spoke always of the price, of the cost, of the gift given and its price. Iollt paid too. . . . The cost was your right hand, Lord Olhor?" she asked with sudden timidity, raising her eyes to his.

"No. I would give both my hands to have saved what I lost."

He got up and went to the window of the tower-room, looking out on the spacious country between the mountains and the distant sea. Down from the high foothills where Breygna Castle stood wound a river, widening and shining among lower hills, vanishing into hazy reaches where one could half make out villages, fields, castle towers, and once again the gleam of the river among blue rainstorms and shafts of sunlight.

"This is the fairest land I ever saw," he said. He was still thinking of Mogien, who would never see it.

"It's not so fair to me as it once was."

"Why, Lady Ganye?"

"Because of the Strangers!"

"Tell me of them, Lady."

"They came here late last winter, many of them riding in great windships, armed with weapons that burn. No one can say what land they come from; there are no tales of them at all. All the land between Viarn River and the sea is theirs now. They killed or drove out all the people of eight domains. We in the hills here are prisoners; we dare not go down even to the old pasturelands with our herds. We fought the Strangers, at first. My husband Ganhing was killed by their burning weapons." Her gaze went for a second to Rocannon's seared, crippled hand; for a second she paused. "In . . . in the time of the first thaw he was killed, and still we have no revenge. We bow our heads and avoid their lands, we the Earthlords! And there is no man to make these Strangers pay for Ganhing's death."

O lovely wrath, Rocannon thought, hearing the trumpets of lost Hallan in her voice. "They will pay, Lady Ganye; they will pay a high price. Though you knew I was no god, did you take me for quite a common man?"

"No, Lord," said she. "Not quite."

The days went by, the long days of the yearlong summer. The white slopes of the peaks above Breygna turned blue, the grain-crops in Breygna fields ripened, were cut and resown, and were ripening again when one afternoon Rocannon sat down by Yahan in the courtyard where a pair of young windsteeds were being trained. "I'm off again to the south, Yahan. You stay here."

"No, Olhor! Let me come—"

Yahan stopped, remembering perhaps that foggy beach where in his longing for adventures he had disobeyed Mogien. Rocannon grinned and said, "I'll do best alone. It won't take long, one way or the other."

"But I am your vowed servant, Olhor. Please let me come."

"Vows break when names are lost. You swore your service to Rokanan, on the other side of the mountains. In this land there are no serfs, and there is no man named Rokanan. I ask you as my friend, Yahan, to say no more to me or to anyone here, but saddle the steed of Hallan for me at daybreak tomorrow."

Loyally, next morning before sunrise Yahan stood waiting for him in the flightcourt, holding the bridle of the one remaining windsteed from Hallan, the gray striped one. It had made its way a few days after them to Breygna, half frozen and starving. It was sleek and full of spirit now, snarling and lashing its striped tail.

"Do you wear the Second Skin, Olhor?" Yahan asked in a whisper, fastening the battle-straps on Rocannon's legs. "They say the Strangers shoot fire at any man who rides near their lands."

"I'm wearing it."

"But no sword? . . ."

"No. No sword. Listen, Yahan, if I don't return, look in the wallet I left in my room. There's some cloth in it, with—with markings in it, and pictures of the land; if any of my people ever come here, give them those, will you? And also the necklace is there." His face darkened and he looked away a moment. "Give that to the Lady Ganye. If I don't come back to do it myself. Goodbye, Yahan; wish me good luck."

"May your enemy die without sons," Yahan said fiercely, in tears, and let the windsteed go. It shot up into the warm, uncolored sky of summer dawn, turned with a great rowing beat of wings, and, catching the north wind, vanished above the hills. Yahan stood watching. From a window high up in Breygna Tower a soft, dark face also watched, for a long time after it was out of sight and the sun had risen.

It was a queer journey Rocannon made, to a place he had never seen and yet knew inside and out with the varying impressions of hundreds of different minds. For though there was no seeing with the mind-sense, there was tactile sensation and perception of space and spatial relationships, of time, motion, and position. From attending to such sensations over and over for hours on end in a hundred days of practice as he sat moveless in his room in Breygna Castle, he had acquired an exact though unvisualized and unverbalized knowledge of every building and area of the enemy base. And from direct sensation and extrapolation from it, he knew what the base was, and why it was here, and how to enter it, and where to find what he wanted from it.

But it was very hard, after the long intense practice, *not* to use the mind-sense as he approached his enemies: to cut it off, deaden it, using only his eyes and ears and intellect. The incident on the mountainside had warned him that at close range sensitive individuals might become aware of his presence, though in a vague way, as a hunch or premonition. He had drawn the helicopter pilot to the mountain like a fish on a line, though the pilot probably had never understood what had made him fly that way or why he had felt compelled to fire on the men he found. Now, entering the huge base alone, Rocannon did not want any attention drawn to himself, none at all, for he came as a thief in the night.

At sunset he had left his windsteed tethered in a hillside clearing, and now after several hours of walking was approaching a group of buildings across a vast, blank plain of cement, the rocket field. There was only one field and seldom used, now that all men and materiel were here. War was not waged with lightspeed rockets when the nearest civilized planet was eight lightyears away.

The base was large, terrifyingly large when seen with one's own eyes, but most of the land and buildings went to housing men. The rebels now had almost their whole army here. While the League wasted its time searching and subduing their home planet, they were staking their gamble on the very high probability of their not being found on this one nameless world among all the worlds of the galaxy. Rocannon knew that some of the giant barracks were empty again; a contingent of soldiers and technicians had been sent out some days ago to take over, as he guessed, a planet they had conquered or had persuaded to join them as allies. Those soldiers would not arrive at that world for almost ten years. The Faradayans were very sure of themselves. They must be doing well in their war. All they had needed to wreck the safety of the League of All Worlds was a well-hidden base, and their six mighty weapons.

He had chosen a night when of all four moons only the little captured asteroid, Heliki, would be in the sky before midnight. It brightened over the hills as he neared a row of hangars, like a black reef on the gray sea of cement, but no one saw him, and he sensed no one near. There were no fences and few guards. Their watch was kept by machines that scanned space for light-years around the Fomalhaut system. What had they to fear, after all, from the Bronze Age aborigines of the little nameless planet?

Heliki shone at its brightest as Rocannon left the shadow of the row of hangars. It was halfway through its waning cycle when he reached his goal: the six FTL ships. They sat like six immense ebony eggs side by side under a vague, high canopy, a camouflage net. Around the ships, looking like toys, stood a scattering of trees, the edge of Viarn Forest.

Now he had to use his mindhearing, safe or not. In the shadow of a group of trees he stood still and very cautiously, trying to keep his eyes and ears alert at the same time, reached out toward the ovoid ships, into them, around them. In each, he had learned at Breygna, a pilot sat ready day and night to move the ships out—probably to Faraday—in case of emergency.

Emergency, for the six pilots, meant only one thing: that the Control Room, four miles away at the east edge of the base, had been sabotaged or bombed out. In that case each was to move his ship out to safety by using its own controls, for these FTLs had controls like any spaceship, independent of any outside, vulnerable computers and power-sources. But to fly them was to commit suicide; no life survived a faster-than-light "trip." So each pilot was not only a highly trained polynomial mathematician, but a sacrificial fanatic. They were a picked lot. All the same, they got bored sitting and waiting for their unlikely blaze of glory. In one of the ships tonight Rocannon sensed the presence of two men. Both were deeply absorbed. Between them was a plane surface cut in squares. Rocannon had picked up the same impression on many earlier nights, and his rational mind registered *chessboard,* while his mindhearing moved on to the next ship. It was empty.

He went quickly across the dim gray field among scattered trees to the fifth ship in line, climbed its ramp and entered the open port. Inside it had no resemblance to a ship of any kind. It was all rocket-hangars and launching pads, computer banks, reactors, a kind of cramped and deathly labyrinth with corridors wide enough to roll citybuster missiles through. Since it did not proceed through spacetime it had no forward or back end, no logic; and he could not read the language of the signs. There was no live mind to reach to as a guide. He spent twenty minutes searching for the control room, methodically, repressing panic, forcing himself not to use the mindhearing lest the absent pilot become uneasy.

Only for a moment, when he had located the control room and found the ansible and sat down before it, did he permit his mind-sense to drift over to the ship that sat east of this one. There he picked up a vivid sensation of a dubious hand hovering over a white Bishop. He withdrew at once. Noting the coordinates at which the ansible sender was set, he changed them to the coordinates of the League HILF Survey Base for Galactic Area 8, at Kerguelen, on the planet New South Georgia—the only coordinates he knew without reference to a handbook. He set the machine to transmit and began to type.

As his fingers (left hand only, awkwardly) struck each key, the letter appeared simultaneously on a small black screen in a room in a city on a planet eight lightyears distant:

URGENT TO LEAGUE PRESIDIUM. The FTL warship base of the Faradayan revolt is on Fomalhaut II, Southwest Continent, 28°28′ North by 121°40′ West, about 3 km. NE of a major river. Base blacked out but should be visible as 4 building-squares 28 barrack groups and hangar on rocket field running E-W. The 6 FTLs are not on the base but in open just SW of rocket field at edge of a forest and are camouflaged with net and light-absorbers. Do not attack indiscriminately as aborigines are not inculpated. This is Gaverel Rocannon of Fomalhaut Ethnographic Survey. I am the only survivor of the expedition. Am sending from ansible aboard grounded enemy FTL. About 5 hours till daylight here.

He had intended to add, "Give me a couple of hours to get clear," but did not. If he were caught as he left, the Faradayans would be warned and might move out the FTLs. He switched the transmitter off and reset the coordinates to their previous destination. As he made his way out along the catwalks in the huge corridors he checked the next ship again. The chessplayers were up and moving about. He broke into a run, alone in the half-lit, meaningless rooms and corridors. He thought he had taken a wrong turning, but went straight to the port, down the ramp, and off at a dead run past the interminable length of the ship, past the interminable length of the next ship, and into the darkness of the forest.

Once under the trees he could run no more, for his breath burned in his chest, and the black branches let no moonlight through. He went on as fast as he could, working back around the edge of the base to the end of the rocket field and then back the way he had come across country, helped out by Heliki's next cycle of brightness and after another hour by Feni rising. He seemed to make no progress through the dark land, and time was running out. If they bombed the base while he was this close shockwave or firestorm would get him, and he struggled through the darkness with the irrepressible fear of the light that might break behind him and destroy him. But why did they not come, why were they so slow?

It was not yet daybreak when he got to the double-peaked hill where he had left his windsteed. The beast, annoyed at being tied up all night in good hunting country, growled at him. He leaned against its warm shoulder, scratching its ear a little, thinking of Kyo.

When he had got his breath he mounted and urged the steed to walk. For a long time it crouched sphinx-like and would not even rise. At last it got up, protesting in a sing-song snarl, and paced northward with maddening slowness. Hills and fields, abandoned villages and hoary trees were now faint all about them, but not till the white of sunrise spilled over the eastern hills would the windsteed fly. Finally it soared up, found a convenient wind, and floated along through the pale, bright dawn. Now and then Rocannon looked back. Nothing was behind him but the peaceful land, mist lying in the riverbottom westward. He listened with the mind-sense, and felt the thoughts and motions and wakening dreams of his enemies, going on as usual.

He had done what he could do. He had been a fool to think he could do anything. What was one man alone, against a people bent on war? Worn out, chewing wearily on his defeat, he rode on toward Breygna, the only place he had to go. He wondered no longer why the League delayed their attack so long. They were not coming. They had thought his message a trick, a trap. Or, for all he knew, he had misremembered the coordinates: one figure wrong had sent his message out into the void where there was neither time nor space. And for that, Raho had died, Iot had died, Mogien had died: for a message that got nowhere. And he was exiled here for the rest of his life, useless, a stranger on an alien world.

It did not matter, after all. He was only one man. One man's fate is not important.

"If it is not, what is?"

He could not endure those remembered words. He looked back once more, to look away from the memory of Mogien's face—and with a cry threw up his crippled arm to shut out the intolerable light, the tall white tree of fire that sprang up, soundless, on the plains behind him.

In the noise and the blast of wind that followed, the windsteed screamed and bolted, then dropped down to earth in terror. Rocannon got free of the saddle and cowered down on the ground with his head in his arms. But he could not shut it out—not the light but the darkness, the darkness that blinded his mind, the knowledge in his own flesh of the death of a thousand men all in one moment. Death, death, death over and over and yet all at once in one moment in his one body and brain. And after it, silence.

He lifted his head and listened, and heard silence.

EPILOGUE

Riding down the wind to the court of Breygna at sundown, he dismounted and stood by his windsteed, a tired man, his gray head bowed. They gathered quickly about him, all the bright-haired people of the castle, asking him what the great fire in the south had been, whether runners from the plains telling of the Strangers' destruction were telling the truth. It was strange how they gathered around him, knowing that he knew. He looked for Ganye among them. When he saw her face he found speech, and said haltingly, "The place of the enemy is destroyed. They will not come back here. Your Lord Ganhing has been avenged. And my Lord Mogien. And your brothers, Yahan; and Kyo's people; and my friends. They are all dead."

They made way for him, and he went on into the castle alone.

In the evening of a day some days after that, a clear blue twilight after thundershowers, he walked with Ganye on the rainwet terrace of the tower. She had asked him if he would leave Breygna now. He was a long time answering.

"I don't know. Yahan will go back to the north, to Hallan, I think. There are lads here who would like to make the voyage by sea. And the Lady of Hallan is waiting for news of her son. . . . But Hallan is not my home. I have none here. I am not of your people."

She knew something now of what he was, and asked, "Will your own people not come to seek you?"

He looked out over the lovely country, the river gleaming in the summer dusk far to the south. "They may," he said. "Eight years from now. They can send death at once, but life is slower. . . . Who are my people? I am not what I was. I have changed; I have drunk from the well in the mountains. And I wish never to be again where I might hear the voices of my enemies."

They walked in silence side by side, seven steps to the parapet; then Ganye, looking up toward the blue, dim bulwark of the mountains, said, "Stay with us here."

Rocannon paused a little and then said, "I will. For a while."

But it was for the rest of his life. When ships of the League returned to the planet, and Yahan guided one of the surveys south to Breygna to find him, he was dead. The people of Breygna mourned their Lord, and his widow, tall and fair-haired, wearing a great blue jewel set in gold at her throat, greeted those who came seeking him. So he never knew that the League had given that world his name.

planet of exile

1

A Handful of Darkness

In the last days of the last moonphase of Autumn a wind blew from the northern ranges through the dying forests of Askatevar, a cold wind that smelled of smoke and snow. Slight and shadowy as a wild animal in her light furs, the girl Rolery slipped through the woods, through the storming of dead leaves, away from the walls that stone by stone were rising on the hillside of Tevar and from the busy fields of the last harvest. She went alone and no one called after her. She followed a faint path that led west, scored and rescored in grooves by the passing southward of the footroots, choked in places by fallen trunks or huge drifts of leaves.

Where the path forked at the foot of the Border Ridge she went on straight, but before she had gone ten steps she turned back quickly towards a pulsing rustle that approached from behind.

A runner came down the northward track, bare feet beating in the surf of leaves, the long string that tied his hair whipping behind him. From the north he came at a steady, pounding, lung-bursting pace, and never glanced at Rolery among the trees but pounded past and was gone. The wind blew him on his way to Tevar with his news—storm, disaster, winter, war. . . . Incurious, Rolery turned and followed her own evasive path, which zigzagged upward among the great, dead, groaning trunks until at last on the ridge-top she saw sky break clear before her, and beneath the sky the sea.

The dead forest had been cleared from the west face of the ridge. Sitting in the shelter of a huge stump, she could look out on the remote and radiant west, the endless gray reaches of the tidal plain, and, a little below her and to the right, walled and red-roofed on its sea-cliffs, the city of the farborns.

High, bright-painted stone houses jumbled window below window and roof below roof down the slanting cliff-top to the brink. Outside the walls and beneath the cliffs where they ran lower south of the town were miles of pastureland and fields, all dyked and terraced, neat as patterned carpets. From the city wall at the brink of the cliff, over dykes and dunes and straight out over the beach and the slick-shining tidal sands for half a mile, striding on immense arches of stone, a causeway went, linking the city to a strange black island among the sands. A sea-stack, it jutted up black and black-shadowed from the sleek planes and shining levels of the sands, grim rock, obdurate, the top of it arched and towered, a carving more fantastic than even wind or sea could make. Was it a house, a statue, a fort, a funeral cairn? What black skill had hollowed it out and built the incredible bridge, back in timepast when the farborns were mighty and made war? Rolery had never paid much heed to the vague tales of witchcraft that went with such mention of the farborns, but now looking at that black place on the sands she saw that it was strange—the first thing truly strange to her that she had ever seen: built in a timepast that had nothing to do with her, by hands that were not kindred flesh and blood, imagined by alien minds. It was sinister, and it drew her. Fascinated, she watched a tiny figure that walked on that high causeway, dwarfed by its great length and height, a little dot or stroke of darkness creeping out to the black tower among the shining sands.

The wind here was less cold; sunlight shone through cloud-rack in the vast west, gilding the streets and roofs below her. The town drew her with its strangeness, and without pausing to summon up courage or decision, reckless, Rolery went lightly and quickly down the mountainside and entered the high gate.

Inside, she walked as light as ever, careless-wilful, but that was mostly from pride: her heart beat hard as she followed the gray, perfectly flat stones of the alien street. She glanced from left to right, and right to left, hastily, at the tall houses all built above the ground, with sharp roofs, and windows of transparent stone—so that tale was true!—and at the narrow dirt-lots in front of some houses where bright-leaved kellem and hadun vines, crimson and orange, went climbing up the painted blue or green walls, vivid among all the gray and drab of the autumnal landscape. Near the eastern gate many of the houses stood empty, color stripping and scabbing from the stone, the glittering windows gone. But farther down the streets and steps the houses were lived in, and she began to pass farborns in the street.

They looked at her. She had heard that farborns would meet one's eyes straight on, but did not put the story to test. At least none of them stopped her; her clothing was not unlike theirs, and some of them, she saw in her quick flicking glances, were not very much darker-skinned than men. But in the faces that she did not look at she sensed the unearthly darkness of the eyes.

All at once the street she walked on ended in a broad open place, spacious and level, all gold-and-shadow-streaked by the westering sun. Four houses stood about this square, houses the size of little hills, fronted with great rows of arches and above these with alternate gray and transparent stones. Only four streets led into this square and each could be shut with a gate that swung from the walls of the four great houses; so the square was a fort within a fort or a town within a town. Above it all a piece of one building stuck straight up into the air and towered there, bright with sunlight.

It was a mighty place, but almost empty of people.

In one sandy corner of the square, itself large as a field, a few farborn boys were playing. Two youths were having a fierce and skilful wrestling match, and a bunch of younger boys in padded coats and caps were as fiercely practicing cut-and-thrust with wooden swords. The wrestlers were wonderful to watch, weaving a slow dangerous dance about each other, then engaging with deft and sudden grace. Along with a couple of farborns, tall and silent in their furs, Rolery stood looking on. When all at once the bigger wrestler went sailing head over heels to land flat on his brawny back she gave a gasp that coincided with his, and then laughed with surprise and admiration. "Good throw, Jonkendy!" a farborn near her called out, and a woman on the far side of the arena clapped her hands. Oblivious, absorbed, the younger boys fought on, thrusting and whacking and parrying.

She had not known the witchfolk bred up warriors, or prized strength and skill. Though she had heard of their wrestling, she had always vaguely imagined them as hunched black and spiderlike in a gloomy den over a potter's wheel, making the delicate bits of pottery and clearstone that found their way into the tents of mankind. And there were stories and rumors and scraps of tales; a hunter was "lucky as a farborn"; a certain kind of earth was called witch-ore because the witchfolk prized it and would trade for it. But scraps were all she knew. Since long before her birth the Men of Askatevar had roamed in the east and north of their range. She had never come with a harvest-load to the storerooms under Tevar Hill, so she had never been on this western border at all till this moonphase, when all the Men of the Range of Askatevar came together with their flocks and families to build the Winter City over the buried granaries. She knew nothing, really, about the alien race, and when she became aware that the winning wrestler, the slender youth called Jonkendy, was staring straight into her face, she turned her head away and drew back in fear and distaste.

He came up to her, his naked body shining black with sweat. "You come from Tevar, don't you?" he asked, in human speech, but sounding half the words wrong. Happy with his victory, brushing sand off his lithe arms, he smiled at her.

"Yes."

"What can we do for you here? Anything you want?"

She could not look at him from so close, of course, but his tone was both friendly and mocking. It was a boyish voice; she thought he was probably younger than she. She would not be mocked. "Yes," she said coolly. "I want to see that black rock on the sands."

"Go on out. The causeway's open."

He seemed to be trying to peer into her lowered face. She turned further from him.

"If anybody stops you, tell them Jonkendy Li sent you," he said, "or should I go with you?"

She would not even reply to this. Head high and gaze down she headed for the street that led from the square towards the causeway. None of these grinning black false-men would dare think she was afraid. . . . ·

Nobody followed. Nobody seemed to notice her, passing her in the short street. She came to the great pillars of the causeway, glanced behind her, looked ahead and stopped.

The bridge was immense, a road for giants. From up on the ridge it had looked fragile, spanning fields and dunes and sand with the light rhythm of its arches; but here she saw that it was wide enough for twenty men to walk abreast, and led straight to the looming black gates of the tower-rock. No rail divided the great walkway from the gulf of air. The idea of walking out on it was simply wrong. She could not do it; it was not a walk for human feet.

A sidestreet led her to a western gate in the city wall. She hurried past long, empty pens and byres and slipped out the gate, intending to go on round the walls and be off home.

But here where the cliffs ran lower, with many stairs cut in them, the fields below lay peaceful and patterned in the yellow afternoon; and just across the dunes lay the wide beach, where she might find the long green seaflowers that women of Askatevar kept in their chests and on feastdays wreathed in their hair. She smelled the queer smell of the sea. She had never walked on the sea-sands in her life. The sun was not low yet. She went down a cliff stairway and through the fields, over the dykes and dunes and ran out at last onto the flat and shining sands that went on and on out of sight to the north and west and south.

Wind blew, faint sun shone. Very far ahead in the west she heard an unceasing sound, an immense, remote voice murmuring, lulling. Firm and level and endless, the sand lay under her feet. She ran for the joy of running, stopped and looked with a laugh of exhilaration at the causeway arches marching solemn and huge beside the tiny wavering line of her footprints, ran on again and stopped again to pick up silvery shells that lay half buried in the sand. Bright as a handful of colored pebbles the farborn town perched on the clifftop behind her. Before she was tired of salt wind and space and solitude, she was out almost as far as the tower-rock, which now loomed dense black between her and the sun.

Cold lurked in that long shadow. She shivered and set off running again to get out of the shadow, keeping a good long ways from the black bulk of rock. She wanted to see how low the sun was getting, how far she must run to see the first waves of the sea.

Faint and deep on the wind a voice rang in her ears, calling something, calling so strangely and urgently that she stopped still and looked back with a qualm of dread at the great black island rising up out of the sand. Was the witchplace calling to her?

On the unrailed causeway, over one of the piers that stuck down into the island rock, high and distant up there, a black figure stood.

She turned and ran, then stopped and turned back. Terror grew in her. Now she wanted to run, and did not. The terror overcame her and she could not move hand or foot but stood shaking, a roaring in her ears. The witch of the black tower was weaving his spider-spell about her. Flinging out his arms he called again the piercing urgent words she did not understand, faint on the wind as a seabird's call, *staak, staak!* The roaring in her ears grew and she cowered down on the sand.

Then all at once, clear and quiet inside her head, a voice said, "Run. Get up and run. To the island—now, quick." And before she knew, she had got to her feet; she was running. The quiet voice spoke again to guide her. Unseeing, sobbing for breath, she reached black stairs cut in the rock and began to struggle up them. At a turning a black figure ran to meet her. She reached up her hand and was half led, half dragged, up one more staircase, then released. She fell against the wall, for her legs would not hold her. The black figure caught her, helped her stand, and spoke aloud in the voice that had spoken inside her skull: "Look," he said, "there it comes."

Water crashed and boiled below them with a roar that shook the solid rock. The waters parted by the island joined white and roaring, swept on, hissed and foamed and crashed on the long slope to the dunes, stilled to a rocking of bright waves.

Rolery stood clinging to the wall, shaking. She could not stop shaking.

"The tide comes in here just a bit faster than a man can run," the quiet voice behind her said. "And when it's in, it's about twenty feet deep here around the Stack. Come on up this way. . . . That's why we lived out here in the old days, you see. Half of the time it's an island. Used to lure an enemy army out onto the sands just before the tide came in, if they didn't know much about the tides . . . Are you all right?"

Rolery shrugged slightly. He did not seem to understand the gesture, so she said, "Yes." She could understand his speech, but he used a good many words she had never heard, and pronounced most of the rest wrong.

"You come from Tevar?"

She shrugged again. She felt sick and wanted to cry, but did not. Climbing the next flight of stairs cut in the black rock, she put her hair straight, and from its shelter glanced up for a split second sideways at the farborn's face. It was strong, rough, and dark, with grim, bright eyes, the dark eyes of the alien.

"What were you doing on the sands? Didn't anyone warn you about the tide?"

"I didn't know," she whispered.

"Your Elders know. Or they used to last Spring when your tribe was living along the coast here. Men have damn short memories." What he said was harsh, but his voice was always quiet and without harshness. "This way now. Don't worry—the whole place is empty. It's been a long time since one of your people set foot on the Stack. . . ."

They had entered a dark door and tunnel and come out into a room which she thought huge till they entered the next one. They passed through gates and courts open to the sky, along arched galleries that leaned far out above the sea, through rooms and vaulted halls, all silent, empty, dwelling places of the sea-wind. The sea rocked its wrinkled silver far below now. She felt light-headed, insubstantial.

"Does nobody live here?" she asked in a small voice.

"Not now."

"It's your Winter City?"

"No, we winter in the town. This was built as a fort. We had a lot of enemies in the old days. . . . Why were you on the sands?"

"I wanted to see . . ."

"See what?"

"The sands. The ocean. I was in your town first, I wanted to see . . ."

"All right! No harm in that." He led her through a gallery so high it made her dizzy. Through the tall, pointed arches crying seabirds flew. Then passing down a last narrow corridor they came out under a gate, and crossed a clanging bridge of swordmetal onto the causeway.

They walked between tower and town, between sky and sea, in silence, the wind pushing them always towards the right. Rolery was cold, and unnerved by the height and strangeness of the walk, by the presence of the dark false-man beside her, walking with her pace for pace.

As they entered the town he said abruptly, "I won't mindspeak you again. I had to then."

"When you said to run—" she began, then hesitated, not sure what he was talking about, or what had happened out on the sands.

"I thought you were one of us," he said as if angry, and then controlled himself. "I couldn't stand and watch you drown. Even if you deserved to. But don't worry. I won't do it again, and it didn't give me any power over you. No matter what your Elders may tell you. So go on, you're free as air and ignorant as ever."

His harshness was real, and it frightened Rolery. Impatient with her fear she inquired, shakily but with impudence, "Am I also free to come back?"

At that the farborn looked at her. She was aware, though she could not look up at his face, that his expression had changed. "Yes. You are. May I know your name, daughter of Askatevar?"

"Rolery of Wold's Kin."

"Wold's your grandfather?—your father? He's still alive?"

"Wold closes the circle in the Stone-Pounding," she said loftily, trying to assert herself against his air of absolute authority. How could a farborn, a false-man, kinless and beneath law, be so grim and lordly?

"Give him greeting from Jakob Agat Alterra. Tell him that I'll come to Te-var tomorrow to speak to him. Farewell, Rolery." And he put out his hand in the salute of equals so that without thinking she did the same, laying her open palm against his.

Then she turned and hurried up the steep streets and steps, drawing her fur hood up over her head, turning from the few farborns she passed. Why did they stare in one's face so, like corpses or fish? Warm-blooded animals and human beings did not go staring in one another's eyes that way. She came out of the landward gate with a great sense of relief, and made her quick way up the ridge in the last reddish sunlight, down through the dying woods, and along the path leading to Tevar. As twilight verged into darkness, she saw across the stubble fields little stars of firelight from the tents encircling the unfinished Winter City on the hill. She hurried on towards warmth and din-ner and humankind. But even in the big sister-tent of her Kin, kneeling by the fire and stuffing herself with stew among the womenfolk and children, still she felt a strangeness lingering in her mind. Closing her right hand, she seemed to hold against her palm a handful of darkness, where his touch had been.

2

In the Red Tent

"This slop's cold," he growled, pushing it away. Then seeing old Kerly's patient look as she took the bowl to reheat it, he called himself a cross old fool. But none of his wives—he had only one left—none of his daughters, none of the women could cook up a bowl of bhan-meal the way Shakatany had done. What a cook she had been, and young . . . his last young wife. And she had died, out there in the eastern range, died young while he went on living and living, waiting for the bitter Winter to come.

A girl came by in a leather tunic stamped with the trifoliate mark of his Kin, a granddaughter probably. She looked a little like Shakatany. He spoke to her, though he did not remember her name. "Was it you that came in late last night, kinswoman?"

He recognized the turn of her head and smile. She was the one he teased, the one that was indolent, impudent, sweet-natured, solitary; the child born out of season. What the devil was her name?

"I bring you a message, Eldest."

"Whose message?"

"He called himself by a big name—Jakat-abat-bolterra? I can't remember it all."

"Alterra? That's what the farborns call their chiefs. Where did you see this man?"

"It wasn't a man, Eldest, it was a farborn. He sent greetings, and a message that he'll come today to Tevar to speak to the Eldest."

"Did he, now?" said Wold, nodding a little, admiring her effrontery. "And you're his message-bearer?"

"He chanced to speak to me. . . ."

"Yes, yes. Did you know, kinswoman, that among the Men of Pernmek Range an unwed woman who speaks to a farborn is . . . punished?"

"Punished how?"

"Never mind."

"The Pernmek men are a lot of kloob-eaters, and they shave their heads.

What do they know about farborns, anyway? They never come to the coast. . . . I heard once in some tent that the Eldest of my Kin had a farborn wife. In other days."

"That was true. In other days." The girl waited, and Wold looked back, far back into another time: timepast, the Spring. Colors, fragrances long faded, flowers that had not bloomed for forty moonphases, the almost forgotten sound of a voice . . . "She was young. She died young. Before Summer ever came." After a while he added, "Besides, that's not the same as an unwed girl speaking to a farborn. There's a difference, kinswoman."

"Why so?"

Though impertinent, she deserved an answer. "There are several reasons, and some are better than others. This mainly: a farborn takes only one wife, so a true-woman marrying him would bear no sons."

"Why would she not, Eldest?"

"Don't women talk in the sister-tent any more? Are you all so ignorant? Because human and farborn can't conceive together! Did you never hear of that? Either a sterile mating or else miscarriages, misformed monsters that don't come to term. My wife, Arilia, who was farborn, died in miscarrying a child. Her people have no rule; their women are like men, they marry whom they like. But among Mankind there is a law: women lie with human men, marry human men, bear human children!"

She looked a little sick and sorry. Presently, looking off at the scurry and bustle on the walls of the Winter City, she said, "A fine law for women who have men to lie with . . ."

She looked to be about twenty moonphases old, which meant she was the one born out of season, right in the middle of the Summer Fallow when children were not born. The sons of Spring would by now be twice or three times her age, married, remarried, prolific; the Fall-born were all children yet. But some Spring-born fellow would take her for third or fourth wife; there was no need for her to complain. Perhaps he could arrange a marriage for her, though that depended on her affiliations. "Who is your mother, kinswoman?"

She looked straight at his belt-clasp and said, "Shakatany was my mother. Have you forgotten her?"

"No, Rolery," he replied after a little while. "I haven't. Listen now, daughter, where did you speak to this Alterra? Was his name Agat?"

"That was part of his name."

"So I knew his father and his father's father. He is of the kin of the woman . . . the farborn we spoke of. He would be perhaps her sister's son or brother's son."

"Your nephew then. My cousin," said the girl, and gave a sudden laugh. Wold also grinned at the grotesque logic of this affiliation.

"I met him when I went to look at the ocean," she explained, "there on the sands. Before, I saw a runner coming from the north. None of the women know. Was there news? Is the Southing going to begin?"

"Maybe, maybe," said Wold. He had forgotten her name again. "Run along, child, help your sisters in the fields there," he said, and forgetting her, and the bowl of bhan he had been waiting for, he got up heavily and went round his great red-painted tent to gaze at the swarming workers on the earth-houses and the walls of the Winter City, and beyond them to the north. The northern sky this morning was very blue, clear, cold, over bare hills.

Vividly he remembered the life in those peak-roofed warrens dug into the earth: the huddled bodies of a hundred sleepers, the old women waking and lighting the fires that sent heat and smoke into all his pores, the smell of boiling wintergrass, the noise, the stink, the close warmth of winter in those burrows under the frozen ground. And the cold cleanly stillness of the world above, wind-scoured or snow-covered, when he and the other young hunters ranged far from Tevar hunting the snowbirds and korio and the fat wespries that followed the frozen rivers down from the remotest north. And over there, right across the valley, from a patch of snowcrop there had risen up the lolling white head of a snowghoul. . . . And before then, before the snow and ice and white beasts of Winter, there had once before been bright weather like this: a bright day of golden wind and blue sky, cold above the hills. And he, no man, only a brat among the brats and women, looking up at flat white faces, red plumes, capes of queer, feathery grayish fur; voices had barked like beasts in words he did not understand, while the men of his Kin and the Elders of Askatevar had answered in stern voices, bidding the flat-faces go on. And before that there had been a man who came running from the north with the side of his face burnt and bloody, crying, "The Gaal, the Gaal! They came through our camp at Pekna! . . ."

Clearer than any present voice he heard that hoarse shout ring across his lifetime, the sixty moonphases that lay between him and that staring, listening brat, between this bright day and that bright day. Where was Pekna? Lost under the rains, the snows; and the thaws of Spring had washed away the bones of the massacred, the rotted tents, the memory, the name.

There would be no massacres this time when the Gaal came south through the Range of Askatevar. He had seen to that. There was some good in outliving your time and remembering old evils. Not one clan or family of the Men of all this Range was left out in the Summerlands to be caught unawares by the Gaal or the first blizzard. They were all here. Twenty hundreds of them, with the little Fall-borns thick as leaves skipping about under your feet, and women chattering and gleaning in the fields like flocks of migratory birds, and men swarming to build up the houses and walls of the Winter City with the old stones on the old foundations, to hunt the last of the migrant beasts, to cut and store endless wood from the forests and peat from the Dry Bog, to round up and settle the hann in great byres and feed them until the winter-grass should begin to grow. All of them, in this labor that had gone on half a moonphase now, had obeyed him, and he had obeyed the old Way of Man. When the Gaal came they would shut the city gates; when the blizzards came they would shut the earth-house doors, and they would survive till Spring. They would survive.

He sat down on the ground behind his tent, lowering himself heavily, sticking out his gnarled, scarred legs into the sunlight. Small and whitish the sun looked, though the sky was flawlessly clear; it seemed half the size of the great sun of Summer, smaller even than the moon. "Sun shrunk to moon, cold comes soon. . . ." The ground was damp with the long rains that had plagued them all this moonphase, and scored here and there with the little ruts left by the migrating footroots. What was it the girl had asked him—about farborns, about the runner, that was it. The fellow had come panting in yesterday—was it yesterday?—with a tale of the Gaal attacking the Winter City of Tlokna, up north there near the Green Mountains. There was lie or panic in that tale. The Gaal never attacked stone walls. Flat-nosed barbarians, in their plumes and dirt, running southward like homeless animals at the approach of Winter—they couldn't take a city. And anyway, Pekna was only a little hunting camp, not a walled city. The runner lied. It was all right. They would survive. Where was the fool woman with his breakfast? Here, now, it was warm, here in the sun. . . .

Wold's eighth wife crept up with a basket of steaming bhan, saw he was asleep, sighed grumpily, and crept away again to the cooking-fire.

That afternoon when the farborn came to his tent, dour guards around him and a ragtag of leering, jeering children trailing behind, Wold remembered what the girl had said, laughing: "Your nephew, my cousin." So he heaved himself up and stood to greet the farborn with averted face and hand held out in the greeting of equals.

As an equal the alien greeted him, unhesitating. They had always that arrogance, that air of thinking themselves as good as men, whether or not they really believed it. This fellow was tall, well-made, still young; he walked like a chief. Except for his darkness and his dark, unearthly eyes, he might have been thought to be human.

"I am Jakob Agat, Eldest."

"Be welcome in my tent and the tents of my Kin, Alterra."

"I hear with my heart," the farborn said, making Wold grin a little; he had not heard anybody say that since his father's time. It was strange how far-borns always remembered old ways, digging up things buried in timepast. How could this young fellow know a phrase that only Wold and perhaps a couple of the other oldest men of Tevar remembered? It was part of the far-borns' strangeness, which was called witchery, and which made people fear the dark folk. But Wold had never feared them.

"A noblewoman of your Kin dwelt in my tents, and I walked in the streets of your city many times in Spring. I remember this. So I say that no man of Tevar will break the peace between our people while I live."

"No man of Landin will break it while I live."

The old chief had been moved by his little speech as he made it; there were tears in his eyes, and he sat down on his chest of painted hide clearing his throat and blinking. Agat stood erect, black-cloaked, dark eyes in a dark face. The young hunters who guarded him fidgeted, children peered whispering and shoving in the open side of the tent. With one gesture Wold blew them all away. The tentside was lowered, old Kerly lit the tentfire and scurried out again, and he was alone with the alien. "Sit down," he said. Agat did not sit down. He said, "I listen," and stood there. If Wold did not ask him to be seated in front of the other humans, he would not be seated when there were none to see. Wold did not think all this nor decide upon it, he merely sensed it through a skin made sensitive by a long lifetime of leading and controlling people.

He sighed and said, "Wife!" in his cracked bass voice. Old Kerly reappeared, staring. "Sit down," Wold said to Agat, who sat down crosslegged by the fire. "Go away," Wold growled to his wife, who vanished.

Silence. Elaborately and laboriously, Wold undid the fastenings of a small leather bag that hung from the waist-strap of his tunic, extracted a tiny lump of solidified gesin-oil, broke from it a still tinier scrap, replaced the lump, retied the bag, and laid the scrap on a hot coal at the edge of the fire. A little curl of bitter greenish smoke went up; Wold and the alien both inhaled deeply and closed their eyes. Wold leaned back against the big pitch-coated urine basket and said, "I listen."

"Eldest, we have had news from the north."

"So have we. There was a runner yesterday." Was it yesterday?

"Did he speak of the Winter City at Tlokna?"

The old man sat looking into the fire a while, breathing deep as if to get a last whiff of the gesin, chewing the inside of his lips, his face (as he well knew) dull as a piece of wood, blank, senile.

"I'd rather not be the bearer of ill news," the alien said in his quiet, grave voice.

"You aren't. We've heard it already. It is very hard, Alterra, to know the truth in stories that come from far away, from other tribes in other ranges. It's eight days' journey even for a runner from Tlokna to Tevar, twice that long with tents and hann. Who knows? The gates of Tevar will be ready to shut, when the Southing comes by. And you in your city that you never leave, surely your gates need no mending?"

"Eldest, it will take very strong gates this time. Tlokna had walls, and gates, and warriors. Now it has none. This is no rumor. Men of Landin were there, ten days ago; they've been watching the borders for the first Gaal. But the Gaal are coming all at once—"

"Alterra, I listen. . . . Now you listen. Men sometimes get frightened and run away before the enemy ever comes. We hear this tale and that tale too. But I am old. I have seen Autumn twice, I have seen Winter come, I have seen the Gaal come south. I will tell you the truth."

"I listen," the alien said.

"The Gaal live in the north beyond the farthest ranges of men who speak our language. They have great grassy Summerlands there, so the story says, beneath mountains that have rivers of ice on their tops. After Mid-Autumn the cold and the beasts of the snow begin to come down into their lands from the farthest north where it is always Winter, and like our beasts the Gaal move south. They bring their tents, but build no cities and save no grain. They come through Tevar Range while the stars of the Tree are rising at sunset and before the Snowstar rises, at the turn from Fall to Winter. If they find families traveling unprotected, hunting camps, unguarded flocks or fields, they'll kill and steal. If they see a Winter City standing built, and warriors on its walls, they go by waving their spears and yelling, and we shoot a few darts into the backsides of the last ones. . . . They go on and on, and stop only somewhere far south of here; some men say it's warmer where they spend the Winter—who knows? But that is the Southing. I know. I've seen it, Alterra, and seen them return north again in the thaws when the forests are growing. They don't attack stone cities. They're like water, water running and noisy, but the stone divides it and is not moved. Tevar is stone."

The young farborn sat with bowed head, thinking, long enough that Wold could glance directly at his face for a moment.

"All you say, Eldest, is truth, entire truth, and has always been true in past Years. But this is . . . a new time. . . . I am a leader among my people, as you are of yours. I come as one chief to another, seeking help. Believe me—listen to me, our people must help each other. There is a great man among the Gaal, a leader, they call him Kubban or Kobban. He has united all their tribes and made an army of them. The Gaal aren't stealing stray hann along their way, they're besieging and capturing the Winter Cities in all the Ranges along the coast, killing the Spring-born men, enslaving the women, leaving Gaal warriors in each city to hold and rule it over the Winter. Come Spring, when the Gaal come north again, they'll stay; these lands will be their lands—these forests and fields and Summerlands and cities and all their people—what's left of them. . . ."

The old man stared aside a while and then said very heavily, in anger, "You talk, I don't listen. You say my people will be beaten, killed, enslaved. My people are men and you're a farborn. Keep your black talk for your own black fate!"

"If men are in danger, we're in worse danger. Do you know how many of us there are in Landin now, Eldest? Less than two thousand."

"So few? What of the other towns? Your people lived on the coast to the north, when I was young."

"Gone. The survivors came to us."

"War? Sickness? You have no sickness, you farborns."

"It's hard to survive on a world you weren't made for," Agat said with grim brevity. "At any rate we're few, we're weak in numbers: we ask to be the allies of Tevar when the Gaal come. And they'll come within thirty days."

"Sooner than that, if there are Gaal at Tlokna now. They're late already, the snow will fall any day. They'll be hurrying."

"They're not hurrying, Eldest. They're coming slowly because they're coming all together—fifty, sixty, seventy thousand of them!"

Suddenly and most horribly, Wold saw what he said: saw the endless horde filing rank behind rank through the mountain passes, led by a tall slab-faced chief, saw the men of Tlokna—or was it of Tevar?—lying slaughtered under the broken walls of their city, ice forming in splinters over puddled blood. . . . He shook his head to clear out these visions. What had come over him? He sat silent a while chewing the inside of his lips.

"Well, I have heard you, Alterra."

"Not entirely, Eldest." This was barbarian rudeness, but the fellow was an alien, and after all a chief of his own kind. Wold let him go ahead. "We have time to prepare. If the men of Askatevar and the men of Allakskat and of Pernmek will make alliance, and accept our help, we can make an army of our own. If we wait in force, ready for the Gaal, on the north border of your three Ranges, then the whole Southing rather than face that much strength might turn aside and go down the mountain trails to the east. Twice in earlier Years our records say they took that eastern way. Since it's late and getting colder, and there's not much game left, the Gaal may turn aside and hurry on if they meet men ready to fight. My guess is that Kubban has no real tactic other than surprise and multitude. We can turn him."

"The men of Pernmek and Allakskat are in their Winter Cities now, like us. Don't you know the Way of Men yet? There are no battles fought in Winter!"

"Tell that law to the Gaal, Eldest! Take your own counsel, but believe my words!" The farborn rose, impelled to his feet by the intensity of his pleading and warning. Wold felt sorry for him, as he often did for young men, who have not seen how passion and plan over and over are wasted, how their lives and acts are wasted between desire and fear.

"I have heard you," he said with stolid kindliness. "The Elders of my people will hear what you've said."

"Then may I come tomorrow to hear—"

"Tomorrow, next day . . ."

"Thirty days, Eldest! Thirty days at most!"

"Alterra, the Gaal will come, and will go. The Winter will come and will not go. What good for a victorious warrior to return to an unfinished house, when the earth turns to ice? When we're ready for Winter we'll worry about the Gaal. . . . Now sit down again." He dug into his pouch again for a second bit of gesin for their closing whiff. "Was your father Agat also? I knew him when he was young. And one of my worthless daughters told me that she met you while she was walking on the sands."

The farborn looked up rather quickly, and then said, "Yes, so we met. On the sands between tides."

3

The True Name of the Sun

What caused the tides along this coast, the great diurnal swinging in and swinging out of fifteen to fifty feet of water? Not one of the Elders of the City of Tevar could answer that question. Any child in Landin could: the moon caused the tides, the pull of the moon. . . .

And moon and earth circled each other, a stately circle taking four hundred days to complete, a moonphase. And together the double planet circled the sun, a great and solemnly whirling dance in the midst of nothingness. Sixty moonphases that dance lasted, twenty-four thousand days, a lifetime, a Year. And the name of the center and sun—the name of the sun was Eltanin: Gamma Draconis.

Before he entered under the gray branches of the forest, Jakob Agat looked up at the sun sinking into a haze above the western ridge and in his mind called it by its true name, the meaning of which was that it was not simply the Sun, but a sun: a star among the stars.

The voice of a child at play rang out behind him on the slopes of Tevar Hill, recalling to him the jeering, sidelong-looking faces, the mocking whispers that hid fear, the yells behind his back—"There's a farborn here! Come and look at him!" Agat, alone under the trees, walked faster, trying to outwalk humiliation. He had been humiliated among the tents of Tevar and had suffered also from the sense of isolation. Having lived all his life in a little community of his own kind, knowing every name and face and heart, it was hard for him to face strangers. Especially hostile strangers of a different species, in crowds, on their own ground. The fear and humiliation now caught up with him so that he stopped walking altogether for a moment. *I'll be damned if I'll go back there!* he thought. *Let the old fool have his way, and sit smoke-drying himself in his stinking tent till the Gaal come. Ignorant, bigoted, quarrelsome, mealy-faced, yellow-eyed barbarians, wood-headed hilfs, let 'em all burn!*

"Alterra?"

The girl had come after him. She stood a few yards behind him on the path, her hand on the striated white trunk of a basuk tree. Yellow eyes blazed with

excitement and mockery in the even white of her face. Agat stood motionless.

"Alterra?" she said again in her light, sweet voice, looking aside.

"What do you want?"

She drew back a bit. "I'm Rolery," she said. "On the sands—"

"I know who you are. Do you know who I am? I'm a false-man, a farborn.
If your tribesmen see you with me they'll either castrate me or ceremonially
rape you—I don't know which rules you follow. Now go home!"

"My people don't do that. And there is kinship between you and me," she
said, her tone stubborn but uncertain.

He turned to go.

"Your mother's sister died in our tents—"

"To our shame," he said, and went on. She did not follow.

He stopped and looked back when he took the left fork up the ridge. Nothing stirred in all the dying forest, except one belated footroot down among
the dead leaves, creeping with its excruciating vegetable obstinacy southward,
leaving a thin track scored behind it.

Racial pride forbade him to feel any shame for his treatment of the girl,
and in fact he felt relief and a return of confidence. He would have to get used
to the hilfs' insults and ignore their bigotry. They couldn't help it; it was their
own kind of obstinacy, it was their nature. The old chief had shown, by his
own lights, real courtesy and patience. He, Jakob Agat, must be equally patient, and equally obstinate. For the fate of his people, the life of mankind
on this world, depended on what these hilf tribes did and did not do in the
next thirty days. Before the crescent moon rose, the history of a race for six
hundred moonphases, ten Years, twenty generations, the long struggle, the
long pull might end. Unless he had luck, unless he had patience.

Dry, leafless, with rotten branches, huge trees stood crowded and aisled for
miles along these hills, their roots withered in the earth. They were ready to
fall under the push of the north wind, to lie under frost and snow for thousands of days and nights, to rot in the long, long thaws of Spring, to enrich
with their vast death the earth where, very deep, very deeply sleeping, their
seeds lay buried now. Patience, patience . . .

In the wind he came down the bright stone streets of Landin to the
Square, and passing the school-children at their exercises in the arena, entered the arcaded, towered building that was called by an old name: the Hall
of the League.

Like the other buildings around the Square, it had been built five Years
ago when Landin was the capital of a strong and flourishing little nation,

the time of strength. The whole first floor was a spacious meeting-hall. All around its gray walls were broad, delicate designs picked out in gold. On the east wall a stylized sun surrounded by nine planets faced the west wall's pattern of seven planets in very long ellipses round their sun. The third planet of each system was double, and set with crystal. Above the doors and at the far end, round dial-faces with fragile and ornate hands told that this present day was the 391st day of the 45th moonphase of the Tenth Local Year of the Colony on Gamma Draconis III. They also told that it was the two hundred and second day of Year 1405 of the League of All Worlds; and that it was the twelfth of August at home.

Most people doubted that there was still a League of All Worlds, and a few paradoxicalists liked to question whether there ever had in fact been a home. But the clocks, here in the Great Assembly and down in the Records Room underground, which had been kept running for six hundred League Years, seemed to indicate by their origin and their steadfastness that there had been a League and that there still was a home, a birthplace of the race of man. Patiently they kept the hours of a planet lost in the abyss of darkness and years. Patience, patience . . .

The other Alterrans were waiting for him in the library upstairs, or came in soon, gathering around the driftwood fire on the hearth: ten of them all together. Seiko and Alla Pasfal lighted the gas jets and turned them low. Though Agat had said nothing at all, his friend Huru Pilotson coming to stand beside him at the fire said, "Don't let 'em get you down, Jakob. A herd of stupid stubborn nomads—they'll never learn."

"Have I been sending?"

"No, of course not." Huru giggled. He was a quick, slight, shy fellow, devoted to Jakob Agat. That he was a homosexual and that Agat was not was a fact well-known to them both, to everybody around them, to everyone in Landin indeed. Everybody in Landin knew everything, and candor, though wearing and difficult, was the only possible solution to this problem of over-communication.

"You expected too much when you left, that's all. Your disappointment shows. But don't let 'em get you, Jakob. They're just hilfs."

Seeing the others were listening, Agat said aloud, "I told the old man what I'd planned to; he said he'd tell their Council. How much he understood and how much he believed, I don't know."

"If he listened at all it's better than I'd hoped," said Alla Pasfal, sharp and frail, with blueblack skin, and white hair crowning her worn face. "Wold's been around as long as I have—longer. Don't expect him to welcome wars and changes."

"But he should be well disposed; he married a human," Dermat said.

"Yes, my cousin Arilia, Jakob's aunt, the exotic one in Wold's female zoo. I remember the courtship," Alla Pasfal said with such bitter sarcasm that Dermat wilted.

"He didn't make any decision about helping us? Did you tell him your plan about going up to the border to meet the Gaal?" Jonkendy Li stammered, hasty and disappointed. He was very young, and had been hoping for a fine war with marchings-forth and trumpets. So had they all. It beat being starved to death or burned alive.

"Give them time. They'll decide," Agat said gravely to the boy.

"How did Wold receive you?" asked Seiko Esmit. She was the last of a great family. Only the sons of the first leader of the Colony had borne that name Esmit. With her it would die. She was Agat's age, a beautiful and delicate woman, nervous, rancorous, repressed. When the Alterrans met, her eyes were always on Agat. No matter who spoke she watched Agat.

"He received me as an equal."

Alla Pasfal nodded approvingly and said, "He always had more sense than the rest of their males." But Seiko went on, "What about the others? Could you just walk through their camp?" Seiko could always dig up his humiliation no matter how well he had buried and forgotten it. His cousin ten times over, his sister-playmate-lover-companion, she possessed an immediate understanding of any weakness in him and any pain he felt, and her sympathy, her compassion closed in on him like a trap. They were too close. Too close, Huru, old Alla, Seiko, all of them. The isolation that had unnerved him today had also given him a glimpse of distance, of solitude, had waked a craving in him. Seiko gazed at him, watching him with clear, soft, dark eyes, sensitive to his every mood and word. The hilf girl, Rolery, had never yet looked at him, never met his gaze. Her look always was aside, away, glancing, golden, alien.

"They didn't stop me," he answered Seiko briefly. "Well, tomorrow maybe they'll decide on our suggestion. Or the next day. How's the provisioning of the Stack been going this afternoon?" The talk became general, though it tended always to center around and be referred back to Jakob Agat. He was younger than several of them, and all ten Alterrans were elected equal in their ten-year terms on the council, but he was evidently and acknowledgedly their leader, their center. No especial reason for this was visible unless it was the vigor with which he moved and spoke; is authority noticeable in the man, or in the men about him? The effects of it, however, showed in him as a certain tension and somberness, the results of a heavy load of responsibility that he had borne for a long time, and that got daily heavier.

"I made one slip," he said to Pilotson, while Seiko and the other women of the council brewed and served the little, hot, ceremonial cupfuls of steeped basuk leaves called *ti*. "I was trying so hard to convince the old fellow that there really is danger from the Gaal, that I think I sent for a moment. Not verbally; but he looked like he'd seen a ghost."

"You've got very powerful sense-projection, and lousy control when you're under strain. He probably did see a ghost."

"We've been out of touch with the hilfs so long—and we're so ingrown here, so damned isolated, I can't trust my control. First I bespeak that girl down on the beach, then I project to Wold—they'll be turning on us as witches if this goes on, the way they did in the first Years. . . . And we've got to get them to trust us. In so short a time. If only we'd known about the Gaal earlier!"

"Well," Pilotson said in his careful way, "since there are no more human settlements up the coast, it's purely due to your foresight in sending scouts up north that we have any warning at all. Your health, Seiko," he added, accepting the tiny, steaming cup she presented.

Agat took the last cup from her tray, and drained it. There was a slight sense-stimulant in freshly brewed ti, so that he was vividly aware of its astringent, clean heat in his throat, of Seiko's intense gaze, of the bare, large, firelit room, of the twilight outside the windows. The cup in his hand, blue porcelain, was very old, a work of the Fifth Year. The handpress books in cases under the windows were old. Even the glass in the windowframes was old. All their luxuries, all that made them civilized, all that kept them Alterran, was old. In Agat's lifetime and for long before there had been no energy or leisure for subtle and complex affirmations of man's skill and spirit. They did well by now merely to preserve, to endure.

Gradually, Year by Year for at least ten generations, their numbers had been dwindling; very gradually, but always there were fewer children born. They retrenched, they drew together. Old dreams of dominion were forgotten utterly. They came back—if the Winters and hostile hilf tribes did not take advantage of their weakness first—to the old center, the first colony, Landin. They taught their children the old knowledge and the old ways, but nothing new. They lived always a little more humbly, coming to value the simple over the elaborate, calm over strife, courage over success. They withdrew.

Agat, gazing into the tiny cup in his hand, saw in its clear, pure translucency, the perfect skill of its making and the fragility of its substance, a kind of epitome of the spirit of his people. Outside the high windows the air was the same translucent blue. But cold: a blue twilight, immense and cold. The old terror of his childhood came over Agat, the terror which, as he became adult, he had reasoned thus: this world on which he had been born, on which his father and forefathers for twenty-three generations had been born, was not his home. His kind was alien. Profoundly, they were always aware of it. They were the farborn. And little by little, with the majestic slowness, the vegetable obstinacy of the process of evolution, this world was killing them—rejecting the graft.

They were perhaps too submissive to this process, too willing to die out. But a kind of submission—their iron adherence to the League Laws—had been their strength from the very beginning; and they were still strong, each one of them. But they had not the knowledge or the skill to combat the sterility and early abortion that reduced their generations. For not all wisdom was written in the League Books, and from day to day and Year to Year a little knowledge would always be lost, supplanted by some more immediately useful bit of information concerning daily existence here and now. And in the end, they could not even understand much of what the books told them. What truly remained of their Heritage, by now? If ever the ship, as in the old hopes and tales, soared down in fire from the stars, would the men who stepped from it know them to be men?

But no ship had come, or would come. They would die; their presence here, their long exile and struggle on this world, would be done with, broken like a bit of clay.

He put the cup very carefully down on the tray, and wiped the sweat off his forehead. Seiko was watching him. He turned from her abruptly and began to listen to Jonkendy, Dermat and Pilotson. Across his bleak rush of foreboding he had recalled briefly, irrelevant and yet seeming both an explanation and a sign, the light, lithe, frightened figure of the girl Rolery, reaching up her hand to him from the dark, sea-besieged stones.

4

The Tall Young Men

The sound of rock pounded on rock, hard and unreverberant, rang out among the roofs and unfinished walls of the Winter City to the high red tents pitched all around it. *Ak ak ak ak,* the sound went on for a long time, until suddenly a second pounding joined it in counterpoint, *kadak ak ak kadak.* Another came in on a higher note, giving a tripping rhythm, then another, another, more, until any measure was lost in the clatter of constant sound, an avalanche of the high dry whack of rock hitting rock in which each individual pounding rhythm was submerged, indistinguishable.

As the sound-avalanche went ceaselessly and stupefyingly on, the Eldest Man of the Men of Askatevar walked slowly from his tent and between the aisles of tents and cookfires from which smoke rose through slanting late-afternoon, late-Autumn light. Stiff and ponderous the old man went alone through the camp of his people and entered the gate of the Winter City, followed a twisting path or street among the tent-like wooden roofs of the houses, which had no sidewalls aboveground, and came to an open place in the middle of the roofpeaks. There a hundred or so men sat, knees to chin, pounding rock on rock, pounding, in a hypnotic toneless trance of percussion. Wold sat down, completing the circle. He picked up the smaller of two heavy waterworn rocks in front of him and with satisfying heaviness whacked it down on the bigger one: *Klak! klak! klak!* To right and left of him the clatter went on and on, a rattling roar of random noise, through which every now and then a snatch of a certain rhythm could be discerned. The rhythm vanished, recurred, a chance concatenation of noise. On its return Wold caught it, fell in with it and held it. Now to him it dominated the clatter. Now his neighbor to the left was beating it, their two stones rising and falling together; now his neighbor to the right. Now others across the circle were beating it, pounding together. It came clear of the noise, conquered it, forced each conflicting voice into its own single ceaseless rhythm, the concord, the hard heartbeat of the Men of Askatevar, pounding on, and on, and on.

This was all their music, all their dance.

A man leaped up at last and walked into the center of the ring. He was bare-chested, black stripes painted up his arms and legs, his hair a black cloud around his face. The rhythm lightened, lessened, died away. Silence.

"The runner from the north brought news that the Gaal follow the Coast Trail and come in great force. They have come to Tlokna. Have you all heard this?"

A rumble of assent.

"Now listen to the man who called this Stone-Pounding," the shaman-herald called out; and Wold got up with difficulty. He stood in his place, gazing straight ahead, massive, scarred, immobile, an old boulder of a man.

"A farborn came to my tent," he said at last in his age-weakened, deep voice. "He is chief of them in Landin. He said the farborns have grown few and ask the help of men."

A rumble from all the heads of clans and families that sat moveless, knees to chin, in the circle. Over the circle, over the wooden roofpeaks about them, very high up in the cold, golden light, a white bird wheeled, harbinger of winter.

"This farborn said the Southing comes not by clans and tribes but all in one horde, many thousands led by a great chief."

"How does he know?" somebody roared. Protocol was not strict in the Stone-Poundings of Tevar; Tevar had never been ruled by its shamans as some tribes were. "He had scouts up north!" Wold roared back. "He said the Gaal besiege Winter Cities and capture them. That is what the runner said of Tlokna. The farborn says that the warriors of Tevar should join with the farborns and with the men of Pernmek and Allakskat, go up in the north of our range, and turn the Southing aside to the Mountain Trail. These things he said and I heard them. Have you all heard?"

The assent was uneven and turbulent, and a clan chief was on his feet at once. "Eldest! from your mouth we hear the truth always. But when did a farborn speak truth? When did men listen to farborns? I hear nothing this farborn said. What if his City perishes in the Southing? No men live in it! Let them perish and then we men can take their Range."

The speaker, Walmek, was a big dark man full of words; Wold had never liked him, and dislike influenced his reply. "I have heard Walmek. Not for the first time. Are the farborns men or not—who knows? Maybe they fell out of the sky as in the tale. Maybe not. No one ever fell out of the sky this Year. . . . They look like men; they fight like men. Their women are like women, I can tell you that! They have some wisdom. It's better to listen to them. . . ." His references to farborn women had them all grinning as they sat in their solemn circle, but he wished he had not said it. It was stupid to remind them of his old ties with the aliens. And it was wrong . . . she had been his wife, after all. . . .

He sat down, confused, signifying he would speak no more.

Some of the other men, however, were impressed enough by the runner's tale and Agat's warning to argue with those who discounted or distrusted the news. One of Wold's Spring-born sons, Umaksuman, who loved raids and forays, spoke right out in favor of Agat's plan of marching up to the border.

"It's a trick to get our men away up north on the Range, caught in the first snow, while the farborns steal our flocks and wives and rob the granaries here. They're not men, there's no good in them!" Walmek ranted. Rarely had he found so good a subject to rant on.

"That's all they've ever wanted, our women. No wonder they're growing few and dying out, all they bear is monsters. They want our women so they can bring up human children as theirs!" This was a youngish family-head, very excited. "Aagh!" Wold growled, disgusted at this mishmash of misinformation, but he kept sitting and let Umaksuman set the fellow straight.

"And what if the farborn spoke truth?" Umaksuman went on. "What if the Gaal come through our Range all together, thousands of them? Are we ready to fight them?"

"But the walls aren't finished, the gates aren't up, the last harvest isn't stored," an older man said. This, more than distrust of the aliens, was the core of the question. If the able men marched off to the north, could the women and children and old men finish all the work of readying the Winter City before winter was upon them? Maybe, maybe not. It was a heavy chance to take on the word of a farborn.

Wold himself had made no decision, and looked to abide by that of the Elders. He liked the farborn Agat, and would guess him neither deluded nor a liar; but there was no telling. All men were alien one to another, at times, not only aliens. You could not tell. Perhaps the Gaal were coming as an army. Certainly the Winter was coming. Which enemy first?

The Elders swayed toward doing nothing, but Umaksuman's faction prevailed to the extent of having runners sent to the two neighboring Ranges, Allakskat and Pernmek, to sound them out on the project of a joint defense. That was all the decision made; the shaman released the scrawny hann he had caught in case a decision for war was reached and must be sealed by lapidation, and the Elders dispersed.

Wold was sitting in his tent with men of his Kin over a good hot pot of bhan, when there was a commotion outside. Umaksuman went out, shouted at everybody to clear out, and reentered the great tent behind the farborn Agat.

"Welcome, Alterra," said the old man, and with a sly glance at his two grandsons, "will you sit with us and eat?"

He liked to shock people; he always had. That was why he had always been running off to the farborns in the old days. And this gesture freed him, in his mind, from the vague shame he suffered since speaking before the other men of the farborn girl who had so long ago been his wife.

Agat, calm and grave as before, accepted and ate enough to show he took the hospitality seriously; he waited till they were all done eating, and Ukwet's wife had scuttled out with the leavings, then he said, "Eldest, I listen."

"There's not much to hear," Wold replied. He belched. "Runners go to Pernmek and Allakskat. But few spoke for war. The cold grows each day now: safety lies inside walls, under roofs. We don't walk about in timepast as your people do, but we know what the Way of Men has always been and is, and hold to it."

"Your way is good," the farborn said, "good enough, maybe, that the Gaal have learned it from you. In past Winters you were stronger than the Gaal because your clans were gathered together against them. Now the Gaal too have learned that strength lies in numbers."

"*If* that news is true," said Ukwet, who was one of Wold's grandsons, though older than Wold's son Umaksuman.

Agat looked at him in silence. Ukwet turned aside at once from that straight, dark gaze.

"If it's not true, then why are the Gaal so late coming south?" said Umaksuman. "What's keeping them? Have they ever waited till the harvests were in before?"

"Who knows?" said Wold. "Last Year they came long before the Snowstar rose, I remember that. But who remembers the Year before last?"

"Maybe they're following the Mountain Trail," said the other grandson, "and won't come through Askatevar at all."

"The runner said they had taken Tlokna," Umaksuman said sharply, "and Tlokna is north of Tevar on the Coast Trail. *Why* do we disbelieve this news, why do we wait to act?"

"Because men who fight wars in Winter don't live till Spring," Wold growled.

"But if they come—"

"If they come, we'll fight."

There was a little pause. Agat for once looked at none of them, but kept his dark gaze lowered like a human.

"People say," Ukwet remarked with a jeering note, sensing triumph, "that the farborns have strange powers. I know nothing about all that, I was born on the Summerlands and never saw farborns before this moonphase, let alone sat to eat with one. But if they're witches and have such powers, why would they need our help against the Gaal?"

"I do not hear you!" Wold thundered, his face purple and his eyes watering. Ukwet hid his face. Enraged by this insolence to a tent-guest, and by his own confusion and indecisiveness which made him argue against both sides, Wold sat breathing heavily, staring with inflamed eyes at the young man, who kept his face hidden.

"I talk," Wold said at last, his voice still loud and deep, free for a little from the huskiness of old age. "I talk: listen! Runners will go up the Coast Trail until they meet the Southing. And behind them, two days behind, but no farther than the border of our Range, warriors will follow—all men born between Mid-Spring and the Summer Fallow. If the Gaal come in force, the warriors will drive them east to the mountains; if not, they will come back to Tevar."

Umaksuman laughed aloud and said, "Eldest, no man leads us but you!"

Wold growled and belched and settled down. "You'll lead the warriors, though," he told Umaksuman dourly.

Agat, who had not spoken for some time, said in his quiet way, "My people can send three hundred and fifty men. We'll go up the old beach road, and join with your men at the border of Askatevar." He rose and held out his hand. Sulky at having been driven into this commitment, and still shaken by his emotion, Wold ignored him. Umaksuman was on his feet in a flash, his hand against the farborn's. They stood there for a moment in the firelight like day and night: Agat dark, shadowy, somber, Umaksuman fair-skinned, light-eyed, radiant.

The decision was made, and Wold knew he could force it upon the other Elders. He knew also that it was the last decision he would ever make. He could send them to war: but Umaksuman would come back the leader of the warriors, and thereby the strongest leader among the Men of Askatevar. Wold's action was his own abdication. Umaksuman would be the young chief. He would close the circle of the Stone-Pounding, he would lead the hunters in Winter, the forays in Spring, the great wanderings of the long days of Summer. His Year was just beginning. . . .

"Go on," Wold growled at them all. "Call the Stone-Pounding for tomorrow, Umaksuman. Tell the shaman to stake out a hann, a fat one with some blood in it." He would not speak to Agat. They left, all the tall young men. He sat crouched on his stiff hams by his fire, staring into the yellow flames as if into the heart of a lost brightness, Summer's irrecoverable warmth.

5

Twilight in the Woods

The farborn came out of Umaksuman's tent and stood a minute talking with the young chief, both of them looking to the north, eyes narrowed against the biting gray wind. Agat moved his outstretched hand as if he spoke of the mountains. A flaw of wind carried a word or two of what he said to Rolery where she stood watching on the path up to the city gate. As she heard him speak, a tremor went through her, a little rush of fear and darkness through her veins, making her remember how that voice had spoken in her mind, in her flesh, calling her to him.

Behind that like a distorted echo in her memory came the harsh command, outward as a slap, when on the forest path he had turned on her, telling her to go, to get away from him.

All of a sudden she put down the baskets she was carrying. They were moving today from the red tents of her nomad childhood into the warren of peaked roofs and underground halls and tunnels and alleys of the Winter City, and all her cousin-sisters and aunts and nieces were bustling and squealing and scurrying up and down the paths and in and out of the tents and the gates with furs and boxes and pouches and baskets and pots. She set down her armload there beside the path and walked off toward the forest.

"Rolery! Ro-o-olery!" shrilled the voices that were forever shrilling after her, accusing, calling, screeching at her back. She never turned, but walked right on. As soon as she was well into the woods she began to run. When all sound of voices was lost in the soughing, groaning silence of the wind-strained trees, and nothing recalled the camp of her people except a faint, bitter scent of woodsmoke in the wind, she slowed down.

Great fallen trunks barred the path now in places, and must be climbed over or crawled under, the stiff dead branches tearing at her clothes, catching her hood. The woods were not safe in this wind; even now, somewhere off up the ridge she heard the muttering crash of a tree falling before the wind's push. She did not care. She felt like going down onto those gray sands again and standing still, perfectly still, to watch the foaming thirty-foot wall of water come down upon her. . . . As suddenly as she had started off, she stopped, and stood still on the twilit path.

The wind blew and ceased and blew. A murky sky writhed and lowered over the network of leafless branches. It was already half dark here. All anger and purpose drained out of the girl, leaving her standing in a kind of scared stupor, hunching her shoulders against the wind. Something white flashed in front of her and she cried out, but did not move. Again the white movement passed, then stilled suddenly above her on a jagged branch: a great beast or bird, winged, pure white, white above and below, with short, sharp hooked lips that parted and closed, and staring silver eyes. Gripping the branch with four naked talons the creature gazed down at her, and she up at it, neither moving. The silver eyes never blinked. Abruptly, great white wings shot out, wider than a man's height, and beat among the branches, breaking them. The creature beat its white wings and screamed, then as the wind gusted launched out into the air and made its way heavily off between the branches and the driving clouds.

"A stormbringer." Agat spoke, standing on the path a few yards behind her. "They're supposed to bring the blizzards."

The great silver creature had driven all her wits away. The little rush of tears that accompanied all strong feelings in her race blinded her a moment. She had meant to stand and mock him, to jeer at him, having seen the resentment under his easy arrogance when people in Tevar slighted him, treated him as what he was, a being of a lower kind. But the white creature, the stormbringer, had frightened her and she broke out, staring straight at him as she had at it, "I hate you, you're not a man, I hate you!"

Then her tears stopped, she looked away, and they both stood there in silence for quite a while.

"Rolery," said the quiet voice, "look at me."

She did not. He came forward, and she drew back crying, "Don't touch me!" in a voice like the stormbringer's scream, her face distorted.

"Get hold of yourself," he said. "Here—take my hand, take it!" He caught her as she struggled to break away, and held both her wrists. Again they stood without moving.

"Let me go," she said at last in her normal voice. He released her at once. She drew a long breath.

"You spoke—I heard you speak inside me. Down there on the sands. Can you do that again?"

He was watching her, alert and quiet. He nodded. "Yes. But I told you then that I never would."

"I still hear it. I feel your voice." She put her hands over her ears.

"I know. . . . I'm sorry. I didn't know you were a hilf—a Tevaran, when I called you. It's against the law. And anyhow it shouldn't have worked. . . ."

"What's a hilf?"

"What we call you."

"What do you call yourselves?"

"Men."

She looked around them at the groaning twilit woods, gray aisles, writhing cloud-roof. This gray world in motion was very strange, but she was no longer scared. His touch, his actual hand's touch canceling the insistent impalpable sense of his presence, had given her calm, which grew as they spoke together. She saw now that she had been half out of her mind this last day and night.

"Can all your people do that . . . speak that way?"

"Some can. It's a skill one can learn. Takes practice. Come here, sit down a while. You've had it rough." He was always harsh and yet there was an edge, a hint of something quite different in his voice now: as if the urgency with which he had called to her on the sands were transmuted into an infinitely restrained, unconscious appeal, a reaching out. They sat down on a fallen basuk-tree a couple of yards off the path. She noticed how differently he moved and sat than a man of her race; the schooling of his body, the sum of his gestures, was very slightly, but completely, unfamiliar. She was particularly aware of his dark-skinned hands, clasped together between his knees. He went on, "Your people could learn mindspeech if they wanted to. But they never have, they call it witchcraft, I think. . . . Our books say that we ourselves learned it from another race, long ago, on a world called Rokanan. It's a skill as well as a gift."

"Can you *hear* my mind when you want?"

"That is forbidden," he said with such finality that her fears on that score were quite disposed of.

"Teach me the skill," she said with sudden childishness.

"It would take all Winter."

"It took you all Fall?"

"And part of Summer too." He grinned slightly.

"What does hilf mean?"

"It's a word from our old language. It means 'Highly intelligent life-form.'"

"Where is another world?"

"Well—there are a lot of them. Out there. Beyond sun and moon."

"Then you did fall out of the sky? What for? How did you get from behind the sun to the seacoast here?"

"I'll tell you if you want to hear, but it's not just a tale, Rolery. There's a lot we don't understand, but what we do know of our history is true."

"I hear," she whispered in the ritual phrase, impressed, but not entirely subdued.

"Well, there were many worlds out among the stars, and many kinds of men living on them. They made ships that could sail the darkness between the worlds, and kept traveling about and trading and exploring. They allied themselves into a League, as your clans ally with one another to make a Range. But there was an enemy of the League of All Worlds. An enemy coming from far off. I don't know how far. The books were written for men who knew more than we know. . . ."

He was always using words that sounded like words, but meant nothing; Rolery wondered what a ship was, what a book was. But the grave, yearning tone in which he told his story worked on her and she listened fascinated.

"For a long time the League prepared to fight that enemy. The stronger worlds helped the weaker ones to arm against the enemy, to make ready. A little as we're trying to make ready to meet the Gaal, here. Mindhearing was one skill they taught, I know, and there were weapons, the books say, fires that could burn up whole planets and burst the stars. . . . Well, during that time my people came from their home-world to this one. Not very many of them. They were to make friends with your peoples and see if they wanted to be a world of the League, and join against the enemy. But the enemy came. The ship that brought my people went back to where it came from, to help in fighting the war, and some of the people went with it, and the . . . the far-speaker with which those men could talk to one another from world to world. But some of the people stayed on here, either to help this world if the enemy came here, or because they couldn't go back again: we don't know. Their records say only that the ship left. A white spear of metal, longer than a whole city, standing up on a feather of fire. There are pictures of it. I think they thought it would come back soon. . . . That was ten Years ago."

"What of the war with the enemy?"

"We don't know. We don't know anything that happened since the day the ship left. Some of us believe the war must have been lost, and others think it was won, but hardly, and the few men left here were forgotten in the years of fighting. Who knows? If we survive, some day we'll find out; if no one ever comes, we'll make a ship and go find out. . . ." He was yearning, ironic. Rolery's head spun with these gulfs of time and space and incomprehension. "This is hard to live with," she said after a while.

Agat laughed, as if startled. "No—it gives us our pride. What is hard is to keep alive on a world you don't belong to. Five Years ago we were a great people. Look at us now."

"They say farborns are never sick, is that true?"

"Yes. We don't catch your sicknesses, and didn't bring any of our own. But we bleed when we're cut, you know. . . . And we get old, we die, like humans. . . ."

"Well of course," she said disgustedly.

He dropped his sarcasm. "Our trouble is that we don't bear enough children. So many abort and are stillborn, so few come to term."

"I heard that. I thought about it. You do so strangely. You conceive children any time of the Year, during the Winter Fallow even—why is that?"

"We can't help it, it's how we are." He laughed again, looking at her, but she was very serious now. "I was born out of season, in the Summer Fallow," she said. "It does happen with us, but very rarely; and you see—when Winter's over I'll be too old to bear a Spring child. I'll never have a son. Some old man will take me for a fifth wife one of these days, but the Winter Fallow has begun, and come Spring I'll be old. . . . So I will die barren. It's better for a woman not to be born at all than to be born out of season as I was. . . . And another thing, it is true what they say, that a farborn man takes only one wife?"

He nodded. Apparently that meant what a shrug meant to her.

"Well, no wonder you're dying out!"

He grinned, but she insisted, "Many wives—many sons. If you were a Tevaran you'd have five or ten children already! Have you any?"

"No, I'm not married."

"But haven't you ever lain with a woman!"

"Well, yes," he said, and then more assertively, "Of course! But when we want children, we marry."

"If you were one of us—"

"But I'm not one of you," he said. Silence ensued. Finally he said, gently enough, "It isn't manners and mores that make the difference. We don't know what's wrong, but it's in the seed. Some doctors have thought that because this sun's different from the sun our race was born under, it affects us, changes the seed in us little by little. And the change kills."

Again there was silence between them for a time. "What was the other world like—your home?"

"There are songs that tell what it was like," he said, but when she asked timidly what a song was, he did not reply. After a while he said, "At home, the world was closer to its sun, and the whole year there wasn't even one moonphase long. So the books say. Think of it, the whole Winter would only last ninety days. . . ." This made them both laugh. "You wouldn't have time to light a fire," Rolery said.

Real darkness was soaking into the dimness of the woods. The path in front of them ran indistinct, a faint gap among the trees leading left to her city, right to his. Here, between, was only wind, dusk, solitude. Night was coming quickly. Night and Winter and war, a time of dying. "I'm afraid of the Winter," she said, very low.

"We all are," he said. "What will it be like? . . . We've only known the sunlight."

There was no one among her people who had ever broken her fearless, careless solitude of mind; having no age-mates, and by choice also, she had always been quite alone, going her own way and caring little for any person. But now as the world had turned gray and nothing held any promise beyond death, now as she first felt fear, she had met him, the dark figure near the tower-rock over the sea, and had heard a voice that spoke in her blood.

"Why will you never look at me?" he asked.

"I will," she said, "if you want me to." But she did not, though she knew his strange shadowy gaze was on her. At last she put out her hand and he took it.

"Your eyes are gold," he said. "I want . . . I want . . . But if they knew we were together, even now . . ."

"Your people?"

"Yours. Mine care nothing about it."

"And mine needn't find out." They both spoke almost in whispers, but urgently, without pauses.

"Rolery, I leave for the north two nights from now."

"I know that."

"When I come back—"

"But when you don't come back!" the girl cried out, under the pressure of the terror that had entered her with Autumn's end, the fear of coldness, of death. He held her against him telling her quietly that he would come back. As he spoke she felt the beating of his heart and the beating of her own. "I want to stay with you," she said, and he was saying, "I want to stay with you."

It was dark around them. When they got up they walked slowly in a grayish darkness. She came with him, towards his city. "Where can we go?" he said with a kind of bitter laugh. "This isn't like love in Summer. . . . There's a hunter's shelter down the ridge a way. . . . They'll miss you in Tevar."

"No," she whispered, "they won't miss me."

6

Snow

The fore-runners had gone; tomorrow the Men of Askatevar would march north on the broad vague trail that divided their Range, while the smaller group from Landin would take the old road up the coast. Like Agat, Umaksuman had judged it best to keep the two forces apart until the eve of fighting. They were allied only by Wold's authority. Many of Umaksuman's men, though veterans of many raids and forays before the Winter Peace, were reluctant to go on this unseasonable war; and a sizable faction, even within his own Kin, so detested this alliance with the farborns that they were ready to make any trouble they could. Ukwet and others had said openly that when they had finished with the Gaal they would finish off the witches. Agat discounted this, foreseeing that victory would modify, and defeat end, their prejudice; but it worried Umaksuman, who did not look so far ahead.

"Our scouts will keep you in sight all along. After all, the Gaal may not wait on the border for us."

"The Long Valley under Cragtop would be a good place for a battle," Umaksuman said with his flashing smile. "Good luck, Alterra!"

"Good luck to you, Umaksuman." They parted as friends, there under the mud-cemented stone gateway of the Winter City. As Agat turned something flickered in the dull afternoon air beyond the arch, a wavering drifting movement. He looked up startled, then turned back. "Look at that."

The native came out from the walls and stood beside him a minute, to see for the first time the stuff of old men's tales. Agat held his hand out palm up. A flickering speck of white touched his wrist and was gone. The long vale of stubble fields and used-up pasture, the creek, the dark inlet of the forest and the farther hills to south and west all seemed to tremble very slightly, to withdraw, as random flakes fell from the low sky, twirling and slanting a little, though the wind was down.

Children's voices cried in excitement behind them among the high-peaked wooden roofs.

"Snow is smaller than I thought," Umaksuman said at last, dreamily.

"I thought it would be colder. The air seems warmer than it did before. . . ." Agat roused himself from the sinister and charming fascination of the twirling fall of the snow. "Till we meet in the north," he said, and pulling his fur collar close around his neck against the queer, searching touch of the tiny flakes, set out on the path to Landin.

A half-kilo into the forest he saw the scarcely marked side path that led to the hunter's shelter, and passing it felt as if his veins were running liquid light. "Come on, come on," he told himself, impatient with his recurrent loss of self-control. He had got the whole thing perfectly straight in the short intervals for thinking he had had today. Last night—had been last night. All right, it was that and nothing more. Aside from the fact that she was, after all, a hilf and he was human, so there was no future in the thing, it was foolish on other counts. Ever since he had seen her face, on the black steps over the tide, he had thought of her and yearned to see her, like an adolescent mooning after his first girl; and if there was anything he hated it was the stupidity, the obstinate stupidity of uncontrolled passion. It led men to take blind risks, to hazard really important things for a mere moment of lust, to lose control over their acts. So, in order to stay in control, he had gone with her last night; that was merely sensible, to get the fit over with. So he told himself once more, walking along very rapidly, his head high, while the snow danced thinly around him. Tonight he would meet her again, for the same reason. At the thought, a flood of warm light and an aching joy ran through his body and mind; he ignored it. Tomorrow he was off to the north, and if he came back, then there would be time enough to explain to the girl that there could be no more such nights, no more lying together on his fur cloak in the shelter in the forest's heart, starlight overhead and the cold and the great silence all around . . . no, no more. . . . The absolute happiness she had given him came up in him like a tide, drowning all thought. He ceased to tell himself anything. He walked rapidly with his long stride in the gathering darkness of the woods, and as he walked, sang under his breath, not knowing that he did so, some old love song of his exiled race.

The snow scarcely penetrated the branches. It was getting dark very early, he thought as he approached the place where the path divided, and this was the last thing in his mind when something caught his ankle in midstride and sent him pitching forward. He landed on his hands and was halfway up when a shadow on his left became a man, silvery-white in the gloom, who knocked him over before he was fairly up. Confused by the ringing in his ears, Agat struggled free of something holding him and again tried to stand up. He seemed to have lost his bearings and did not understand what was happening, though he had an impression that it had happened before, and also that it was not actually happening. There were several more of the silvery-looking men with stripes down their legs and arms, and they held him by the arms while another one came up and struck him with something across the mouth. There was pain, the darkness was full of pain and rage. With a furious and skilful convulsion of his whole body he got free of the silvery men, catching one under the jaw with his fist and sending him out of the scene backward: but there were more and more of them and he could not get free a second time. They hit him and when he hid his face in his arms against the mud of the path they kicked his sides. He lay pressed against the blessed harmless mud, trying to hide, and heard somebody breathing very strangely. Through that noise he also heard Umaksuman's voice. Even he, then . . . But he did not care, so long as they would go away, would let him be. It was getting dark very early.

It was dark: pitch dark. He tried to crawl forward. He wanted to get home to his people who would help him. It was so dark he could not see his hands. Soundlessly and unseen in the absolute blackness, snow fell on him and around him on the mud and leaf-mold. He wanted to get home. He was very cold. He tried to get up, but there was no west or east, and sick with pain he put his head down on his arm. "Come to me," he tried to call in the mind-speech of Alterra, but it was too hard to call so far into the darkness. It was easier to lie still right here. Nothing could be easier.

In a high stone house in Landin, by a driftwood fire, Alla Pasfal lifted her head suddenly from her book. She had a distinct impression that Jakob Agat was sending to her, but no message came. It was queer. There were all too many queer by-products and aftereffects and inexplicables involved in mindspeech; many people here in Landin never learned it, and those who did used it very sparingly. Up north in Atlantika colony they had mindspoken more freely. She herself was a refugee from Atlantika and remembered how in the terrible Winter of her childhood she had mindspoken with the others all the time. And after her mother and father died in the famine, for a whole moonphase after, over and over again she had felt them sending to her, felt their presence in her mind—but no message, no words, silence.

"Jakob!" She bespoke him, long and hard, but there was no answer.

At the same time, in the Armory checking over the expedition's supplies once more, Huru Pilotson abruptly gave way to the uneasiness that had been preying on him all day and burst out, "What the hell does Agat think he's doing!"

"He's pretty late," one of the Armory boys affirmed. "Is he over at Tevar again?"

"Cementing relations with the mealy-faces," Pilotson said, gave a mirth-less giggle, and scowled. "All right, come on, let's see about the parkas."

At the same time, in a room paneled with wood like ivory satin, Seiko Esmit burst into a fit of silent crying, wringing her hands and struggling not to send to him, not to bespeak him, not even to whisper his name aloud: "Jakob!"

At the same time Rolery's mind went quite dark for a while. She simply crouched motionless where she was.

She was in the hunter's shelter. She had thought, with all the confusion of the move from the tents into the warren-like Kinhouses of the city, that her absence and very late return had not been observed last night. But today was different; order was reestablished and her leaving would be seen. So she had gone off in broad daylight as she so often did, trusting that no one would take special notice of that; she had gone circuitously to the shelter, curled down there in her furs and waited till dark should fall and finally he should come. The snow had begun to fall; watching it made her sleepy; she watched it, wondering sleepily what she would do tomorrow. For he would be gone. And everyone in her clan would know she had been out all night. That was tomorrow. It would take care of itself. This was tonight, tonight . . . and she dozed off, till suddenly she woke with a great start, and crouched there a little while, her mind blank, dark.

Then abruptly she scrambled up and with flint and tinderbox lighted the basket-lantern she had brought with her. By its tiny glow she headed down-hill till she struck the path, then hesitated, and turned west. Once she stopped and said, "Alterra . . ." in a whisper. The forest was perfectly quiet in the night. She went on till she found him lying across the path.

The snow, falling thicker now, streaked across the lantern's dim, small glow. The snow was sticking to the ground now instead of melting, and it had stuck in a powdering of white all over his torn coat and even on his hair. His hand, which she touched first, was cold and she knew he was dead. She sat down on the wet, snow-rimmed mud by him and took his head on her knees.

He moved and made a kind of whimper, and with that Rolery came to her-self. She stopped her silly gesture of smoothing the powdery snow from his hair and collar, and sat intent for a minute. Then she eased him back down, got up, automatically tried to rub the sticky blood from her hand, and with the lantern's aid began to seek around the sides of the path for something. She found what she needed and set to work.

Soft, weak sunlight slanted down across the room. In that warmth it was hard to wake up and he kept sliding back down into the waters of sleep, the deep tideless lake. But the light always brought him up again; and finally he was awake, seeing the high gray walls about him and the slant of sunlight through glass.

He lay still while the shaft of watery golden light faded and returned, slipped from the floor and pooled on the farther wall, rising higher, reddening. Alla Pasfal came in, and seeing he was awake signed to someone behind her to stay out. She closed the door and came to kneel by him. Alterran houses were sparsely furnished; they slept on pallets on the carpeted floor, and for chairs used at most a thin cushion. So Alla knelt, and looked down at Agat, her worn, black face lighted strongly by the reddish shaft of sun. There was no pity in her face as she looked at him. She had borne too much, too young, for compassion and scruple ever to rise from very deep in her, and in her old age she was quite pitiless. She shook her head a little from side to side as she said softly, "Jakob . . . What have you done?"

He found that his head hurt him when he tried to speak, so having no real answer he kept still.

"What have you done?"

"How did I get home?" he asked at last, forming the words so poorly with his smashed mouth that she raised her hand to stop him. "How you got here—is that what you asked? She brought you. The hilf girl. She made a sort of travois out of some branches and her furs, and rolled you onto it and hauled you over the ridge and to the Land Gate. At night in the snow. Nothing left on her but her breeches—she had to tear up her tunic to tie you on. Those hilfs are tougher than the leather they dress in. She said the snow made it easier to pull. . . . No snow left now. That was the night before last. You've had a pretty good rest all in all."

She poured him a cup of water from the jug on a tray nearby and helped him drink. Close over him her face looked very old, delicate with age. She said to him with the mindspeech, unbelievingly, *How could you do this? You were always a proud man, Jakob!*

He replied the same way, wordlessly. Put into words what he told her was: *I can't get on without her.*

The old woman flinched physically away from the sense of his passion, and as if in self-defense spoke aloud: "But what a time to pick for a love affair, for a romance! When everyone depended on you—"

He repeated what he had told her, for it was the truth and all he could tell her. She bespoke him with harshness: *But you're not going to marry her, so you'd better learn to get on without her.*

He replied only, *No.*

She sat back on her heels a while. When her mind opened again to his it was with a great depth of bitterness. *Well, go ahead, what's the difference. At this point whatever we do, any of us, alone or together, is wrong. We can't do the right thing, the lucky thing. We can only go on committing suicide, little by little, one by one. Till we're all gone, till Alterra is gone, all the exiles dead . . .*

"Alla," he broke in aloud, shaken by her despair, "the . . . the men went . . . ?"

"What men? Our army?" She said the words sarcastically. "Did they march north yesterday—without you?"

"Pilotson—"

"If Pilotson had led them anywhere it would have been to attack Tevar. To avenge you. He was crazy with rage yesterday."

"And they . . . ?"

"The hilfs? No, of course they didn't go. When it became known that Wold's daughter is running off to sleep with a farborn in the woods, Wold's faction comes in for a certain amount of ridicule and discredit—you can see that? Of course, it's easier to see it after the fact; but I should have thought—"

"For God's sake, Alla."

"All right. Nobody went north. We sit here and wait for the Gaal to arrive when they please."

Jakob Agat lay very still, trying to keep himself from falling headfirst, backwards, into the void that lay under him. It was the blank and real abyss of his own pride: the self-deceiving arrogance from which all his acts had sprung: the lie. If he went under, no matter. But what of his people whom he had betrayed?

Alla bespoke him after a while: *Jakob, it was a very little hope at best. You did what you could. Man and unman can't work together. Six hundred home-years of failure should tell you that. Your folly was only their pretext. If they hadn't turned on us over it, they would have found something else very soon. They're our enemies as much as the Gaal. Or the Winter. Or the rest of this planet that doesn't want us. We can make no alliances but among ourselves. We're on our own. Never hold your hand out to any creature that belongs to this world.*

He turned his mind away from hers, unable to endure the finality of her despair. He tried to lie closed in on himself, withdrawn, but something worried him insistently, dragged at his consciousness, until suddenly it came clear, and struggling to sit up he stammered, "Where is she? You didn't send her back—"

Clothed in a white Alterran robe, Rolery sat crosslegged, a little farther away from him than Alla had been. Alla was gone; Rolery sat there busy with some work, mending a sandal it seemed. She had not seemed to notice that he spoke; perhaps he had only spoken in dream. But she said presently in her light voice, "That old one upset you. She could have waited. What can you do now? . . . I think none of them knows how to take six steps without you."

The last red of the sunlight made a dull glory on the wall behind her. She sat with a quiet face, eyes cast down as always, absorbed in mending a sandal.

In her presence both guilt and pain eased off and took their due proportion. With her, he was himself. He spoke her name aloud.

"Oh, sleep now; it hurts you to talk," she said with a flicker of her timid mockery.

"Will you stay?" he asked.

"Yes."

"As my wife," he insisted, reduced by necessity and pain to the bare essential. He imagined that her people would kill her if she went back to them; he was not sure what his own people might do to her. He was her only defense, and he wanted the defense to be certain.

She bowed her head as if in acceptance; he did not know her gestures well enough to be sure. He wondered a little at her quietness now. The little while he had known her she had always been quick with motion and emotion. But it had been a very little while. . . . As she sat there working away her quietness entered into him, and with it he felt his strength begin to return.

7

The Southing

Bright above the roofpeaks burned the star whose rising told the start of Winter, as cheerlessly bright as Wold remembered it from his boyhood sixty moonphases ago. Even the great, slender crescent moon opposite it in the sky seemed paler than the Snowstar. A new moonphase had begun, and a new season. But not auspiciously.

Was it true what the farborns used to say, that the moon was a world like Askatevar and the other Ranges, though without living creatures, and the stars too were worlds, where men and beasts lived and Summer and Winter came? . . . What sort of men would dwell on the Snowstar? Terrible beings, white as snow, with pallid lipless mouths and fiery eyes, stalked through Wold's imagination. He shook his head and tried to pay attention to what the other Elders were saying. The forerunners had returned after only five days with various rumors from the north; and the Elders had built a fire in the great court of Tevar and held a Stone-Pounding. Wold had come last and closed the circle, for no other man dared; but it was meaningless, humiliating to him. For the war he had declared was not being fought, the men he had sent had not gone, and the alliance he had made was broken.

Beside him, as silent as he, sat Umaksuman. The others shouted and wrangled, getting nowhere. What did they expect? No rhythm had risen out of the pounding of stones, there had been only clatter and conflict. After that, could they expect to agree on anything? Fools, fools, Wold thought, glowering at the fire that was too far away to warm him. The others were mostly younger, they could keep warm with youth and with shouting at one another. But he was an old man and furs did not warm him, out under the glaring Snowstar in the wind of Winter. His legs ached now with cold, his chest hurt, and he did not know or care what they were all quarreling about.

Umaksuman was suddenly on his feet. "Listen!" he said, and the thunder of his voice (*He got that from me,* thought Wold) compelled them, though there were audible mutters and jeers. So far, though everybody had a fair idea what had happened, the immediate cause or pretext of their quarrel with Landin had not been discussed outside the walls of Wold's Kinhouse; it had simply been announced that Umaksuman was not to lead the foray, that there was to be no foray, that there might be an attack from the farborns. Those of other houses who knew nothing about Rolery or Agat knew what was actually involved: a power struggle between factions in the most power-ful clan. This was covertly going on in every speech made now in the Stone-Pounding, the subject of which was, nominally, whether the farborns were to be treated as enemies when met beyond the walls.

Now Umaksuman spoke: "Listen, Elders of Tevar! You say this, you say that, but you have nothing left to say. The Gaal are coming: within three days they are here. Be silent and go sharpen your spears, go look to our gates and walls, because the enemy comes, they come down on us—see!" He flung out his arm to the north, and many turned to stare where he pointed, as if ex-pecting the hordes of the Southing to burst through the wall that moment, so urgent was Umaksuman's rhetoric.

"Why didn't you look to the gate your kinswoman went out of, Umak-suman?"

Now it was said.

"She's your kinswoman too, Ukwet," Umaksuman said wrathfully.

One of them was Wold's son, the other his grandson; they spoke of his daughter. For the first time in his life Wold knew shame, bald, helpless shame before all the best men of his people. He sat moveless, his head bowed down.

"Yes, she is; and because of me, no shame rests on our Kin! I and my brothers knocked the teeth out of the dirty face of that one she lay with, and I had him down to geld him as he-animals should be gelded, but then you stopped us, Umaksuman. You stopped us with your fool talk—"

"I stopped you so that we wouldn't have the farborns to fight along with the Gaal, you fool! She's of age to sleep with a man if she chooses, and this is no—"

"He was no man, kinsman, and I am no fool."

"You are a fool, Ukwet, for you jumped at this as a chance to make quar-rel with the farborns, and so lost us our one chance to turn aside the Gaal!"

"I do not hear you, liar, traitor!"

They met with a yell in the middle of the circle, axes drawn. Wold got up. Men sitting near him looked up expecting him, as Eldest and clan-chief, to stop the fight. But he did not. He turned away from the broken circle and in silence, with his stiff, ponderous shuffle, went down the alley between the high slant roofs, under projecting eaves, to the house of his Kin.

He clambered laboriously down earthen stairs into the stuffy, smoky

warmth of the immense dug-out room. Boys and womenfolk came asking him
if the Stone-Pounding was over and why he came alone. "Umaksuman and
Ukwet are fighting," he said to get rid of them, and sat down by the fire, his
legs right in the firepit. No good would come of this. No good would come of
anything any more. When crying women brought in the body of his grandson Ukwet, a thick path of blood dropping behind them from the ax-split
skull, he looked on without moving or speaking. "Umaksuman killed him,
his kinsman, his brother," Ukwet's wives shrilled at Wold, who never raised
his head. Finally he looked around at them heavily like an old animal beset
by hunters, and said in a thick voice, "Be still. . . . Can't you be still. . . ."

It snowed again next day. They buried Ukwet, the first-dead of the Winter, and
the snow fell on the corpse's face before the grave was filled. Wold thought
then and later of Umaksuman, outlawed, alone in the hills, in the snow. Which
was better off?

His tongue was very thick and he did not like to talk. He stayed by the fire
and was not sure, sometimes, whether outside it was day or night. He did not
sleep well; he seemed somehow always to be waking up. He was just waking
up when the noise began outside, up above ground.

Women came shrieking in from the side-rooms, grabbing up their little
Fall-born brats. "The Gaal, the Gaal!" they screeched. Others were quiet as
befitted women of a great house, and put the place in order and sat down to
wait.

No man came for Wold.

He knew he was no longer a chief; but was he no longer a man? Must he
stay with the babies and women by the fire, in a hole in the ground?

He had endured public shame, but the loss of his own self-respect he could
not endure, and shaking a little he got up and began to rummage in his old
painted chest for his leather vest and his heavy spear, the spear with which
he had killed a snowghoul singlehanded, very long ago. He was stiff and heavy
now and all the bright seasons had passed since then, but he was the same
man, the same that had killed with that spear in the snow of another winter.
Was he not the same man? They should not have left him here by the fire,
when the enemy came.

His fool womenfolk came squealing around him, and he got mixed up and
angry. But old Kerly drove them all off, gave him back his spear that one of
them had taken from him, and fastened at his neck the cape of gray korio-fur
she had made for him in Autumn. There was one left who knew what a man
was. She watched him in silence and he felt her grieving pride. So he walked

very erect. She was a cross old woman and he was a foolish old man, but pride remained. He climbed up into the cold, bright noon, hearing beyond the walls the calling of foreign voices.

Men were gathered on the square platform over the smokehole of the House of Absence. They made way for him when he hoisted himself up the ladder. He was wheezing and trembling so that at first he could see nothing. Then he saw. For a while he forgot everything in the unbelievable sight.

The valley that wound from north to south along the base of Tevar Hill to the river-valley east of the forest was full—full as the river in the flood-time, swarming, overrunning with people. They were moving southward, a sluggish, jumbled, dark flood, stretching and contracting, stopping and starting, with yells, cries, calls, creaking, snapping whips, the hoarse bray of hann, the wail of babies, the tuneless chanting of travois-pullers; the flash of color from a rolled-up red felt tent, a woman's painted bangles, a red plume, a spearhead; the stink, the noise, the movement—always the movement, moving southward, the Southing. But in all timepast there had never been a Southing like this, so many all together. As far as eye could follow up the widening valley northward there were more coming, and behind them more, and behind them more. And these were only the women and the brats and the baggage-train. . . . Beside that slow torrent of people the Winter City of Tevar was nothing. A pebble on the edge of a river in flood.

At first Wold felt sick; then he took heart, and said presently, "This is a wonderful thing. . . ." And it was, this migration of all the nations of the north. He was glad to have seen it. The man next to him, an Elder, Anweld of Siokman's Kin, shrugged and answered quietly, "But it's the end of us."

"If they stop here."

"These won't. But the warriors come behind."

They were so strong, so safe in their numbers, that their warriors came behind. . . .

"They'll need our stores and our herds tonight, to feed all those," Anweld went on. "As soon as these get by, they'll attack."

"Send our women and children out into the hills to the west, then. This City is only a trap against such a force."

"I listen," Anweld said with a shrug of assent.

"Now—quickly—before the Gaal encircle us."

"This has been said and heard. But others say we can't send our women out to fend for themselves while we stay in the shelter of the walls."

"Then let's go with them!" Wold growled. "Can the Men of Tevar decide nothing?"

"They have no leader," Anweld said. "They follow this man and that man and no man." To say more would be to seem to blame Wold and his kinsmen; he said no more except, "So we wait here to be destroyed."

"I'm going to send my womenfolk off," Wold said, irked by Anweld's cool hopelessness, and he left the mighty spectacle of the Southing, to lower himself down the ladder and go tell his kinfolk to save themselves while there was some chance. He meant to go with them. For there was no fighting such odds, and some, some few of the people of Tevar must survive.

But the younger men of his clan did not agree and would not take his orders. They would stand and fight.

"But you'll die," said Wold, "and your women and children might go free— if they're not here with you." His tongue was thick again. They could hardly wait for him to finish.

"We'll beat off the Gaal," said a young grandson. "We are warriors!"

"Tevar is a strong city, Eldest," another said, persuasive, flattering. "You told us and taught us to build it well."

"It will stand against Winter," Wold said. "Not against ten thousand warriors. I would rather see my women die of the cold in the bare hills, than live as whores and slaves of the Gaal." But they were not listening, only waiting for him to be done talking.

He went outside again, but was too weary now to climb the ladders to the platform again. He found himself a place to wait out of the way of the coming and going in the narrow alleys: a niche by a supporting buttress of the south wall, not far from the gate. If he clambered up on the slanting mudbrick buttress he could look over the wall and watch the Southing going by; when the wind got under his cape he could squat down, chin on knees, and have some shelter in the angle. For a while the sun shone on him there. He squatted in its warmth and did not think of much. Once or twice he glanced up at the sun, the Winter sun, old, weak in its old age.

Winter grasses, the short-lived hasty-flowering little plants that would thrive between the blizzards until Mid-Winter when the snow did not melt and nothing lived but the rootless snowcrop, already were pushing up through the trampled ground under the wall. Always something lived, each creature biding its time through the great Year, flourishing and dying down to wait again.

The long hours went by.

There was crying and shouting at the northwest corner of the walls. Men went running by through the ways of the little city, alleys wide enough for one man only under the overhanging eaves. Then the roar of shouting was behind Wold's back and outside the gate to his left. The high wooden slide-gate, that lifted from inside by means of long pulleys, rattled in its frame. They were ramming a log against it. Wold got up with difficulty; he had got so stiff sitting there in the cold that he could not feel his legs. He leaned a minute on his spear, then got a footing with his back against the buttress and held his spear ready, not with the thrower but poised to use at short range.

The Gaal must be using ladders, for they were already inside the city over at the north side, he could tell by the noise. A spear sailed clear over the roofs, overshot with a thrower. The gate rattled again. In the old days they had had no ladders and rams, they came not by thousands but in ragged tribes, cowardly barbarians, running south before the cold, not staying to live and die on their own Range as true men did. . . . There came one with a wide, white face and a red plume in his horn of pitch-smeared hair, running to open the gate from within. Wold took a step forward and said, "Stop there!" The Gaal looked around, and the old man drove his six-foot iron-headed spear into his enemy's side under the ribs, clear in. He was still trying to pull it back out of the shivering body when, behind him, the gate of the city began to split. That was a hideous sight, the wood splitting like rotten leather, the snout of a thick log poking through. Wold left his spear in the Gaal's belly and ran down the alley, heavily, stumbling, towards the House of his Kin. The peaked wooden roofs of the city were all on fire ahead of him.

In the Alien City

The strangest thing in all the strangeness of this house was the painting on the wall of the big room downstairs. When Agat had gone and the rooms were deathly still she stood gazing at this picture till it became the world and she the wall. And the world was a network: a deep network, like interlacing branches in the woods, like inter-running currents in water, silver, gray, black, shot through with green and rose and a yellow like the sun. As one watched the network one saw in it, among it, woven into it and weaving it, little and great patterns and figures, beasts, trees, grasses, men and women and other creatures, some like farborns and some not; and strange shapes, boxes set on round legs, birds, axes, silver spears and feathers of fire, faces that were not faces, stones with wings and a tree whose leaves were stars.

"What is that?" she asked the farborn woman whom Agat had asked to look after her, his kinswoman; and she in her way that was an effort to be kind replied, "A painting, a picture—your people make pictures, don't they?"

"Yes, a little. What is it telling of?"

"Of the other worlds and our home. You see the people in it. . . . It was painted long ago, in the first Year of our exile, by one of the sons of Esmit."

"What is that?" Rolery pointed, from a respectful distance.

"A building—the Great Hall of the League on the world called Davenant."

"And that?"

"An erkar."

"I listen again," Rolery said politely—she was on her best manners at every moment now—but when Seiko Esmit seemed not to understand the formality, she asked, "What is an erkar?"

The farborn woman pushed out her lips a little and said indifferently, "A . . . thing to ride in, like a . . . well, you don't even use wheels, how can I tell you? You've seen our wheeled carts? Yes? Well, this was a cart to ride in, but it flew in the sky."

"Can your people make such cars now?" Rolery asked in pure wonderment, but Seiko took the question wrong. She replied with rancor, "No. How could we keep such skills here, when the Law commanded us not to rise above your level? For six hundred years your people have failed to learn the use of wheels!"

Desolate in this strange place, exiled from her people and now alone without Agat, Rolery was frightened of Seiko Esmit and of every person and every thing she met. But she would not be scorned by a jealous woman, an older woman. She said, "I ask to learn. But I think your people haven't been here for six hundred years."

"Six hundred home-years is ten Years here." After a moment Seiko Esmit went on, "You see, we don't know all about the erkars and many other things that used to belong to our people, because when our ancestors came here they were sworn to obey a law of the League, which forbade them to use many things different from the things the native people used. This was called Cultural Embargo. In time we would have taught you how to make things—like wheeled carts. But the Ship left. There were few of us here, and no word from the League, and we found many enemies among your nations in those days. It was hard for us to keep the Law and also to keep what we had and knew. So perhaps we lost much skill and knowledge. We don't know."

"It was a strange law," Rolery murmured.

"It was made for your sakes—not ours," Seiko said in her hurried voice, in the hard distinct farborn accent like Agat's. "In the Canons of the League, which we study as children, it is written: *No Religion or Congruence shall be disseminated, no technique or theory shall be taught, no cultural set or pattern shall be exported, nor shall paraverbal speech be used with any non-Communicant high-intelligence life-form, or any Colonial Planet, until it be judged by the Area Council with the consent of the Plenum that such a planet be ready for Control or for Membership. . . .* It means, you see, that we were to live exactly as you live. In so far as we do not, we have broken our own Law."

"It did us no harm," Rolery said. "And you not much good."

"You cannot judge us," Seiko said with that rancorous coldness; then controlling herself once more, "There's work to be done now. Will you come?"

Submissive, Rolery followed Seiko. But she glanced back at the painting as they left. It had a greater wholeness than any object she had ever seen. Its somber, silvery, unnerving complexity affected her somewhat as Agat's presence did; and when he was with her, she feared him, but nothing else. Nothing, no one.

The fighting men of Landin were gone. They had some hope, by guerilla attacks and ambushes, of harrying the Gaal on southward towards less aggressive victims. It was a bare hope, and the women were working to ready the town for siege. Seiko and Rolery reported to the Hall of the League on the great square, and there were assigned to help round up the herds of hann from the long fields south of town. Twenty woman went together; each as she left the Hall was given a packet of bread and hann-milk curd, for they would be gone all day. As forage grew scant the herds had ranged far south between the beach and the coastal ridges. The women hiked about eight miles south and then beat back, zigzagging to and fro, collecting and driving the little, silent, shaggy beasts in greater and greater numbers.

Rolery saw the farborn women in a new light now. They had seemed delicate, childish, with their soft light clothes, their quick voices and quick minds. But here they were out in the ice-rimmed stubble of the hills, in furs and trousers like human women, driving the slow, shaggy herds into the north wind, working together, cleverly and with determination. They were wonderful with the beasts, seeming to lead rather than drive them, as if they had some mastery over them. They came up the road to the Sea Gate after the sun had set, a handful of women in a shaggy sea of trotting, high-haunched beasts. When Landin walls came in sight a woman lifted up her voice and sang. Rolery had never heard a voice play this game with pitch and time. It made her eyes blink and her throat ache, and her feet on the dark road kept the music's time. The singing went from voice to voice up and down the road; they sang about a lost home they had never known, about weaving cloth and sewing jewels on it, about warriors killed in war; there was a song about a girl who went mad for love and jumped into the sea, "O the waves they roll far out before the tide . . ." Sweet-voiced, making song out of sorrow, they came with the herds, twenty women walking in the windy dark. The tide was in, a soughing blackness over the dunes to their left. Torches on the high walls flared before them, making the city of exile an island of light.

All food in Landin was strictly rationed now. People ate communally in one of the great buildings around the square, or if they chose took their rations home to their houses. The women who had been herding were late. After a hasty dinner in the strange building called Thiatr, Rolery went with Seiko Esmit to the house of the woman Alla Pasfal. She would rather have gone to Agat's empty house and been alone there, but she did whatever she was asked to do. She was no longer a girl, and no longer free. She was the wife of an Alterran, and a prisoner on sufferance. For the first time in her life, she obeyed.

No fire burned in the hearth, yet the high room was warm; lamps without wicks burned in glass cages on the wall. In this one house, as big as a whole Kinhouse of Tevar, one old woman lived by herself. How did they bear the loneliness? And how did they keep the warmth and light of summer inside the walls? And all Year long they lived in these houses, all their lives, never wandering, never living in tents out on the Range, on the broad Summerlands, wandering. . . . Rolery pulled her groggy head erect and stole a glance at the old one, Pasfal, to see if her sleepiness had been seen. It had. The old one saw everything; and she hated Rolery.

So did they all, the Alterrans, these farborn Elders. They hated her because they loved Jakob Agat with a jealous love; because he had taken her to wife; because she was human and they were not.

One of them was saying something about Tevar, something very strange that she did not believe. She looked down, but fright must have showed in her face, for one of the men, Dermat Alterra, stopped listening to the others and said, "Rolery, you didn't know that Tevar was lost?"

"I listen," she whispered.

"Our men were harrying the Gaal from the west all day," the farborn explained. "When the Gaal warriors attacked Tevar, we attacked their baggage-line and the camps their women were putting up east of the forest. That drew some of them off, and some of the Tevarans got out—but they and our men got scattered. Some of them are here now; we don't really know what the rest are doing, except it's a cold night and they're out there in the hills. . . ."

Rolery sat silent. She was very tired, and did not understand. The Winter City was taken, destroyed. Could that be true? She had left her people; now her people were all dead, or homeless in the hills in the Winter night. She was left alone. The aliens talked and talked in their hard voices. For a while Rolery had an illusion, which she knew for an illusion, that there was a thin film of blood on her hands and wrists. She felt a little sick, but was not sleepy any longer; now and then she felt herself entering the outskirts, the first stage, of Absence for a minute. The bright, cold eyes of the old one, Pasfal the witch, stared at her. She could not move. There was nowhere to go. Everyone was dead.

Then there was a change. It was like a small light far off in darkness. She said aloud, though so softly only those nearest her heard, "Agat is coming here."

"Is he bespeaking you?" Alla Pasfal asked sharply.

Rolery gazed for a moment at the air beside the old woman she feared; she was not seeing her. "He's coming here," she repeated.

"He's probably not sending, Alla," said the one called Pilotson. "They're in steady rapport, to some degree."

"Nonsense, Huru."

"Why nonsense? He told us he sent to her very hard, on the beach, and got through; she must be a Natural. And that established a rapport. It's happened before."

"Between human couples, yes," the old woman said. "An untrained child can't receive or send a paraverbal message, Huru; a Natural is the rarest thing in the world. And this is a hilf, not a human!"

Rolery meanwhile had got up, slipped away from the circle and gone to the door. She opened it. Outside was empty darkness and the cold. She looked up the street, and in a moment could make out a man coming down it at a weary jogtrot. He came into the shaft of yellow light from the open door, and putting out his hand to catch hers, out of breath, said her name. His smile showed three front teeth gone; there was a blackened bandage around his head under his fur cap; he was grayish with fatigue and pain. He had been out in the hills since the Gaal had entered Askatevar Range, three days and two nights ago. "Get me some water to drink," he told Rolery softly, and then came on into the light, while the others all gathered around him.

Rolery found the cooking-room and in it the metal reed with a flower on top which you turned to make water run out of the reed; Agat's house also had such a device. She saw no bowls or cups set out anywhere, so she caught the water in a hollow of the loose hem of her leather tunic, and brought it thus to her husband in the other room. He gravely drank from her tunic. The others stared and Pasfal said sharply, "There are cups in the cupboard." But she was a witch no longer; her malice fell like a spent arrow. Rolery knelt beside Agat and heard his voice.

9

The Guerillas

The weather had warmed again after the first snow. There was sun, a little rain, northwest wind, light frost at night, much as it had been all the last moon-phase of Autumn. Winter was not so different from what went before; it was a bit hard to believe the records of previous Years that told of ten-foot snow-falls, and whole moonphases when the ice never thawed. Maybe that came later. The problem now was the Gaal. . . .

Paying very little attention to Agat's guerillas, though he had inflicted some nasty wounds on their army's flanks, the northerners had poured at a fast march down through Askatevar Range, encamped east of the forest, and now on the third day were assaulting the Winter City. They were not destroying it, however; they were obviously trying to save the granaries from the fire, and the herds, and perhaps the women. It was only the men they slaughtered. Per-haps, as reported, they were going to try to garrison the place with a few of their own men. Come Spring the Gaal returning from the south could march from town to town of an Empire.

It was not like the hilfs, Agat thought as he lay hidden under an immense fallen tree, waiting for his little army to take their positions for their own assault on Tevar. He had been in the open, fighting and hiding, two days and nights now. A cracked rib from the beating he had taken in the woods, though well bound up, hurt, and so did a shallow scalp-wound from a Gaal slingshot yesterday; but with immunity to infection wounds healed very fast, and Agat paid scant attention to anything less than a severed artery. Only a concus-sion had got him down at all. He was thirsty at the moment and a bit stiff, but his mind was pleasantly alert as he got this brief enforced rest. It wasn't like the hilfs, this planning ahead. Hilfs did not consider either time or space in the linear, imperialistic fashion of his own species. Time to them was a lan-tern lighting a step before, a step behind—the rest was indistinguishable dark. Time was this day, this one day of the immense Year. They had no historical vocabulary; there was merely today and "timepast." They looked ahead only to the next season at most. They did not look down over time but were in it as the lamp in the night, as the heart in the body. And so also with space: space to them was not a surface on which to draw boundaries but a Range, a heartland, centered on the self and clan and tribe. Around the Range were areas that brightened as one approached them and dimmed as one departed; the farther, the fainter. But there were no lines, no limits. This planning ahead, this trying to keep hold of a conquered place across both space and time, was untypical; it showed—what? An autonomous change in a hilf culture-pattern, or an infection from the old northern colonies and forays of Man?

It would be the first time, Agat thought sardonically, that they ever learned an idea from us. Next we'll be catching their colds. And that'll kill us off; and our ideas might well kill them off. . . .

There was in him a deep and mostly unconscious bitterness against the Tevarans, who had smashed his head and ribs, and broken their covenant; and whom he must now watch getting slaughtered in their stupid little mud city under his eyes. He had been helpless to fight against them, now he was almost helpless to fight for them. He detested them for forcing helplessness upon him.

At that moment—just as Rolery was starting back towards Landin behind the herds—there was a rustle in the dry leaf-dust in the hollow behind him. Before the sound had ceased he had his loaded dartgun trained on the hollow.

Explosives were forbidden by the Law of Cultural Embargo, which had become a basic ethos of the Exiles; but some native tribes, in the early Years of fighting, had used poisoned spears and darts. Freed by this from taboo, the doctors of Landin had developed some effective poisons which were still in the hunting-fighting repertory. There were stunners, paralyzers, slow and quick killers; this one was lethal and took five seconds to convulse the nervous system of a large animal, such as a Gaal. The mechanism of the dartgun was neat and simple, accurate within a little over fifty meters. "Come on out," Agat called to the silent hollow, and his still swollen lips stretched out in a grin. All things considered, he was ready to kill another hilf.

"Alterra?"

A hilf rose to his full height among the dead gray bushes of the hollow, his arms by his sides. It was Umaksuman.

"Hell!" Agat said, lowering his gun, but not all the way. Repressed violence shook him a moment with a spastic shudder.

"Alterra," the Tevaran said huskily, "in my father's tent we were friends."

"And afterwards—in the woods?"

The native stood there silent, a big, heavy figure, his fair hair filthy, his face clayey with hunger and exhaustion.

"I heard your voice, with the others. If you had to avenge your sister's honor, you could have done it one at a time." Agat's finger was still on the trigger; but when Umaksuman answered, his expression changed. He had not hoped for an answer.

"I was not with the others. I followed them, and stopped them. Five days ago I killed Ukwet, my nephew-brother, who led them. I have been in the hills since then."

Agat uncocked his gun and looked away.

"Come on up here," he said after a while. Only then did both of them realize that they had been standing up talking out loud, in these hills full of Gaal scouts. Agat gave a long noiseless laugh as Umaksuman slithered into the niche under the log with him. "Friend, enemy, what the hell," he said. "Here." He passed the hilf a hunk of bread from his wallet. "Rolery is my wife, since three days ago."

Silent, Umaksuman took the bread, and ate it as a hungry man eats.

"When they whistle from the left, over there, we're going to go in all together, heading for that breach in the walls at the north corner, and make a run through the town, to pick up any Tevarans we can. The Gaal are looking for us around the Bogs where we were this morning, not here. It's the only time we're going for the town. You want to come?"

Umaksuman nodded.

"Are you armed?"

Umaksuman lifted his ax. Side by side, not speaking, they crouched watching the burning roofs, the tangles and spurts of motion in the wrecked alleys of the little town on the hill facing them. A gray sky was closing off the sunlight; smoke was acrid on the wind.

Off to their left a whistle shrilled. The hillsides west and north of Tevar sprang alive with men, little scattered figures crouch-running down into the vale and up the slope, piling over the broken wall and into the wreckage and confusion of the town.

As the men of Landin met at the wall they joined into squads of five to twenty men, and these squads kept together, whether in attacking groups of Gaal looters with dartguns, bolos and knives, or in picking up whatever Tevaran women and children they found and making for the gate with them. They went so fast and sure that they might have rehearsed the raid; the Gaal, occupied in cleaning out the last resistance in the town, were taken off guard.

Agat and Umaksuman kept pace, and a group of eight or ten coalesced with them as they ran through the Stone-Pounding Square, then down a narrow tunnel-alley to a lesser square, and burst into one of the big Kinhouses. One after another leapt down the earthen stairway into the dark interior. White-faced men with red plumes twined in their horn-like hair came yelling and swinging axes, defending their loot. The dart from Agat's gun shot straight into the open mouth of one; he saw Umaksuman take the arm off a Gaal's shoulder as an axman lops a branch from a tree. Then there was silence. Women crouched in silence in the half-darkness. A baby bawled and bawled. "Come with us!" Agat shouted. Some of the women moved towards him, and seeing him, stopped.

Umaksuman loomed up beside him in the dim light from the doorway, heavy laden with some burden on his back. "Come, bring the children!" he roared, and at the sound of his known voice they all moved. Agat got them grouped at the stairs with his men strung out to protect them, then gave the word. They broke from the Kinhouse and made for the gate. No Gaal stopped their run—a queer bunch of women, children, men, led by Agat with a Gaal ax running cover for Umaksuman, who carried on his shoulders a great dangling burden, the old chief, his father Wold.

They made it out the gate, ran the gauntlet of a Gaal troop in the old tenting-place, and with other such flying squads of Landin men and refugees in front of them and behind them, scattered into the woods. The whole run through Tevar had taken about five minutes.

There was no safety in the forest. Gaal scouts and troops were scattered along the road to Landin. The refugees and rescuers fanned out singly and in pairs southward into the woods. Agat stayed with Umaksuman, who could not defend himself carrying the old man. They struggled through the underbrush. No enemy met them among the gray aisles and hummocks, the fallen trunks and tangled dead branches and mummied bushes. Somewhere far behind them a woman's voice screamed and screamed.

It took them a long time to work south and west in a half-circle through the forest, over the ridges and back north at last to Landin. When Umaksuman could not go any farther, Wold walked, but he could go only very slowly. When they came out of the trees at last they saw the lights of the City of Exile flaring far off in the windy dark above the sea. Half dragging the old man, they struggled along the hillside and came to the Land Gate.

"Hilfs coming!" Guards sang out before they got within clear sight, spotting Umaksuman's fair hair. Then they saw Agat, and the voices cried, "The Alterra, the Alterra!"

They came to meet him and brought him into the city, men who had fought beside him, taken his orders, saved his skin for these three days of guerilla-fighting in the woods and hills.

They had done what they could, four hundred of them against an enemy that swarmed like the vast migrations of the beasts—fifteen thousand men, Agat had guessed. Fifteen thousand warriors, between sixty or seventy thousand Gaal in all, with their tents and cookpots and travois and hann and fur rugs and axes and armlets and cradleboards and tinderboxes, all their scant belongings, and their fear of the Winter, and their hunger. He had seen Gaal women in their encampments gathering the dead lichen off logs and eating it. It did not seem probable that the little City of Exile still stood, untouched by this flood of violence and hunger, with torches alight above its gates of iron and carved wood, and men to welcome him home.

Trying to tell the story of the last three days, he said, "We came around behind their line of march, yesterday afternoon." The words had no reality; neither had this warm room, the faces of men and women he had known all his life, listening to him. "The . . . the ground behind them, where the whole migration had come down some of the narrow valleys—it looked like the ground after a landslide. Raw dirt. Nothing. Everything trodden to dust, to nothing . . ."

"How can they keep going? What do they eat?" Huru muttered.

"The Winter stores in the cities they take. The land's all stripped by now, the crops are in, the big game gone south. They must loot every town on their course and live off the hann-herds, or starve before they get out of the snow-lands."

"Then they'll come here," one of the Alterrans said quietly.

"I think so. Tomorrow or next day." This was true, but it was not real either. He passed his hand over his face, feeling the dirt and stiffness and the un-healed soreness of his lips. He had felt he must come make his report to the government of his city, but now he was so tired that he could not say anything more, and did not hear what they were saying. He turned to Rolery, who knelt in silence beside him. Not raising her amber eyes, she said very softly, "You should go home, Alterra."

He had not thought of her all those endless hours of fighting and running and shooting and hiding in the woods. He had known her for two weeks; had talked with her at any length perhaps three times; had lain with her once; had taken her as his wife in the Hall of Law in the early morning three days ago, and an hour later had left to go with the guerillas. He knew nothing much about her, and she was not even of his species. And in a couple of days more they would probably both be dead. He gave his noiseless laugh and put his hand gently on hers. "Yes, take me home," he said. Silent, delicate, alien, she rose, and waited for him as he took his leave of the others.

He had told her that Wold and Umaksuman, with about two hundred more of her people, had escaped or been rescued from the violated Winter City and were now in refugee quarters in Landin. She had not asked to go to them. As they went up the steep street together from Alla's house to his, she asked, "Why did you enter Tevar to save the people?"

"Why?" It seemed a strange question to him. "Because they wouldn't save themselves."

"That's no reason, Alterra."

She seemed submissive, the shy native wife who did her lord's will. Actually, he was learning, she was stubborn, wilful, and very proud. She spoke softly, but said exactly what she meant.

"It is a reason, Rolery. You can't just sit there watching the bastards kill off people slowly. Anyhow, I want to fight—to fight back. . . ."

"But your town: how do you feed these people you brought here? If the Gaal lay siege, or afterwards, in Winter?"

"We have enough. Food's not our worry. All we need is men."

He stumbled a little from weariness. But the clear cold night had cleared his mind, and he felt the rising of a small spring of joy that he had not felt for a long time. He had some sense that this little relief, this lightness of spirit, was given him by her presence. He had been responsible for everything so long. She the stranger, the foreigner, of alien blood and mind, did not share his power or his conscience or his knowledge or his exile. She shared nothing at all with him, but had met him and joined with him wholly and immediately across the gulf of their great difference: as if it were that difference, the alienness between them, that let them meet, and that in joining them together, freed them.

They entered his unlocked front door. No light burned in the high narrow house of roughly dressed stone. It had stood here for three Years, a hundred and eighty moonphases; his great-grandfather had been born in it, and his grandfather, and his father, and himself. It was as familiar to him as his own body. To enter it with her, the nomad woman whose only home would have been this tent or that on one hillside or another, or the teeming burrows under the snow, gave him a peculiar pleasure. He felt a tenderness towards her which he hardly knew how to express. Without intent he said her name not aloud but paraverbally. At once she turned to him in the darkness of the hall; in the darkness, she looked into his face. The house and city were silent around them. In his mind he heard her say his own name, like a whisper in the night, like a touch across the abyss.

"You bespoke me," he said aloud, unnerved, marveling. She said nothing but once more he heard in his mind, along his blood and nerves, her mind that reached out to him: *Agat, Agat . . .*

10

The Old Chief

The old chief was tough. He survived stroke, concussion, exhaustion, exposure, and disaster with intact will, and nearly intact intelligence.

Some things he did not understand, and others were not present to his mind at all times. He was if anything glad to be out of the stuffy darkness of the Kinhouse, where sitting by the fire had made such a woman of him; he was quite clear about that. He liked—he had always liked—this rock-founded, sunlit, windswept city of the farborns, built before anybody alive was born and still standing changeless in the same place. It was a much better built city than Tevar. About Tevar he was not always clear. Sometimes he remembered the yells, the burning roofs, the hacked and disemboweled corpses of his sons and grandsons. Sometimes he did not. The will to survive was very strong in him.

Other refugees trickled in, some of them from sacked Winter Cities to the north; in all there were now about three hundred of Wold's race in the farborns' town. It was so strange to be weak, to be few, to live on the charity of pariahs, that some of the Tevarans, particularly among the middle-aged men, could not take it. They sat in Absence, legs crossed, the pupils of their eyes shrunk to a dot, as if they had been rubbing themselves with gesin-oil. Some of the women, too, who had seen their men cut into gobbets in the streets and by the hearths of Tevar, or who had lost children, grieved themselves into sickness or Absence. But to Wold the collapse of the Tevaran world was only part of the collapse of his own life. Knowing that he was very far along the way to death, he looked with great benevolence on each day and on all younger men, human or farborn: they were the ones who had to keep fighting.

Sunlight shone now in the stone streets, bright on the painted housefronts, though there was a vague dirty smear along the sky above the dunes northward. In the great square, in front of the house called Thiatr where all the humans were quartered, Wold was hailed by a farborn. It took him a while to recognize Jakob Agat. Then he cackled a bit and said, "Alterra! you used to be a handsome fellow. You look like a Pernmek shaman with his front teeth pulled. Where is . . ." He forgot her name. "Where's my kinswoman?"

"In my house, Eldest."

"This is shameful," Wold said. He did not care if he offended Agat. Agat was his lord and leader now, of course; but the fact remained that it was shameful to keep a mistress in one's own tent or house. Farborn or not, Agat should observe the fundamental decencies.

"She's my wife. Is that the shame?"

"I hear wrongly, my ears are old," Wold said, wary.

"She is my wife."

Wold looked up, meeting Agat's gaze straight on for the first time. Wold's eyes were dull yellow like the winter sun, and no white showed under the slanting lids. Agat's eyes were dark, iris and pupil dark, white-cornered in the dark face: strange eyes to meet the gaze of, unearthly.

Wold looked away. The great stone houses of the farborns stood all about him, clean and bright and ancient in the sunlight.

"I took a wife from you, Farborn," he said at last, "but I never thought you'd take one from me. . . . Wold's daughter married among the false-men, to bear no sons—"

"You've got no cause to mourn," the young farborn said unmoving, set as a rock. "I am your equal, Wold. In all but age. You had a farborn wife once. Now you've got a farborn son-in-law. If you wanted one you can swallow the other."

"It is hard," the old man said with dour simplicity. There was a pause. "We are not equals, Jakob Agat. My people are dead or broken. You are a chief, a lord. I am not. But I am a man, and you are not. What likeness between us?"

"At least no grudge, no hate," Agat said, still unmoving.

Wold looked about him and at last, slowly, shrugged assent.

"Good, then we can die well together," the farborn said with his surprising laugh. You never knew when a farborn was going to laugh. "I think the Gaal will attack in a few hours, Eldest."

"In a few—?"

"Soon. When the sun's high maybe." They were standing by the empty arena. A light discus lay abandoned by their feet. Agat picked it up and without intent, boyishly, sailed it across the arena. Gazing where it fell he said, "There's about twenty of them to one of us. So if they get over the walls or through the gate . . . I'm sending all the Fallborn children and their mothers out to the Stack. With the drawbridges raised there's no way to take it, and it's got water and supplies to last five hundred people about a moonphase.

There ought to be some men with the womenfolk. Will you choose three or four of your men, and the women with young children, and take them there? They must have a chief. Does this plan seem good to you?"

"Yes. But I will stay here," the old man said.

"Very well, Eldest," Agat said without a flicker of protest, his harsh, scarred young face impassive. "Please choose the men to go with your women and children. They should go very soon. Kemper will take our group out."

"I'll go with them," Wold said in exactly the same tone, and Agat looked just a trifle disconcerted. So it was possible to disconcert him. But he agreed quietly. His deference to Wold was courteous pretense, of course—what reason had he to defer to a dying man who even among his own defeated tribe was no longer a chief?—but he stuck with it no matter how foolishly Wold replied. He was truly a rock. There were not many men like that. "My lord, my son, my like," the old man said with a grin, putting his hand on Agat's shoulder, "send me where you want me. I have no more use, all I can do is die. Your black rock looks like an evil place to die, but I'll do it there if you want. . . ."

"Send a few men to stay with the women, anyway," Agat said, "good steady ones that can keep the women from panicking. I've got to go up to the Land Gate, Eldest. Will you come?"

Agat, lithe and quick, was off. Leaning on a farborn spear of bright metal, Wold made his way slowly up the streets and steps. But when he was only halfway he had to stop for breath, and then realized that he should turn back and send the young mothers and their brats out to the island, as Agat had asked. He turned and started down. When he saw how his feet shuffled on the stones he knew that he should obey Agat and go with the women to the black island, for he would only be in the way here.

The bright streets were empty except for an occasional farborn hurrying purposefully by. They were all ready or getting ready, at their posts and duties. If the clansmen of Tevar had been ready, if they had marched north to meet the Gaal, if they had looked ahead into a coming time the way Agat seemed to do . . . No wonder people called farborns witchmen. But then, it was Agat's fault that they had not marched. He had let a woman come between allies. If he, Wold, had known that the girl had ever spoken again to Agat, he would have had her killed behind the tents, and her body thrown into the sea, and Tevar might still be standing. . . . She came out of the door of a high stone house, and seeing Wold, stood still.

He noticed that though she had tied back her hair as married women did, she still wore leather tunic and breeches stamped with the trifoliate day-flower, clanmark of his Kin.

They did not look into each other's eyes.

She did not speak. Wold said at last—for past was past, and he had called Agat "son"—"Do you go to the black island or stay here, kinswoman?"

"I stay here, Eldest."

"Agat sends me to the black island," he said, a little vague, shifting his stiff weight as he stood there in the cold sunlight, in his bloodstained furs, leaning on the spear.

"I think Agat fears the women won't go unless you lead them, you or Umaksuman. And Umaksuman leads our warriors, guarding the north wall."

She had lost all her lightness, her aimless, endearing insolence; she was urgent and gentle. All at once he recalled her vividly as a little child, the only little one in all the Summerlands, Shakatany's daughter, the Summerborn. "So you are the Alterra's wife?" he said, and this idea coming on top of the memory of her as a wild, laughing child confused him again so he did not hear what she answered.

"Why don't all of us in the city go to the island, if it can't be taken?"

"Not enough water, Eldest. The Gaal would move into this city, and we would die on the rock."

He could see, across the roofs of the League Hall, a glimpse of the causeway. The tide was in; waves glinted beyond the black shoulder of the island fort.

"A house built upon sea-water is no house for men," he said heavily. "It's too close to the land under the sea.... Listen now, there was a thing I meant to say to Arilia—to Agat. Wait. What was it, I've forgotten. I can't hear my mind...." He pondered, but nothing came. "Well, no matter. Old men's thoughts are like dust. Goodbye, daughter."

He went on, shuffling halt and ponderous across the Square to the Thiatr, where he ordered the young mothers to collect their children and come. Then he led his last foray—a flock of cowed women and little crying children following him and the three younger men he chose to come with him—across the vasty dizzy air-road to the black and terrible house.

It was cold there, and silent. In the high vaults of the rooms there was no sound at all but the sound of the sea sucking and mouthing at the rocks below. His people huddled together all in one huge room. He wished old Kerly were there, she would have been a help, but she was lying dead in Tevar or in the forests. A couple of courageous women got the others going at last;

they found grain to make bhan-meal, water to boil it, wood to boil the water. When the women and children of the farborns came with their guard of ten men, the Tevarans could offer them hot food. Now there were five or six hundred people in the fort, filling it up pretty full, so it echoed with voices and there were brats underfoot everywhere, almost like the women's side of a Kinhouse in the Winter City. But from the narrow windows, through the transparent rock that kept out the wind, one looked down and down to the water spouting on the rocks below, the waves smoking in the wind.

The wind was turning and the dirtiness in the northern sky had become a haze, so that around the little pale sun there hung a great pale circle: the snowcircle. That was it, that was what he had meant to tell Agat. It was going to snow. Not a shake of salt like last time, but snow, winter snow. The blizzard . . . The word he had not heard or said for so long made him feel strange. To die, then, he must return across the bleak, changeless landscape of his boyhood, he must reenter the white world of the storms.

He still stood at the window, but did not see the noisy water below. He was remembering Winter. A lot of good it would do the Gaal to have taken Tevar, and Landin too. Tonight and tomorrow they could feast on hann and grain. But how far would they get, when the snow began to fall? The real snow, the blizzard that leveled the forests and filled the valleys; and the winds that followed, bitter cold. They would run when that enemy came down the roads at them! They had stayed North too long. Wold suddenly cackled out loud, and turned from the darkening window. He had outlived his chiefdom, his sons, his use, and had to die here on a rock in the sea; but he had great allies, and great warriors served him—greater than Agat, or any man. Storm and Winter fought for him, and he would outlive his enemies.

He strode ponderously to the hearth, undid his gesin-pouch, dropped a tiny fragment on the coals and inhaled three deep breaths. After that he bellowed, "Well, women! Is the slop ready?" Meekly they served him; contentedly he ate.

11

The Siege of the City

All the first day of the siege Rolery's job had been with those who kept the men on the walls and roofs supplied with lances—long, crude, unfinished slivers of holngrass weighing a couple of pounds, one end slashed to a long point. Well aimed, one would kill, and even from unskilled hands a rain of them was a good deterrent to a group of Gaal trying to raise a ladder against the curving landward wall. She had brought bundles of these lances up endless stairs, passed them up as one of a chain of passers on other stairs, run with them through the windy streets, and her hands still bristled with hair-thin, stinging splinters. But now since daybreak she had been hauling rocks for the *katapuls,* the rock-throwing-things like huge slingshots, which were set up inside the Land Gate. When the Gaal crowded up to the gate to use their rams, the big rocks whizzing and whacking down among them scattered and rescattered them. But to feed the katapuls took an awful pile of rocks. Boys kept at work prising paving-stones up from the nearby streets, and her crew of women ran these eight or ten at a time on a little roundlegged box to the men working the katapuls. Eight women pulled together, harnessed to ropes. The heavy box with its dead load of stone would seem immovable, until at last as they all pulled its round legs would suddenly turn, and with it clattering and jolting behind, they would pull it uphill to the gate all in one straining rush, dump it, then stand panting a minute and wipe the hair out of their eyes, and drag the bucking, empty cart back for more. They had done this all morning. Rocks and ropes had blistered Rolery's hard hands raw. She had torn squares from her thin leather skirt and bound them on her palms with sandal-thongs; it helped, and others imitated her.

"I wish you hadn't forgotten how to make erkars," she shouted to Seiko Esmit once as they came clattering down the street at a run with the unwieldy cart jouncing behind them. Seiko did not answer; perhaps she did not hear. She kept at this grueling work—there seemed to be no soft ones among the farborns—but the strain they were under told on Seiko; she worked like one in a trance. Once as they neared the gate the Gaal began shooting fire-brands that fell smoking and smoldering on the stones and the tile roofs. Seiko had struggled in the ropes like a beast in a snare, cowering as the flaming things shot over. "They go out, this city won't burn," Rolery had said softly, but Seiko turning her unseeing face had said, "I'm afraid of fire, I'm afraid of fire. . . ."

But when a young crossbowman up on the wall, struck in the face by a Gaal slingshot, had been thrown backwards off his narrow ledge and crashed down spread-eagled beside them, knocking over two of the harnessed women and spattering their skirts with his blood and brains, it had been Seiko who went to him and took that smashed head on her knees, whispering goodbye to the dead man. "That was your kinsman?" Rolery asked as Seiko resumed her harness and they went on. The Alterran woman said, "We are all kinsmen in the City. He was Jonkendy Li—the youngest of the Council."

A young wrestler in the arena in the great square, shining with sweat and triumph, telling her to walk where she liked in his city. He was the first farborn that had spoken to her.

She had not seen Jakob Agat since the night before last, for each person left in Landin, human and farborn, had his job and place, and Agat's was everywhere, holding a city of fifteen hundred against a force of fifteen thousand. As the day wore on and weariness and hunger lowered her strength, she began to see him too sprawled out on bloody stones, down at the other main attack-point, the Sea Gate above the cliffs. Her crew stopped work to eat bread and dried fruit brought by a cheerful lad hauling a roundleg-cart of provisions; a serious little maiden lugging a skin of water gave them to drink. Rolery took heart. She was certain that they would all die, for she had seen, from the rooftops, the enemy blackening the hills: there was no end to them, they had hardly begun the siege yet. She was equally certain that Agat could not be killed, and that since he would live, she would live. What had death to do with him? He was life; her life. She sat on the cobbled street comfortably chewing hard bread. Mutilation, rape, torture and horror encompassed her within a stone's throw on all sides, but there she sat chewing her bread. So long as they fought back with all their strength, with all their heart, as they were doing, they were safe at least from fear.

But not long after came a very bad time. As they dragged their lumbering load towards the gate, the sound of the clattering cart and all sounds were drowned out by an incredible howling noise outside the gate, a roar like that of an earthquake, so deep and loud as to be felt in the bone, not heard. And the gate leaped on its iron hinges, shuddering. She saw Agat then, for a moment. He was running, leading a big group of archers and dartgunners up from the lower part of town, yelling orders to another group on the walls as he ran.

All the women scattered, ordered to take refuge in streets nearer the center of town. *Howw, howw, howw!* went the crowd-voice at the Land Gate, a noise so huge it seemed the hills themselves were making it, and would rise and shake the city off the cliffs into the sea. The wind was bitter cold. Her crew was scattered, all was confusion. She had no work to lay her hand to. It was getting dark. The day was not that old, it was not time yet for darkness. All at once she saw that she was in fact going to die, believed in her death; she stood still and cried out under her breath, there in the empty street between the high, empty houses.

On a side street a few boys were prising up stones and carrying them down to build up the barricades that had been built across the four streets that led into the main square, reinforcing the gates. She joined them, to keep warm, to keep doing something. They labored in silence, five or six of them, doing work too heavy for them.

"Snow," one of them said, pausing near her. She looked up from the stone she was pushing foot by foot down the street, and saw the white flakes whirling before her, falling thicker every moment. They all stood still. Now there was no wind, and the monstrous voice howling at the gate fell silent. Snow and darkness came together, bringing silence.

"Look at it," a boy's voice said in wonder. Already they could not see the end of the street. A feeble yellowish glimmer was the light from the League Hall, only a block away.

"We've got all Winter to look at the stuff," said another lad. "If we live that long. Come on! They must be passing out supper at the Hall."

"You coming?" the youngest one said to Rolery.

"My people are in the other house, Thiatr, I think."

"No, we're all eating in the Hall, to save work. Come on." The boys were shy, gruff, comradely. She went with them.

The night had come early; the day came late. She woke in Agat's house, beside him, and saw gray light on the gray walls, slits of dimness leaking through the shutters that hid the glass windows. Everything was still, entirely still. Inside the house and outside it there was no noise at all. How could a besieged city be so silent? But siege and Gaals seemed very far off, kept away by this strange daybreak hush. Here there was warmth, and Agat beside her lost in sleep. She lay very still.

Knocking downstairs, hammering at the door, voices. The charm broke; the best moment passed. They were calling Agat. She roused him, a hard job; at last, still blind with sleep, he got himself on his feet and opened window and shutter, letting in the light of day.

The third day of siege, the first of storm. Snow lay a foot deep in the streets and was still falling, ceaseless, sometimes thick and calm, mostly driving on a hard north wind. Everything was silenced and transformed by snow. Hills, forest, fields, all were gone; there was no sky. The near rooftops faded off into white. There was fallen snow, and falling snow, for a little ways, and then you could not see at all.

Westward, the tide drew back and back into the silent storm. The causeway curved out into void. The Stack could not be seen. No sky, no sea. Snow drove down over the dark cliffs, hiding the sands.

Agat latched shutter and window and turned to her. His face was still relaxed with sleep, his voice was hoarse. "They can't have gone," he muttered. For that was what they had been calling up to him from the street: "The Gaal have gone, they've pulled out, they're running south. . . ."

There was no telling. From the walls of Landin nothing could be seen but the storm. But a little way farther into the storm there might be a thousand tents set up to weather it out; or there might be none.

A few scouts went over the walls on ropes. Three returned saying they had gone up the ridge to the forest and found no Gaal; but they had come back because they could not see even the city itself from a hundred yards off. One never came back. Captured, or lost in the storm?

The Alterrans met in the library of the Hall; as was customary, any citizen who wished came to hear and deliberate with them. The Council of the Alterrans was eight now, not ten. Jonkendy Li was dead and so was Haris, the youngest and the oldest. There were only seven present, for Pilotson was on guard duty. But the room was crowded with silent listeners.

"They're not gone. . . . They're not close to the city. . . . Some . . . some are . . ." Alla Pasfal spoke thickly, the pulse throbbed in her neck, her face was muddy gray. She was best trained of all the farborns at what they called mindhearing: she could hear men's thoughts farther than any other, and could listen to a mind that did not know she heard it.

That is forbidden, Agat had said long ago—a week ago?—and he had spoken against this attempt to find out if the Gaal were still encamped near Landin. "We've never broken that law," he said, "never in all the Exile." And he said, "We'll know where the Gaal are as soon as the snow lets up; meanwhile we'll keep watch."

But others did not agree with him, and they overrode his will. Rolery was confused and distressed when she saw him withdraw, accepting their choice. He had tried to explain to her why he must; he said he was not the chief of the city or the Council, that ten Alterrans were chosen and ruled together, but it all made no sense to Rolery. Either he was their leader or he was not; and if he was not, they were lost.

Now the old woman writhed, her eyes unseeing, and tried to speak in words her unspeakable half-glimpses into alien minds whose thoughts were in an alien speech, her brief inarticulate grasp of what another being's hands touched—"I hold—I hold—line—rope—" she stammered.

Rolery shivered in fear and distaste; Agat sat turned from Alla, withdrawn. At last Alla was still, and sat for a long time with bowed head.

Seiko Esmit poured out for each of the seven Alterrans and Rolery the tiny ceremonial cup of ti; each, barely touching it with his lips, passed it on to a fellow-citizen, and he to another till it was empty. Rolery looked fascinated at the bowl Agat gave to her, before she drank and passed it on. Blue, leaf-frail, it let the light pass through it like a jewel.

"The Gaal have gone," Alla Pasfal said aloud, raising her ravaged face. "They are on the move now, in some valley between two ranges—that came very clear."

"Giln Valley," one of the men murmured. "About ten kilos south from the Bogs."

"They are fleeing from the Winter. The walls of the city are safe."

"But the law is broken," Agat said, his hoarsened voice cutting across the murmur of hope and jubilation. "Walls can be mended. Well, we'll see. . . ."

Rolery went with him down the staircase and through the vast Assembly Room, crowded now with trestles and tables, for the communal dining-hall was there under the golden clocks and the crystal patterns of planets circling their suns. "Let's go home," he said, and pulling on the big hooded fur coats that had been issued to everyone from the storerooms underneath the Old Hall, they went out together into the blinding wind in the Square. They had not gone ten steps when out of the blizzard a grotesque figure plastered with red-streaked white burst on them, shouting, "The Sea Gate, they're inside the walls, at the Sea Gate—"

Agat glanced once at Rolery and was gone into the storm. In a moment the clangor of metal on metal broke out from the tower overhead, booming, snow-muffled. They called that great noise the *bell,* and before the siege began all had learned its signals. Four, five strokes, then silence, then five again, and again: all men to the Sea Gate, the Sea Gate . . .

Rolery dragged the messenger out of the way, under the arcades of the League Hall, before men came bursting from the doors, coatless or struggling into their coats as they ran, armed and unarmed, pelting into the whirling snow, vanishing in it before they were across the Square.

No more came. She could hear some noise in the direction of the Sea Gate, seeming very remote through the sound of the wind and the hushing of the snow. The messenger leaned on her, in the shelter of the arcade. He was bleeding from a deep wound in his neck, and would have fallen if she had let him. She recognized his face; he was the Alterran called Pilotson, and she used his name to rouse him and keep him going as she tried to get him inside the building. He staggered with weakness and muttered as if still trying to deliver his message, "They broke in, they're inside the walls. . . ."

12

The Siege of the Square

The high, narrow Sea Gate clashed to, the bolts shot home. The battle in the storm was over. But the men of the city turned and saw, over the red-stained drifts in the street and through the still-falling snow, shadows running.

They took up their dead and wounded hastily and returned to the Square. In this blizzard no watch could be kept against ladders, climbers; you could not see along the walls more than fifteen feet to either hand. A Gaal or a group of them had slipped in, right under the noses of the guards, and opened the Sea Gate to the assault. That assault had been driven out, but the next one could come anywhere, at any time, in greater force.

"I think," Umaksuman said, walking with Agat towards the barricade between the Thiatr and the College, "that most of the Gaal went on south today."

Agat nodded. "They must have. If they don't move on they starve. What we face now is an occupying force left behind to finish us off and live on our stores. How many do you think?"

"Not more than a thousand were there at the gate," the native said doubtfully. "But there may be more. And they'll all be inside the walls—There!" Umaksuman pointed to a quick cowering shape that the snow-curtains revealed for a moment halfway up the street. "You that way," the native muttered and vanished abruptly to the left. Agat circled the block from the right, and met Umaksuman in the street again. "No luck," he said.

"Luck," the Tevaran said briefly, and held up a bone-inlaid Gaal ax which he had not had a minute ago. Over their heads the bell of the Hall tower kept sending out its soft dull clanging through the snow: one, two—one, two—one, two—Retreat to the Square, to the Square . . . All who had fought at the Sea Gate, and those who had been patrolling the walls and the Land Gate, or asleep in their houses or trying to watch from the roofs, had come or were coming to the city's heart, the Square between the four great buildings. One by one they were let through the barricades. Umaksuman and Agat came along at last, knowing it was folly to stay out now in these streets where shadows ran. "Let's go, Alterra!" the native urged him, and Agat came, but reluctantly. It was hard to leave his city to the enemy.

The wind was down now. Sometimes, through the queer complex hush of the storm, people in the Square could hear glass shattering, the splintering of an ax against a door, up one of the streets that led off into the falling snow. Many of the houses had been left unlocked, open to the looters: they would find very little in them beyond shelter from the snow. Every scrap of food had been turned in to the Commons here in the Hall a week ago. The water mains and the natural-gas mains to all buildings except the four around the Square had been shut off last night. The fountains of Landin stood dry, under their rings of icicles and burdens of snow. All stores and granaries were underground, in the vaults and cellars dug generations ago beneath the Old Hall and the League Hall. Empty, icy, lightless, the deserted houses stood, offering nothing to the invaders.

"They can live off our herds for a moonphase—even without feed for them, they'll slaughter the hann and dry the meat—" Dermat Alterra had met Agat at the very door of the League Hall, full of panic and reproach.

"They'll have to catch the hann first," Agat growled in reply.

"What do you mean?"

"I mean that we opened the byres a few minutes ago, while we were there at the Sea Gate, and let 'em go. Paol Herdsman was with me and he sent out a panic. They ran like a shot, right out into the blizzard."

"You let the hann go—the herds? What do we live on the rest of the winter—if the Gaal leave?"

"Did Paol mindsending to the hann panic you too, Dermat?" Agat fired at him. "D'you think we can't round up our own animals? What about our grain stores, hunting, snowcrop—what the devil's wrong with you!"

"Jakob," murmured Seiko Esmit, coming between him and the older man. He realized he had been yelling at Dermat, and tried to get hold of himself. But it was damned hard to come in from a bloody fight like that defense of the Sea Gate and have to cope with a case of male hysteria. His head ached violently; the scalp wound he had got in one of their raids on the Gaal camp still hurt, though it should have healed already; he had got off unhurt at the Sea Gate, but he was filthy with other men's blood. Against the high, unshuttered windows of the library the snow streaked and whispered. It was noon; it seemed dusk. Beneath the windows lay the Square with its well-guarded barricades. Beyond those lay the abandoned houses, the defenseless walls, the city of snow and shadows.

That day of their retreat to the Inner City, the fourth day of siege, they stayed inside their barricades; but already that night, when the snowfall thinned for a while, a reconnoitering party slipped out via the roofs of the College. The blizzard grew worse again around daybreak, or a second storm perhaps followed right on the first, and under cover of the snow and cold the men and boys of Landin played guerilla in their own streets. They went out by twos or threes, prowling the streets and roofs and rooms, shadows among the shadows. They used knives, poisoned darts, bolos, arrows. They broke into their own homes and killed the Gaal who sheltered there, or were killed by them.

Having a good head for heights, Agat was one of the best at playing the game from roof to roof. Snow made the steep-pitched tiles pretty slippery, but the chance to pick off Gaal with darts was irresistible, and the chances of getting killed no higher than in other versions of the sport, streetcorner dodging or house-haunting.

The sixth day of siege, the fourth of storm: this day the snowfall was fine, sparse, wind-driven. Thermometers down in the basement Records Room of Old Hall, which they were using now as a hospital, read −4°C. outside, and the anemometers showed gusts well over a hundred kmh. Outside it was terrible, the wind lashing that fine snow at one's face like gravel, whirling it in through the smashed glass of windows whose shutters had been torn off to build a campfire, drifting it across splintered floors. There was little warmth and little food anywhere in the city, except inside the four buildings around the Square. The Gaal huddled in empty rooms, burning mats and broken doors and shutters and chests in the middle of the floor, waiting out the storm. They had no provisions—what food there was had gone with the Southing. When the weather changed they would be able to hunt, and finish off the townsfolk, and thereafter live on the city's winter stores. But while the storm lasted, the attackers starved.

They held the causeway, if it was any good to them. Watchers in the League Tower had seen their one hesitant foray out to the Stack, which ended promptly in a rain of lances and a raised drawbridge. Very few of them had been seen venturing on the low-tide beaches below the cliffs of Landin; probably they had seen the tide come roaring in, and had no idea how often and when it would come next, for they were inlanders. So the Stack was safe, and some of the trained paraverbalists in the city had been in touch with one or another of the men and women out on the island, enough to know they were getting on well, and to tell anxious fathers that there were no children sick. The Stack was all right. But the city was breached, invaded, occupied; more than a hundred of its people already killed in its defense, and the rest trapped in a few buildings. A city of snow, and shadows, and blood.

Jakob Agat crouched in a gray-walled room. It was empty except for a lit-ter of torn felt matting and broken glass over which fine snow had sifted. The house was silent. There under the windows where the pallet had been, he and Rolery had slept one night; she had waked him in the morning. Crouching there, a housebreaker in his own house, he thought of Rolery with bitter ten-derness. Once—it seemed far back in time, twelve days ago maybe—he had said in this same room that he could not get on without her; and now he had no time day or night even to think of her. Then let me think of her now, at least think of her, he said ragefully to the silence; but all he could think was that she and he had been born at the wrong time. In the wrong season. You cannot begin a love in the beginning of the season of death.

Wind whistled peevishly at the broken windows. Agat shivered. He had been hot all day, when he was not freezing cold. The thermometer was still dropping, and a lot of the rooftop guerillas were having trouble with what the old men said was frostbite. He felt better if he kept moving. Thinking did no good. He started for the door out of a lifetime's habit, then getting hold of himself went softly to the window by which he had entered. In the ground-floor room of the house next door a group of Gaal were camped. He could see the back of one near the window. They were a fair people; their hair was darkened and made stiff with some kind of pitch or tar, but the bowed, mus-cular neck Agat looked down on was white. It was strange how little chance he had had actually to see his enemies. You shot from a distance, or struck and ran, or as at the Sea Gate fought too close and fast to look. He wondered if their eyes were yellowish or amber like those of the Tevarans; he had an impression that they were gray, instead. But this was no time to find out. He climbed up on the sill, swung out on the gable, and left his home via the roof.

His usual route back to the Square was blocked: the Gaal were begin-ning to play the rooftop game too. He lost all but one of his pursuers quickly enough, but that one, armed with a dart-blower, came right after him, leap-ing an eight-foot gap between two houses that had stopped the others. Agat had to drop down into an alley, pick himself up and run for it.

A guard on the Esmit Street barricade, watching for just such escapes, flung down a rope ladder to him, and he swarmed up it. Just as he reached the top a dart stung his right hand. He came sliding down inside the barricade, pulled the thing out and sucked the wound and spat. The Gaal did not poison their darts or arrows, but they picked up and used the ones the men of Landin shot at them, and some of these, of course, were poisoned. It was a rather neat demonstration of one reason for the canonical Law of Embargo. Agat had a very bad couple of minutes waiting for the first cramp to hit him; then decided he was lucky, and thereupon began to feel the pain of the messy little wound in his hand. His shooting hand, too.

Dinner was being dished out in the Assembly Hall, beneath the golden clocks. He had not eaten since daybreak. He was ravening hungry until he sat down at one of the tables with his bowl of hot bhan and salt meat; then he could not eat. He did not want to talk, either, but it was better than eating, so he talked with everyone who gathered around him, until the alarm rang out on the bell in the tower above them: another attack.

As usual, the assault moved from barricade to barricade; as usual it did not amount to much. Nobody could lead a prolonged attack in this bitter weather. What they were after in these shifting, twilight raids was the chance of slipping even one or two of their men over a momentarily unguarded barricade into the Square, to open the massive iron doors at the back of Old Hall. As darkness came, the attackers melted away. The archers shooting from upper windows of the Old Hall and College held their fire and presently called down that the streets were clear. As usual, a few defenders had been hurt or killed: one crossbowman picked off at his window by an arrow from below, one boy who, climbing too high on the barricade to shoot down, had been hit in the belly with an iron-headed lance; several minor injuries. Every day a few more were killed or wounded, and there were less to guard and fight. The subtraction of a few from too few . . .

Hot and shivering again, Agat came in from this action. Most of the men who had been eating when the alarm came went back and finished eating. Agat had no interest in food now except to avoid the smell of it. His scratched hand kept bleeding afresh whenever he used it, which gave him an excuse to go down to the Records Room, underneath Old Hall, to have the bonesetter tie it up for him.

It was a very large, low-ceilinged room, kept at even warmth and even soft light night and day, a good place to keep old instruments and charts and papers, and an equally good place to keep wounded men. They lay on improvised pallets on the felted floor, little islands of sleep and pain dotted about in the silence of the long room. Among them he saw his wife coming towards him, as he had hoped to see her. The sight, the real certain sight of her, did not rouse in him that bitter tenderness he felt when he thought about her: instead it simply gave him intense pleasure.

"Hullo, Rolery," he mumbled and turned away from her at once to Seiko and the bonesetter Wattock, asking how Huru Pilotson was. He did not know what to do with delight any more, it overcame him.

"His wound grows," Wattock said in a whisper. Agat stared at him, then

realized he was speaking of Pilotson. "Grows?" he repeated uncomprehending and went over to kneel at Pilotson's side.

Pilotson was looking up at him.

"How's it going, Huru?"

"You made a very bad mistake," the wounded man said.

They had known each other and been friends all their lives. Agat knew at
once and unmistakably what would be on Pilotson's mind: his marriage. But
he did not know what to answer. "It wouldn't have made much difference,"
he began finally, then stopped; he would not justify himself.

Pilotson said, "There aren't enough, there aren't enough."

Only then did Agat realize that his friend was out of his head. "It's all right,
Huru!" he said so authoritatively that Pilotson after a moment sighed and shut
his eyes, seeming to accept this blanket reassurance. Agat got up and rejoined
Wattock. "Look, tie this up, will you, to stop the bleeding. —What's wrong
with Pilotson?"

Rolery brought cloth and tape. Wattock bandaged Agat's hand with a couple
of expert turns. "Alterra," he said, "I don't know. The Gaal must be using a
poison our antidotes can't handle. I've tried 'em all. Pilotson Alterra isn't the
only one. The wounds don't close; they swell up. Look at this boy here. It's
the same thing." The boy, a street-guerilla of sixteen or so, was moaning and
struggling like one in nightmare. The spear-wound in his thigh showed no
bleeding, but red streaks ran from it under the skin, and the whole wound
was strange to look at and very hot to the touch.

"You've tried antidotes?" Agat asked, looking away from the boy's tormented face.

"All of them. Alterra, what it reminds me of is the wound you got, early
in Fall, from the *klois* you treed. Remember that? Perhaps they make some
poison from the blood or glands of klois. Perhaps these wounds will go away
as that did. Yes, that's the scar. When he was a young fellow like this one,"
Wattock explained to Seiko and Rolery, "he went up a tree after a klois, and
the scratches it gave him didn't seem much, but they puffed up and got hot
and made him sick. But in a few days it all went off again."

"This one won't get well," Rolery said very softly to Agat.

"Why do you say that?"

"I used to . . . to watch the medicine-woman of my clan. I learned a little . . .
Those streaks, on his leg there, those are what they call death-paths."

"You know this poison, then, Rolery?"

"I don't think it's poison. Any deep wound can do it. Even a small wound
that doesn't bleed, or that gets dirty. It's the evil of the weapon—"

"That is superstition," the old bonesetter said fiercely.

"We don't get the weapon-evil, Rolery," Agat told her, drawing her rather defensively away from the indignant old doctor. "We have an—"

"But the boy and Pilotson Alterra do have it! Look here—" She took him over to where one of the wounded Tevarans sat, a cheerful little middle-aged fellow, who willingly showed Agat the place where his left ear had been before an ax took it off. The wound was healing, but was puffed, hot, oozing. . . .

Unconsciously, Agat put his hand up to his own throbbing, untended scalp-wound.

Wattock had followed them. Glaring at the unoffending hilf, he said, "What the local hilfs call 'weapon-evil' is, of course, bacterial infection. You studied it in school, Alterra. As human beings are not susceptible to infection by any local bacterial or viral life-forms, the only harm we can suffer is damage to vital organs, exsanguination, or chemical poisoning, for which we have antidotes—"

"But the boy is dying, Elder," said Rolery in her soft, unyielding voice. "The wound was not washed out before it was sewed together—"

The old doctor went rigid with fury. "Get back among your own kind and don't tell me how to care for humans—"

"That's enough," Agat said.

Silence.

"Rolery," Agat said, "if you can be spared here a while, I thought we might go . . ." He had been about to say, "go home." "To get some dinner, maybe," he finished vaguely.

She had not eaten; he sat with her in the Assembly Room, and ate a little. Then they put on their coats to cross the unlit, wind-whistling Square to the College building, where they shared a classroom with two other couples. The dormitories in Old Hall were more comfortable, but most of the married couples of which the wife had not gone out to the Stack preferred at least this semiprivacy, when they could have it. One woman was sound asleep behind a row of desks, bundled up in her coat. Tables had been up-ended to seal the broken windows from stones and darts and wind. Agat and his wife put their coats down on the unmatted floor for bedding. Before she let him sleep, Rolery gathered clean snow from a windowsill and washed the wounds in his hand and scalp with it. It hurt, and he protested, short-tempered with fatigue; but she said, "You are the Alterra—you don't get sick—but this will do no harm. No harm . . ."

13

The Last Day

In his feverish sleep, in the cold darkness of the dusty room, Agat spoke aloud sometimes, and once when she was asleep he called to her from his own sleep, reaching out across the unlit abyss, calling her name from farther and farther away. His voice broke her dreaming and she woke. It was still dark.

Morning came early: light shone in around the upturned tables, white streaks across the ceiling. The woman who had been there when they came in last night still slept on in exhaustion, but the other couple, who had slept on one of the writing-tables to avoid the drafts, roused up. Agat sat up, looked around, and said in his hoarse voice, with a stricken look, "The storm's over. . . ." Sliding one of the tables aside a little they peered out and saw the world again: the trampled Square, snow-mounded barricades, great shuttered facades of the four buildings, snow-covered roofs beyond them, and a glimpse of the sea. A white and blue world, brilliantly clear, the shadows blue and every point touched by the early sunlight dazzling white.

It was very beautiful; but it was as if the walls that protected them had been torn down in the night.

Agat was thinking what she thought, for he said, "We'd better get on over to the Hall before they realize they can sit up on the rooftops and use us for target-practice."

"We can use the basement tunnels to get from one building to another," one of the others said. Agat nodded. "We will," he said. "But the barricades have got to be manned. . . ."

Rolery procrastinated till the others had gone, then managed to persuade the impatient Agat to let her look at his head-wound again. It was improved or at least no worse. His face still showed the beating he had got from her kinsmen; her own hands were bruised from handling rocks and ropes, and full of sores that the cold had made worse. She rested her battered hands on his battered head and began to laugh. "Like two old warriors," she said. "O Jakob Agat, when we go to the country under the sea, will you have your front teeth back?"

He looked up at her, not understanding, and tried to smile, but failed.

"Maybe when a farborn dies he goes back to the stars—to the other worlds," she said, and ceased to smile.

"No," he said, getting up. "No, we stay right here. Come along, my wife."

For all the brilliant light from the sun and sky and snow, the air outside was so cold it hurt to breathe. They were hurrying across the Square to the arcades of the League Hall when a noise behind them made them turn, Agat with his dartgun drawn, both ready to duck and run. A strange shrieking figure seemed to fly up over the barricade and crashed down headfirst inside it, not twenty feet from them: a Gaal, two lances bristling out between his ribs. Guards on the barricades stared and shouted, archers loaded their crossbows in haste, glancing up at a man who was yelling down at them from a shuttered window on the east side of the building above them. The dead Gaal lay face down in the bloody, trampled snow, in the blue shadow of the barricade.

One of the guards came running up to Agat, shouting, "Alterra, it must be the signal for an attack—" Another man, bursting out of the door of the College, interrupted him, "No, I saw it, it was chasing him, that's why he was yelling like that—"

"Saw what? Did he attack like that all by himself?"

"He was running from it—trying to save his life! Didn't you see it, you on the barricade? No wonder he was yelling. White, runs like a man, with a neck like—God, like this, Alterra! It came around the corner after him, and then turned back."

"A snowghoul," Agat said, and turned for confirmation to Rolery. She had heard Wold's tales, and nodded. "White, and tall, and the head going from side to side . . ." She imitated Wold's grisly imitation, and the man who had seen the thing from the window cried, "That's it." Agat mounted the barricade to try and get a sight of the monster. She stayed below, looking down at the dead man, who had been so terrified that he had run on his enemy's lances to escape. She had not seen a Gaal up close, for no prisoners were taken, and her work had been underground with the wounded. The body was short and thin, rubbed with grease till the skin, whiter than her own, shone like fat meat; the greased hair was interbraided with red feathers. Ill-clothed, with a felt rag for a coat, the man lay sprawled in his abrupt death, face buried as if still hiding from the white beast that had hunted him. The girl stood motionless near him in the bright, icy shadow of the barricade.

"There!" she heard Agat shout, above her on the slanting, stepped inner face of the wall, built of paving-stones and rocks from the sea-cliffs. He came down to her, his eyes blazing, and hurried her off to the League Hall. "Saw it just for a second as it crossed Otake Street. It was running, it swung its head towards us. Do the things hunt in packs?"

She did not know; she only knew Wold's story of having killed a snowghoul singlehanded, among last Winter's mythic snows. They brought the news and the question into the crowded refectory. Umaksuman said positively that snowghouls often ran in packs, but the farborns would not take a hilf's word, and had to go look in their *books*. The book they brought in said that snowghouls had been seen after the first storm of the Ninth Winter running in a pack of twelve to fifteen.

"How do the books say? They make no sound. It is like the mindspeech you speak to me?"

Agat looked at her. They were at one of the long tables in the Assembly Room, drinking the hot, thin grass-soup the farborns liked; ti, they called it.

"No—well, yes, a little. Listen, Rolery, I'll be going outside in a minute. You go back to the hospital. Don't mind Wattock's temper. He's an old man and he's tired. He knows a lot, though. Don't cross the Square if you have to go to another building, use the tunnels. Between the Gaal archers and those creatures . . ." He gave a kind of laugh. "What next, I wonder?" he said.

"Jakob Agat, I wanted to ask you. . . ."

In the short time she had known him, she had never learned for certain how many pieces his name came into, and which pieces she should use.

"I listen," he said gravely.

"Why is it that you don't speak mindspeech to the Gaal? Tell them to—to go. As you told me on the beach to run to the Stack. As your herdsman told the hann . . ."

"Men aren't hann," he said; and it occurred to her that he was the only one of them all that spoke of her people and his own and the Gaal all as men.

"The old one—Pasfal—she listened to the Gaal, when the big army was starting on south."

"Yes. People with the gift and the training can listen in, even at a distance, without the other mind's knowing it. That's a bit like what any person does in a crowd of people, he feels their fear or joy; there's more to mindhearing than that, but it's without words. But the mindspeech, and receiving mindspeech, is different. An untrained man, if you bespeak him, will shut his mind to it before he knows he's heard anything. Especially if what he hears isn't what he himself wants or believes. Non-Communicants have perfect defenses, usually. In fact to learn paraverbal communication is mainly to learn how to break down one's own defenses."

"But the animals hear?"

"To some extent. That's done without words again. Some people have that knack for projecting to animals. It's useful in herding and hunting, all right. Did you never hear that farborns were lucky hunters?"

"Yes, it's why they're called witches. But am I like a hann, then? I heard you."

"Yes. And you bespoke me—once, in my house. It happens sometimes between two people: there are no barriers, no defenses." He drained his cup and looked up broodingly at the pattern of sun and jeweled circling worlds on the long wall across the room. "When that happens," he said, "it's necessary that they love each other. Necessary . . . I can't send my fear or hate against the Gaal. They wouldn't hear. But if I turned it on you, I could kill you. And you me, Rolery. . . ."

Then they came wanting him out in the Square, and he must leave her. She went down to look after the Tevaran men in the hospital, which was her assigned job, and also to help the wounded farborn boy to die: a hard death that took all day. The old bonesetter let her take care of the boy. Wattock was bitter and rageful, seeing all his skill useless. "We humans don't die your foul death!" he stormed once. "The boy was born with some blood defect!" She did not care what he said. Neither did the boy, who died in pain, holding onto her hand.

New wounded were brought down into the big, quiet room, one or two at a time. Only by this did they know that there must be bitter fighting, up in the sunlight on the snow. Umaksuman was carried down, knocked unconscious by a Gaal slingshot. Great-limbed and stately he lay, and she looked at him with a dull pride: a warrior, a brother. She thought him near death, but after a while he sat up, shaking his head, and then stood up. "What place is this?" he demanded, and she almost laughed when she answered. Wold's kin were hard to kill off. He told her that the Gaal were running an attack against all the barricades at once, a ceaseless push, like the great attack on the Land Gate when the whole force of them had tried to scale the walls on one another's shoulders. "They are stupid warriors," he said, rubbing the great lump over his ear. "If they sat up on the roofs around this Square for a week and shot at us with arrows, we wouldn't have men enough left to hold the barricades. All they know is to come running all at once, yelling. . . ." He rubbed his head again, said, "What did they do with my spear?" and went back up to the fighting.

The dead were not brought down here, but laid in an open shed in the Square till they could be burned. If Agat had been killed, she would not know it. When bearers came with a new patient she looked up with a surge of hope: if it were Agat wounded, then he was not dead. But it was never him. She wondered if, when he was killed, he would cry out to her mind before he died; and if that cry would kill her.

Late in the unending day the old woman Alla Pasfal was carried down. With certain other old men and women of the farborns, she had demanded the dangerous job of bringing arms to the defenders of the barricades, which meant running across the Square with no shelter from the enemy's fire. A Gaal lance had pierced her throat from side to side. Wattock could do very little for her. A little, black, old woman, she lay dying among the young men. Caught by her gaze, Rolery went to her, a basin of bloody vomit in her hands. Hard, dark, and depthless as rock the old eyes gazed at her; and Rolery looked straight back, though it was not a thing her people did.

The bandaged throat rattled, the mouth twisted.

To break down one's own defenses . . .

"I listen!" Rolery said aloud, in the formal phrase of her people, in a shaking voice.

They will go, Alla Pasfal's voice, tired and faint, said in her mind: *They'll try to follow the others south. They fear us, the snowghouls, the houses and streets. They are afraid, they will go after this attack. Tell Jakob. I can hear, I can hear them. Tell Jakob they will go—tomorrow—*

"I'll tell him," Rolery said, and broke into tears. Moveless, speechless, the dying woman stared at her with eyes like dark stones.

Rolery went back to her job, for the hurt men needed attention and Wattock had no other assistant. And what good would it do to go seek out Agat up there in the bloody snow and the noise and haste, to tell him, before he was killed, that a mad old woman dying had said they would survive?

She went on about her work with tears still running down her face. One of the farborns, badly wounded but eased by the wonderful medicine Wattock used, a little ball that, swallowed, made pain lessen or cease, asked her, "Why are you crying?" He asked it drowsily, curiously, as one child might ask another. "I don't know," Rolery told him. "Go to sleep." But she did know, though vaguely, that she was crying because hope was intolerably painful, breaking through into the resignation in which she had lived for days; and pain, since she was only a woman, made her weep.

There was no way at all of knowing it down here, but the day must be ending, for Seiko Esmit came with hot food on a tray for her and Wattock and those of the wounded that could eat. She waited to take the bowls back, and Rolery said to her, "The old one, Pasfal Alterra, is dead."

Seiko only nodded. Her face was tight and strange. She said in a high voice, "They're shooting firebrands now, and throwing burning stuff down from the roofs. They can't break in so they're going to burn the buildings and the stores and then we all can starve together in the cold. If the Hall catches fire you'll be trapped down here. Burnt alive."

Rolery ate her food and said nothing. The hot bhanmeal had been flavored with meat juice and chopped herbs. The farborns under siege were better cooks than her people in the midst of Autumn plenty. She finished up her bowl, and also the half-bowlful a wounded man left, and another scrap or two, and brought the tray back to Seiko, only wishing there had been more.

No one else came down for a long time. The men slept, and moaned in their sleep. It was warm; the heat of the gas-fires rose up through the gratings, making it comfortable as a fire-warmed tent. Through the breathing of the men sometimes Rolery could hear the tick, tick, tick of the round-faced things on the walls. These, and the glass cases pushed back against the wall, and the high rows of *books,* winked in gold and brown glimmerings in the soft, steady light of the gas-flares.

"Did you give him the analgesic?" Wattock whispered, and she shrugged yes, rising from beside one of the men. The old bonesetter looked half a Year older than he was, as he squatted down beside Rolery at a study table to cut bandages, of which they had run short. He was a very great doctor, in Rolery's eyes. To please him in his fatigue and discouragement she asked him, "Elder, if it's not the weapon-evil that makes a wound rot, what thing does?"

"Oh—creatures. Little beasts, too small to see. I could only show 'em to you with a special glass, like that one in the case over there. They live nearly everywhere; they're on the weapon, in the air, on the skin. If they get into the blood, the body resists 'em and the battle is what causes the swelling and all that. So the books say. It's nothing that ever concerned me as a doctor."

"Why don't the creatures bite farborns?"

"Because they don't like foreigners." Wattock snorted at his small joke. "We are foreign, you know. We can't even digest food here unless we take periodic doses of certain enzymoids. We have a chemical structure that's very slightly different from the local organic norm, and it shows up in the cytoplasm— You don't know what that is. Well, what it means is, we're made of slightly different stuff than you hilfs are."

"So that you're dark-skinned and we light?"

"No, that's unimportant. Totally superficial variations, color and eye-structure and all that. No, the difference is on a lower level, and is very small—

one molecule in the hereditary chain," Wattock said with relish, warming to his lecture. "It causes no major divergence from the Common Hominid Type in you hilfs; so the first colonists wrote, and they knew. But it means that we can't interbreed with you; or digest local organic food without help; or react to your viruses. . . . Though as a matter of fact, this enzymoid business is a bit overdone. Part of the effort to do exactly as the First Generation did. Pure superstition, some of that. I've seen people come in from long hunting-trips, or the Atlantika refugees last Spring, who hadn't taken an enzymoid shot or pill for two or three moonphases, but weren't failing to digest. Life tends to adapt, after all." As he said this Wattock got a very odd expression, and stared at her. She felt guilty, since she had no idea what he had been explaining to her: none of the key words were words in her language.

"Life what?" she inquired timidly.

"Adapts. Reacts. Changes! Given enough pressure, and enough generations, the favorable adaptation tends to prevail. . . . Would the solar radiation work in the long run towards a sort of local biochemical norm? . . . All the stillbirths and miscarriages then would be overadaptations, or maybe incompatibility between the mother and a normalized fetus. . . ." Wattock stopped waving his scissors and bent to his work again, but in a moment he was looking up again in his unseeing, intense way and muttering, "Strange, strange, strange! . . . That would imply, you know, that cross-fertilization might take place."

"I listen again," Rolery murmured.

"That men and hilfs could breed together!"

This she understood at last, but did not understand whether he said it as a fact or a wish or a dread. "Elder, I am too stupid to hear you," she said.

"You understand him well enough," said a weak voice nearby: Pilotson Alterra, lying awake. "So you think we've finally turned into a drop in the bucket, Wattock?" Pilotson had raised up on his elbow. His dark eyes glittered in his gaunt, hot, dark face.

"If you and several of the others do have infected wounds, then the fact's got to be explained somehow."

"Damn adaptation then. Damn your crossbreeding and fertility!" the sick man said, and looked at Rolery. "So long as we've bred true we've been Man. Exiles, Alterrans, humans. Faithful to the knowledge and the Laws of Man. Now, if we can breed with the hilfs, the drop of our human blood will be lost before another Year's past. Diluted, thinned out to nothing. Nobody will set these instruments, or read these books. Jakob Agat's grandsons will sit pounding two rocks together and yelling, till the end of time. . . . Damn you stupid barbarians, can't you leave men alone—alone!" He was shaking with fever and fury. Old Wattock, who had been fiddling with one of his little hollow darts, filling it up, now reached over in his smooth doctorly way and shot poor Pilotson in the forearm. "Lie down, Huru," he said, and with a puzzled expression the wounded man obeyed. "I don't care if I die of your filthy infections," he said in a thickening voice, "but your filthy brats, keep them away from here, keep 'em out of the . . . out of the City. . . ."

"That'll hold him down a while," Wattock said, and sighed. He sat in silence while Rolery went on preparing bandages. She was deft and steady at such work. The old doctor watched her with a brooding face.

When she straightened up to ease her back she saw the old man too had fallen asleep, a dark pile of skin and bones hunched up in the corner behind the table. She worked on, wondering if she had understood what he said, and if he had meant it: that she could bear Agat's son.

She had totally forgotten that Agat might very well be dead already, for all she knew. She sat there among the sleep of wounded men, under the ruined city full of death, and brooded speechlessly on the chance of life.

14

The First Day

The cold gripped harder as night fell. Snow that had thawed in sunlight froze as slick ice. Concealed on nearby roofs or in attics, the Gaal shot over their pitch-tipped arrows that arched red and gold like birds of fire through the cold twilit air. The roofs of the four beleaguered buildings were of copper, the walls of stone; no fire caught. The attacks on the barricades ceased, no more arrows of iron or fire were shot. Standing up on the barricade, Jakob Agat saw the darkening streets slant off empty between dark houses.

At first the men in the Square waited for a night attack, for the Gaal were plainly desperate; but it grew colder, and still colder. At last Agat ordered that only the minimum watch be kept, and let most of the men go to have their wounds looked after, and get food and rest. If they were exhausted, so must the Gaal be, and they at least were clothed against this cold while the Gaal were not. Even desperation would not drive the northerners out into this awful, starlit clarity, in their scant rags of fur and felt. So the defenders slept, many at their posts, huddled in the halls and by the windows of warm buildings. And the besiegers, without food, pressed around campfires built in high stone rooms; and their dead lay stiff-limbed in the ice-crusted snow below the barricades.

Agat wanted no sleep. He could not go inside the buildings, leaving the Square where all day long they had fought for their lives, and which now lay so still under the Winter constellations. The Tree; and the Arrow; and the Track of five stars; and the Snowstar itself, fiery above the eastern roofs: the stars of Winter. They burned like crystals in the profound, cold blackness overhead.

He knew this was the last night—his own last night, or his city's, or the last night of battle—which one, he did not know. As the hours wore on, and the Snowstar rose higher, and utter silence held the Square and the streets around it, a kind of exultation got hold of him. They slept, all the enemies within these city walls, and it was as if he alone waked; as if the city belonged, with all its sleepers and all its dead, to him alone. This was his night.

He would not spend it locked in a trap within a trap. With a word to the sleepy guard, he mounted the Esmit Street barricade and swung himself down on the other side. "Alterra!" someone called after him in a hoarse whisper; he only turned and gestured that they keep a rope ready for him to get back up on, and went on, right up the middle of the street. He had a conviction of his invulnerability with which it would be bad luck to argue. He accepted it, and walked up the dark street among his enemies as if he were taking a stroll after dinner.

He passed his house but did not turn aside. Stars eclipsed behind the black roofpeaks and reappeared, their reflections glittering in the ice underfoot. Near the upper end of town the street narrowed and turned a little between houses that had been deserted since before Agat was born, and then opened out suddenly into the little square under the Land Gate. The catapults still stood there, partly wrecked and dismantled for firewood by the Gaal, each with a heap of stones beside it. The high gates themselves had been opened at one point, but were bolted again now and frozen fast. Agat climbed up the steps beside one of the gate-towers to a post on the wall; he remembered looking down from that post, just before the snow began, on the whole battle-force of the Gaal, a roaring tide of men like the seatide down on the beach. If they had had more ladders it would have all been over with that day. . . . Now nothing moved; nothing made any sound. Snow, silence, starlight over the slope and the dead, ice-laden trees that crowned it.

He looked back westward, over the whole City of Exile: a little clutter of roofs dropping down away from his high post to the wall over the sea-cliff. Above that handful of stone the stars moved slowly westward. Agat sat motionless, cold even in his clothing of leather and heavy furs, whistling a jig-tune very softly.

Finally he felt the day's weariness catching up with him, and descended from his perch. The steps were icy. He slipped on the next to bottom step, caught himself from falling by grabbing the rough stone of the wall, and then still staggering looked up at some movement that had caught his eyes across the little square.

In the black gulf of a street opening between two house-walls, something white moved, a slight swaying motion like a wave seen in the dark. Agat stared, puzzled. Then it came out into the vague gray of the starlight: a tall, thin, white figure running towards him very quickly as a man runs, the head on the long, curving neck swaying a little from side to side. As it came it made a little wheezing, chirping sound.

His dartgun had been in his hand all along, but his hand was stiff from yesterday's wound, and the glove hampered him: he shot and the dart struck, but the creature was already on him, the short clawed forearms reaching out, the head stuck forward with its weaving, swaying motion, a round toothed mouth gaping open. He threw himself down right against its legs in an effort to trip it and escape the first lunge of that snapping mouth, but it was quicker than he. Even as he went down it turned and caught at him, and he felt the claws on the weak-looking little arms tear through the leather of his coat and clothing, and felt himself pinned down. A terrible strength bent his head back, baring his throat; and he saw the stars whirl in the sky far up above him, and go out.

And then he was trying to pull himself up on hands and knees, on the icy stones beside a great, reeking bulk of white fur that twitched and trembled. Five seconds it took the poison on the dart-tip to act; it had almost been a second too long. The round mouth still snapped open and shut, the legs with their flat, splayed, snowshoe feet pumped as if the snowghoul were still running. Snowghouls hunt in packs, Agat's memory said suddenly, as he stood trying to get his breath and nerve back. Snowghouls hunt in packs. . . . He reloaded his gun clumsily but methodically, and, with it held ready, started back down Esmit Street; not running lest he slip on the ice, but not strolling, either. The street was still empty, and serene, and very long.

But as he neared the barricade, he was whistling again.

He was sound asleep in the room in the College when young Shevik, their best archer, came to rouse him up, whispering urgently, "Come on, Alterra, come on, wake up, you've got to come. . . ." Rolery had not come in during the night; the others who shared the room were all still asleep.

"What is it, what's wrong?" Agat mumbled, on his feet and struggling into his torn coat already.

"Come on to the Tower," was all Shevik said.

Agat followed him, at first with docility, then, waking up fully, with beginning understanding. They crossed the Square, gray in the first bleak light, ran up the circular stairs of the League Tower, and looked out over the city. The Land Gate was open.

The Gaal were gathered inside it, and going out of it. It was hard to see them in the half-light before sunrise; there were between a thousand and two thousand of them, the men watching with Agat guessed, but it was hard to tell. They were only shadowy blots of motion under the walls and on the snow. They strung out from the Gate in knots and groups, one after another disappearing under the walls and then reappearing farther away on the hillside, going at a jogtrot in a long irregular line, going south. Before they had gone far the dim light and the folds of the hill hid them; but before Agat stopped watching, the east had grown bright, and a cold radiance reached halfway up the sky.

The houses and the steep streets of the city lay very quiet in the morning light.

Somebody began to ring the bell, right over their heads in the tower there, a steady rapid clamor and clangor of bronze on bronze, bewildering. Hands over their ears, the men in the tower came running down, meeting other men and women halfway. They laughed and they shouted after Agat and caught at him, but he ran on down the rocking stairs, the insistent jubilation of the bell still hammering at him, and into the League Hall. In the big, crowded, noisy room where golden suns swam on the walls and the years and Years were told on golden dials, he searched for the alien, the stranger, his wife. He finally found her, and taking her hands he said, "They're gone, they're gone, they're gone . . ."

Then he turned and roared it with all the force of his lungs at everybody— "They're gone!"

They were all roaring at him and at one another, laughing and crying. After a minute he said to Rolery, "Come on with me—out to the Stack." Restless, exultant, bewildered, he wanted to be on the move, to get out into the city and make sure it was their own again. No one else had left the Square yet, and as they crossed the west barricade Agat drew his dartgun. "I had an adventure last night," he said to Rolery, and she, looking at the gaping rent in his coat, said, "I know."

"I killed it."

"A snowghoul?"

"Right."

"Alone?"

"Yes. Both of us, fortunately."

The solemn look on her face as she hurried along beside him made him laugh out loud with pleasure.

They came out onto the causeway, running out in the icy wind between the bright sky and the dark, foam-laced water.

The news of course had already been given, by the bell and by mind-speech, and the drawbridge of the Stack was lowered as soon as Agat set foot on the bridge. Men and women and little sleepy, fur-bundled children came running to meet them, with more shouts, questions, and embraces.

Behind the women of Landin, the women of Tevar hung back, afraid and unrejoicing. Agat saw Rolery going to one of these, a young woman with wild hair and dirt-smudged face. Most of them had hacked their hair short and looked unkempt and filthy, even the few hilf men who had stayed out at the Stack. A little disgusted by this grimy spot on his bright morning of victory, Agat spoke to Umaksuman, who had come out to gather his tribesmen together. They stood on the drawbridge, under the sheer wall of the black fort. Hilf men and women had collected around Umaksuman, and Agat lifted up his voice so they all could hear. "The Men of Tevar kept our walls side by side with the Men of Landin. They are welcome to stay with us or to go, to live with us or leave us, as they please. The gates of my city are open to you, all Winter long. You are free to go out them, but welcome within them!"

"I hear," the native said, bowing his fair head.

"But where's the Eldest, Wold? I wanted to tell him—"

Then Agat saw the ash-smeared faces and ragged heads with a new eye. They were in mourning. In understanding that, he remembered his own dead, his friends, his kinsmen; and the arrogance of triumph went out of him.

Umaksuman said, "The Eldest of my Kin went under the sea with his sons who died in Tevar. Yesterday he went. They were building the dawn-fire when they heard the bell and saw the Gaal going south."

"I would watch this fire," Agat said, asking Umaksuman's permission. The Tevaran hesitated, but an older man beside him said firmly, "Wold's daughter is this one's wife: he has clan right."

So they let him come, with Rolery and all that were left of her people, to a high terrace outside a gallery on the seaward side of the Stack. There on a pyre of broken wood the body of the old man lay, age-deformed and powerful, wrapped in a red cloth, death's color. A young child set the torch and the fire burnt red and yellow, shaking the air, paled by the cold early light of the sun. The tide was drawing out, grinding and thundering at the rocks below the sheer black walls. East over the hills of Askatevar Range and west over the sea the sky was clear, but northward a bluish dusk brooded: Winter.

Five thousand nights of Winter, five thousand days of it: the rest of their youth and maybe the rest of their lives.

Against that distant, bluish darkness in the north, no triumph showed up at all. The Gaal seemed a little scurry of vermin, gone already, fleeing before the true enemy, the true lord, the white lord of the Storms. Agat stood by Rolery in front of the sinking death-fire, in the high sea-beleaguered fort, and it seemed to him then that the old man's death and the young man's victory were the same thing. Neither grief nor pride had so much truth in them as did joy, the joy that trembled in the cold wind between sky and sea, bright and brief as fire. This was his fort, his city, his world; these were his people. He was no exile here.

"Come," he said to Rolery as the fire sank down to ashes, "come, let's go home."

city of illusions

1

Imagine darkness.

In the darkness that faces outward from the sun a mute spirit woke. Wholly involved in chaos, he knew no pattern. He had no language, and did not know the darkness to be night.

As unremembered light brightened about him he moved, crawling, running sometimes on all fours, sometimes pulling himself erect, but not going anywhere. He had no way through the world in which he was, for a way implies a beginning and an end. All things about him were tangled, all things resisted him. The confusion of his being was impelled to movement by forces for which he knew no name: terror, hunger, thirst, pain. Through the dark forest of things he blundered in silence till the night stopped him, a greater force. But when the light began again he groped on. When he broke out into the sudden broad sunlight of the Clearing he rose upright and stood a moment. Then he put his hands over his eyes and cried out aloud.

Weaving at her loom in the sunlit garden, Parth saw him at the forest's edge. She called to the others with a quick beat of her mind. But she feared nothing, and by the time the others came out of the house she had gone across the Clearing to the uncouth figure that crouched among the high, ripe grasses. As they approached they saw her put her hand on his shoulder and bend down to him, speaking softly.

She turned to them with a wondering look, saying, "Do you see his eyes . . . ?"

They were strange eyes, surely. The pupil was large; the iris, of a grayed amber color, was oval lengthwise so that the white of the eye did not show at all. "Like a cat," said Garra. "Like an egg all yolk," said Kai, voicing the slight distaste of uneasiness roused by that small, essential difference. Otherwise the stranger seemed only a man, under the mud and scratches and filth he had got over his face and naked body in his aimless struggle through the forest; at most he was a little paler-skinned than the brown people who now surrounded him, discussing him quietly as he crouched in the sunlight, cowering and shaking with exhaustion and fear.

Though Parth looked straight into his strange eyes no spark of human recognition met her there. He was deaf to their speech, and did not understand their gestures.

"Mindless or out of his mind," said Zove. "But also starving; we can remedy that." At this Kai and young Thurro half-led half-dragged the shambling fellow into the house. There they and Parth and Buckeye managed to feed and clean him, and got him onto a pallet, with a shot of sleep-dope in his veins to keep him there.

"Is he a Shing?" Parth asked her father.

"Are you? Am I? Don't be naive, my dear," Zove answered. "If I could answer that question I could set Earth free. However, I hope to find out if he's mad or sane or imbecile, and where he came from, and how he came by those yellow eyes. Have men taken to breeding with cats and falcons in humanity's degenerate old age? Ask Kretyan to come up to the sleeping-porches, daughter."

Parth followed her blind cousin Kretyan up the stairs to the shady, breezy balcony where the stranger slept. Zove and his sister Karell, called Buckeye, were waiting there. Both sat cross-legged and straight-backed, Buckeye playing with her patterning frame, Zove doing nothing at all: a brother and sister getting on in years, their broad, brown faces alert and very tranquil. The girls sat down near them without breaking the easy silence. Parth was a reddish-brown color with a flood of long, bright, black hair. She wore nothing but a pair of loose silvery breeches. Kretyan, a little older, was dark and frail; a red band covered her empty eyes and held her thick hair back. Like her mother she wore a tunic of delicately woven figured cloth. It was hot. Midsummer afternoon burned on the gardens below the balcony and out on the rolling fields of the Clearing. On every side, so close to this wing of the house as to shadow it with branches full of leaves and wings, so far in other directions as to be blued and hazed by distance, the forest surrounded them.

The four people sat still for quite a while, together and separate, unspeaking but linked. "The amber bead keeps slithering off into the Vastness pattern," Buckeye said with a smile, setting down her frame with its jewel-strung, crossing wires.

"All your beads end up in Vastness," her brother said. "An effect of your suppressed mysticism. You'll end up like our mother, see if you don't, able to see the patterns on an empty frame."

"Suppressed fiddlediddle," Buckeye remarked. "I never suppressed anything in my life."

"Kretyan," said Zove, "the man's eyelids move. He may be in a dreaming cycle."

The blind girl moved closer to the pallet. She reached out her hand, and Zove guided it gently to the stranger's forehead. They were all silent again. All listened. But only Kretyan could hear.

She lifted her bowed, blind head at last.

"Nothing," she said, her voice a little strained.

"Nothing?"

"A jumble—a void. He has no mind."

"Kretyan, let me tell you how he looks. His feet have walked, his hands have worked. Sleep and the drug relax his face, but only a thinking mind could use and wear a face into these lines."

"How did he look when he was awake?"

"Afraid," said Parth. "Afraid, bewildered."

"He may be an alien," Zove said, "not a Terran man, though how that could be— But he may think differently than we. Try once more, while he still dreams."

"I'll try, uncle. But I have no sense of any mind, of any true emotion or direction. A baby's mind is frightening but this . . . is worse—darkness and a kind of empty jumble—"

"Well, then keep out," Zove said easily. "No-mind is an evil place for mind to stay."

"His darkness is worse than mine," said the girl. "This is a ring, on his hand. . . ." She had laid her hand a moment on the man's, in pity or as if asking his unconscious pardon for her eavesdropping on his dreams.

"Yes, a gold ring without marking or design. It was all he wore on his body. And his mind stripped naked as his flesh. So the poor brute comes to us out of the forest—sent by whom?"

All the family of Zove's House except the little children gathered that night in the great hall downstairs, where high windows stood open to the moist night air. Starlight and the presence of trees and the sound of the brook all entered into the dimly lit room, so that between each person and the next, and between the words they said, there was a certain space for shadows, night-wind, and silence.

"Truth, as ever, avoids the stranger," the Master of the House said to them in his deep voice. "This stranger brings us a choice of several unlikelihoods. He may be an idiot born, who blundered here by chance; but then, who lost him? He may be a man whose brain has been damaged by accident, or tampered with by intent. Or he may be a Shing masking his mind behind a seeming amentia. Or he may be neither man nor Shing; but then, what is he? There's no proof or disproof for any of these notions. What shall we do with him?"

"See if he can be taught," said Zove's wife Rossa.

The Master's eldest son Metock spoke: "If he can be taught, then he is to be distrusted. He may have been sent here to be taught, to learn our ways, insights, secrets. The cat brought up by the kindly mice."

"I am not a kindly mouse, my son," the Master said. "Then you think him a Shing?"

"Or their tool."

"We're all tools of the Shing. What would you do with him?"

"Kill him before he wakes."

The wind blew faintly, a whippoorwill called out in the humid, starlit Clearing.

"I wonder," said the Oldest Woman, "if he might be a victim, not a tool. Perhaps the Shing destroyed his mind as punishment for something he did or thought. Should we then finish their punishment?"

"It would be truer mercy," Metock said.

"Death is a false mercy," the Oldest Woman said bitterly.

So they discussed the matter back and forth for some while, equably but with a gravity that included both moral concern and a heavier, more anxious care, never stated but only hinted at whenever one of them spoke the word *Shing*. Parth took no part in the discussion, being only fifteen, but she listened intently. She was bound by sympathy to the stranger and wanted him to live.

Ranya and Kretyan joined the group; Ranya had been running what physiological tests she could on the stranger, with Kretyan standing by to catch any mental response. They had little to report as yet, other than that the stranger's nervous system and the sense areas and basic motor capacity of his brain seemed normal, though his physical responses and motor skill compared with those of a year-old child, perhaps, and no stimulus of localities in the speech area had got any response at all. "A man's strength, a baby's coordination, an empty mind," Ranya said.

"If we don't kill him like a wild beast," said Buckeye, "then we shall have to tame him like a wild beast. . . ."

Kretyan's brother Kai spoke up. "It seems worth trying. Let some of us younger ones have charge of him; we'll see what we can do. We don't have to teach him the Inner Canons right away, after all. At least teaching him not to wet the bed comes first. . . . I want to know if he's human. Do you think he is, Master?"

Zove spread out his big hands. "Who knows? Ranya's blood-tests may tell us. I never heard that any Shing had yellow eyes, or any visible differences from Terran men. But if he is neither Shing nor human, what is he? No being from the Other Worlds that once were known has walked on Earth for twelve hundred years. Like you, Kai, I think I would risk his presence here among us out of pure curiosity. . . ."

So they let their guest live.

At first he was little trouble to the young people who looked after him. He regained strength slowly, sleeping much, sitting or lying quietly most of the time he was awake. Parth named him Falk, which in the dialect of the Eastern Forest meant "yellow," for his sallow skin and opal eyes.

One morning several days after his arrival, coming to an unpatterned stretch in the cloth she was weaving, she left her sunpowered loom to purr away by itself down in the garden and climbed up to the screened balcony where "Falk" was kept. He did not see her enter. He was sitting on his pallet gazing intently up at the haze-dimmed summer sky. The glare made his eyes water and he rubbed them vigorously with his hand, then seeing his hand stared at it, the back and the palm. He clenched and extended the fingers, frowning. Then he raised his face again to the white glare of the sun and slowly, tentative, reached his open hand up towards it.

"That's the sun, Falk," Parth said. "Sun. . . ."

"Sun," he repeated, gazing at it, centered on it, the void and vacancy of his being filled with the light of the sun and the sound of its name.

So his education began.

Parth came up from the cellars and passing through the Old Kitchen saw Falk hunched up in one of the window-bays, alone, watching the snow fall outside the grimy glass. It was a tennight now since he had struck Rossa and they had to lock him up till he calmed down. Ever since then he had been dour and would not speak. It was strange to see his man's face dulled and blunted by a child's sulky obstinate suffering. "Come on in by the fire, Falk," Parth said, but did not stop to wait for him. In the great hall by the fire she did wait a little, then gave him up and looked for something to raise her own low spirits. There was nothing to do; the snow fell, all the faces were too familiar, all the books told of things long ago and far away that were no longer true. All around the silent house and its fields lay the silent forest, endless, monotonous, indifferent; winter after winter, and she would never leave this house, for where was there to go, what was there to do . . . ?

On one of the empty tables Ranya had left her tëanb, a flat, keyed instrument,

said to be of Hainish origin. Parth picked out a tune in the melancholic
Stepped Mode of the Eastern Forest, then retuned the instrument to its native scale and began anew. She had no skill with the tëanb and found the notes
slowly, singing the words, spinning them out to keep the melody going as she
sought the next note.

> Beyond the sound of wind in trees
> beyond the storm-enshadowed seas,
> on stairs of sunlit stone the fair
> daughter of Airek stands . . .

She lost the tune, then found it again:

> . . . stands,
> silent, with empty hands.

A legend, who knew how old, from a world incredibly remote, its words and
tune had been part of man's heritage for centuries. Parth sang on very softly,
alone in the great firelit room, snow and twilight darkening the windows.

There was a sound behind her and she turned to see Falk standing there.
There were tears in his strange eyes. He said, "Parth—stop—"

"Falk, what's wrong?"

"It hurts me," he said, turning away his face that so clearly revealed the incoherent and defenseless mind.

"What a compliment to my singing," she teased him, but she was moved,
and sang no more. Later that night she saw Falk stand by the table on which
the tëanb lay. He raised his hand to it but dared not touch it, as if fearing to
release the sweet relentless demon within it that had cried out under Parth's
hands and changed her voice to music.

"My child learns faster than yours," Parth said to her cousin Garra, "but yours
grows faster. Fortunately."

"Yours is quite big enough," Garra agreed, looking down across the kitchen-
garden to the brookside where Falk stood with Garra's year-old baby on his
shoulder. The early summer afternoon sang with the shrilling of crickets and
gnats. Parth's hair clung in black locks to her cheeks as she tripped and reset
and tripped the catches of her loom. Above her patterning shuttle rose the
heads and necks of a row of dancing herons, silver thread on gray. At seventeen she was the best weaver among the women. In winter her hands were

always stained with the chemicals of which her threads and yarns were made and the dyes that colored them, and all summer she wove at her sunpowered loom the delicate and various stuff of her imagination.

"Little spider," said her mother nearby, "a joke is a joke. But a man is a man."

"And you want me to go along with Metock to Kathol's house and trade my heron-tapestry for a husband. I know," said Parth.

"I never said it—did I?" inquired her mother, and went weeding on away between the lettuce-rows.

Falk came up the path, the baby on his shoulder squinting in the glare and smiling benignly. He put her down on the grass and said, as if to a grown person, "It's hotter up here, isn't it?" Then turning to Parth with the grave candor that was characteristic of him he asked, "Is there an end to the forest, Parth?"

"So they say. The maps are all different. But that way lies the sea at last—and that way the prairie."

"Prairie?"

"Open lands, grasslands. Like the Clearing but going on for a thousand miles to the mountains."

"The mountains?" he asked, innocently relentless as any child.

"High hills, with snow on their tops all year. Like this." Pausing to reset her shuttle, Parth put her long, round, brown fingers together in the shape of a peak.

Falk's yellow eyes lit up suddenly, and his face became intense. "Below the white is blue, and below that the—the lines—the hills far away—"

Parth looked at him, saying nothing. A great part of all he knew had come straight from her, for she had always been the one who could teach him. The remaking of his life had been an effect and a part of the growth of her own. Their minds were very closely interwoven.

"I see it—have seen it. I remember it," the man stammered.

"A projection, Falk?"

"No. Not from a book. In my mind. I do remember it. Sometimes going to sleep I see it. I don't know its name: the Mountain."

"Can you draw it?"

Kneeling beside her he sketched quickly in the dust the outline of an irregular cone, and beneath it two lines of foothills. Garra craned to see the sketch, asking, "And it's white with snow?"

"Yes. It's as if I see it through something—a big window, big and high up. . . . Is it from your mind, Parth?" he asked a little anxiously.

"No," the girl said. "None of us in the house have ever seen high mountains. I think there are none this side of the Inland River. It must be far from here, very far." She spoke like one on whom a chill had fallen.

Through the edge of dreams a sawtooth sound cut, a faint jagged droning, eerie. Falk roused and sat up beside Parth; both gazed with strained, sleepy eyes northward where the remote sound throbbed and faded and first light paled the sky above the darkness of the trees. "An aircar," Parth whispered. "I heard one once before, long ago. . . ." She shivered. Falk put his arm around her shoulders, gripped by the same unease, the sense of a remote, uncomprehended, evil presence passing off there in the north through the edge of daylight.

The sound died away; in the vast silence of the forest a few birds piped up for the sparse dawn-chorus of autumn. Light in the east brightened. Falk and Parth lay back down in the warmth and the infinite comfort of each other's arms; only half wakened, Falk slipped back into sleep. When she kissed him and slipped away to go about the day's work he murmured, "Don't go yet . . . little hawk, little one. . . ." But she laughed and slipped away, and he drowsed on a while, unable as yet to come up out of the sweet lazy depths of pleasure and of peace.

The sun shone bright and level in his eyes. He turned over, then sat up yawning and stared into the deep, red-leaved branches of the oak that towered up beside the sleeping-porch. He became aware that in leaving Parth had turned on the sleepteacher beside his pillow; it was muttering softly away, reviewing Cetian number theory. That made him laugh, and the cold of the bright November morning woke him fully. He pulled on his shirt and breeches—heavy, soft, dark cloth of Parth's weaving, cut and fitted for him by Buckeye—and stood at the wooden rail of the porch looking across the Clearing to the brown and red and gold of the endless trees.

Fresh, still, sweet, the morning was as it had been when the first people on this land had waked in their frail, pointed houses and stepped outside to see the sun rise free of the dark forest. Mornings are all one, and autumn always autumn, but the years men count are many. There had been a first race on this land . . . and a second, the conquerors; both were lost, conquered and conquerors, millions of lives, all drawn together to a vague point on the horizon of past time. The stars had been gained, and lost again. Still the years went on, so many years that the forest of archaic times, destroyed utterly during the era when men had made and kept their history, had grown up again. Even in the obscure vast history of a planet the time it takes to make a forest counts. It takes a while. And not every planet can do it; it is no common effect, that tangling of the sun's first cool light in the shadow and complexity of innumerable wind-stirred branches. . . .

Falk stood rejoicing in it, perhaps the more intensely because for him behind this morning there were so few other mornings, so short a stretch of remembered days between him and the dark. He listened to the remarks made by a chickadee in the oak, then stretched, scratched his head vigorously, and went off to join the work and company of the house.

Zove's House was a rambling, towering, intermitted chalet-castle-farmhouse of stone and timber; some parts of it had stood a century or so, some longer. There was a primitiveness to its aspect: dark staircases, stone hearths and cellars, bare floors of tile or wood. But nothing in it was unfinished; it was perfectly fireproof and weatherproof; and certain elements of its fabric and function were highly sophisticated devices or machines—the pleasant, yellowish fusion-lights, the libraries of music, words and images, various automatic tools or devices used in house-cleaning, cooking, washing, and farmwork, and some subtler and more specialized instruments kept in workrooms in the East Wing. All these things were part of the house, built into it or along with it, made in it or in another of the forest houses. The machinery was heavy and simple, easy to repair; only the knowledge behind its power-source was delicate and irreplaceable.

One type of technological device was notably lacking. The library evinced a skill with electronics that had become practically instinctive; the boys liked to build little tellies to signal one another with from room to room. But there was no television, telephone, radio, telegraph transmitting or receiving beyond the Clearing. There were no instruments of communication over distance. There were a couple of homemade air-cushion sliders in the East Wing, but again they featured mainly in the boys' games. They were hard to handle in the woods, on wilderness trails. When people went to visit and trade at another house they went afoot, perhaps on horseback if the way was very long.

The work of the house and farm was light, no hard burden to anyone. Comfort did not rise above warmth and cleanliness, and the food was sound but monotonous. Life in the house had the drab levelness of communal existence, a clean, serene frugality. Serenity and monotony rose from isolation. Forty-four people lived here together. Kathol's House, the nearest, was nearly thirty miles to the south. Around the Clearing, mile after mile uncleared, unexplored, indifferent, the forest went on. The wild forest, and over it the sky. There was no shutting out the inhuman here, no narrowing man's life, as in the cities of earlier ages, to within man's scope. To keep anything at all of a

complex civilization intact here among so few was a singular and very perilous achievement, though to most of them it seemed quite natural: it was the
way one did; no other way was known. Falk saw it a little differently than did
the children of the house, for he must always be aware that he had come out
of that immense unhuman wilderness, as sinister and solitary as any wild
beast that roamed it, and that all he had learned in Zove's House was like a
single candle burning in a great field of darkness.

At breakfast—bread, goat's-milk cheese and brown ale—Metock asked him
to come with him to the deer-blinds for the day. That pleased Falk. The Elder Brother was a very skillful hunter, and he was becoming one himself; it
gave him and Metock, at last, a common ground. But the Master intervened:
"Take Kai today, my son. I want to talk with Falk."

Each person of the household had his own room for a study or workroom
and to sleep in in freezing weather; Zove's was small, high, and light, with
windows west and north and east. Looking across the stubble and fallow of
the autumnal fields to the forest, the Master said, "Parth first saw you there,
near that copper beech, I think. Five and a half years ago. A long time! Is it
time we talked?"

"Perhaps it is, Master," Falk said, diffident.

"It's hard to tell, but I guessed you to be about twenty-five when you first
came. What have you now of those twenty-five years?"

Falk held out his left hand a moment: "A ring," he said.

"And the memory of a mountain?"

"The memory of a memory." Falk shrugged. "And often, as I've told you, I
find for a moment in my mind the sound of a voice, or the sense of a motion,
a gesture, a distance. These don't fit into my memories of my life here with
you. But they make no whole, they have no meaning."

Zove sat down in the windowseat and nodded for Falk to do the same. "You
had no growing to do; your gross motor skills were unimpaired. But even
given that basis, you have learned with amazing quickness. I've wondered
if the Shing, in controlling human genetics in the old days and weeding out
so many as colonists, were selecting us for docility and stupidity, and if you
spring from some mutant race that somehow escaped control. Whatever you
were, you were a highly intelligent man. . . . And now you are one again. And
I should like to know what you yourself think about your mysterious past."

Falk was silent a minute. He was a short, spare, well-made man; his very
lively and expressive face just now looked rather somber or apprehensive,
reflecting his feelings as candidly as a child's face. At last, visibly summoning up his resolution, he said, "While I was studying with Ranya this past

summer, she showed me how I differ from the human genetic norm. It's only a twist or two of a helix . . . a very small difference. Like the difference between *wei* and *o*." Zove looked up with a smile at the reference to the Canon which fascinated Falk, but the younger man was not smiling. "However, I am unmistakably not human. So I may be a freak; or a mutant, accidental or intentionally produced; or an alien. I suppose most likely I am an unsuccessful genetic experiment, discarded by the experimenters. . . . There's no telling. I'd prefer to think I'm an alien, from some other world. It would mean that at least I'm not the only creature of my kind in the universe."

"What makes you sure there are other populated worlds?"

Falk looked up, startled, going at once with a child's credulity but a man's logic to the conclusion: "Is there reason to think the other Worlds of the League were destroyed?"

"Is there reason to think they ever existed?"

"So you taught me yourself, and the books, the histories—"

"You believe them? You believe all we tell you?"

"What else can I believe?" He flushed red. "Why would you lie to me?"

"We might lie to you day and night about everything, for either of two good reasons. Because we are Shing. Or because we think you serve them."

There was a pause. "And I might serve them and never know it," Falk said, looking down.

"Possibly," said the Master. "You must consider that possibility, Falk. Among us, Metock has always believed you to be a programmed mind, as they call it. —But all the same, he's never lied to you. None of us has, knowingly. The River Poet said a thousand years ago, 'In truth manhood lies. . . .'" Zove rolled the words out oratorically, then laughed. "Double-tongued, like all poets. Well, we've told you what truths and facts we know, Falk. But perhaps not all the guesses and the legends, the stuff that comes before the facts. . . ."

"How could you teach me those?"

"We could not. You learned to see the world somewhere else—some other world, maybe. We could help you become a man again, but we could not give you a true childhood. That, one has only once. . . ."

"I feel childish enough, among you," Falk said with a somber ruefulness.

"You're not childish. You are an inexperienced man. You are a cripple, because there *is* no child in you, Falk; you are cut off from your roots, from your source. Can you say that this is your home?"

"No," Falk answered, wincing. Then he said, "I have been very happy here."

The Master paused a little, but returned to his questioning. "Do you think our life here is a good one, that we follow a good way for men to go?"

"Yes."

"Tell me another thing. Who is our enemy?"

"The Shing."

"Why?"

"They broke the League of All Worlds, took choice and freedom from men, wrecked all man's works and records, stopped the evolution of the race. They are tyrants, and liars."

"But they don't keep us from leading our good life here."

"We're in hiding—we live apart, so that they'll let us be. If we tried to build any of the great machines, if we gathered in groups or towns or nations to do any great work together, then the Shing would infiltrate and ruin the work and disperse us. I tell you only what you told me and I believed, Master!"

"I know. I wondered if behind the fact you had perhaps sensed the . . . legend, the guess, the hope. . . ."

Falk did not answer.

"We hide from the Shing. Also we hide from what we were. Do you see that, Falk? We live well in the houses—well enough. But we are ruled utterly by fear. There was a time we sailed in ships between the stars, and now we dare not go a hundred miles from home. We keep a little knowledge, and do nothing with it. But once we used that knowledge to weave the pattern of life like a tapestry across night and chaos. We enlarged the chances of life. We did man's work."

After another silence Zove went on, looking up into the bright November sky: "Consider the worlds, the various men and beasts on them, the constellations of their skies, the cities they built, their songs and ways. All that is lost, lost to us, as utterly as your childhood is lost to you. What do we really know of the time of our greatness? A few names of worlds and heroes, a ragtag of facts we've tried to patch into a history. The Shing law forbids killing, but they killed knowledge, they burned books, and what may be worse, they falsified what was left. They slipped in the Lie, as always. We aren't sure of anything concerning the Age of the League; how many of the documents are forged? You must remember, you see, wherein the Shing are our Enemy. It's easy enough to live one's whole life without ever seeing one of them—knowingly; at most one hears an aircar passing by far away. Here in the forest they let us be, and it may be the same now all over the Earth, though we don't know. They let us be so long as we stay here, in the cage of our ignorance and the wilderness, bowing when they pass by above our heads. But they don't trust us. How could they, even after twelve hundred years? There is no trust in them, because there is no truth in them. They honor no compact, break any promise, perjure, betray, and lie inexhaustibly; and certain records from the time of the Fall of the League hint that they could mind-lie. It was the Lie that defeated all the races of the League and left us subject to the Shing. Remember that, Falk. Never believe the truth of anything the Enemy has said."

"I will remember, Master, if I ever meet the Enemy."

"You will not, unless you go to them."

The apprehensiveness in Falk's face gave way to a listening, still look. What he had been waiting for had arrived. "You mean leave the house," he said.

"You have thought of it yourself," Zove said as quietly.

"Yes, I have. But there is no way for me to go. I want to live here. Parth and I—"

He hesitated, and Zove struck in, incisive and gentle. "I honor the love grown between you and Parth, your joy and your fidelity. But you came here on the way to somewhere else, Falk. You are welcome here; you have always been welcome. Your partnership with my daughter must be childless; even so, I have rejoiced in it. But I do believe that the mystery of your being and your coming here is a great one, not lightly to be put aside; that you walk a way that leads on; that you have work to do. . . ."

"What work? Who can tell me?"

"What was kept from us and stolen from you, the Shing will have. That you can be sure of."

There was an aching, scathing bitterness in Zove's voice that Falk had never heard.

"Will those who speak no truth tell me the truth for the asking? And how will I recognize what I seek when I find it?"

Zove was silent a little while, and then said with his usual ease and control, "I cling to the notion, my son, that in you lies some hope for man. I do not like to give up that notion. But only you can seek your own truth; and if it seems to you that your way ends here, then that, perhaps, *is* the truth."

"If I go," Falk said abruptly, "will you let Parth go with me?"

"No, my son."

A child was singing down in the garden—Garra's four-year-old, turning inept somersaults on the path and singing shrill, sweet nonsense. High up, in the long wavering V of the great migrations, skein after skein of wild geese went over southward.

"I was to go with Metock and Thurro to fetch home Thurro's bride," Falk said. "We planned to go soon, before the weather changes. If I go, I'll go on from Ransifel House."

"In winter?"

"There are houses west of Ransifel, no doubt, where I can ask shelter if I need it."

He did not say and Zove did not ask why west was the direction he would go.

"There may be; I don't know. I don't know if they would give shelter to strangers as we do. If you go you will be alone, and must be alone. Outside this house there is no safe place for you on Earth."

He spoke, as always, absolutely truthfully . . . and paid the cost of truth in self-control and pain. Falk said with quick reassurance, "I know that, Master. It's not safety I'd regret—"

"I will tell you what I believe about you. I think you came from a lost world; I think you were not born on Earth. I think you came here, the first Alien to return in a thousand years or more, bringing us a message or a sign. The Shing stopped your mouth, and turned you loose in the forests so that none might say they had killed you. You came to us. If you go I will grieve and fear for you, knowing how alone you go. But I will hope for you, and for ourselves! If you had words to speak to men, you'll remember them, in the end. There must be a hope, a sign: we cannot go on like this forever."

"Perhaps my race was never a friend of mankind," Falk said, looking at Zove with his yellow eyes. "Who knows what I came here to do?"

"You'll find those who know. And then you'll do it. I don't fear it. If you serve the Enemy, so do we all: all's lost and nothing's to lose. If not, then you have what we men have lost: a destiny; and in following it you may bring hope to us all. . . ."

2

Zove had lived sixty years, Parth twenty; but she seemed, that cold afternoon in the Long Fields, old in a way no man could be old, ageless. She had no comfort from ideas of ultimate star-spanning triumph or the prevalence of truth. Her father's prophetic gift in her was only lack of illusion. She knew Falk was going. She said only, "You won't come back."

"I will come back, Parth."

She held him in her arms but she did not listen to his promise.

He tried to bespeak her, though he had little skill in telepathic communication. The only Listener in the house was blind Kretyan; none of them was adept at the nonverbal communication, mindspeech. The techniques of learning mindspeech had not been lost, but they were little practiced. The great virtue of that most intense and perfect form of communication had become its peril for men.

Mindspeech between two intelligences could be incoherent or insane, and could of course involve error, misbelief; but it could not be misused. Between thought and spoken word is a gap where intention can enter, the symbol be twisted aside, and the lie come to be. Between thought and sent-thought is no gap; they are one act. There is no room for the lie.

In the late years of the League, the tales and fragmentary records Falk had studied seemed to show, the use of mindspeech had been widespread and the telepathic skills very highly developed. It was a skill Earth had come to late, learning its techniques from some other race; the Last Art, one book called it. There were hints of troubles and upheavals in the government of the League of All Worlds, rising perhaps from that prevalence of a form of communication that precluded lying. But all that was vague and half-legendary, like all man's history. Certainly since the coming of the Shing and the downfall of the League, the scattered community of man had mistrusted trust and used the spoken word. A free man can speak freely, but a slave or fugitive must be able to hide truth and lie. So Falk had learned in Zove's House, and so it was that he had had little practice in the attunement of minds. But he tried now to bespeak Parth so she would know he was not lying: "Believe me, Parth, I will come back to you!"

But she wouldn't hear. "No, I won't mindspeak," she said aloud.

"Then you're keeping your thoughts from me."

"Yes, I am. Why should I give you my grief? What's the good of truth? If you had lied to me yesterday, I'd still believe that you were only going to Ransifel and would be back home in a tennight. Then I'd still have ten days and nights. Now I have nothing left, not a day, not an hour. It's all taken, all over. What good is truth?"

"Parth, will you wait for me one year?"

"No."

"Only a year—"

"A year and a day, and you'll return riding a silver steed to carry me to your kingdom and make me its queen. No, I won't wait for you, Falk. Why must I wait for a man who will be lying dead in the forest, or shot by Wanderers out on the prairie, or brainless in the City of the Shing, or gone off a hundred years to another star? What should I wait for? You needn't think I'll take another man. I won't. I'll stay here in my father's house. I'll dye black thread and weave black cloth to wear, black to wear and black to die in. But I won't wait for anyone, or anything. Never."

"I had no right to ask you," he said with the humility of pain—and she cried, "O Falk, I don't reproach you!"

They were sitting together on the slight slope above the Long Field. Goats and sheep grazed over the mile of fenced pasture between them and the forest. Yearling colts pranced and tagged around the shaggy mares. A gray November wind blew.

Their hands lay together. Parth touched the gold ring on his left hand. "A ring is a thing given," she said. "Sometimes I've thought, have you? that you may have had a wife. Think, if she was waiting for you. . . ." She shivered.

"What of it?" he said. "What do I care about what may have been, what I was? Why should I go from here? All that I am now is yours, Parth, came from you, your gift—"

"It was freely given," the girl said in tears. "Take it and go. Go on. . . ." They held each other, and neither would break free.

The house lay far behind hoar black trunks and intertangling leafless branches. The trees closed in behind the trail.

The day was gray and cool, silent except for the drone of wind through branches, a meaningless whisper without locality that never ceased. Metock led the way, setting a long easy pace. Falk followed and young Thurro came last. They were all three dressed light and warm in hooded shirt and breeches of an unwoven stuff called wintercloth, over which no coat was needed even in snow. Each carried a light backpack of gifts and trade-goods, sleeping-bag, enough dried concentrated food to see him through a month's blizzard. Buckeye, who had never left the house of her birth, had a great fear of perils and delays in the forest and had supplied their packs accordingly. Each wore a laser-beam gun; and Falk carried some extras—another pound or two of food; medicines, compass, a second gun, a change of clothing, a coil of rope; a little book given him two years ago by Zove—amounting in all to about fifteen pounds of stuff, his earthly possessions. Easy and tireless Metock loped on ahead, and ten yards or so behind he followed, and after him came Thurro. They went lightly, with little sound, and behind them the trees gathered motionless over the faint, leaf-strewn trail.

They would come to Ransifel on the third day. At evening of the second day they were in country different from that around Zove's House. The forest was more open, the ground broken. Gray glades lay along hillsides above brush-choked streams. They made camp in one of these open places, on a south-facing slope, for the north wind was blowing stronger with a hint of winter in it. Thurro brought armloads of dry wood while the other two cleared away the gray grass and piled up a rough hearth of stones. As they worked Metock said, "We crossed a divide this afternoon. The stream down there runs west. To the Inland River, finally."

Falk straightened up and looked westward, but the low hills rose up soon and the low sky closed down, leaving no distant view.

"Metock," he said, "I've been thinking there's no point in my going on to Ransifel. I may as well be on my way. There seemed to be a trail leading west along the big stream we crossed this afternoon. I'll go back and follow it."

Metock glanced up; he did not mindspeak, but his thought was plain enough: *Are you thinking of running back home?*

Falk did use mindspeech for his reply: "No, damn it, I'm not!"

"I'm sorry," the Elder Brother said aloud, in his grim, scrupulous way. He had not tried to hide the fact that he was glad to see Falk go. To Metock nothing mattered much but the safety of the house; any stranger was a threat, even the stranger he had known for five years, his hunting-companion and his sister's lover. But he went on, "They'll make you welcome at Ransifel. Why not start from there?"

"Why not from here?"

"Your choice." Metock worked a last rock into place, and Falk began to build up the fire. "If that was a trail we crossed, I don't know where it comes from or goes. Early tomorrow we'll cross a real path, the old Hirand Road. Hirand House was a long way west, a week on foot at least; nobody's gone there for sixty or seventy years. I don't know why. But the trail was still plain last time I came this way. The other might be an animal track, and lead you straying or leave you in a swamp."

"All right, I'll try the Hirand Road."

There was a pause, then Metock asked, "Why are you going west?"

"Because Es Toch is in the west."

The name seldom spoken sounded flat and strange out here under the sky. Thurro coming up with an armload of wood glanced around uneasily. Metock asked nothing more.

That night on the hillside by the campfire was Falk's last with those who were to him his brothers, his own people. Next morning they were on the trail again a little after sunrise, and long before noon they came to a wide, overgrown trace leading to the left off the path to Ransifel. There was a kind of gateway to it made by two great pines. It was dark and still under their boughs where they stopped.

"Come back to us, guest and brother," young Thurro said, troubled even in his bridegroom's self-absorption by the look of that dark, vague way Falk would be taking. Metock said only, "Give me your water-flask, will you," and in exchange gave Falk his own flask of chased silver. Then they parted, they going north and he west.

After he had walked a while Falk stopped and looked back. The others were out of sight; the Ransifel trail was already hidden behind the young trees and brush that overgrew the Hirand Road. The road looked as though it was used, if infrequently, but had not been kept up or cleared for many years. Around Falk nothing was visible but the forest, the wilderness. He stood alone under the shadows of the endless trees. The ground was soft with the fall of a thousand years; the great trees, pines and hemlocks, made the air dark and quiet. A fleck or two of sleet danced in the dying wind.

Falk eased the strap of his pack a bit and went on.

By nightfall it seemed to him that he had been gone from the house for a long, long time, that it was immeasurably far behind him, that he had always been alone.

His days were all the same. Gray winter light; a wind blowing; forest-clad hills and valleys, long slopes, brush-hidden streams, swampy lowlands. Though badly overgrown the Hirand Road was easy to follow, for it led in long straight shafts or long easy curves, avoiding the bogs and the heights. In the hills Falk realized it followed the course of some great ancient highway, for its way had been cut right through the hills, and two thousand years had not effaced it wholly. But the trees grew on it and beside it and all about it, pine and hemlock, vast holly-thickets on the slopes, endless stands of beech, oak, hickory, alder, ash, elm, all overtopped and crowned by the lordly chestnuts only now losing their last dark-yellow leaves, dropping their fat brown burrs along the path. At night he cooked the squirrel or rabbit or wild hen he had bagged from among the infinity of little game that scurried and flitted here in the kingdom of the trees; he gathered beechnuts and walnuts, roasted the chestnuts on his campfire coals. But the nights were bad. There were two evil dreams that followed him each day and always caught up with him by midnight. One was of being stealthily pursued in the darkness by a person he could never see. The other was worse. He dreamed that he had forgotten to bring something with him, something important, essential, without which he would be lost. From this dream he woke and knew that it was true: he was lost; it was himself he had forgotten. He would build up his fire then if it was not raining and would crouch beside it, too sleepy and dream-bemused to take up the book he carried, the Old Canon, and seek comfort in the words which declared that when all ways are lost the Way lies clear. A man all alone is a miserable thing. And he knew he was not even a man but at best a kind of half-being, trying to find his wholeness by setting out aimlessly to cross a continent under uninterested stars. The days were all the same, but they were a relief after the nights.

He was still keeping count of their number, and it was on the eleventh day from the crossroads, the thirteenth of his journey, that he came to the end of the Hirand Road. There had been a clearing, once. He found a way through great tracts of wild bramble and second-growth birch thickets to four crumbling black towers that stuck high up out of the brambles and vines and mummied thistles: the chimneys of a fallen house. Hirand was nothing now, a name. The road ended at the ruin.

He stayed around the fallen place a couple of hours, kept there simply by the bleak hint of human presence. He turned up a few fragments of rusted machinery, bits of broken pottery which outlive even men's bones, a scrap of rotted cloth which fell to dust in his hands. At last he pulled himself together and looked for a trail leading west out of the clearing. He came across a strange thing, a field a half-mile square covered perfectly level and smooth with some glassy substance, dark violet colored, unflawed. Earth was creeping over its edges and leaves and branches had scurfed it over, but it was unbroken, unscratched. It was as if the great level space had been flooded with melted amethyst. What had it been—a launching-field for some unimaginable vehicle, a mirror with which to signal other worlds, the basis of a force-field? Whatever it was, it had brought doom on Hirand. It had been a greater work than the Shing permitted men to undertake.

Falk went on past it and entered the forest, following no path now.

These were clean woods of stately, wide-aisled deciduous trees. He went on at a good pace the rest of that day, and the next morning. The country was growing hilly again, the ridges all running north-south across his way, and around noon, heading for what looked from one ridge like the low point of the next, he became embroiled in a marshy valley full of streams. He searched for fords, floundered in boggy watermeadows, all in a cold heavy rain. Finally as he found a way up out of the gloomy valley the weather began to break up, and as he climbed the ridge the sun came out ahead of him under the clouds and sent a wintry glory raying down among the naked branches, brightening them and the great trunks and the ground with wet gold. That cheered him; he went on sturdily, figuring to walk till day's end before he camped. Everything was bright now and utterly silent except for the drip of rain from twig-ends and the far-off wistful whistle of a chickadee. Then he heard, as in his dream, the steps that followed behind him to his left.

A fallen oak that had been an obstacle became in one startled moment a defense: he dropped down behind it and with drawn gun spoke aloud: "Come on out!"

For a long time nothing moved.

"Come out!" Falk said with the mindspeech, then closed to reception, for he was afraid to receive. He had a sense of strangeness; there was a faint, rank odor on the wind.

A wild boar walked out of the trees, crossed his tracks, and stopped to snuff the ground. A grotesque, magnificent pig, with powerful shoulders, razor back, trim, quick, filthy legs. Over snout and tusk and bristle, little bright eyes looked up at Falk.

"Aah, aah, aah, man, aah," the creature said, snuffling.

Falk's tense muscles jumped, and his hand tightened on the grip of his laser-pistol. He did not shoot. A wounded boar was hideously quick and dangerous. He crouched there absolutely still.

"Man, man," said the wild pig, the voice thick and flat from the scarred snout, "think to me. Think to me. Words are hard for me."

Falk's hand on the pistol shook now. Suddenly he spoke aloud: "Don't speak, then. I will not mindspeak. Go on, go your pig's way."

"Aah, aah, man, bespeak me!"

"Go or I will shoot." Falk stood up, his gun pointing steadily. The little bright hog-eyes watched the gun.

"It is wrong to take life," said the pig.

Falk had got his wits back and this time made no answer, sure that the beast understood no words. He moved the gun a little, recentered its aim, and said, "Go!" The boar dropped its head, hesitated. Then with incredible swiftness, as if released by a cord breaking, it turned and ran the way it had come.

Falk stood still a while, and when he turned and went on he kept his gun ready in his hand. His hand shook again, a little. There were old tales of beasts that spoke, but the people of Zove's House had thought them only tales. He felt a brief nausea and an equally brief wish to laugh out loud. "Parth," he whispered, for he had to talk to somebody, "I just had a lesson in ethics from a wild pig. . . . Oh, Parth, will I ever get out of the forest? Does it ever end?"

He worked his way on up the steepening, brushy slopes of the ridge. At the top the woods thinned out and through the trees he saw sunlight and the sky. A few paces more and he was out from under the branches, on the rim of a green slope that dropped down to a sweep of orchards and plow-lands and at last to a wide, clear river. On the far side of the river a herd of fifty or more cattle grazed in a long fenced meadow, above which hayfields and orchards rose steepening towards the tree-rimmed western ridge. A short way south of where Falk stood the river turned a little around a low knoll, over the shoulder of which, gilt by the low, late sun, rose the red chimneys of a house.

It looked like a piece of some other, golden age caught in that valley and overlooked by the passing centuries, preserved from the great wild disorder of the desolate forest. Haven, companionship, and above all, order: the work of man. A kind of weakness of relief filled Falk, at the sight of a wisp of smoke rising from those red chimneys. A hearthfire . . . He ran down the long hillside and through the lowest orchard to a path that wandered along beside the riverbank among scrub alder and golden willows. No living thing was to be seen except the red-brown cattle grazing across the water. The silence of peace filled the wintry, sunlit valley. Slowing his pace, he walked between kitchen-gardens to the nearest door of the house. As he came around the knoll the place rose up before him, walls of ruddy brick and stone reflecting in the quickened water where the river curved. He stopped, a little daunted, thinking he had best hail the house aloud before he went any farther. A movement in an open window just above the deep doorway caught his eye. As he stood half hesitant, looking up, he felt a sudden deep, thin pain sear through his chest just below the breastbone: he staggered and then dropped, doubling up like a swatted spider.

The pain had been only for an instant. He did not lose consciousness, but he could not move or speak.

People were around him; he could see them, dimly, through waves of non-seeing, but could not hear any voices. It was as if he had gone deaf, and his body was entirely numb. He struggled to think through this deprivation of the senses. He was being carried somewhere and could not feel the hands that carried him; a horrible giddiness overwhelmed him, and when it passed he had lost all control of his thoughts, which raced and babbled and chattered. Voices began to gabble and drone inside his mind, though the world drifted and ebbed dim and silent about him. Who are you are you where do you come from Falk going where going are you I don't know are you a man west going I don't know where the way eyes a man not a man . . . Waves and echoes and flights of words like sparrows, demands, replies, narrowing, overlapping, lapping, crying, dying away to a gray silence.

A surface of darkness lay before his eyes. An edge of light lay along it.

A table; the edge of a table. Lamp-lit, in a dark room.

He began to see, to feel. He was in a chair, in a dark room, by a long table on which a lamp stood. He was tied into the chair: he could feel the cord cut into the muscles of his chest and arms as he moved a little. Movement: a man sprang into existence at his left, another at his right. They were sitting like him, drawn up to the table. They leaned forward and spoke to each other across him. Their voices sounded as if they came from behind high walls a great way off, and he could not understand the words.

He shivered with cold. With the sensation of cold he came more closely in touch with the world and began to regain control of his mind. His hearing was clearer, his tongue was loosed. He said something which was meant to be, "What did you do to me?"

There was no answer, but presently the man on his left stuck his face quite close to Falk's and said loudly, "Why did you come here?"

Falk heard the words; after a moment he understood them; after another moment he answered. "For refuge. The night."

"Refuge from what?"

"Forest. Alone."

He was more and more penetrated with cold. He managed to get his heavy, clumsy hands up a little, trying to button his shirt. Below the straps that bound him in the chair, just below his breastbone was a little painful spot.

"Keep your hands down," the man on his right said out of the shadows. "It's more than programming, Argerd. No hypnotic block could stand up to penton that way."

The one on his left, slab-faced and quick-eyed, a big man, answered in a weak sibilant voice: "You can't say that—what do we know about their tricks? Anyhow, how can you estimate his resistance—what is he? You, Falk, where is this place you came from, Zove's House?"

"East. I left . . ." The number would not come to mind. "Fourteen days ago, I think."

How did they know the name of his house, his name? He was getting his wits back now, and did not wonder very long. He had hunted deer with Metock using hypodermic darts, which could make even a scratch-wound a kill. The dart that had felled him, or a later injection when he was helpless, had been some drug which must relax both the learned control and the primitive unconscious block of the telepathic centers of the brain, leaving him open to paraverbal questioning. They had ransacked his mind. At the idea, his feeling of coldness and sickness increased, complicated by helpless outrage. Why this violation? Why did they assume he would lie to them before they even spoke to him?

"Did you think I was a Shing?" he asked.

The face of the man on his right, lean, long-haired, bearded, sprang suddenly into the lamplight, the lips drawn back, and his open hand struck Falk across the mouth, jolting his head back and blinding him a moment with the shock. His ears rang; he tasted blood. There was a second blow and a third. The man kept hissing many times over. "You do not say that name, don't say it, you do not say it, you don't say it—"

Falk struggled helplessly to defend himself, to get free. The man on his left spoke sharply. Then there was silence for some while.

"I meant no harm coming here," Falk said at last, as steadily as he could through his anger, pain, and fear.

"All right," said the one on the left, Argerd, "go on and tell your little story. What did you mean in coming here?"

"To ask for a night's shelter. And ask if there's any trail going west."

"Why are you going west?"

"Why do you ask? I told you in mindspeech, where there's no lying. You know my mind."

"You have a strange mind," Argerd said in his weak voice. "And strange eyes. Nobody comes here for a night's shelter or to ask the way or for anything else. Nobody comes here. When the servants of the Others come here, we kill them. We kill toolmen, and the speaking beasts, and Wanderers and pigs and vermin. We don't obey the law that says it's wrong to take life—do we, Drehnem?"

The bearded one grinned, showing brownish teeth.

"We are men," Argerd said. "Men, free men, killers. What are you, with your half-mind and your owl's eyes, and why shouldn't we kill you? Are you a man?"

In the brief span of his memory, Falk had not met directly with cruelty or hate. The few people he had known had been, if not fearless, not ruled by fear; they had been generous and familiar. Between these two men he knew he was defenseless as a child, and the knowledge both bewildered and enraged him.

He sought some defense or evasion and found none. All he could do was speak the truth. "I don't know what I am or where I came from. I'm going to try to find out."

"Going where?"

He looked from Argerd to the other one, Drehnem. He knew they knew the answer, and that Drehnem would strike again if he said it.

"Answer!" the bearded one muttered, half rising and leaning forward.

"To Es Toch," Falk said, and again Drehnem struck him across the face, and again he took the blow with the silent humiliation of a child punished by strangers.

"This is no good; he's not going to say anything different from what we got from him under penton. Let him up."

"Then what?" said Drehnem.

"He came for a night's shelter; he can have it. Get up!"

The strap that held him into the chair was loosened. He got shakily onto his feet. When he saw the door and the black down-pitch of the stairs they forced him towards, he tried to resist and break free, but his muscles would not yet obey him. Drehnem arm-twisted him down into a crouch and pushed him through the doorway. The door slammed shut as he turned staggering to keep his footing on the stairs.

It was dark, black dark. The door was as if sealed shut, no handle on this side, no mote or hint of light coming under it, no sound. Falk sat down on the top step and put his head down on his arms.

Gradually the weakness of his body and the confusion in his mind wore off. He raised his head, straining to see. His night-vision was extraordinarily acute, a function, Ranya had long ago pointed out, of his large-pupiled, large-irised eyes. But only flecks and blurs of after-images tormented his eyes; he could see nothing, for there was no light. He stood up and step by step felt his slow way down the narrow, unseen descent.

Twenty-one steps, two, three—level. Dirt. Falk went slowly forward, one hand extended, listening.

Though the darkness was a kind of physical pressure, a constraint, deluding him constantly with the notion that if he only looked hard enough he would see, he had no fear of it in itself. Methodically, by pace and touch and hearing, he mapped out a part of the vast cellar he was in, the first room of a series which, to judge by echoes, seemed to go on indefinitely. He found his way directly back to the stairs, which because he had started from them were home base. He sat down, on the lowest step this time, and sat still. He was hungry and very thirsty. They had taken his pack, and left him nothing.

It's your own fault, Falk told himself bitterly, and a kind of dialogue began in his mind:

What did I do? Why did they attack me?

Zove told you: trust nobody. They trust nobody, and they're right.

Even someone who comes alone asking for help?

With your face—your eyes? When it's obvious even at a glance that you're not a normal human being?

All the same, they could have given me a drink of water, said the perhaps childish, still fearless part of his mind.

You're damned lucky they didn't kill you at sight, his intellect replied, and got no further answer.

All the people of Zove's House had of course got accustomed to Falk's looks, and guests were rare and circumspect, so that he had never been forced into particular awareness of his physical difference from the human norm. It had seemed so much less of a difference and barrier than the amnesia and ignorance that had isolated him so long. Now for the first time he realized that a stranger looking into his face would not see the face of a man.

The one called Drehnem had been afraid of him, and had struck him because he was afraid and repelled by the alien, the monstrous, the inexplicable.

It was only what Zove had tried to tell him when he had said with such grave and almost tender warning, "You must go alone, you can only go alone."

There was nothing for it, now, but sleep. He curled up as well as he could on the bottom step, for the dirt floor was damp, and closed his eyes on the darkness.

Some time later in timelessness he was awakened by the mice. They ran about making a faint tiny scrabble, a zigzag scratch of sound across the black, whispering in very small voices very close to the ground, "It is wrong to take life it is wrong to take life hello heeellllooo don't kill us don't kill."

"I will!" Falk roared and all the mice were still.

It was hard to go to sleep again; or perhaps what was hard was to be sure whether he was asleep or awake. He lay and wondered whether it was day or night; how long they would leave him here and if they meant to kill him, or use that drug again until his mind was destroyed, not merely violated; how long it took thirst to change from discomfort to torment; how one might go about catching mice in the dark without trap or bait; how long one could stay alive on a diet of raw mouse.

Several times, to get a vacation from his thoughts, he went exploring again. He found a great up-ended vat or tun and his heart leaped with hope, but it rang hollow: splintered boards near the bottom scratched his hands as he groped around it. He could find no other stairs or doors in his blind explorations of the endless unseen walls.

He lost his bearings finally and could not find the stairs again. He sat on the ground in the darkness and imagined rain falling, out in the forest of his lonely journeying, the gray light and the sound of rain. He spoke in his mind all he could remember of the Old Canon, beginning at the beginning:

> *The way that can be gone*
> *is not the eternal Way. . . .*

His mouth was so dry after a while that he tried to lick the damp dirt floor for its coolness; but to the tongue it was dry dust. The mice scuttled up quite close to him sometimes, whispering.

Far away down long corridors of darkness bolts clashed and metal clanged, a bright piercing clangor of light. Light—

Vague shapes and shadows, vaultings, arches, vats, beams, openings, bulked and loomed into dim reality about him. He struggled to his feet and made his way, unsteady but running, towards the light.

It came from a low doorway, through which, when he got close, he could see an upswell of ground, treetops, and the rosy sky of evening or morning, which dazzled his eyes like a midsummer noon. He stopped inside the door because of that dazzlement, and because a motionless figure stood just outside.

"Come out," said the weak, hoarse voice of the big man, Argerd.

"Wait. I can't see yet."

"Come out. And keep going. Don't even turn your head, or I'll bum it off your neck."

Falk came into the doorway, then hesitated again. His thoughts in the dark served some purpose now. If they did let him go, he had thought, it would mean that they were afraid to kill him.

"Move!"

He took the chance. "Not without my pack," he said, his voice faint in his dry throat.

"This is a laser."

"You might as well use it. I can't get across the continent without my own gun."

Now it was Argerd who hesitated. At last, his voice going up almost into a shriek, he yelled to someone: "Gretten! Gretten! Bring the stranger's stuff down here!"

A long pause. Falk stood in the darkness just inside the door, Argerd, motionless, just outside it. A boy came running down the grassy slope visible from the door, tossed Falk's pack down and disappeared.

"Pick it up," Argerd ordered; Falk came out into the light and obeyed. "Now get going."

"Wait," Falk muttered, kneeling and looking hastily through the disarrayed, unstrapped pack. "Where's my book?"

"Book?"

"The Old Canon. A handbook, not electronic—"

"You think we'd let you leave here with that?"

Falk stared. "Don't you people recognize the Canons of Man when you see them? What did you take it for?"

"You don't know and won't find out what we know, and if you don't get going I'll burn your hands off. Get up and go on, go straight on, get moving!" The shrieking note was in Argerd's voice again, and Falk realized he had nearly driven him too far. As he saw the look of hate and fear in Argerd's heavy, intelligent face the contagion of it caught him, and hastily he closed and shouldered his pack, walked past the big man and started up the grassy rise from the door of the cellars. The light was that of evening, a little past sunset. He walked towards it. A fine elastic strip of pure suspense seemed to connect the back of his head to the nose of the laser-pistol Argerd held, stretching out, stretching out as he walked on. Across a weedy lawn, across a bridge of loose planks over the river, up a path between the pastures and then between orchards. He reached the top of the ridge. There he glanced back for one moment, seeing the hidden valley as he had first seen it, full of a golden evening light, sweet and peaceful, high chimneys over the sky-reflecting river. He hastened on into the gloom of the forest, where it was already night.

Thirsty and hungry, sore and downhearted, Falk saw his aimless journey through the Eastern Forest stretching on ahead of him with no vague hope, now, of a friendly hearth somewhere along the way to break the hard, wild monotony. He must not seek a road but avoid all roads, and hide from men and their dwelling-places like any wild beast. Only one thing cheered him up a bit, besides a creek to drink from and some travel-ration from his pack, and that was the thought that though he had brought his trouble on himself, he had not knuckled under. He had bluffed the moral boar and the brutal man on their own ground, and got away with it. That did hearten him; for he knew himself so little that all his acts were also acts of self-discovery, like those of a boy, and knowing that he lacked so much he was glad to learn that at least he was not without courage.

After drinking and eating and drinking again he went on, in a broken moonlight that sufficed his eyes, till he had put a mile or so of broken country between himself and the house of Fear, as he thought of the place. Then, worn out, he lay down to sleep at the edge of a little glade, building no fire or shelter, lying gazing up at the moon-washed winter sky. Nothing broke the silence but now and again the soft query of a hunting owl. And this desolation seemed to him restful and blessed after the scurrying, voice-haunted, lightless prison-cellar of the house of Fear.

As he pushed on westward through the trees and the days, he kept no more count of one than of the other. Time went on; and he went on.

The book was not the only thing he had lost; they had kept Metock's silver water-flask, and a little box, also of silver, of disinfectant salve. They could only have kept the book because they wanted it badly, or because they took it for some kind of code or mystery. There was a period when the loss of it weighed unreasonably on him, for it seemed to him it had been his one true link with the people he had loved and trusted, and once he told himself, sitting by his fire, that next day he would turn back and find the house of Fear again and get his book. But he went on, next day. He was able to go west, with compass and sun for guides, but could never have refound a certain place in the vastness of these endless hills and valleys of the forest. Not Argerd's hidden valley; not the Clearing where Parth might be weaving in the winter sunlight, either. It was all behind him, lost.

Maybe it was just as well that the book was gone. What would it have meant to him here, that shrewd and patient mysticism of a very ancient civilization, that quiet voice speaking from amidst forgotten wars and disasters? Mankind had outlived disaster; and he had outrun mankind. He was too far away, too much alone. He lived entirely now by hunting; that slowed his daily pace. Even when game is not gun-shy and is very plentiful, hunting is not a business one can hurry. Then one must clean and cook the game, and sit and suck the bones beside the fire, full-bellied for a while and drowsy in the winter cold; and build up a shelter of boughs and bark against the rain; and sleep; and next day go on. A book had no place here, not even that old Canon of Unaction. He would not have read it; he was ceasing, really, to think. He hunted and ate and walked and slept, silent in the forest silence, a gray shadow slipping westward through the cold wilderness.

The weather was more and more often bleak. Often lean feral cats, beautiful little creatures with their pied or striped fur and green eyes, waited within sight of his campfire for the leavings of his meat, and came forward with sly, shy fierceness to carry off the bones he tossed them: their rodent prey was scarce now, hibernating through the cold. No beasts since the house of Fear had spoken to or bespoken him. The animals in the lovely, icy, lowland woods he was now crossing had never been tampered with, had never seen or scented man, perhaps. And as it fell farther and farther behind him he saw its strangeness more clearly, that house hidden in its peaceful valley, its very foundations alive with mice that squeaked in human speech, its people revealing a great knowledge, the truth-drug, and a barbaric ignorance. The Enemy had been there.

That the Enemy had ever been here was doubtful. Nobody had ever been here. Nobody ever would be. Jays screamed in the gray branches. Frost-rimed brown leaves crackled underfoot, the leaves of hundreds of autumns. A tall stag looked at Falk across a little meadow, motionless, questioning his right to be there.

"I won't shoot you. Bagged two hens this morning," Falk said.

The stag stared at him with the lordly self-possession of the speechless, and walked slowly off. Nothing feared Falk, here. Nothing spoke to him. He thought that in the end he might forget speech again and become as he had been, dumb, wild, unhuman. He had gone too far away from men and had come where the dumb creatures ruled and men had never come.

At the meadow's edge he stumbled over a stone, and on hands and knees read weatherworn letters carved in the half-buried block: CK O.

Men had come here; had lived here. Under his feet, under the icy, hummocky terrain of leafless bush and naked tree, under the roots, there was a city. Only he had come to the city a millennium or two too late.

3

The days of which Falk kept no count had grown very short, and had perhaps already passed Year's End, the winter solstice. Though the weather was not so bad as it might have been in the years when the city had stood aboveground, this being a warmer meteorological cycle, still it was mostly bleak and gray. Snow fell often, not so thickly as to make the going hard, but enough to make Falk know that if he had not had his wintercloth clothing and sleeping-bag from Zove's House he would have suffered more than mere discomfort from the cold. The north wind blew so unwearyingly bitter that he tended always to be pushed a little southwards by it, picking the way south of west when there was a choice, rather than face into the wind.

In the dark wretched afternoon of one day of sleet and rain he came slogging down a south-trending stream-valley, struggling through thick brambly undergrowth over rocky, muddy ground. All at once the brush thinned out, and he was brought to a sudden halt. Before him lay a great river, dully shining, peppered with rain. Rainy mist half obscured the low farther bank. He was awed by the breadth, the majesty of this great silent westward drive of dark water under the low sky. At first he thought it must be the Inland River, one of the few landmarks of the inner continent known by rumor to the eastern Forest Houses; but it was said to run south marking the western edge of the kingdom of the trees. Surely this was a tributary of the Inland River, then. He followed it, for that reason, and because it kept him out of the high hills and provided both water and good hunting; moreover it was pleasant to have, sometimes, a sandy shore for a path, with the open sky overhead instead of the everlasting leafless darkness of branches. So following the river he went west by south through a rolling land of woods, all cold and still and colorless in the grip of winter.

One of these mornings by the river he shot a wild hen, so common here in their squawking, low-flying flocks that they provided his staple meat. He had only winged the hen and it was not dead when he picked it up. It beat its

wings and cried in its piercing bird-voice, "Take—life—take—life—take—"
Then he wrung its neck.

The words rang in his mind and would not be silenced. Last time a beast
had spoken to him he had been on the threshold of the house of Fear. Somewhere in these lonesome gray hills there were, or had been, men: a group in
hiding like Argerd's household, or savage Wanderers who would kill him
when they saw his alien eyes, or toolmen who would take him to their Lords
as a prisoner or slave. Though at the end of it all he might have to face those
Lords, he would find his own way to them, in his own time, and alone. Trust
no one, avoid men! He knew his lesson now. Very warily he went that day,
alert, so quiet that often the water-birds that thronged the shores of the river
rose up startled almost under his feet.

He crossed no path and saw no sign at all that any human beings dwelt or
ever came near the river. But towards the end of the short afternoon a flock
of the bronze-green wild fowl rose up ahead of him and flew out over the
water clucking and calling together in a gabble of human words.

A little farther on he stopped, thinking he had scented woodsmoke on the
wind.

The wind was blowing upriver to him, from the northwest. He went with
double caution. Then as the night rose up among the tree-trunks and blurred
the dark reaches of the river, far ahead of him along the brushy, willow-tangled
shore a light glimmered, and vanished, and shone again.

It was not fear or even caution that stopped him now, standing in his tracks
to stare at that distant glimmer. Aside from his own solitary campfire this was
the first light he had seen lit in the wilderness since he had left the Clearing.
It moved him very strangely, shining far off there across the dusk.

Patient in his fascination as any forest animal, he waited till full night
had come and then made his way slowly and noiselessly along the riverbank,
keeping in the shelter of the willows, until he was close enough to see the
square of a window yellow with firelight and the peak of the roof above it,
snow-rimmed, pine-overhung. Huge over black forest and river Orion stood.
The winter night was very cold and silent. Now and then a fleck of dry snow
dislodged from a branch drifted down towards the black water and caught
the sparkle of the firelight as it fell.

Falk stood gazing at the light in the cabin. He moved a little closer, then
stood motionless for a long time.

The door of the cabin creaked open, laying down a fan of gold on the
dark ground, stirring up powdery snow in puffs and spangles. "Come on

into the light," said a man standing, vulnerable, in the golden oblong of the doorway.

Falk in the darkness of the thickets put his hand on his laser, and made no other movement.

"I mindheard you. I'm a Listener. Come on. Nothing to fear here. Do you speak this tongue?"

Silence.

"I hope you do, because I'm not going to use mindspeech. There's nobody here but me, and you," said the quiet voice. "I hear without trying, as you hear with your ears, and I still hear you out there in the dark. Come and knock if you want to get under a roof for a while."

The door closed.

Falk stood still for some while. Then he crossed the few dark yards to the door of the little cabin, and knocked.

"Come in!"

He opened the door and entered into warmth and light.

An old man, gray hair braided long down his back, knelt at the hearth building up the fire. He did not turn to look at the stranger, but laid his firewood methodically. After a while he said aloud in a slow chant,

> *"I alone am confused*
> *confused*
> *desolate*
> *Oh, like the sea*
> *adrift*
> *Oh, with no harbor*
> *to anchor in. . . ."*

The gray head turned at last. The old man was smiling; his narrow, bright eyes looked sidelong at Falk.

In a voice that was hoarse and hesitant because he had not spoken any words for a long time, Falk replied with the next verse of the Old Canon:

> *"Everyone is useful*
> *only I alone*
> *am inept*
> *outlandish.*
> *I alone differ from others*

but I seek
the milk of the Mother
the Way. . . ."

"Ha ha ha!" said the old man. "Do you, Yellow Eyes? Come on, sit down, here by the hearth. Outlandish, yes yes, yes indeed. You are outlandish. How far out the land?—who knows? How long since you washed in hot water? Who knows? Where's the damned kettle? Cold tonight in the wide world, isn't it, cold as a traitor's kiss. Here we are; fill that from the pail there by the door, will you, then I'll put it on the fire, so. I'm a Thurro-dowist, you know what that is I see, so you won't get much comfort here. But a hot bath's hot, whether the kettle's boiled with hydrogen fusion or pine-knots, eh? Yes, you really are outlandish, lad, and your clothes could use a bath too, weatherproof though they may be. What's that?—rabbits? Good. We'll stew 'em tomorrow with a vegetable or two. Vegetables are one thing you can't hunt down with a laser-gun. And you can't store cabbages in a backpack. I live alone here, my lad, alone and all alonio. Because I am a great, a very great, the greatest Listener, I live alone, and talk too much. I wasn't born here, like a mushroom in the woods; but with other men I never could shut out the minds, all the buzz and grief and babble and worry and all the different ways they went, as if I had to find my way through forty different forests all at once. So I came to live alone in the real forest with only the beasts around me, whose minds are brief and still. No death lies in their thoughts. And no lies lie in their thoughts. Sit down; you've been a long time coming here and your legs are tired."

Falk sat down on the wooden hearth-bench. "I thank you for your hospitality," he said, and was about to name himself when the old man spoke: "Never mind. I can give you plenty of good names, good enough for this part of the world. Yellow Eyes, Outlander, Guest, anything will do. Remember I'm a Listener, not a paraverbalist. I get no words or names. I don't want them. That there was a lonely soul out there in the dark, I knew, and I know how my lighted window shone into your eyes. Isn't that enough, more than enough? I don't need names. And my name is All-Alonio. Right? Now pull up to the fire, get warm."

"I'm getting warm," Falk said.

The old man's gray braid flipped across his shoulders as he moved about, quick and frail, his soft voice running on; he never asked a real question, never paused for an answer. He was fearless and it was impossible to fear him.

Now all the days and nights of journeying through the forest drew together and were behind Falk. He was not camping: he had come to a place. He need not think at all about the weather, the dark, the stars and beasts and trees. He could sit stretching out his legs to a bright hearth, could eat in company with another, could bathe in front of the fire in a wooden tub of hot water. He did not know which was the greatest pleasure, the warmth of that water washing dirt and weariness away, or the warmth that washed his spirit here, the absurd elusive vivid talk of the old man, the miraculous complexity of human conversation after the long silence of the wilderness.

He took as true what the old man told him, that he was able to sense Falk's emotions and perceptions, that he was a mindhearer, an empath. Empathy was to telepathy somewhat as touch to sight, a vaguer, more primitive, and more intimate sense. It was not subject to fine learned control to the degree that telepathic communication was; conversely, involuntary empathy was not uncommon even among the untrained. Blind Kretyan had trained herself to mindhear, having the gift by nature. But it was no such gift as this. It did not take Falk long to make sure that the old man was in fact constantly aware to some degree of what his visitor was feeling and sensing. For some reason this did not bother Falk, whereas the knowledge that Argerd's drug had opened his mind to telepathic search had enraged him. It was the difference in intent; and more.

"This morning I killed a hen," he said, when for a little the old man was silent, warming a rough towel for him by the leaping fire. "It spoke, in this speech. Some words of . . . of the Law. Does that mean anyone is near here, who teaches language to the beasts and fowls?" He was not so relaxed, even getting out of the hot bath, as to say the Enemy's name—not after his lesson in the house of Fear.

By way of answer the old man merely asked a question for the first time: "Did you eat the hen?"

"No," said Falk, toweling himself dry in the firelight that reddened his skin to the color of new bronze. "Not after it talked. I shot the rabbits instead."

"Killed it and didn't eat it? Shameful, shameful." The old man cackled, then crowed like a wild cock. "Have you no reverence for life? You must understand the Law. It says you mustn't kill unless you must kill. And hardly even then. Remember that in Es Toch. Are you dry? Clothe your nakedness, Adam of the Yaweh Canon. Here, wrap this around you, it's no fine artifice like your own clothes, it's only deerhide tanned in piss, but at least it's clean."

"How do you know I'm going to Es Toch?" Falk asked, wrapping the soft leather robe about him like a toga.

"Because you're not human," said the old man. "And remember, I am the Listener. I know the compass of your mind, outlandish as it is, whether I will or no. North and south are dim; far back in the east is a lost brightness; to the west there lies darkness, a heavy darkness. I know that darkness. Listen. Listen to me, because I don't want to listen to you, dear guest and blunderer. If I wanted to listen to men talk I wouldn't live here among the wild pigs like a wild pig. I have this to say before I go to sleep. Now listen: There are not very many of the Shing. That's a great piece of news and wisdom and advice. Remember it, when you walk in the awful darkness of the bright lights of Es Toch. Odd scraps of information may always come in handy. Now forget the east and west, and go to sleep. You take the bed. Though as a Thurro-dowist I am opposed to ostentatious luxury, I applaud the simpler pleasures of existence, such as a bed to sleep on. At least, every now and then. And even the company of a fellow man, once a year or so. Though I can't say I miss them as you do. Alone's not lonely. . . ." And as he made himself a sort of pallet on the floor he quoted in an affectionate singsong from the Younger Canon of his creed: "'I am no more lonely than the mill brook, or a weathercock, or the north star, or the south wind, or an April shower, or a January thaw, or the first spider in a new house. . . . I am no more lonely than the loon on the pond that laughs so loud, or than Walden Pond itself. . . .'"

Then he said, "Good night!" and said no more. Falk slept that night the first sound, long sleep he had had since his journey had begun.

He stayed two more days and nights in the riverside cabin, for his host made him very welcome and he found it hard to leave the little haven of warmth and company. The old man seldom listened and never answered questions, but in and out of his ever-running talk certain facts and hints glanced and vanished. He knew the way west from here and what lay along it—for how far, Falk could not make sure. Clear to Es Toch, it seemed; perhaps even beyond? What lay beyond Es Toch? Falk himself had no idea, except that one would come eventually to the Western Sea, and on beyond that to the Great Continent, and eventually on around again to the Eastern Sea and the forest. That the world was round, men knew, but there were no maps left. Falk had a notion that the old man might have been able to draw one; but where he got such a notion he scarcely knew, for his host never spoke directly of anything he himself had done or seen beyond this little river-bank clearing.

"Look out for the hens, downriver," said the old man, apropos of nothing, as they breakfasted in the early morning before Falk set off again. "Some of them can talk. Others can listen. Like us, eh? I talk and you listen. Because, of course, I am the Listener and you are the Messenger. Logic be damned. Remember about the hens, and mistrust those that sing. Roosters are less to be mistrusted; they're too busy crowing. Go alone. It won't hurt you. Give my regards to any Princes or Wanderers you may meet, particularly Henstrella. By the way, it occurred to me in between your dreams and my own last night that you've walked quite enough for exercise and might like to take my slider. I'd forgotten I had it. I'm not going to use it, since I'm not going anywhere, except to die. I hope someone comes by to bury me, or at least drag me outside for the rats and ants, once I'm dead. I don't like the prospect of rotting around in here after all the years I've kept the place tidy. You can't use a slider in the forest, of course, now there are no trails left worth the name, but if you want to follow the river it'll take you along nicely. And across the Inland River too, which isn't easy to cross in the thaws, unless you're a catfish. It's in the lean-to if you want it. I don't."

The people of Kathol's House, the settlement nearest Zove's, were Thurrodowists; Falk knew that one of their principles was to get along, as long as they could do so sanely and unfanatically, without mechanical devices and artifices. That this old man, living much more primitively than they, raising poultry and vegetables because he did not even own a gun to hunt with, should possess a bit of fancy technology like a slider, was queer enough to make Falk for the first time look up at him with a shadow of doubt.

The Listener sucked his teeth and cackled. "You never had any reason to trust me, outlandish laddie," he said. "Nor I you. After all, things can be hidden from even the greatest Listener. Things can be hidden from a man's own mind, can't they, so that he can't lay the hands of thought upon them. Take the slider. My traveling days are done. It carries only one, but you'll be going alone. And I think you've got a longer journey to make than you can ever go by foot. Or by slider, for that matter."

Falk asked no question, but the old man answered it:

"Maybe you have to go back home," he said.

Parting from him in the icy, misty dawn under the ice-furred pines, Falk in regret and gratitude offered his hand as to the Master of a House; so he had been taught to do; but as he did so he said, "*Tiokioi . . .*"

"What name do you call me, Messenger?"

"It means . . . it means *father*, I think. . . ." The word had come on his lips unbidden, incongruous. He was not sure he knew its meaning, and had no idea what language it was in.

"Goodbye, poor trusting fool! You will speak the truth and the truth will set you free. Or not, as the case may be. Go all alonio, dear fool; it's much the best way to go. I will miss your dreams. Goodbye, goodbye. Fish and visitors stink after three days. Goodbye!"

Falk knelt on the slider, an elegant little machine, black paristolis inlaid with a three-dimensional arabesque of platinum wire. The ornamentation all but concealed the controls, but he had played with a slider at Zove's House, and after studying the control-arcs a minute he touched the left arc, moved his finger along it till the slider had silently risen about two feet, and then with the right arc sent the little craft slipping over the yard and the riverbank till it hovered above the scummy ice of the backwater below the cabin. He looked back then to call goodbye, but the old man had already gone into the cabin and shut the door. And as Falk steered his noiseless craft down the broad dark avenue of the river, the enormous silence closed in around him again.

Icy mist gathered on the wide curves of water ahead of him and behind him, and hung among the gray trees on either bank. Ground and trees and sky were all gray with ice and fog. Only the water, sliding along a little slower than he slid airborne above it, was dark. When on the following day snow began to fall the flakes were dark against the sky, white against the water before they vanished, endlessly falling and vanishing in the endless current.

This mode of travel was twice the speed of walking, and safer and easier— too easy indeed, monotonous, hypnotic. Falk was glad to come ashore when he had to hunt or to make camp. Waterbirds all but flew into his hands, and animals coming down to the shore to drink glanced at him as if he on the slider were a crane or heron skimming past, and offered their defenseless flanks and chests to his hunting gun. Then all he could do was skin, hack up, cook, eat, and build himself a little shelter for the night against snow or rain with boughs or bark and the up-ended slider as a roof; he slept, at dawn ate cold meat left from last night, drank from the river, and went on. And on.

He played games with the slider to beguile the eventless hours: taking her up above fifteen feet where wind and air-layers made the air-cushion unreliable and might tilt the slider right over unless he compensated instantly with the controls and his own weight; or forcing her down into the water in a wild commotion of foam and spray so she slapped and skipped and skittered all over the river, bucking like a colt. A couple of falls did not deter Falk from his amusements. The slider was set to hover at one foot if uncontrolled, and all he had to do was clamber back on, get to shore and make a fire if he had got chilled, or if not, simply go on. His clothes were weatherproof, and in any case the river could get him little wetter than the rain. The wintercloth kept him fairly warm; he was never really warm. His little campfires were strictly cookingfires. There was not enough dry wood in the whole Eastern Forest, probably, for a real fire, after the long days of rain, wet snow, mist, and rain again.

He became adept at slapping the slider downriver in a series of long, loud fish-leaps, diagonal bounces ending in a whack and a jet of spray. The noisiness of the process pleased him sometimes as a break in the smooth silent monotony of sliding along above the water between the trees and hills. He came whacking around a bend, banking his curves, with delicate flicks of the control-arcs, then braked to a sudden soundless halt in mid-air. Far ahead down the steely-shining reach of the river a boat was coming towards him.

Each craft was in full view of the other; there was no slipping past in secret behind screening trees. Falk lay flat on the slider, gun in hand, and steered down the right bank of the river, up at ten feet so he had height advantage on the people in the boat.

They were coming along easily with one little triangular sail set. As they drew nearer, though the wind was blowing downriver, he could faintly hear the sound of their singing.

They came still nearer, paying no heed to him, still singing.

As far back as his brief memory went, music had always both drawn him and frightened him, filling him with a kind of anguished delight, a pleasure too near torment. At the sound of a human voice singing he felt most intensely that he was not human, that this game of pitch and time and tone was alien to him, not a thing forgotten but a thing new to him, beyond him. But by that strangeness it drew him, and now unconsciously he slowed the slider to listen. Four or five voices sang, chiming and parting and interweaving in a more artful harmony than any he had heard. He did not understand the words. All the forest, the miles of gray water and gray sky, seemed to listen with him in intense, uncomprehending silence.

The song died away, chiming and fading into a little gust of laughter and talk. The slider and the boat were nearly abreast now, separated by a hundred yards or more. A tall, very slender man erect in the stern hailed Falk, a clear voice ringing easily across the water. Again he caught none of the words. In the steely winter light the man's hair and the hair of the four or five others in the boat shone fulvous gold, all the same, as if they were all of one close kin, or one kind. He could not see the faces clearly, only the red-gold hair, the slender figures bending forward to laugh and beckon. He could not make sure how many there were. For a second, one face was distinct, a woman's face, watching him across the moving water and the wind. He had slowed the slider to a hover, and the boat too seemed to rest motionless on the river.

"Follow us," the man called again, and this time, recognizing the language, Falk understood. It was the old League tongue, Galaktika. Like all Foresters, Falk had learned it from tapes and books, for the documents surviving from the Great Age were recorded in it, and it served as a common speech among men of different tongues. The forest dialect was descended from Galaktika, but had grown far from it over a thousand years, and by now differed even from House to House. Travelers once had come to Zove's House from the coast of the Eastern Sea, speaking a dialect so divergent that they had found it easier to speak Galaktika with their hosts, and only then had Falk heard it used as a living tongue; otherwise it had only been the voice of a sound-book, or the murmur of the sleepteacher in his ear in the dark of a winter morning. Dreamlike and archaic it sounded now in the clear voice of the steersman. "Follow us, we go to the city!"

"To what city?"

"Our own," the man called, and laughed.

"The city that welcomes the traveler," another called; and another, in the tenor that had rung so sweetly in their singing, spoke more softly: "Those that mean no harm find no harm among us." And a woman called as if she smiled as she spoke, "Come out of the wilderness, traveler, and hear our music for a night."

The name they called him meant traveler, or messenger.

"Who are you?" he asked.

Wind blew and the broad river ran. The boat and the airboat hovered motionless amid the flow of air and water, together and apart as if in an enchantment.

"We are men."

With that reply the charm vanished, blown away like a sweet sound or fragrance in the wind from the east. Falk felt again a maimed bird struggle in his hands crying out human words in its piercing unhuman voice: now as then a chill went through him, and without hesitation, without decision, he touched the silver arc and sent the slider forward at full speed.

No sound came to him from the boat, though now the wind blew from them to him, and after a few moments, when hesitation had had time to catch up with him, he slowed his craft and looked back. The boat was gone. There was nothing on the broad dark surface of the water, clear back to the distant bend.

After that Falk played no more loud games, but went on as swiftly and silently as he might; he lit no fire at all that night, and his sleep was uneasy. Yet something of the charm remained. The sweet voices had spoken of a city, *elonaae* in the ancient tongue, and drifting downriver alone in mid-air and mid-wilderness Falk whispered the word aloud. Elonaae, the Place of Man: myriads of men gathered together, not one house but thousands of houses, great dwelling-places, towers, walls, windows, streets and the open places where streets met, the trading-houses told of in books where all the ingenuities of men's hands were made and sold, the palaces of government where the mighty met to speak together of the great works they did, the fields from which ships shot out across the years to alien suns: had Earth ever borne so wonderful a thing as the Places of Man?

They were all gone now. There remained only Es Toch, the Place of the Lie. There was no city in the Eastern Forest. No towers of stone and steel and crystal crowded with souls rose up from among the swamps and alder-groves, the rabbit-warrens and deer-trails, the lost roads, the broken, buried stones.

Yet the vision of a city remained with Falk almost like the dim memory of something he had once known. By that he judged the strength of the lure, the illusion which he had blundered safely through, and he wondered if there would be more such tricks and lures as he went on always westward, towards their source.

The days and the river went on, flowing with him, until on one still gray afternoon the world opened slowly out and out into an awesome breadth, an immense plain of muddy waters under an immense sky: the confluence of the Forest River with the Inland River. It was no wonder they had heard of the Inland River even in the deep ignorance of their isolation hundreds of miles back east in the Houses: it was so huge even the Shing could not hide it. A vast and shining desolation of yellow-gray waters spread from the last crowns and islets of the flooded forest on and on west to a far shore of hills. Falk soared like one of the river's low-flying blue herons over the meetingplace of the waters. He landed on the western bank and was, for the first time in his memory, out of the forest.

To north, west, and south lay rolling land, clumped with many trees, full of brush and thickets in the lowlands, but an open country, wide open. Falk with easy self-delusion looked west, straining his eyes to see the mountains. This open land, the prairie, was believed to be very wide, a thousand miles perhaps; but no one in Zove's House really knew.

He saw no mountains, but that night he saw the rim of the world where it cut across the stars. He had never seen a horizon. His memory was all encircled with a boundary of leaves, of branches. But out here nothing was between him and the stars, which burned from the Earth's edge upwards in a huge bowl, a dome built of black patterned with fire. And beneath his feet the circle was completed; hour by hour the tilting horizon revealed the fiery patterns that lay eastward and beneath the Earth. He spent half the long winter night awake, and was awake again when that tilting eastern edge of the world cut across the sun and daylight struck from outer space across the plains.

That day he went on due west by the compass, and the next day, and the next. No longer led by the meanderings of the river, he went straight and fast. Running the slider was no such dull game as it had been over the water; here above uneven ground it bucked and tipped at each drop and rise unless he was very alert every moment at the controls. He liked the vast openness of sky and prairie, and found loneliness a pleasure with so immense a domain to be alone in. The weather was mild, a calm sunlit spell of late winter. Thinking back to the forest he felt as if he had come out of stifling, secret darkness into light and air, as if the prairies were one enormous Clearing. Wild red cattle in herds of tens of thousands darkened the far plains like cloud-shadows. The ground was everywhere dark, but in places misted faintly with green where the first tiny double-leaved shoots of the hardiest grasses were opening; and above and below the ground was a constant scurrying and burrowing of little beasts, rabbits, badgers, coneys, mice, feral cats, moles, stripe-eyed arcturies, antelope, yellow yappers, the pests and pets of fallen civilizations. The huge sky whirred with wings. At dusk along the rivers flocks of white cranes settled, the water between the reeds and leafless cottonwoods mirroring their long legs and long uplifted wings.

Why did men no longer journey forth to see their world? Falk wondered, sitting by his campfire that burned like a tiny opal in the vast blue vault of the prairie twilight. Why did such men as Zove and Metock hide in the woods, never once in their lives coming out to see the wide splendor of the Earth? He now knew something that they, who had taught him everything, did not know: that a man could see his planet turn among the stars. . . .

Next day under a lowering sky and through a cold wind from the north he went on, guiding the slider with a skill soon become habit. A herd of wild cattle covered half the plains south of his course, every one of the thousands and thousands of them standing facing the wind, white faces lowered in front of shaggy red shoulders. Between him and the first ranks of the herd for a mile the long gray grass bowed under the wind, and a gray bird flew towards him, gliding with no motion of its wings. He watched it, wondering at its straight gliding flight—not quite straight, for it turned without a wingbeat to intercept his course. It was coming very fast, straight at him. Abruptly he was alarmed, and waved his arm to frighten the creature away, then threw himself down flat and veered the slider, too late. The instant before it struck he saw the blind featureless head, the glitter of steel. Then the impact, a shriek of exploding metal, a sickening backward fall. And no end to the falling.

4

"Kessnokaty's old woman says it's going to snow," his friend's voice murmured near him. "We should be ready, if there comes a chance for us to run away."

Falk did not reply but sat listening with sharpened hearing to the noises of the camp: voices in a foreign tongue, distance-softened; the dry sound of somebody nearby scraping a hide; the thin bawl of a baby; the snapping of the tentfire.

"Horressins!" someone outside summoned him, and he got up promptly, then stood still. In a moment his friend's hand was on his arm and she guided him to where they wanted him, the communal fire in the center of the circle of tents, where they were celebrating a successful hunt by roasting a whole bull. A shank of beef was shoved into his hands. He sat down on the ground and began to eat. Juices and melted fat ran down his jaws but he did not wipe them off. To do so was beneath the dignity of a Hunter of the Mzurra Society of the Basnasska Nation. Though a stranger, a captive, and blind, he was a Hunter, and was learning to comport himself as such.

The more defensive a society, the more conformist. The people he was among walked a very narrow, a tortuous and cramped Way, across the broad free plains. So long as he was among them he must follow all the twistings of their ways exactly. The diet of the Basnasska consisted of fresh half-raw beef, raw onions, and blood. Wild herdsmen of the wild cattle, like wolves they culled the lame, the lazy and unfit from the vast herds, a lifelong feast of meat, a life with no rest. They hunted with hand-lasers and warded strangers from their territory with bombirds like the one that had destroyed Falk's slider, tiny impact-missiles programmed to home in on anything that contained a fusion element. They did not make or repair these weapons themselves, and handled them only after purifications and incantations; where they obtained them Falk had not found out, though there was occasional mention of a yearly pilgrimage, which might be connected with the weapons. They had no agriculture and no domestic animals; they were illiterate and did not know, except perhaps through certain myths and hero-legends, any of the history of humankind. They informed Falk that he had not come out of the forest, because the forest was inhabited only by giant white snakes. They practiced a monotheistic religion whose rituals involved mutilation, castration and human sacrifice.

It was one of the outgrowth-superstitions of their complex creed that had induced them to take Falk alive and make him a member of the tribe. Normally, since he carried a laser and thus was above slave-status, they would have cut out his stomach and liver to examine for auguries, and then let the women hack him up as they pleased. However, a week or two before his capture an old man of the Mzurra Society had died. There being no as-yet-unnamed infant in the tribe to receive his name, it was given to the captive, who, blinded, disfigured, and only conscious at intervals, still was better than nobody; for so long as Old Horressins kept his name his ghost, evil like all ghosts, would return to trouble the ease of the living. So the name was taken from the ghost and given to Falk, along with the full initiations of a Hunter, a ceremony which included whippings, emetics, dances, the recital of dreams, tattooing, antiphonal free-association, feasting, sexual abuse of one woman by all the males in turn, and finally nightlong incantations to The God to preserve the new Horressins from harm. After this they left him on a horsehide rug in a cowhide tent, delirious and unattended, to die or recover, while the ghost of Old Horressins, nameless and powerless, went whining away on the wind across the plains.

The woman, who, when he had first recovered consciousness, had been busy bandaging his eyes and looking after his wounds, also came whenever she could to care for him. He had only seen her when for brief moments in the semi-privacy of his tent he could lift the bandage which her quick wits had provided him when he was first brought in. Had the Basnasska seen those eyes of his open, they would have cut out his tongue so he could not name his own name, and then burned him alive. She had told him this, and other matters he needed to know about the Nation of the Basnasska; but not much about herself. Apparently she had not been with the tribe very much longer than himself; he gathered that she had been lost on the prairie, and had joined the tribe rather than starve to death. They were willing to accept another she-slave for the use of the men, and she had proved skillful at doctoring, so they let her live. She had reddish hair, her voice was very soft, her name was Estrel. Beyond this he knew nothing about her; and she had not asked him anything at all about himself, not even his name.

He had escaped lightly, all things considered. Paristolis, the Noble Matter of ancient Cetian science, would not explode nor take fire, so the slider had not blown up under him, though its controls were wrecked. The bursting missile had chewed the left side of his head and upper body with fine shrapnel, but Estrel was there with the skill and a few of the materials of medicine. There was no infection; he recuperated fast, and within a few days of his blood-christening as Horressins he was planning escape with her.

But the days went on and no chances came. A defensive society: a wary, jealous people, all their actions rigidly scheduled by rite, custom, and tabu. Though each Hunter had his tent, women were held in common and all a man's doings were done with other men; they were less a community than a club or herd, interdependent members of one entity. In this effort to attain security, independence and privacy of course were suspect; Falk and Estrel had to snatch at any chance to talk for a moment. She did not know the forest dialect, but they could use Galaktika, which the Basnasska spoke only in a pidgin form.

"The time to try," she said once, "might be during a snowstorm, when the snow would hide us and our tracks. But how far could we get on foot in a blizzard? You've got a compass; but the cold . . ."

Falk's wintercloth clothing had been confiscated, along with everything else he possessed, even the gold ring he had always worn. They had left him one gun: that was integral with his being a Hunter and could not be taken from him. But the clothes he had worn so long now covered the bony ribs and shanks of the Old Hunter Kessnokaty and he had his compass only because Estrel had got it and hidden it before they went through his pack. He and she were well enough clothed in Basnasska buckskin shirts and leggings, with boots and parkas of red cowhide; but nothing was adequate shelter from one of the prairie blizzards, with their hard subfreezing winds, except walls, roof, and a fire.

"If we can get across into Samsit territory, just a few miles west of here, we could hole up in an Old Place I know there and hide till they give up looking. I thought of trying it before you came. But I had no compass and was afraid of getting lost in the storm. With a compass, and a gun, we might make it. . . . We might not."

"If it's our best chance," Falk said, "we'll take it."

He was not quite so naive, so hopeful and easily swayed, as he had been before his capture. He was a little more resistant and resolute. Though he had suffered at their hands he had no special grudge against the Basnasska; they had branded him once and for all down both his arms with the blue tattoo-slashes of their kinship, branding him as a barbarian, but also as a man. That was all right. But they had their business, and he had his. The hard individual will developed in him by his training in the Forest House demanded that he get free, that he get on with his journey, with what Zove had called *man's work*. These people were not going anywhere, nor did they come from anywhere, for they had cut their roots in the human past. It was not only the extreme precariousness of his existence among the Basnasska that made him impatient to get out; it was also a sense of suffocation, of being cramped and immobilized, which was harder to endure than the bandage that blanked his vision.

That evening Estrel stopped by his tent to tell him that it had begun to snow, and they were settling their plan in whispers when a voice spoke at the flap of the tent. Estrel translated quietly: "He says, 'Blind Hunter, do you want the Red Woman tonight?'" She added no explanation. Falk knew the rules and etiquette of sharing the women around; his mind was busy with the matter of their talk, and he replied with the most useful of his short list of Basnasska words—"Mieg!"—no.

The male voice said something more imperative. "If it goes on snowing, tomorrow night, maybe," Estrel murmured in Galaktika. Still thinking, Falk did not answer. Then he realized she had risen and gone, leaving him alone in the tent. And after that he realized that she was the Red Woman, and that the other man had wanted her to copulate with.

He could simply have said Yes instead of No; and when he thought of her cleverness and gentleness towards him, the softness of her touch and voice, and the utter silence in which she hid her pride or shame, then he winced at his failure to spare her, and felt himself humiliated as her fellow man, and as a man.

"We'll go tonight," he said to her next day in the drifted snow beside the Women's Lodge. "Come to my tent. Let a good part of the night pass first."

"Kokteky has told me to come to his tent tonight."

"Can you slip away?"

"Maybe."

"Which tent is Kokteky's?"

"Behind the Mzurra Society Lodge to the left. It has a patched place over the flap."

"If you don't come I'll come get you."

"Another night there might be less danger—"

"And less snow. Winter's getting on; this may be the last big storm. We'll go tonight."

"I'll come to your tent," she said with her unarguing, steady submissiveness.

He had left a slit in his bandage through which he could dimly see his way about, and he tried to see her now; but in the dull light she was only a gray shape in grayness.

In the late dark of that night she came, quiet as the windblown snow against the tent. They each had ready what they had to take. Neither spoke. Falk fastened his oxhide coat, pulled up and tied the hood, and bent to unseal the doorflap. He started aside as a man came pushing in from outside, bent double to clear the low gap—Kokteky, a burly shaven-headed Hunter, jealous of his status and his virility. "Horressins! The Red Woman—" he began, then saw her in the shadows across the embers of the fire. At the same moment he saw how she and Falk were dressed, and their intent. He backed up to close off the doorway or to escape from Falk's attack, and opened his mouth to shout. Without thought, reflex-quick and certain, Falk fired his laser at pointblank range, and the brief flick of mortal light stopped the shout in the Basnasska's mouth, burnt away mouth and brain and life in one moment, in perfect silence.

Falk reached across the embers, caught the woman's hand, and led her over the body of the man he had killed into the dark.

Fine snow on a light wind sifted and whirled, taking their breaths with cold. Estrel breathed in sobs. His left hand holding her wrist and his right his gun, Falk set off west among the scattered tents, which were barely visible as slits and webs of dim orange. Within a couple of minutes even these were gone, and there was nothing at all in the world but night and snow.

Hand-lasers of Eastern Forest make had several settings and functions: the handle served as a lighter, and the weapon-tube converted to a not very efficient flashlight. Falk set his gun to give a glow by which they could read the compass and see the next few steps ahead, and they went on, guided by the mortal light.

On the long rise where the Basnasska winter-camp stood the wind had thinned the snowcover, but as they went on, unable to pick their course ahead, the compass West their one guideline in the confusion of the snowstorm that mixed air and ground into one whirling mess, they got onto lower land. There were four- and five-foot drifts through which Estrel struggled gasping like a spent swimmer in high seas. Falk pulled out the rawhide drawstring of his hood and tied it around his arm, giving her the end to hold, and then went ahead, making her a path. Once she fell and the tug on the line nearly pulled him down; he turned and had to seek for a moment with the light before he saw her crouching in his tracks, almost at his feet. He knelt, and in the wan, snowstreaked sphere of light saw her face for the first time clearly. She was whispering, "This is more than I bargained for. . . ."

"Get your breath a while. We're out of the wind in this hollow."

They crouched there together in a tiny bubble of light, around which hundreds of miles of wind-driven snow hurtled in darkness over the plains.

She whispered something which at first he did not understand: "Why did you kill the man?"

Relaxed, his senses dulled, drawing up resources of strength for the next stage of their slow, hard escape, Falk made no response. Finally with a kind of grin he muttered, "What else . . . ?"

"I don't know. You had to."

Her face was white and drawn with strain; he paid no attention to what she said. She was too cold to rest there, and he got to his feet, pulling her up with him. "Come on. It can't be much farther to the river."

But it was much farther. She had come to his tent after some hours of darkness, as he thought of it—there was a word for *hours* in the forest tongue, though its meaning was imprecise and qualitative, since a people without business and communication across time and space have no use for timepieces—and the winter night had still a long time to run. They went on, and the night went on.

As the first gray began to leaven the whirling black of the storm they struggled down a slope of frozen tangled grass and shrubs. A mighty groaning bulk rose up straight in front of Falk and plunged off into the snow. Somewhere nearby they heard the snorting of another cow or bull, and then for a minute the great creatures were all about them, white muzzles and wild liquid eyes catching the light, the driven snow hillocky and bulking with flanks and shaggy shoulders. Then they were through the herd, and came down to the bank of the little river that separated Basnasska from Samsit territory. It was fast, shallow, unfrozen. They had to wade, the current tugging at their feet over loose stones, pulling at their knees, icily rising till they struggled waist-deep through burning cold. Estrel's legs gave way under her before they were clear across. Falk hauled her up out of the water and through the ice-crusted reedbeds of the west bank, and then again crouched down by her in blank exhaustion among the snowmounded bushes of the overhanging shore. He switched off his lightgun. Very faint, but very large, a stormy day was gaining on the dark.

"We have to go on, we've got to have a fire."

She did not reply.

He held her in his arms against him. Their boots and leggings and parkas from the shoulders down were frozen stiff already. The woman's face, bowed against his arm, was deathly white.

He spoke her name, trying to rouse her. "Estrel! Estrel, come on. We can't stay here. We can get on a little farther. It won't be so hard. Come on, wake up, little one, little hawk, wake up. . . ." In his great weariness he spoke to her as he had used to speak to Parth, at daybreak, a long time ago.

She obeyed him at last, struggling to her feet with his help, getting the line into her frozen gloves, and step by step following him across the shore, up the low bluffs, and on through the tireless, relentless, driving snow.

They kept along the rivercourse, going south, as she had told him they would do when they had planned their run. He had no real hope they could find anything in this spinning whiteness, as featureless as the night storm had been. But before long they came to a creek tributary to the river they had crossed, and turned up it, rough going, for the land was broken. They struggled on. It seemed to Falk that by far the best thing to do would be to lie down and fall asleep, and he was only unable to do this because there was someone who was counting on him, someone a long way off, a long time ago, who had sent him on a journey; he could not lie down, for he was accountable to someone. . . .

There was a croaking whisper in his ear, Estrel's voice. Ahead of them a clump of high cottonwood boles loomed like starving wraiths in the snow, and Estrel was tugging at his arm. They began to stumble up and down the north side of the snow-choked creek just beyond the cottonwoods, searching for something. "A stone," she kept saying, "a stone," and though he did not know why they needed a stone, he searched and scrabbled in the snow with her. They were both crawling on hands and knees when at last she came on the landmark she was after, a snowmounded block of stone a couple of feet high.

With her frozen gloves she pushed away the dry drifts from the east side of the block. Incurious, listless with fatigue, Falk helped her. Their scraping bared a metal rectangle, level with the curiously level ground. Estrel tried to open it. A hidden handle clicked, but the edges of the rectangle were frozen shut. Falk spent his last strength straining to lift the thing, till finally he came to his wits and unsealed the frozen metal with the heatbeam in the handle of his gun. Then they lifted up the door and looked down a neat steep set of stairs, weirdly geometric amidst this howling wilderness, to a shut door.

"It's all right," his companion muttered, and going down the stairs— crawling backwards, as on a ladder, because she could not trust her legs—she pushed the door open, and then looked up at Falk. "Come on!" she said.

He came down, pulling the trapdoor to above him as she directed. It was abruptly utterly dark, and crouching on the steps Falk hastily pressed the stud of his handgun for light. Below him Estrel's white face glimmered. He came down and followed her in the door, into a place that was very dark and very big, so big his light could only hint at the ceiling and the nearer walls. It was silent, and the air was dead, flowing past them in a faint unchanging draft.

"There should be wood over here," Estrel's soft, strain-hoarsened voice said somewhere to his left. "Here. We need a fire; help me with this. . . ."

Dry wood was stacked in high piles in a corner near the entrance. While he got a blaze going, building it up inside a circle of blackened stones nearer the center of the cavern, Estrel crept off into some farther corner and returned dragging a couple of heavy blankets. They stripped and rubbed down, then huddled in the blankets, inside their Basnasska sleep-rolls, up close to the fire. It burned hot as if in a chimney, drawn up by a high draft that also carried off the smoke. There was no warming the great room or cave, but the firelight and heat relaxed and cheered them. Estrel got dried meat out of her bag, and they munched as they sat, though their lips were sore with frostbite and they were too tired to be hungry. Gradually the warmth of the fire began to soak into their bones.

"Who else has used this place?"

"Anyone that knows of it, I suppose."

"There was a mighty house here once, if this was the cellar," Falk said, looking into the shadows that flickered and thickened into impenetrable black at a distance from the fire, and thinking of the great basements under the house of Fear.

"They say there was a whole city here. It goes on a long way from the door, they say. I don't know."

"How did you know of it—are you a Samsit woman?"

"No."

He asked no further, recalling the code; but presently she said in her submissive way, "I am a Wanderer. We know many places like this, hiding places. . . . I suppose you've heard of the Wanderers."

"A little," said Falk, stretching out and looking across the fire at his companion. Tawny hair curled about her face as she sat huddled in the shapeless bag, and a pale jade amulet at her throat caught the firelight.

"They know little of us in the forest."

"No Wanderers came as far east as my house. What was told of them there fits the Basnasska better—savages, hunters, nomads." He spoke sleepily, laying his head down on his arm.

"Some Wanderers might be called savages. Others not. The Cattle-Hunters are all savages and know nothing beyond their own territories, these Bas-nasska and Samsit and Arksa. We go far. We go east to the forest, and south to the mouth of the Inland River, and west over the Great Mountains and the Western Mountains even to the sea. I myself have seen the sun set in the sea, behind the chain of blue isles that lies far off the coast, beyond the drowned valleys of California, earthquake-whelmed. . . ." Her soft voice had slipped into the cadence of some archaic chant or plaint. "Go on," Falk murmured, but she was still, and before long he was fast asleep. For a while she watched his sleeping face. At last she pushed the embers together, whispered a few words as if in prayer to the amulet chained around her neck, and curled down to sleep across the fire from him.

When he woke she was making a stand of bricks over the fire to support a kettle filled with snow. "It looks like late afternoon outside," she said, "but it could be morning, or noon for that matter. The storm's as thick as ever. They can't track us. And if they did, still they couldn't get in this place. . . . This kettle was in the cache with the blankets. And there's a bag of dried peas. We'll do well enough here." The hard, delicate face turned to him with a faint smile. "It's dark, though. I don't like the thick walls and the dark."

"It's better than bandaged eyes. Though you saved my life with that ban-dage. Blind Horressins was better off than dead Falk." He hesitated and then asked, "What moved you to save me?"

She shrugged, still with the faint, reluctant smile. "Fellow prisoners . . . They always say Wanderers are clever at ruses and disguises. Did you not hear them call me Fox Woman? Let me look at those hurts of yours. I brought my bag of tricks."

"Are Wanderers all good healers, too?"

"We have certain skills."

"And you know the Old Tongue; you have not forgotten man's old way, like the Basnasska."

"Yes, we all know Galaktika. Look there, the rim of your ear was frostbit-ten yesterday. Because you took the tie from your hood for me to hold."

"I can't look at it," Falk said amiably, submitting to her doctoring. "I don't need to, usually."

As she dressed the still unhealed cut on his left temple she glanced once or twice sidelong at his face, and at last she ventured: "There are many Foresters with such eyes as yours, no doubt."

"None."

Evidently the code prevailed. She asked nothing, and he, having resolved to confide in no one, volunteered nothing. But his own curiosity got the better of him and he said, "They don't frighten you, then, these cat-eyes?"

"No," she answered in her quiet way. "You frightened me only once. When you shot—so fast—"

"He would have raised the whole camp."

"I know, I know. But we carry no guns. You shot so quick, I was frightened—it was like a terrible thing I saw once, when I was a child. A man who killed another with a gun, quicker than thought, like that. He was one of the Razes."

"Razes?"

"Oh, one meets with them in the Mountains sometimes."

"I know very little of the Mountains."

She explained, though as if unwillingly. "You know the Law of the Lords. They do not kill—you know. When there is a murderer in their city, they cannot kill him to stop him, so they make him into a Raze. It is something they do to the mind. They can turn him loose and he starts to live anew, innocent. This man I spoke of was older than you, but had a mind like a little child. But he got a gun in his hands, and his hands knew how to use it, and he—shot a man very close up, like you did—"

Falk was silent. He glanced across the fire at his handgun, lying atop his pack, the marvelous little tool that had started his fires, provided his meat, and lighted his darkness all his long way. There had been no knowledge in his hands of how to use the thing—had there? Metock had taught him how to shoot. He had learned from Metock, and grown skillful by hunting. He was sure of it. He could not be a mere freak and criminal given a second chance by the arrogant charity of the Lords of Es Toch. . . .

Yet was that no more plausible than his own vague dreams and notions of his origin?

"How do they do this to a man's mind?"

"I do not know."

"They might do it," he said harshly, "not only to criminals, but to—to rebels?"

"What are rebels?"

She spoke Galaktika much more fluently than he, but she had never heard that word.

She had finished dressing his hurt and was carefully tucking her few medicaments away in her pouch. He turned around to her so abruptly that she looked up startled, drawing back a little.

"Have you ever seen eyes like mine, Estrel?"

"No."

"You know—the City?"

"Es Toch? Yes, I have been there."

"Then you have seen the Shing?"

"You are no Shing."

"No. But I am going among them." He spoke fiercely. "But I dread—" He stopped.

Estrel closed the medicine-pouch and put it in her pack. "Es Toch is strange to men from the lonely houses and the far lands," she said at last in her soft, careful voice. "But I have walked its streets with no harm; many people live there, in no fear of the Lords. You need not go in dread. The Lords are very powerful, but much is told of Es Toch that is not true. . . ."

Her eyes met his. With sudden decision, summoning what paraverbal skill he had, he bespoke her for the first time: "Then tell me what is true of Es Toch!"

She shook her head, answering aloud, "I have saved your life and you mine, and we are companions, and fellow-Wanderers perhaps for a while. But I will not bespeak you or any person met by chance; not now, nor ever."

"Do you think me a Shing after all?" he asked ironically, a little humiliated, knowing she was right.

"Who can be sure?" she said, and then added with her faint smile, "Though I would find it hard to believe of you. . . . There, the snow in the kettle has melted down. I'll go up and get more. It takes so much to make a little water, and we are both thirsty. You . . . you are called Falk?"

He nodded, watching her.

"Don't mistrust me, Falk," she said. "Let me prove myself to you. Mind-speech proves nothing; and trust is a thing that must grow, from actions, across the days."

"Water it, then," said Falk, "and I hope it grows."

Later, in the long night and silence of the cavern, he roused from sleep to see her sitting hunched by the embers, her tawny head bowed on her knees. He spoke her name.

"I'm cold," she said. "There's no warmth left. . . ."

"Come over to me." He spoke sleepily, smiling. She did not answer, but presently she came to him across the red-lit darkness, naked except for the pale jade stone between her breasts. She was slight, and shaking with the cold. In his mind which was in certain aspects that of a very young man he had resolved not to touch her, who had endured so much from the savages; but she murmured to him, "Make me warm, let me have solace." And he blazed up like fire in the wind, all resolution swept away by her presence and her utter compliance. She lay all night in his arms, by the ashes of the fire.

Three more days and nights in the cavern, while the blizzard renewed and spent itself overhead, Falk and Estrel passed in sleep and lovemaking. She was always the same, yielding, acquiescent. He, having only the memory of the pleasant and joyful love he had shared with Parth, was bewildered by the insatiability and violence of the desire Estrel roused in him. Often the thought of Parth came to him accompanied by a vivid image, the memory of a spring of clear, quick water that rose among rocks in a shadowy place in the forest near the Clearing. But no memory quenched his thirst, and again he would seek satisfaction in Estrel's fathomless submissiveness and find, at least, exhaustion. Once it all turned to uncomprehended anger. He accused her: "You only take me because you think you have to, that I'd have raped you otherwise."

"And you would not?"

"No!" he said, believing it. "I don't want you to serve me, to obey me— Isn't it warmth, human warmth, we both want?"

"Yes," she whispered.

He would not come near her for a while; he resolved he would not touch her again. He went off by himself with his lightgun to explore the strange place they were in. After several hundred paces the cavern narrowed, becoming a high, wide, level tunnel. Black and still, it led him on perfectly straight for a long time, then turned without narrowing or branching and around the dark turning went on and on. His steps echoed dully. Nothing caught any brightness or cast any shadow from his light. He walked till he was weary and hungry, then turned. It was all the same, leading nowhere. He came back to Estrel, to the endless promise and unfulfillment of her embrace.

The storm was over. A night's rain had laid the black earth bare, and the last hollowed drifts of snow dripped and sparkled. Falk stood at the top of the stairway, sunlight on his hair, wind fresh on his face and in his lungs. He felt like a mole done hibernating, like a rat come out of a hole. "Let's go," he called to Estrel, and went back down to the cavern only to help her pack up quickly and clear out.

He had asked her if she knew where her people were, and she had answered, "Probably far ahead in the west, by now."

"Did they know you were crossing Basnasska territory alone?"

"Alone? It's only in fairytales from the Time of the Cities that women ever go anywhere alone. A man was with me. The Basnasska killed him." Her delicate face was set, unexpressive.

Falk began to explain to himself, then, her curious passivity, the want of response that had seemed almost a betrayal of his strong feeling. She had borne too much and could no longer respond. Who was the companion the Basnasska had killed? It was none of Falk's business to know, until she wanted to tell him. But his anger was gone and from that time on he treated Estrel with confidence and with tenderness.

"Can I help you look for your people?"

She said softly, "You are a kind man, Falk. But they will be far ahead, and I cannot comb all the Western Plains. . . ."

The lost, patient note in her voice moved him. "Come west with me, then, till you get news of them. You know what way I take."

It was still hard for him to say the name "Es Toch," which in the tongue of the forest was an obscenity, abominable. He was not yet used to the way Estrel spoke of the Shing city as a mere place among other places.

She hesitated, but when he pressed her she agreed to come with him. That pleased him, because of his desire for her and his pity for her, because of the loneliness he had known and did not wish to know again. They set off together through the cold sunshine and the wind. Falk's heart was light at being outside, at being free, at going on. Today the end of the journey did not matter. The day was bright, the broad bright clouds sailed overhead, the way itself was its end. He went on, the gentle, docile, unwearying woman walking by his side.

5

They crossed the Great Plains on foot—which is soon said, but was not soon or easily done. The days were longer than the nights and the winds of spring were softening and growing mild when they first saw, even from afar, their goal: the barrier, paled by snow and distance, the wall across the continent from north to south. Falk stood still then, gazing at the mountains.

"High in the mountains lies Es Toch," Estrel said, gazing with him. "There I hope we each shall find what we seek."

"I often fear it more than I hope it. . . . Yet I'm glad to have seen the mountains."

"We should go on from here."

"I'll ask the Prince if he is willing that we go tomorrow."

But before leaving her he turned and looked eastward at the desert land beyond the Prince's gardens a while, as if looking back across all the way he and she had come together.

He knew still better now how empty and mysterious a world men inhabited in these later days of their history. For days on end he and his companion had gone and never seen one trace of human presence.

Early in their journey they had gone cautiously, through the territories of the Samsit and other Cattle-Hunter nations, which Estrel knew to be as predatory as the Basnasska. Then, coming to more arid country, they were forced to keep to ways which others had used before, in order to find water; still, when there were signs of people having recently passed, or living nearby, Estrel kept a sharp lookout, and sometimes changed their course to avoid even the risk of being seen. She had a general, and in places a remarkably specific, knowledge of the vast area they were crossing; and sometimes when the terrain worsened and they were in doubt which direction to take, she would say, "Wait till dawn," and going a little away would pray a minute to her amulet, then come back, roll up in her sleeping-bag and sleep serenely: and the way she chose at dawn was always the right one. "Wanderer's instinct," she said when Falk admired her guessing. "Anyway, so long as we keep near water and far from human beings, we are safe."

But once, many days west of the cavern, following the curve of a deep stream-valley they came so abruptly upon a settlement that the guards at the place were around them before they could run. Heavy rain had hidden any sight or sound of the place before they reached it. When the people offered no violence and proved willing to take them in for a day or two, Falk was glad of it, for walking and camping in that rain had been a miserable business.

This tribe or people called themselves the Bee-Keepers. A strange lot, literate and laser-armed, all clothed alike, men and women, in long shifts of yellow wintercloth marked with a brown cross on the breast, they were hospitable and uncommunicative. They gave the travelers beds in their barrack-houses, long, low, flimsy buildings of wood and clay, and plentiful food at their common table; but they spoke so little, to the strangers and among themselves, that they seemed almost a community of the dumb. "They're sworn to silence. They have vows and oaths and rites, no one knows what it's all about," Estrel said, with the calm uninterested disdain which she seemed to feel for most kinds of men. The Wanderers must be proud people, Falk thought. But the Bee-Keepers went her scorn one better: they never spoke to her at all. They would talk to Falk, "Does your she want a pair of our shoes?"—as if she were his horse and they had noticed she wanted shoeing. Their own women used male names, and were addressed and referred to as men. Grave girls, with clear eyes and silent lips, they lived and worked as men among the equally grave and sober youths and men. Few of the Bee-Keepers were over forty and none were under twelve. It was a strange community, like the winter barracks of some army encamped here in the midst of utter solitude in the truce of some unexplained war; strange, sad, and admirable. The order and frugality of their living reminded Falk of his forest home, and the sense of a hidden but flawless, integral dedication was curiously restful to him. They were so sure, these beautiful sexless warriors, though what they were so sure of they never told the stranger.

"They recruit by breeding captured savage women like sows, and bringing up the brats in groups. They worship something called the Dead God, and placate him with sacrifice—murder. They are nothing but the vestige of some ancient superstition," Estrel said, when Falk had said something in favor of the Bee-Keepers to her. For all her submissiveness she apparently resented being treated as a creature of a lower species. Arrogance in one so passive both touched and entertained Falk, and he teased her a little:

"Well, I've seen you at nightfall mumbling to your amulet. Religions differ. . . ."

"Indeed they do," she said, but she looked subdued.

"Who are they armed against, I wonder?"

"Their Enemy, no doubt. As if they could fight the Shing. As if the Shing need bother to fight them!"

"You want to go on, don't you?"

"Yes. I don't trust these people. They keep too much hidden."

That evening, he went to take his leave of the head of the community, a gray-eyed man called Hiardan, younger perhaps than himself. Hiardan received his thanks laconically, and then said in the plain, measured way the Bee-Keepers had, "I think you have spoken only truth to us. For this I thank you. We would have welcomed you more freely and spoken to you of things known to us, if you had come alone."

Falk hesitated before he answered. "I am sorry for that. But I would not have got this far but for my guide and friend. And . . . you live here all together, Master Hiardan. Have you ever been alone?"

"Seldom," said the other. "Solitude is soul's death: man is mankind. So our saying goes. But also we say, do not put your trust in any but brother and hive-twin, known since infancy. That is our rule. It is the only safe one."

"But I have no kinsmen, and no safety, Master," Falk said, and bowing soldierly in the Bee-Keepers' fashion, he took his leave, and next morning at daybreak went on westward with Estrel.

From time to time as they went they saw other settlements or encampments, none large, all wide-scattered—five or six of them perhaps in three or four hundred miles. At some of these Falk left to himself would have stopped. He was armed, and they looked harmless: a couple of nomad tents by an ice-rimmed creek, or a little solitary herdboy on a great hillside watching the half-wild red oxen, or, away off across the rolling land, a mere feather of bluish smoke beneath the illimitable gray sky. He had left the forest to seek, as it were, some news of himself, some hint of what he was or guide towards what he had been in the years he could not remember; how was he to learn if he dared not risk asking? But Estrel was afraid to stop even at the tiniest and poorest of these prairie settlements. "They do not like Wanderers," she said, "nor any strangers. Those that live so much alone are full of fear. In their fear they would take us in and give us food and shelter. But then in the night they would come and bind and kill us. You cannot go to them, Falk"—and she glanced at his eyes—"and tell them *I am your fellow-man*. . . . They know we are here; they watch. If they see us move on tomorrow they won't trouble us.

But if we don't move on, or if we try to go to them, they'll fear us. It is fear that kills."

Windburned and travelweary, his hood pushed back so the keen, glowing wind from the red west stirred his hair, Falk sat, arms across his knees, near their campfire in the lee of a knobbed hill. "True enough," he said, though he spoke wistfully, his gaze on that far-off wisp of smoke.

"Perhaps that's the reason why the Shing kill no one." Estrel knew his mood and was trying to hearten him, to change his thoughts.

"Why's that?" he asked, aware of her intent, but unresponsive.

"Because they are not afraid."

"Maybe." She had got him to thinking, though not very cheerfully. Eventually he said, "Well, since it seems I must go straight to them to ask my questions, if they kill me I'll have the satisfaction of knowing that I frightened them. . . ."

Estrel shook her head. "They will not. They do not kill."

"Not even cockroaches?" he inquired, venting the ill-temper of his weariness on her. "What do they do with cockroaches, in their City—disinfect them and set them free again, like the Razes you told me about?"

"I don't know," Estrel said; she always took his questions seriously. "But their law is reverence for life, and they do keep the law."

"They don't revere human life. Why should they?—they're not human."

"But that is why their rule is reverence for all life—isn't it? And I was taught that there have been no wars on Earth or among the worlds since the Shing came. It is humans that murder one another!"

"There are no humans that could do to me what the Shing did. I honor life, I honor it because it's a much more difficult and uncertain matter than death; and the most difficult and uncertain quality of all is intelligence. The Shing kept their law and let me live, but they killed my intelligence. Is that not murder? They killed the man I was, the child I had been. To play with a man's mind so, is that reverence? Their law is a lie, and their reverence is mockery."

Abashed by his anger, Estrel knelt by the fire cutting up and skewering a rabbit he had shot. The dusty reddish hair curled close to her bowed head; her face was patient and remote. As ever, she drew him to her by compunction and desire. Close as they were, yet he never understood her; were all women so? She was like a lost room in a great house, like a carven box to which he did not have the key. She kept nothing from him and yet her secrecy remained, untouched.

Enormous evening darkened over rain-drenched miles of earth and grass. The little flames of their fire burned red-gold in the clear blue dusk.

"It's ready, Falk," said the soft voice.

He rose and came to her beside the fire. "My friend, my love," he said, taking her hand a moment. They sat down side by side and shared their meat, and later their sleep.

As they went farther west the prairies began to grow dryer, the air clearer. Estrel guided them southward for several days in order to avoid an area which she said was, or had been, the territory of a very wild nomad people, the Horsemen. Falk trusted her judgment, having no wish to repeat his experience with the Basnasska. On the fifth and sixth day of this southward course they crossed through a hilly region and came into dry, high terrain, flat and treeless, forever windswept. The gullies filled with torrents during the rain, and next day were dry again. In summer this must be semi-desert; even in spring it was very dreary.

As they went on they twice passed ancient ruins, mere mounds and hummocks, but aligned in the spacious geometry of streets and squares. Fragments of pottery, flecks of colored glass and plastic were thick in the spongy ground around these places. It had been two or three thousand years, perhaps, since they had been inhabited. This vast steppe-land, good only for cattle-grazing, had never been resettled after the diaspora to the stars, the date of which in the fragmentary and falsified records left to men was not definitely known.

"Strange to think," Falk said as they skirted the second of these long-buried towns, "that there were children playing here and . . . women hanging out the washing . . . so long ago. In another age. Farther away from us than the worlds around a distant star."

"The Age of Cities," Estrel said, "the Age of War. . . . I never heard tell of these places, from any of my people. We may have come too far south, and be heading for the Deserts of the South."

So they changed course, going west and a little north, and the next morning came to a big river, orange and turbulent, not deep but dangerous to cross, though they spent the whole day seeking a ford.

On the western side, the country was more arid than ever. They had filled their flasks at the river, and as water had been a problem by excess rather than default, Falk thought little about it. The sky was clear now, and the sun shone all day; for the first time in hundreds of miles they did not have to resist the cold wind as they walked, and could sleep dry and warm. Spring came quick and radiant to the dry land; the morning star burned above the dawn and wildflowers bloomed under their steps. But they did not come to any stream or spring for three days after crossing the river.

In their struggle through the flood Estrel had taken some kind of chill. She said nothing about it, but she did not keep up her untiring pace, and her face began to look wan. Then dysentery attacked her. They made camp early. As she lay beside their brushwood fire in the evening she began to cry, a couple of dry sobs only, but that was much for one who kept emotion so locked within herself.

Uneasy, Falk tried to comfort her, taking her hands; she was hot with fever. "Don't touch me," she said. "Don't, don't. I lost it, I lost it, what shall I do?"

And he saw then that the cord and amulet of pale jade were gone from her neck.

"I must have lost it crossing the river," she said controlling herself, letting him take her hand.

"Why didn't you tell me—"

"What good?"

He had no answer to that. She was quiet again, but he felt her repressed, feverish anxiety. She grew worse in the night and by morning was very ill. She could not eat, and though tormented by thirst could not stomach the rabbit-blood which was all he could offer her to drink. He made her as comfortable as he could and then taking their empty flasks set off to find water.

Mile after mile of wiry, flower-speckled grass and clumped scrub stretched off, slightly rolling, to the bright hazy edge of the sky. The sun shone very warm; desert larks went up singing from the earth. Falk went at a fast steady pace, confident at first, then dogged, quartering out a long sweep north and east of their camp. Last week's rains had already soaked deep into this soil, and there were no streams. There was no water. He must go on and seek west of the camp. Circling back from the east he was looking out anxiously for the camp when, from a long low rise, he saw something miles off to westward, a smudge, a dark blur that might be trees. A moment later he spotted the nearer smoke of the campfire, and set off towards it at a jogging run, though he was tired, and the low sun hammered its light in his eyes, and his mouth was dry as chalk.

Estrel had kept the fire smoldering to guide him back. She lay by it in her worn-out sleeping-bag. She did not lift her head when he came to her.

"There are trees not too far to the west of here; there may be water. I went the wrong way this morning," he said, getting their things together and slipping on his pack. He had to help Estrel get to her feet; he took her arm and they set off. Bent, with a blind look on her face, she struggled along beside him for a mile and then for another mile. They came up one of the long swells of land. "There!" Falk said; "there—see it? It's trees, all right—there must be water there."

But Estrel had dropped to her knees, then lain down on her side in the grass, doubled up on her pain, her eyes shut. She could not walk farther.

"It's two or three miles at most, I think. I'll make a smudge-fire here, and you can rest; I'll go fill the flasks and come back—I'm sure there's water there, and it won't take long." She lay still while he gathered all the scrub-wood he could and made a little fire and heaped up more of the green wood where she could put it on the fire. "I'll be back soon," he said, and started away. At that she sat up, white and shivering, and cried out, "No! don't leave me! You mustn't leave me alone—you mustn't go—"

There was no reasoning with her. She was sick and frightened beyond the reach of reason. Falk could not leave her there, with the night coming; he might have, but it did not seem to him that he could. He pulled her up, her arm over his shoulder, half pulling and half carrying her, and went on.

On the next rise he came in sight of the trees again, seeming no nearer. The sun was setting away off ahead of them in a golden haze over the ocean of land. He was carrying Estrel now, and every few minutes he had to stop and lay his burden down and drop down beside her to get breath and strength. It seemed to him that if he only had a little water, just enough to wet his mouth, it would not be so hard.

"There's a house," he whispered to her, his voice dry and whistling. Then again, "It's a house, among the trees. Not much farther. . . ." This time she heard him, and twisted her body feebly and struggled against him, moaning, "Don't go there. No, don't go there. Not to the houses. Ramarren mustn't go to the houses. Falk—" She took to crying out weakly in a tongue he did not know, as if crying for help. He plodded on, bent down under her weight.

Through the late dusk light shone out sudden and golden in his eyes: light shining through high windows, behind high dark trees.

A harsh, howling noise rose up, in the direction of the light, and grew louder, coming closer to him. He struggled on, then stopped, seeing shadows running at him out of the dusk, making that howling, coughing clamor. Heavy shadow-shapes as high as his waist encircled him, lunging and snapping at him where he stood supporting Estrel's unconscious weight. He could not draw his gun and dared not move. The lights of the high windows shone serenely, only a few hundred yards away. He shouted, "Help us! Help!" but his voice was only a croaking whisper.

Other voices spoke aloud, calling sharply from a distance. The dark shadow-beasts withdrew, waiting. People came to him where, still holding Estrel against him, he had dropped to his knees. "Take the woman," a man's voice said; another said clearly, "What have we here?—a new pair of toolmen?"

They commanded him to get up, but he resisted, whispering, "Don't hurt her—she's sick—"

"Come on, then!" Rough and expeditious hands forced him to obey. He let them take Estrel from him. He was so dizzy with fatigue that he made no sense of what happened to him and where he was until a good while had passed. They gave him his fill of cool water, that was all he knew, all that mattered.

He was sitting down. Somebody whose speech he could not understand was trying to get him to drink a glassful of some liquid. He took the glass and drank. It was stinging stuff, strongly scented with juniper. A glass—a little glass of slightly clouded green: he saw that clearly, first. He had not drunk from a glass since he had left Zove's House. He shook his head, feeling the volatile liquor clear his throat and brain, and looked up.

He was in a room, a very large room. A long expanse of polished stone floor vaguely mirrored the farther wall, on which or in which a great disk of light glowed soft yellow. Radiant warmth from the disk was palpable on his lifted face. Halfway between him and the sunlike circle of light a tall, massive chair stood on the bare floor; beside it, unmoving, silhouetted, a dark beast crouched.

"What are you?"

He saw the angle of nose and jaw, the black hand on the arm of the chair. The voice was deep, and hard as stone. The words were not in the Galaktika he had now spoken for so long but in his own tongue, the forest speech, though a different dialect of it. He answered slowly with the truth.

"I do not know what I am. My self-knowledge was taken from me six years ago. In a Forest House I learned the way of man. I go to Es Toch to try to learn my name and nature."

"You go to the Place of the Lie to find out the truth? Tools and fools run over weary Earth on many errands, but that beats all for folly or a lie. What brought you to my Kingdom?"

"My companion—"

"Will you tell me that she brought you here?"

"She fell sick; I was seeking water. Is she—"

"Hold your tongue. I am glad you did not say she brought you here. Do you know this place?"

"No."

"This is the Kansas Enclave. I am its Master. I am its Lord, its Prince and God. I am in charge of what happens here. Here we play one of the great games. King of the Castle it's called. The rules are very old, and are the only laws that bind me. I make the rest."

The soft tame sun glowed from floor to ceiling and from wall to wall behind the speaker as he rose from his chair. Overhead, far up, dark vaults and beams held the unflickering golden light reflected among shadows. The radiance silhouetted a hawk nose, a high slanting forehead, a tall, powerful, thin frame, majestic in posture, abrupt in motion. As Falk moved a little the mythological beast beside the throne stretched and snarled. The juniper-scented liquor had volatilized his thoughts; he should be thinking that madness caused this man to call himself a king, but was thinking rather that kingship had driven this man mad.

"You have not learned your name, then?"

"They called me Falk, those who took me in."

"To go in search of his true name: what better way has a man ever gone? No wonder it brought you past my gate. I take you as a Player of the Game," said the Prince of Kansas. "Not every night does a man with eyes like yellow jewels come begging at my door. To refuse him would be cautious and ungracious, and what is royalty but risk and grace? They called you Falk, but I do not. In the game you are the Opalstone. You are free to move. Griffon, be still!"

"Prince, my companion—"

"—is a Shing or a tool or a woman: what do you keep her for? Be still, man; don't be so quick to answer kings. I know what you keep her for. But she has no name and does not play in the game. My cowboys' women are looking after her, and I will not speak of her again." The Prince was approaching him, striding slowly across the bare floor as he spoke. "My companion's name is Griffon. Did you ever hear in the old Canons and Legends of the animal called dog? Griffon is a dog. As you see, he has little in common with the yellow yappers that run the plains, though they are kin. His breed is extinct, like royalty. Opalstone, what do you most wish for?"

The Prince asked this with shrewd, abrupt geniality, looking into Falk's face. Tired and confused and bent on speaking truth, Falk answered: "To go home."

"To go home . . ." The Prince of Kansas was black as his silhouette or his shadow, an old, jet-black man seven feet tall with a face like a swordblade. "To go home . . ." He had moved away a little to study the long table near Falk's chair. All the top of the table, Falk now saw, was sunk several inches into a frame, and contained a network of gold and silver wires upon which beads were strung, so pierced that they could slip from wire to wire and, at certain points, from level to level. There were hundreds of beads, from the size of a baby's fist to the size of an apple seed, made of clay and rock

and wood and metal and bone and plastic and glass and amethyst, agate, to-
paz, turquoise, opal, amber, beryl, crystal, garnet, emerald, diamond. It was
a patterning frame, such as Zove and Buckeye and others of the House possessed. Thought to have come originally from the great culture of Davenant,
though it was now very ancient on Earth, the thing was a fortune-teller, a
computer, an implement of mystical discipline, a toy. In Falk's short second
life he had not had time to learn much about patterning frames. Buckeye
had once remarked that it took forty or fifty years to get handy with one; and
hers, handed down from old in her family, had been only ten inches square,
with twenty or thirty beads. . . .

A crystal prism struck an iron sphere with a clear, tiny clink. Turquoise
shot to the left and a double link of polished bone set with garnets looped
off to the right and down, while a fire-opal blazed for a moment in the dead
center of the frame. Black, lean, strong hands flashed over the wires, playing
with the jewels of life and death. "So," said the Prince, "you want to go home.
But look! Can you read the frame? Vastness. Ebony and diamond and crystal, all the jewels of fire: and the Opalstone among them, going on, going out.
Farther than the King's House, farther than the Wallwindow Prison, farther
than the hills and hollows of Kopernik, the stone flies among the stars. Will
you break the frame, time's frame? See there!"

The slide and flicker of the bright beads blurred in Falk's eyes. He held to
the edge of the great patterning frame and whispered, "I cannot read it. . . ."

"This is the game you play, Opalstone, whether you can read it or not. Good,
very good. My dogs have barked at a beggar tonight and he proves a prince of
starlight. Opalstone, when I come asking water from your wells and shelter
within your walls, will you let me in? It will be a colder night than this. . . .
And a long time from now! You come from very, very long ago. I am old but
you are much older; you should have died a century ago. Will you remember a century from now that in the desert you met a king? Go on, go on, I
told you you are free to move here. There are people to serve you if you need
them."

Falk found his way across the long room to a curtained portal. Outside it
in an anteroom a boy waited; he summoned others. Without surprise or ser-
vility, deferent only in that they waited for Falk to speak first, they provided
him a bath, a change of clothing, supper, and a clean bed in a quiet room.

Thirteen days in all he lived in the Great House of the Enclave of Kansas,
while the last light snow and the scattered rains of spring drove across the
desert lands beyond the Prince's gardens. Estrel, recovering, was kept in one
of the many lesser houses that clustered behind the great one. He was free to

be with her when he chose . . . free to do anything he chose. The Prince ruled his domain absolutely, but in no way was his rule enforced: rather it was accepted as an honor; his people chose to serve him, perhaps because they found, in thus affirming the innate and essential grandeur of one person, that they reaffirmed their own quality as men. There were not more than two hundred of them, cowboys, gardeners, makers and menders, their wives and children. It was a very little kingdom. Yet to Falk, after a few days, there was no doubt that had there been no subjects at all, had he lived there quite alone, the Prince of Kansas would have been no more and no less a prince. It was, again, a matter of quality.

This curious reality, this singular validity of the Prince's domain, so fascinated and absorbed him that for days he scarcely thought of the world outside, that scattered, violent, incoherent world he had been traveling through so long. But talking on the thirteenth day with Estrel and having spoken of going, he began to wonder at the relation of the Enclave with all the rest, and said, "I thought the Shing suffered no lordship among men. Why should they let him guard his boundaries here, calling himself prince and king?"

"Why should they not let him rave? This Enclave of Kansas is a great territory, but barren and without people. Why should the Lords of Es Toch interfere with him? I suppose to them he is like a silly child, boasting and babbling."

"Is he that to you?"

"Well—did you see when the ship came over, yesterday?"

"Yes, I saw."

An aircar—the first Falk had ever seen, though he had recognized its throbbing drone—had crossed directly over the house, up very high so that it was in sight for some minutes. The people of the Prince's household had run out into the gardens beating pans and clappers, the dogs and children had howled, the Prince on an upper balcony had solemnly fired off a series of deafening firecrackers, until the ship had vanished in the murky west.

"They are as foolish as the Basnasska, and the old man is mad."

Though the Prince would not see her, his people had been very kind to her; the undertone of bitterness in her soft voice surprised Falk. "The Basnasska have forgotten the old way of man," he said; "these people maybe remember it too well." He laughed. "Anyway, the ship did go on over."

"Not because they scared it away with firecrackers, Falk," she said seriously, as if trying to warn him of something.

He looked at her a moment. She evidently saw nothing of the lunatic, poetic dignity of those firecrackers, which ennobled even a Shing aircar with the quality of a solar eclipse. In the shadow of total calamity why not set off a firecracker? But since her illness and the loss of her jade talisman she had been anxious and joyless, and the sojourn here which pleased Falk so was a trial to her. It was time they left. "I shall go speak to the Prince of our going," he told her gently, and leaving her there under the willows, now beaded yellow-green with leaf-buds, he walked up through the gardens to the great house. Five of the long-legged, heavy-shouldered black dogs trotted along with him, an honor guard he would miss when he left this place.

The Prince of Kansas was in his throne-room, reading. The disk that covered the east wall of the room by day shone cool mottled silver, a domestic moon; only at night did it glow with soft solar warmth and light. The throne, of polished petrified wood from the southern deserts, stood in front of it. Only on the first night had Falk seen the Prince seated on the throne. He sat now in one of the chairs near the patterning-frame, and at his back the twenty-foot-high windows looking to the west were uncurtained. There the far, dark mountains stood, tipped with ice.

The Prince raised his swordblade face and heard what Falk had to say. Instead of answering he touched the book he had been reading, not one of the beautiful decorated projector-scrolls of his extraordinary library but a little handwritten book of bound paper. "Do you know this Canon?"

Falk looked where he pointed and saw the verse,

What men fear
must be feared.
O desolation!
It has not yet
not yet reached its limit!

"I know it, Prince. I set out on this journey of mine with it in my pack. But I cannot read the page to the left, in your copy."

"Those are the symbols it was first written in, five or six thousand years ago: the tongue of the Yellow Emperor—my ancestor. You lost yours along the way? Take this one, then. But you'll lose it too, I expect; in following the Way the way is lost. O desolation! Why do you always speak the truth, Opalstone?"

"I'm not sure." In fact, though Falk had gradually determined that he would not lie no matter whom he spoke to or how chancy the truth might seem, he did not know why he had come to this decision. "To—to use the enemy's weapon is to play the enemy's game. . . ."

"Oh, they won their game long ago. —So you're off? Go on, then; no doubt it's time. But I shall keep your companion here a while."

"I told her I would help her find her people, Prince."

"Her people?" The hard, shadowy face turned to him. "What do you take her for?"

"She is a Wanderer."

"And I am a green walnut, and you a fish, and those mountains are made of roasted sheepshit! Have it your way. Speak the truth and hear the truth. Gather the fruits of my flowery orchards as you walk westward, Opalstone, and drink the milk of my thousand wells in the shade of giant ferntrees. Do I not rule a pleasant kingdom? Mirages and dust straight west to the dark. Is it lust or loyalty that makes you hold to her?"

"We have come a long way together."

"Mistrust her!"

"She has given me help, and hope; we are companions. There is trust between us—how can I break it?"

"Oh fool, oh desolation!" said the Prince of Kansas. "I'll give you ten women to accompany you to the Place of the Lie, with lutes and flutes and tambourines and contraceptive pills. I'll give you five good friends armed with firecrackers. I'll give you a dog—in truth I will, a living extinct dog, to be your true companion. Do you know why dogs died out? Because they were loyal, because they were trusting. Go alone, man!"

"I cannot."

"Go as you please. The game here's done." The Prince rose, went to the throne beneath the moon-circle, and seated himself. He never turned his head when Falk tried to say farewell.

6

With his lone memory of a lone peak to embody the word "mountain," Falk had imagined that as soon as they reached the mountains they would have reached Es Toch; he had not realized they would have to clamber over the rooftree of a continent. Range behind range the mountains rose; day after day the two crept upward into the world of the heights, and still their goal lay farther up and farther on to the southwest. Among the forests and torrents and the cloud-conversant slopes of snow and granite there was every now and then a little camp or village along the way. Often they could not avoid these as there was but one path to take. They rode past on their mules, the Prince's princely gift at their going, and were not hindered. Estrel said that the mountain people, living here on the doorstep of the Shing, were a wary lot who would neither molest nor welcome a stranger, and were best left alone.

Camping was a cold business, in April in the mountains, and the once they stopped at a village was a welcome relief. It was a tiny place, four wooden houses by a noisy stream in a canyon shadowed by great storm-wreathed peaks; but it had a name, Besdio, and Estrel had stayed there once years ago, she told him, when she had been a girl. The people of Besdio, a couple of whom were light-skinned and tawny-haired like Estrel herself, spoke with her briefly. They talked in the language which the Wanderers used; Falk had always spoken Galaktika with Estrel and had not learned this Western tongue. Estrel explained, pointing east and west; the mountain people nodded coolly, studying Estrel carefully, glancing at Falk only out of the corner of their eyes. They asked few questions, and gave food and a night's shelter ungrudgingly but with a cool, incurious manner that made Falk vaguely uneasy.

The cowshed where they were to sleep was warm, however, with the live heat of the cattle and goats and poultry crowded there in sighing, odorous, peaceable companionship. While Estrel talked a little longer with their hosts in the main hut, Falk betook himself to the cowshed and made himself at home. In the hayloft above the stalls he made a luxurious double bed of hay and spread their bedrolls on it. When Estrel came he was already half asleep, but he roused himself enough to remark, "I'm glad you came . . . I smell something kept hidden here, but I don't know what."

"It's not all I smell."

This was as close as Estrel had ever come to making a joke, and Falk looked at her with a bit of surprise. "You are happy to be getting close to the City, aren't you?" he asked. "I wish I were."

"Why shouldn't I be? There I hope to find my kinsfolk; if I do not, the Lords will help me. And there you will find what you seek too, and be restored into your heritage."

"My heritage? I thought you thought me a Raze."

"You? Never! Surely you don't believe, Falk, that it was the Shing that meddled with your mind? You said that once, down on the plains, and I did not understand you then. How could you think yourself a Raze, or any common man? You are not Earth-born!"

Seldom had she spoken so positively. What she said heartened him, concurring with his own hope, but her saying it puzzled him a little, for she had been silent and troubled for a long time now. Then he saw something swing from a leather cord around her neck: "They gave you an amulet." That was the source of her hopefulness.

"Yes," she said, looking down at the pendant with satisfaction. "We are of the same faith. Now all will go well for us."

He smiled a little at her superstition, but was glad it gave her comfort. As he went to sleep he knew she was awake, lying looking into the darkness full of the stink and the gentle breath and presence of the animals. When the cock crowed before daylight he half-roused and heard her whispering prayers to her amulet in the tongue he did not know.

They went on, taking a path that wound south of the stormy peaks. One great mountain bulwark remained to cross, and for four days they climbed, till the air grew thin and icy, the sky dark blue, and the sun of April shone dazzling on the fleecy backs of clouds that grazed the meadows far beneath their way. Then, the summit of the pass attained, the sky darkened and snow fell on the naked rocks and blanked out the great bare slopes of red and gray. There was a hut for wayfarers in the pass, and they and their mules huddled in it till the snow stopped and they could begin the descent.

"Now the way is easy," Estrel said, turning to look at Falk over her mule's jogging rump and his mule's nodding ears; and he smiled, but there was a dread in him that only grew as they went on and down, towards Es Toch.

Closer and closer they came, and the path widened into a road; they saw huts, farms, houses. They saw few people, for it was cold and rainy, keeping people indoors under a roof. The two wayfarers jogged on down the lonely road through the rain. The third morning from the summit dawned bright, and after they had ridden a couple of hours Falk halted his mule, looking questioningly at Estrel.

"What is it, Falk?"

"We have come—this is Es Toch, isn't it?"

The land had leveled out all about them, though distant peaks closed the horizon all around, and the pastures and plowlands they had been riding through had given way to houses, houses and still more houses. There were huts, cabins, shanties, tenements, inns, shops where goods were made and bartered for, children everywhere, people on the highway, people on side-roads, people afoot, on horses and mules and sliders, coming and going: it was crowded yet scanty, slack and busy, dirty, dreary and vivid under the bright dark sky of morning in the mountains.

"It is a mile or more yet to Es Toch."

"Then what is this city?"

"This is the outskirts of the city."

Falk stared about him, dismayed and excited. The road he had followed so far from the house in the Eastern Forest had become a street, leading only too quickly to its end. As they sat their mules in the middle of the street people glanced at them, but none stayed and none spoke. The women kept their faces averted. Only some of the ragged children stared, or pointed shouting and then ran, vanishing up a filth-encumbered alley or behind a shack. It was not what Falk had expected; yet what had he expected? "I did not know there were so many people in the world," he said at last. "They swarm about the Shing like flies on dung."

"Fly-maggots flourish in dung," Estrel said dryly. Then, glancing at him, she reached across and put her hand lightly on his. "These are the outcasts and the hangers-on, the rabble outside the walls. Let us go on to the City, the true City. We have come a long way to see it. . . ."

They rode on; and soon they saw, jutting up over the shanty roofs, the walls of windowless green towers, bright in the sunlight.

Falk's heart beat hard; and he noticed that Estrel spoke a moment to the amulet she had been given in Besdio.

"We cannot ride the mules inside the city," she said. "We can leave them here." They stopped at a ramshackle public stable; Estrel talked persuasively a while in the Western tongue with the man who kept the place, and when Falk asked what she had been asking him she said, "To keep our mules as surety."

"Surety?"

"If we don't pay for their keep, he will keep them. You have no money, have you?"

"No," Falk said humbly. Not only did he have no money, he had never seen money; and though Galaktika had a word for the thing, his forest dialect did not.

The stable was the last building on the edge of a field of rubble and refuse which separated the shantytown from a high, long wall of granite blocks. There was one entrance to Es Toch for people on foot. Great conical pillars marked the gate. On the left-hand pillar an inscription in Galaktika was carved: REVERENCE FOR LIFE. On the right was a longer sentence in characters Falk had never seen. There was no traffic through the gate, and no guard.

"The pillar of the Lie and the pillar of the Secret," he said aloud as he walked between them, refusing to let himself be overawed; but then he entered Es Toch, and saw it, and stood still saying nothing.

The City of the Lords of Earth was built on the two rims of a canyon, a tremendous cleft through the mountains, narrow, fantastic, its black walls striped with green plunging terrifically down half a mile to the silver tinsel strip of a river in the shadowy depths. On the very edges of the facing cliffs the towers of the city jutted up, hardly based on earth at all, linked across the chasm by delicate bridge-spans. Towers, roadways and bridges ceased and the wall closed the city off again just before a vertiginous bend of the canyon. Helicopters with diaphanous vanes skimmed the abyss, the sliders flickered along the half-glimpsed streets and slender bridges. The sun, still not far above the massive peaks to eastward, seemed scarcely to cast shadows here; the great green towers shone as if translucent to the light.

"Come," Estrel said, a pace ahead of him, her eyes shining. "There's nothing to fear here, Falk."

He followed her. There was no one on the street, which descended between lower buildings toward the cliff-edge towers. Once he glanced back at the gate, but he could no longer see the opening between the pillars.

"Where do we go?"

"There's a place I know, a house where my people come." She took his arm, the first time she had ever done so in all the way they had walked together, and clinging to him kept her eyes lowered as they came down the long zigzag street. Now to their right the buildings loomed up high as they neared the city's heart, and to the left, without wall or parapet, the dizzy gorge dropped away full of shadows, a black gap between the luminous perching towers.

"But if we need money here—"

"They'll look after us."

People brightly and strangely dressed passed them on sliders; the landing-ledges high up the sheer-walled buildings flickered with helicopters. High over the gorge an aircar droned, going up.

"Are these all . . . Shing?"

"Some."

Unconsciously he was keeping his free hand on his laser. Estrel without looking at him, but smiling a little, said, "Do not use your lightgun here, Falk. You came here to gain your memory, not to lose it."

"Where are we going, Estrel?"

"Here."

"This? This is a palace."

The luminous greenish wall towered up windowless, featureless, into the sky. Before them a square doorway stood open.

"They know me here. Don't be afraid. Come on with me."

She clung to his arm. He hesitated. Looking back up the street he saw several men, the first he had seen on foot, loitering towards them, watching them. That scared him, and with Estrel he entered the building, passing through inner automatic portals that slid apart at their approach. Just inside, possessed by a sense of misjudgment, having made a hideous error, he stopped. "What is this place? Estrel—"

It was a high hall, full of a thick greenish light, dim as an underwater cave; there were doorways and corridors, down which men approached, hurrying towards him. Estrel had broken away from him. In panic he turned to the doors behind him: they were shut now. They had no handles. Dim figures of men broke into the hall, running at him and shouting. He backed up against the shut doors and reached for his laser. It was gone. It was in Estrel's hands. She stood behind the men as they surrounded Falk, and as he tried to break through them and was seized, and fought and was beaten, he heard for a moment a sound he had never heard before: her laugh.

A disagreeable sound rang in Falk's ears; a metallic taste filled his mouth. His head swam when he raised it, and his eyes would not focus, and he could not seem to move freely. Presently he realized that he was waking from unconsciousness, and thought he could not move because he had been hurt or drugged. Then he made out that his wrists were shackled together on a short chain, his ankles likewise. But the swimming in his head grew worse. There was a great voice booming in his ears now, repeating the same thing over and over: *ramarren-ramarren-ramarren.* He struggled and cried out, trying to get away from the booming voice which filled him with terror. Lights flashed in his eyes, and through the sound roaring in his head he heard someone scream in his own voice, "I am not—"

When he came to again everything was utterly still. His head ached, and still he could not see very clearly; but there were no shackles on his arms and legs now, if there ever had been any, and he knew he was being protected, sheltered, looked after. They knew who he was and he was welcome. His own people were coming for him, he was safe here, cherished, beloved, and all he need do now was rest and sleep, rest and sleep, while the soft, deep stillness murmured tenderly in his head, *marren-marren-marren.* . . .

He woke. It took a while, but he woke, and managed to sit up. He had to bury his acutely aching head in his arms for a while to get over the vertigo the movement caused, and at first was aware only that he was sitting on the floor of some room, a floor which seemed to be warm and yielding, almost soft, like the flank of some great beast. Then he lifted his head, and got his eyes into focus, and looked about him.

He was alone, in the midst of a room so uncanny that it revived his dizziness for a while. There was no furniture. Walls, floor and ceiling were all of the same translucent stuff, which appeared soft and undulant like many thicknesses of pale green veiling, but was tough and slick to the touch. Queer carvings and crimpings and ridges forming ornate patterns all over the floor were, to the exploring hand, nonexistent; they were eye-deceiving paintings, or lay beneath a smooth transparent surface. The angles where walls met were thrown out of true by optical-illusion devices of crosshatching and pseudo-parallels used as decoration; to pull the corners into right angles took an effort of will, which was perhaps an effort of self-deception, since they might, after all, not be right angles. But none of this teasing subtlety of decoration so disoriented Falk as the fact that the entire room was translucent. Vaguely, with the effect of looking into a depth of very green pond-water, underneath him another room was visible. Overhead was a patch of light that might be the moon, blurred and greened by one or more intervening ceilings. Through one wall of the room strings and patches of brightness were fairly distinct, and he could make out the motion of the lights of helicopters or aircars. Through the other three walls these outdoor lights were much dimmer, blurred by the veilings of further walls, corridors, rooms. Shapes moved in those other rooms. He could see them but there was no identifying them: features, dress, color, size, all was blurred away. A blot of shadow somewhere in the green depths suddenly rose and grew less, greener, dimmer, fading into the maze of vagueness. Visibility without discrimination, solitude without privacy. It was extraordinarily beautiful, this masked shimmer of lights and shapes through inchoate planes of green, and extraordinarily disturbing.

All at once in a brighter patch on the near wall Falk caught a glimpse of movement. He turned quickly and with a shock of fear saw something at last vivid, distinct: a face, a seamed, savage, staring face set with two inhuman yellow eyes.

"A Shing," he whispered in blank dread. The face mocked him, the terrible lips mouthing soundlessly *A Shing*, and he saw that it was the reflection of his own face.

He got up stiffly and went to the mirror and passed his hand over it to make sure. It was a mirror, half-concealed by a molded frame painted to appear flatter than it actually was.

He turned from it at the sound of a voice. Across the room from him, not too clear in the dim, even light from hidden sources, but solid enough, a figure stood. There was no doorway visible, but a man had entered, and stood looking at him: a very tall man, a white cape or cloak dropping from wide shoulders, white hair, clear, dark, penetrating eyes. The man spoke; his voice was deep and very gentle. "You are welcome here, Falk. We have long awaited you, long guided and guarded you." The light was growing brighter in the room, a clear, swelling radiance. The deep voice held a note of exaltation. "Put away fear and be welcome among us, O Messenger. The dark road is behind you and your feet are set upon the way that leads you home!" The brilliance grew till it dazzled Falk's eyes; he had to blink and blink again, and when he looked up, squinting, the man was gone.

There came unbidden into his mind words spoken months ago by an old man in the forest: *The awful darkness of the bright lights of Es Toch.*

He would not be played with, drugged, deluded any longer. A fool he had been to come here, and he would never get away alive; but he would not be played with. He started forward to find the hidden doorway to follow the man. A voice from the mirror said, "Wait a moment more, Falk. Illusions are not always lies. You seek truth."

A seam in the wall split and opened into a door; two figures entered. One, slight and small, strode in; he wore breeches fitted with an ostentatious codpiece, a jerkin, a close-fitting cap. The second, taller, was heavily robed and moved mincingly, posing like a dancer; long, purplish-black hair streamed down to her waist—his waist, it must be for the voice though very soft was deep. "We are being filmed, you know, Strella."

"I know," said the little man in Estrel's voice. Neither of them so much as glanced at Falk; they behaved as if they were alone. "Go on with what you were about to say, Kradgy."

"I was about to ask you why it took you so long."

"So long? You are unjust, my Lord. How could I track him in the forest east of Shorg?—it is utter wilderness. The stupid animals were no help; all they do these days is babble the Law. When you finally dropped me the manfinder I was two hundred miles north of him. When I finally caught up he was heading straight into Basnasska territory. You know the Council has them furnished with bombirds and such so that they can thin out the Wanderers and the Solia-pachim. So I had to join the filthy tribe. Have you not heard my reports? I sent them in all along, till I lost my sender crossing a river south of Kansas Enclave. And my mother in Besdio gave me another. Surely they kept my reports on tape?"

"I never listen to reports. In any case, it was all time and risk wasted, since you did not in all these weeks succeed in teaching him not to fear us."

"Estrel," Falk said. "Estrel!"

Grotesque and frail in her transvestite clothes, Estrel did not turn, did not hear. She went on speaking to the robed man. Choked with shame and anger Falk shouted her name, then strode forward and seized her shoulder—and there was nothing there, a blur of lights in the air, a flicker of color, fading.

The door-slit in the wall still stood open, and through it Falk could see into the next room. There stood the robed man and Estrel, their backs to him. He said her name in a whisper, and she turned and looked at him. She looked into his eyes without triumph and without shame, calmly, passively, detached and uncaring, as she had looked at him all along.

"Why—why did you lie to me?" he said. "Why did you bring me here?" He knew why; he knew what he was and always had been in Estrel's eyes. It was not his intelligence that spoke, but his self-respect and his loyalty, which could not endure or admit the truth in this first moment.

"I was sent to bring you here. You wanted to come here."

He tried to pull himself together. Standing rigid, not moving towards her, he asked, "Are you a Shing?"

"I am," said the robed man, affably smiling. "I am a Shing. All Shing are liars. Am I, then, a Shing lying to you, in which case of course I am not a Shing, but a non-Shing, lying? Or is it a lie that all Shing lie? But I am a Shing, truly; and truly I lie. Terrans and other animals have been known to tell lies also; lizards change color, bugs mimic sticks and flounders lie by lying still, looking pebbly or sandy depending on the bottom which underlies them. Strella, this one is even stupider than the child."

"No, my Lord Kradgy, he is very intelligent," Estrel replied, in her soft, passive way. She spoke of Falk as a human being speaks of an animal.

She had walked beside Falk, eaten with him, slept with him. She had slept in his arms. . . . Falk stood watching her, silent; and she and the tall one also stood silent, unmoving, as if awaiting a signal from him to go on with their performance.

He could not feel rancor towards her. He felt nothing towards her. She had turned to air, to a blur and flicker of light. His feeling was all towards himself: he was sick, physically sick, with humiliation.

Go alone, Opalstone, said the Prince of Kansas. Go alone, said Hiardan the Bee-Keeper. Go alone, said the old Listener in the forest. Go alone, my son, said Zove. How many others would have guided him aright, helped him on his quest, armed him with knowledge, if he had come across the prairies alone? How much might he have learned, if he had not trusted Estrel's guidance and good faith?

Now he knew nothing, except that he had been measurelessly stupid, and that she had lied. She had lied to him from the start, steadily, from the moment she told him she was a Wanderer—no, from before that: from the moment she had first seen him and had pretended not to know who or what he was. She had known all along, and had been sent to make sure he got to Es Toch; and to counteract, perhaps, the influence those who hated the Shing had had and might have upon his mind. But then why, he thought painfully, standing there in one room gazing at her in another, why had she stopped lying, now?

"It does not matter what I say to you now," she said, as if she had read his thoughts.

Possibly she had. They had never used mindspeech; but if she was a Shing and had the mental powers of the Shing, the extent of which was only a matter of rumor and speculation among men, she might have been attuned to his thoughts all along, all the weeks of their traveling. How could he tell? There was no use asking her. . . .

There was a sound behind him. He turned, and saw two people standing at the other end of the room, near the mirror. They wore black gowns and white hoods, and were twice the height of ordinary men.

"You are too easily fooled," said one giant.

"You must know you have been fooled," said the other.

"You are half a man only."

"Half a man cannot know the whole truth."

"He who hates is mocked and fooled."

"He who kills is razed and tooled."

"Where do you come from, Falk?"

"What are you, Falk?"

"Where are you, Falk?"

"Who are you, Falk?"

Both giants raised their hoods, showing that there was nothing inside but shadow, and backed into the wall, and through it, and vanished.

Estrel ran to him from the other room, flung her arms about him, pressing herself against him, kissing him hungrily, desperately. "I love you, I have loved you since I first saw you. Trust me, Falk, trust me!" Then she was torn from him, wailing, "Trust me!" and was drawn away as if pulled by some mighty, invisible force, as if blown by a great wind, whirled about, blown through a slit doorway that closed silently behind her, like a mouth closing.

"You realize," said the tall male in the other room, "that you are under the influence of hallucinatory drugs." His whispering, precise voice held an undertone of sarcasm and ennui. "Trust yourself least of all. Eh?" He then lifted his long robes and urinated copiously; after which he wandered out, rearranging his robes and smoothing his long flowing hair.

Falk stood watching the greenish floor of the other room gradually absorb the urine till it was quite gone.

The sides of the door were very slowly drawing together, closing the slit. It was the only way out of the room in which he was trapped. He broke from his lethargy and ran through the slit before it shut. The room in which Estrel and the other one had stood was exactly the same as the one he had left, perhaps a trifle smaller and dimmer. A slit-door stood open in its far wall, but was closing very slowly. He hurried across the room and through it, and into a third room which was exactly like the others, perhaps a trifle smaller and dimmer. The slit in its far wall was closing very slowly, and he hurried through it into another room, smaller and dimmer than the last, and from it squeezed through into another small, dim room, and from it crawled into a small dim mirror and fell upwards, screaming in sick terror, towards the white, seamed, staring moon.

He woke, feeling rested, vigorous, and confused, in a comfortable bed in a bright, windowless room. He sat up, and as if that had given a signal two men came hurrying from behind a partition, big men with a staring, bovine look to them. "Greetings Lord Agad! Greetings Lord Agad!" they said one after the other, and then, "Come with us, please, come with us, please." Falk stood up, stark naked, ready to fight—the only thing clear in his mind at the moment was his fight and defeat in the entrance hall of the palace—but they offered no violence. "Come on, please," they repeated antiphonally, until he came with them. They led him, still naked, out of the room, up a long blank corridor, through a mirror-walled hall, up a staircase that turned out to be a ramp painted to look like stairs, through another corridor and up more ramps, and finally into a spacious, furnished room with bluish-green walls, one of which was glowing with sunlight. One of the men stopped outside the room; the other entered with Falk. "There's clothes, there's food, there's drink. Now you—now you eat, drink. Now you—now you ask for need. All right?" He stared persistently but without any particular interest at Falk.

There was a pitcher of water on the table, and the first thing Falk did was drink his fill, for he was very thirsty. He looked around the strange, pleasant room with its furniture of heavy, glass-clear plastic and its windowless, translucent walls, and then studied his guard or attendant with curiosity. A big, blank-faced man, with a gun strapped to his belt. "What is the Law?" he asked on impulse.

Obediently and with no surprise the big, staring fellow answered, "Do not take life."

"But you carry a gun."

"Oh, this gun, it makes you all stiff, not dead," said the guard, and laughed. The modulations of his voice were arbitrary, not connected with the meaning of the words, and there was a slight pause between the words and the laugh. "Now you eat, drink, get clean. Here's good clothes. See, here's clothes."

"Are you a Raze?"

"No. I am a Captain of the Bodyguard of the True Lords, and I key in to the Number Eight computer. Now you eat, drink, get clean."

"I will if you leave the room."

A slight pause. "Oh yes, very well, Lord Agad," said the big man, and again laughed as if he had been tickled. Perhaps it tickled when the computer spoke through his brain. He withdrew. Falk could see the vague hulking shapes of the two guards through the inner wall of the room; they waited one on either side of the door in the corridor. He found the washroom and washed up. Clean clothes were laid out on the great soft bed that filled one end of the room; they were loose long robes patterned wildly with red, magenta, and violet, and he examined them with distaste, but put them on. His battered backpack lay on the table of gold-mounted glassy plastic, its contents seemingly untouched, but his clothes and guns were not in evidence. A meal was laid out, and he was hungry. How long had it been since he had entered the doors that closed behind him? He had no idea, but his hunger told him it had been some while, and he fell to. The food was queer stuff, highly flavored, mixed, sauced, and disguised, but he ate it all and looked for more. There being no more, and since he had done what he had been asked to do, he examined the room more carefully. He could not see the vague shadows of the guards on the other side of the semi-transparent, bluish-green wall any longer, and was going to investigate when he stopped short. The barely visible vertical slit of the door was widening, and a shadow moved behind it. It opened to a tall oval, through which a person stepped into the room.

A girl, Falk thought at first, then saw it was a boy of sixteen or so, dressed in loose robes like those he wore himself. The boy did not come close to Falk, but stopped, holding out his hands palm upwards, and spouted a whole rush of gibberish.

"Who are you?"

"Orry," said the young man, "Orry!" and more gibberish. He looked frail and excited; his voice shook with emotion. He then dropped down on both knees and bowed his head low, a bodily gesture that Falk had never seen, though its meaning was unmistakable: it was the full and original gesture, of which, among the Bee-Keepers and the subjects of the Prince of Kansas, he had seen certain vestigial remnants.

"Speak in Galaktika," Falk said fiercely, shocked and uneasy. "Who are you?"

"I am Har-Orry-Prech-Ramarren," the boy whispered.

"Get up. Get off your knees. I don't— Do you know me?"

"Prech Ramarren, do you not remember me? I am Orry, Har Weden's son—"

"What is my name?"

The boy raised his head, and Falk stared at him—at his eyes, which looked straight into his own. They were of a gray-amber color, except for the large dark pupil: all iris, without visible white, like the eyes of a cat or a stag, like no eyes Falk had ever seen, except in the mirror last night.

"Your name is Agad Ramarren," the boy said, frightened and subdued.

"How do you know it?"

"I—I have always known it, prech Ramarren."

"Are you of my race? Are we of the same people?"

"I am Har Weden's son, prech Ramarren! I swear to you I am!"

There were tears in the gray-gold eyes for a moment. Falk himself had always tended to react to stress with a brief blinding of tears; Buckeye had once reproved him for being embarrassed by this trait, saying it appeared to be a purely physiological reaction, probably racial.

The confusion, bewilderment, disorientation Falk had undergone since he had entered Es Toch now left him unequipped to question and judge this latest apparition. Part of his mind said, *That is exactly what they want: they want you confused to the point of total credulity.* At this point he did not know whether Estrel—Estrel whom he knew so well and loved so loyally—was a friend or a Shing or a tool of the Shing, whether she had ever told him the truth or ever lied to him, whether she had been trapped here with him or had lured him here into a trap. He remembered a laugh; he also remembered a desperate embrace, a whisper. . . . What then was he to make of this boy, this boy looking at him in awe and pain with unearthly eyes like his own: would he turn if touched to a blur of lights? Would he answer questions with lies, or truth?

Amidst all illusions, errors and deceptions there remained, it seemed to Falk, only one way to take: the way he had followed all along, from Zove's House on. He looked at the boy again and told him the truth.

"I do not know you. If I should remember you, I do not, because I remember nothing longer ago than four or five years." He cleared his throat, turned away again, sat down on one of the tall spindly chairs, motioned for the boy to do the same.

"You . . . do not remember Werel?"

"Who is Werel?"

"Our home. Our world."

That hurt. Falk said nothing.

"Do you remember the—the journey here, prech Ramarren?" the boy asked, stammering. There was incredulity in his voice; he seemed not to have taken in what Falk had told him. There was also a shaken, yearning note, checked by respect or fear.

Falk shook his head.

Orry repeated his question with a slight change: "You do remember our journey to Earth, prech Ramarren?"

"No. When was the journey?"

"Six Terran years ago. —Forgive me, please, prech Ramarren. I did not know—I was over by the California Sea and they sent an aircar for me, an automatic; it did not say what I was wanted for. Then Lord Kradgy told me one of the Expedition had been found, and I thought— But he did not tell me this about your memory— You remember . . . only . . . only the Earth, then?"

He seemed to be pleading for a denial. "I remember only the Earth," Falk said, determined not to be swayed by the boy's emotion, or his naiveté, or the childish candor of his face and voice. He must assume that this Orry was not what he seemed to be.

But if he was?

I will not be fooled again, Falk thought bitterly.

Yes you will, another part of his mind retorted; *you will be fooled if they want to fool you, and there is no way you can prevent it. If you ask no questions of this boy lest the answer be a lie, then the lie prevails entirely, and nothing comes of all your journey here but silence and mockery and disgust. You came to learn your name. He gives you a name: accept it.*

"Will you tell me who . . . who we are?"

The boy eagerly began again in his gibberish, then checked himself at Falk's uncomprehending gaze. "You don't remember how to speak Kelshak, prech Ramarren?" He was almost plaintive.

Falk shook his head. "Kelshak is your native language?"

The boy said, "Yes," adding timidly, "And yours, prech Ramarren."

"What is the word for 'father' in Kelshak?"

"Hiowech. Or wawa—for babies." A flicker of an ingenuous grin passed over Orry's face.

"What would you call an old man whom you respected?"

"There are a lot of words like that—kinship words—Prevwa, kioinap, ska n-gehoy . . . Let me think, prechna. I haven't spoken Kelshak for so long. . . . A prechnoweg—a higher-level non-relative could be tiokioi, or previotio—"

"Tiokioi. I said the word once, not . . . knowing where I learned it. . . ."

It was no real test. There was no test here. He had never told Estrel much about his stay with the old Listener in the forest, but they might have learned every memory in his brain, everything he had ever said or done or thought, while he was drugged in their hands this past night or nights. There was no knowing what they had done; there was no knowing what they could do, or would. Least of all could he know what they wanted. All he could do was go ahead trying to get at what he wanted.

"Are you free to come and go here?"

"Oh, yes, prech Ramarren. The Lords have been very kind. They have long been seeking for any . . . other survivors of the Expedition. Do you know, prechna, if any of the others . . ."

"I do not know."

"All that Kradgy had time to tell me, when I got here a few minutes ago,

was that you had been living in the forest in the eastern part of this continent, with some wild tribe."

"I'll tell you that if you want to know. But tell me some things first. I do
not know who I am, who you are, what the Expedition was, what Werel is."

"We are Kelshy," the boy said with constraint, evidently embarrassed at explaining on so low a level to one he considered his superior, in age of course,
but also in more than age. "Of the Kelshak Nation, on Werel—we came here
on the ship *Alterra*—"

"Why did we come here?" Falk asked, leaning forward.

And slowly, with digressions and backtrackings and a thousand question-
interruptions, Orry went on, till he was worn out with talking and Falk with
hearing, and the veil-like walls of the room were glowing with evening light;
then they were silent for a while, and dumb servants brought in food and drink
for them. And all the time he ate and drank Falk kept gazing in his mind at
the jewel that might be false and might be priceless, the story, the pattern, the
glimpse—true vision or not—of the world he had lost.

7

A sun like a dragon's eye, orange-yellow, like a fire-opal with seven glittering pendants swinging slowly through their long ellipses. The green third planet took sixty of Earth's years to complete its year: *Lucky the man who sees his second spring,* Orry translated a proverb of that world. The winters of the northern hemisphere, tilted by the angle of the ecliptic away from the sun while the planet was at its farthest from the sun, were cold, dark, terrible: the vast summers, half a lifetime long, were measurelessly opulent. Giant tides of the planet's deep seas obeyed a giant moon that took four hundred days to wax and wane; the world was rife with earthquakes, volcanoes, plants that walked, animals that sang, men who spoke and built cities: a catalogue of wonders. To this miraculous though not unusual world had come, twenty years ago, a ship from outer space. Twenty of its great years, Orry meant: something over twelve hundred Terran years.

Colonists and hilfers of the League of All Worlds, the people on that ship were committing their work and lives to the new-found planet, remote from the ancient central worlds of the League, in the hope of bringing its native intelligent species eventually into the League, a new ally in the War To Come. Such had been the policy of the League ever since, generations before, warnings had come from beyond the Hyades of a great wave of conquerors that moved from world to world, from century to century, closer toward the farflung cluster of eighty planets that so proudly called itself the League of All Worlds. Terra, near the edge of the League heart-zone and the nearest League planet to the new-found planet Werel, had supplied all the colonists on this first ship. There were to have been other ships from other worlds of the League, but none ever came: the War came first.

The colonists' only communication with Earth, with the Prime World Davenant, and the rest of the League, was by the ansible, the instantaneous transmitter, aboard their ship. No ship, said Orry, had ever flown faster than light—here Falk corrected him. Warships had indeed been built on the ansible principle, but they had been only automatic death-machines, incredibly costly and carrying no living creatures. Lightspeed, with its foreshortening of time for the voyager, was the limit of human voyaging, then and now. So the colonists of Werel were a very long way from home and wholly dependent on their ansible for news. They had only been on Werel five years when they were informed that the Enemy had come, and immediately after that the communications grew confused, contradictory, intermittent, and soon ceased altogether. About a third of the colonists chose to take the ship and fly back across the great gap of years to Earth, to rejoin their people. The rest stayed on Werel, self-marooned. In their lifetimes they could never know what had become of their home world and the League they served, or who the Enemy was, and whether he ruled the League or had been vanquished. Without ship or communicator, isolated, they stayed, a small colony surrounded by curious and hostile High-Intelligence Life Forms of a culture inferior, but an intelligence equal, to their own. And they waited, and their sons' sons waited, while the stars stayed silent over them. No ship ever came, no word. Their own ship must have been destroyed, the records of the new planet lost. Among all the stars the little orange-yellow opal was forgotten.

The colony thrived, spreading up a pleasant sea-coast land from its first town, which was named Alterra. Then after several years—Orry stopped and corrected himself, "Nearly six centuries, Earth-style, I mean. It was the Tenth Year of the Colony, I think. I was just beginning to learn history; but Father and . . . and you, prech Ramarren, used to tell me these things, before we made the Voyage, to explain it all to me. . . ." After several centuries, then, the colony had come onto hard days. Few children were conceived, still fewer born alive. Here again the boy paused, explaining finally, "I remember your telling me that the Alterrans didn't know what was happening to them, they thought it was some bad effect of inbreeding, but actually it was a sort of selection. The Lords, here, say it couldn't have been that, that no matter how long an alien colony is established on a planet they remain alien. With gene-manipulation they can breed with natives, but the children will always be sterile. So I don't know what it was that happened to the Alterrans—I was only a child when you and Father were trying to tell me the story—I do remember you spoke of selection towards a . . . viable type. . . . Anyhow, the colonists were getting near extinction when what was left of them finally managed to make an alliance with a native Werelian nation, Tevar. They wintered-through together, and when the Spring breeding season came, they found that Tevarans and Alterrans could reproduce. Enough of them, at least, to found a hybrid

race. The Lords say that is not possible. But I remember you telling it to me."
The boy looked worried and a little vague.

"Are we descendants of that race?"

"You are descended from the Alterra Agat, who led the colony through the
Winter of the Tenth Year! We learned about Agat even in boy-school. That is
your name, prech Ramarren—Agad of Charen. I am of no such lineage, but
my great-grandmother was of the family Esmy of Kiow—that is an Alterran
name. Of course, in a democratic society as Earth's, these distinctions are
meaningless, aren't they . . . ?" Again Orry looked worried, as if some vague
conflict was occurring in his mind. Falk steered him back to the history of
Werel, filling out with guesses and extrapolation the childish narrative that
was all Orry could supply.

The new mixed stock and mixed culture of the Tevar-Alterran nation flour-
ished in the years after that perilous Tenth Winter. The little cities grew; a
mercantile culture was established on the single north-hemisphere continent.
Within a few generations it was spreading to the primitive peoples of the
southern continents, where the problem of keeping alive through the Winter
was more easily solved. Population went up; science and technology began
their exponential climb, guided and aided always by the Books of Alterra,
the ship's library, the mysteries of which grew explicable as the colonists' remote descendants relearned lost knowledge. They had kept and copied those
books, generation after generation, and learned the tongue they were written
in—Galaktika, of course. Finally, the moon and sister-planets all explored,
the sprawl of cities and the rivalries of nations controlled and balanced by
the powerful Kelshak Empire in the old Northland, at the height of an age of
peace and vigor the Empire had built and sent forth a lightspeed ship.

That ship, the *Alterra,* left Werel eighteen and a half years after the ship
of the Colony from Earth landed: twelve hundred years, Earth style. Its crew
had no idea what they would find on Earth. Werel had not yet been able to
reconstruct the principles of the ansible transmitter, and had hesitated to
broadcast radio-signals that would betray their location to a possible hostile
world ruled by the Enemy the League had feared. To get information living
men must go, and return, crossing the long night to the ancient home of the
Alterrans.

"How long was that voyage?"

"Over two Werelian years—maybe a hundred and thirty or forty light-
years—I was only a boy, a child, prech Ramarren, and some things I didn't
understand, and much wasn't told me—"

Falk did not see why this ignorance should embarrass the lad; he was much more struck by the fact that Orry, who looked fifteen or sixteen, had been alive for perhaps a hundred and fifty years. And himself?

The *Alterra,* Orry went on, had left from a base near the old coast-town Tevar, her coordinates set for Terra. She had carried nineteen people, men, women and children, Kelshak for the most part and claiming Colonist descent: the adults selected by the Harmonious Council of the Empire for training, intelligence, courage, generosity, and arlesh.

"I don't know a word for it in Galaktika. It's just arlesh." Orry smiled his ingenuous smile. "Rale is . . . the right thing to do, like learning things at school, or like a river following its course, and arlesh derives from rale, I guess."

"Tao?" asked Falk; but Orry had never heard of the Old Canon of Man.

"What happened to the ship? What happened to the other seventeen people?"

"We were attacked at the Barrier. The Shing got there only after the *Alterra* was destroyed and the attackers were dispersing. They were rebels, in planetary cars. The Shing rescued me off one. They didn't know whether the rest of us had been killed or carried off by the rebels. They kept searching, over the whole planet, and about a year ago they heard a rumor about a man living in the Eastern Forest—that sounded like it might be one of us. . . ."

"What do you remember of all this—the attack and so on?"

"Nothing. You know how lightspeed flight affects you—"

"I know that for those in the ship, no time passes. But I have no idea how that feels."

"Well, I don't really remember it very clearly. I was just a boy—nine years old, Earth style. And I'm not sure anybody could remember it clearly. You can't tell how—how things relate. You see and hear, but it doesn't hang together— nothing *means* anything—I can't explain it. It's horrible, but only like a dream. But then coming down into planetary space again, you go through what the Lords call the Barrier, and that blacks out the passengers, unless they're prepared for it. Our ship wasn't. None of us had come to when we were attacked, and so I don't remember it, any—any more than you, prech Ramarren. When I came to I was aboard a Shing vessel."

"Why were you brought along as a boy?"

"My father was the captain of the expedition. My mother was on the ship too. You know, otherwise, prech Ramarren—well, if one came back one's people would all have been dead, long long ago. Not that it mattered—my parents are dead, now, anyhow. Or maybe they were treated like you, and . . . and wouldn't recognize me if we met. . . ."

"What was my part in the expedition?"

"You were our navigator."

The irony of that made Falk wince, but Orry went on in his respectful, naive fashion, "Of course, that means you set the ship's course, the coordinates—you were the greatest prosteny, a mathematician-astronomer, in all Kelshy. You were prechnowa to all of us aboard except my father, Har Weden. You are of the Eighth Order, prech Ramarren! You—you remember something of that—?"

Falk shook his head.

The boy subsided, saying at last, sadly, "I can't really believe that you don't remember, except when you do that."

"Shake my head?"

"On Werel we shrug for no. This way."

Orry's simplicity was irresistible. Falk tried the shrug; and it seemed to him that he found a certain rightness in it, a propriety, that could persuade him that it was indeed an old habit. He smiled, and Orry at once cheered up. "You are so like yourself, prech Ramarren, and so different! Forgive me. But what did they do, what did they do to make you forget so much?"

"They destroyed me. Surely I'm like myself. I am myself. I'm Falk. . . ." He put his head in his hands. Orry, abashed, was silent. The quiet, cool air of the room glowed like a blue-green jewel around them; the western wall was lambent with late sunlight.

"How closely do they watch you here?"

"The Lords like me to carry a communicator if I go off by aircar." Orry touched the bracelet on his left wrist, which appeared to be simple gold links. "It can be dangerous, after all, among the natives."

"But you're free to go where you like?"

"Yes, of course. This room of yours is just like mine, across the canyon." Orry looked puzzled again. "We have no enemies here, you know, prech Ramarren," he ventured.

"No? Where are our enemies, then?"

"Well—outside—where you came from—"

They stared at each other in mutual miscomprehension.

"You think men are our enemies—Terrans, human beings? You think it was they that destroyed my mind?"

"Who else?" Orry said, frightened, gaping.

"The aliens—the Enemy—the Shing!"

"But," the boy said with timid gentleness, as if realizing at last how utterly his former lord and teacher was ignorant and astray, "there never was an Enemy. There never was a War."

The room trembled softly like a tapped gong to an almost sub-aural vibration, and a moment afterward a voice, disembodied, spoke: *The Council meets.* The slit-door parted and a tall figure entered, stately in white robes and an ornate black wig. The eyebrows were shaven and repainted high; the face, masked by makeup to a matte smoothness, was that of a husky man of middle age. Orry rose quickly from the table and bowed, whispering, "Lord Abundibot."

"Har Orry," the man acknowledged, his voice also damped to a creaking whisper, then turned to Falk. "Agad Ramarren. Be welcome. The Council of Earth meets, to answer your questions and consider your requests. Behold now . . ." He had glanced at Falk only for a second, and did not approach either Werelian closely. There was a queer air about him of power and also of utter self-containment, self-absorption. He was apart, unapproachable. All three of them stood motionless a moment; and Falk, following the others' gaze, saw that the inner wall of the room had blurred and changed, seeming to be now a depth of clear grayish jelly in which lines and forms twitched and flickered. Then the image came clear, and Falk caught his breath. It was Estrel's face, ten times lifesize. The eyes gazed at him with the remote composure of a painting.

"I am Strella Siobelbel." The lips of the image moved, but the voice had no locality, a cold, abstract whisper trembling in the air of the room. "I was sent to bring to the City in safety the member of the Werel Expedition said to be living in the east of Continent One. I believe this to be the man."

And her face, fading, was replaced by Falk's own.

A disembodied voice, sibilant, inquired, "Does Har Orry recognize this person?"

As Orry answered, his face appeared on the screen. "This is Agad Ramarren, Lords, the Navigator of the *Alterra.*"

The boy's face faded and the screen remained blank, quivering, while many voices whispered and rustled in the air, like a brief multitudinous discussion among spirits, speaking an unknown tongue. This was how the Shing held their Council: each in his own room, apart, with only the presence of whispering voices. As the incomprehensible questioning and replying went on, Falk murmured to Orry, "Do you know this tongue?"

"No, prech Ramarren. They always speak Galaktika to me."

"Why do they talk this way, instead of face to face?"

"There are so many of them—thousands and thousands meet in the Council of Earth, Lord Abundibot told me. And they are scattered over the planet in many places, though Es Toch is the only city. That is Ken Kenyek, now."

The buzz of disembodied voices had died away and a new face had appeared on the screen, a man's face, with dead white skin, black hair, pale eyes. "Agad Ramarren, we are met in Council, and you have been brought into our Council, that you may complete your mission to Earth and, if you desire, return to your home. The Lord Pelleu Abundibot will bespeak you."

The wall abruptly blanked, returned to its normal translucent green. The tall man across the room was gazing steadily at Falk. His lips did not move, but Falk heard him speak, not in a whisper now but clearly—singularly clearly. He could not believe it was mindspeech, yet it could be nothing else. Stripped of the character and timbre, the incarnateness of voice, this was comprehensibility pure and simple, reason addressing reason.

"We mindspeak so that you may hear only truth. For it is not true that we who call ourselves Shing, or any other man, can pervert or conceal truth in paraverbal speech. The Lie that men ascribe to us is itself a lie. But if you choose to use voicespeech do so, and we will do likewise."

"I have no skill at bespeaking," Falk said aloud after a pause. His living voice sounded loud and coarse after the brilliant, silent mind-contact. "But I hear you well enough. I do not ask for the truth. Who am I to demand the truth? But I should like to hear what you choose to tell me."

Young Orry looked shocked. Abundibot's face registered nothing at all. Evidently he was attuned to both Falk and Orry—a rare feat in itself, in Falk's experience—for Orry was quite plainly listening as the telepathic speech began again.

"Men razed your mind and then taught you what they wished you to know—what they wish to believe. So taught, you distrust us. We feared it would be so. But ask what you will, Agad Ramarren of Werel; we will answer with the truth."

"How long have I been here?"

"Six days."

"Why was I drugged and befooled at first?"

"We were attempting to restore your memory. We failed."

Do not believe him, do not believe him, Falk told himself so urgently that no doubt the Shing, if he had any empathic skill at all, received the message clearly. That did not matter. The game must be played, and played their way, though they made all the rules and had all the skill. His ineptitude did not matter. His honesty did. He was staked now totally on one belief: that an honest man cannot be cheated, that truth, if the game be played through right to the end, will lead to truth.

"Tell me why I should trust you," he said.

The mindspeech, pure and clear as an electronically produced musical note, began again, while the sender Abundibot, and he and Orry, stood motionless as pieces on a chessboard.

"We whom you know as Shing are men. We are Terrans, born on Earth of human stock, as was your ancestor Jacob Agat of the First Colony on Werel. Men have taught you what they believe about the history of Earth in the twelve centuries since the Colony on Werel was founded. Now we—men also—will teach you what we know.

"No Enemy ever came from distant stars to attack the League of All Worlds. The League was destroyed by revolution, civil war, by its own corruption, militarism, despotism. On all the worlds there were revolts, rebellions, usurpations; from the Prime World came reprisals that scorched planets to black sand. No more lightspeed ships went out into so risky a future: only the FTLs, the missile-ships, the world-busters. Earth was not destroyed, but half its people were, its cities, its ships and ansibles, its records, its culture—all in two terrible years of civil war between the Loyalists and the Rebels, both armed with the unspeakable weapons developed by the League to fight an alien enemy.

"Some desperate men on Earth, dominating the struggle for a moment but knowing further counter-revolt and wreckage and ruin was inevitable, employed a new weapon. They lied. They invented a name for themselves, and a language, and some vague tales of the remote home-world they came from, and then they went spreading the rumor over Earth, in their own ranks and the Loyalist camps as well, that the Enemy had come. The civil war was all due to the Enemy. The Enemy had infiltrated everywhere, had wrecked the League and was running Earth, was in power now and was going to stop the war. And they had achieved all this by their one unexpectable, sinister, alien power: the power to mind-lie.

"Men believed the tale. It suited their panic, their dismay, their weariness. Their world in ruins around them, they submitted to an Enemy whom they were glad to believe supernatural, invincible. They swallowed the bait of peace.

"And they have lived since then in peace.

"We of Es Toch tell a little myth, which says that in the beginning the

Creator told a great lie. For there was nothing at all, but the Creator spoke, saying, It exists. And behold, in order that the lie of God might be God's truth, the universe at once began to exist. . . .

"If human peace depended on a lie, there were those willing to maintain the lie. Since men insisted that the Enemy had come and ruled the Earth, we called ourselves the Enemy, and ruled. None came to dispute our lie or wreck our peace; the worlds of the League are all sundered, the age of interstellar flight is past; once in a century, perhaps, some ship from a far world blunders here, like yours. There are rebels against our rule, such as those who attacked your ship at the Barrier. We try to control such rebels, for, rightly or wrongly, we bear and have borne for a millennium the burden of human peace. For having told a great lie, we must now uphold a great law. You know the law that we—men among men—enforce: the one Law, learned in humanity's most terrible hour."

The brilliant toneless mindspeech ceased; it was like the switching off of a light. In the silence like darkness which followed, young Orry whispered aloud, "Reverence for Life."

Silence again. Falk stood motionless, trying not to betray in his face or in his perhaps overheard thoughts the confusion and irresolution he felt. Was all he had learned false? Had mankind indeed no Enemy?

"If this history is the true one," he said at last, "why do you not tell it and prove it to men?"

"We are men," came the telepathic answer. "There are thousands upon thousands of us who know the truth. We are those who have power and knowl-edge, and use them for peace. There come dark ages, and this is one of them, all through man's history, when people will have it that the world is ruled by demons. We play the part of demons in their mythologies. When they begin to replace mythology with reason, we help them; and they learn the truth."

"Why do you tell me these things?"

"For truth's sake, and for your own."

"Who am I to deserve the truth?" Falk repeated coldly, looking across the room into Abundibot's masklike face.

"You were a messenger from a lost world, a colony of which all record was lost in the Years of Trouble. You came to Earth, and we, the Lords of Earth, failed to protect you. This is a shame and a grief to us. It was men of Earth who attacked you, killed or mindrazed all your company—men of Earth, of the planet to which, after so many centuries, you were returning. They were rebels from Continent Three, which is neither so primitive nor so sparsely in-habited as this Continent One; they were using stolen interplanetary cars;

they assumed that any lightspeed ship must belong to the 'Shing,' and so attacked it without warning. This we could have prevented, had we been more alert. We owe to you any reparation we can make."

"They have sought for you and the others all these years," Orry put in, earnest and a little pleading; obviously he very much wanted Falk to believe it all, to accept it, and to—to do what?

"You tried to restore my memory," Falk said. "Why?"

"Is that not what you came seeking here: your lost self?"

"Yes. It is. But I . . ." He did not even know what questions to ask; he could neither believe nor disbelieve all he had been told. There seemed to be no standard to judge it all by. That Zove and the others had lied to him was inconceivable, but that they themselves were deceived and ignorant was certainly possible. He was incredulous of everything Abundibot affirmed, and yet it had been mindsent, in clear immediate mindspeech where lying was impossible— or was it possible? If a liar says he is not lying—Falk gave it all up again. Looking once more at Abundibot he said, "Please do not bespeak me. I—I would rather hear your voice. You found, I think you said, that you could not restore my memory?"

Abundibot's muted, creaking whisper in Galaktika came strangely after the fluency of his sending. "Not by the means we used."

"By other means?"

"Possibly. We thought you had been given a parahypnotic block. Instead, you were mindrazed. We do not know where the rebels learned that technique, which we keep a close secret. An even closer secret is the fact that a razed mind can be restored." A smile appeared for a moment on the heavy, masklike face, then disappeared completely. "With our psychocomputer techniques, we think we can effect the restoration in your case. However, this incurs the permanent total blocking of the replacement-personality; and this being so we did not wish to proceed without your consent."

The replacement-personality . . . It meant nothing particular. What did it mean?

Falk felt a little cold creep over him, and he said carefully, "Do you mean that, in order to remember what I was, I must . . . forget what I am?"

"Unfortunately that is the case. We regret it very much. The loss, however, of a replacement-personality of a few years' growth is, though regrettable, perhaps not too high a price to pay for the repossession of a mind such as yours obviously was, and, of course, for the chance of completing your great mission across the stars and returning at last to your home with the knowledge you so gallantly came to seek."

Despite his rusty, unused-sounding whisper, Abundibot was as fluent in speaking as in mindspeaking; his words poured out and Falk caught the meaning, if he caught it, only on the third or fourth bounce. . . . "The chance— of completing—?" he repeated, feeling a fool, and glancing at Orry as if for support. "You mean, you would send me—us—back to . . . this planet I am supposed to have come from?"

"We would consider it an honor and a beginning of the reparation due you to give you a lightspeed ship for the voyage home to Werel."

"Earth is my home," Falk said with sudden violence. Abundibot was silent. After a minute the boy spoke: "Werel is mine, prech Ramarren," he said wistfully. "And I can never go back to it without you."

"Why not?"

"I don't know where it is. I was a child. Our ship was destroyed, the course-computers and all were blown up when we were attacked. I can't recalculate the course!"

"But these people have lightspeed ships and course-computers! What do you mean? What star does Werel circle, that's all you need to know."

"But I don't know it."

"This is nonsense," Falk began, pushed by mounting incredulity into anger. Abundibot held up his hand in a curiously potent gesture. "Let the boy explain, Agad Ramarren," he whispered.

"Explain that he doesn't know the name of his planet's sun?"

"It's true, prech Ramarren," Orry said shakily, his face crimson. "If—if you were only yourself, you'd know it without being told. I was in my ninth moonphase—I was still First Level. The Levels . . . Well, our civilization, at home, it's different from anything here, I guess. Now that I see it by the light of what the Lords here try to do, and democratic ideals, I realize it's very backward in some ways. But anyhow, there are the Levels, that cut across all the Orders and ranks, and make up the Basic Harmony of—prechnoye. . . . I don't know how to say it in Galaktika. Knowledge, I guess. Anyway I was on the First Level, being a child, and you were Eighth Level and Order. And each Level has—things you don't learn, and things you aren't told, and can't be told or understand, until you enter into it. And below the Seventh Level, I think, you don't learn the True Name of the World or the True Name of the Sun—they're just the world, Werel, and the sun, prahan. The True Names are the old ones—they're in the Eighth Analect of the Books of Alterra, the books of the Colony. They're in Galaktika, so that they'd mean something to the Lords here. But I couldn't tell them, because I didn't know; all I know is 'sun' and 'world,' and that wouldn't get me home—nor you, if you can't remember what you knew! Which sun? Which world? Oh, you've got to let them give you your memory back, prech Ramarren! Do you see?"

"As through a glass," Falk said, "darkly."

And with the words from the Yaweh Canon he remembered all at once, certain and vivid amidst his bewilderment, the sun shining above the Clearing, bright on the windy, branch-embowered balconies of the Forest House. Then it was not his name he had come here to learn, but the sun's, the true name of the sun.

8

The strange unseen Council of the Lords of Earth was over. In parting Abundibot had said to Falk, "The choice is yours: to remain Falk, our guest on Earth, or to regain your heritage and complete your destiny as Agad Ramarren of Werel. We wish that the choice be made knowingly and in your own time. We await your decision and will abide by it." Then to Orry: "Make your kinsman free of the City, Har Orry, and let all he and you desire be known to us." The slit-door opened behind Abundibot and he withdrew, his tall bulky figure vanishing so abruptly outside the doorway that it seemed to have been flicked off. Had he in fact been there in substance, or only as some kind of projection? Falk was not sure. He wondered if he had yet seen a Shing, or only the shadows and images of the Shing.

"Is there anywhere we can walk—out of doors?" he asked the boy abruptly, sick of the indirect and insubstantial ways and walls of this place, and also wondering how far their freedom actually extended.

"Anywhere, prech Ramarren. Out in the streets—or shall we take a slider? Or there is a garden here in the Palace."

"A garden will do."

Orry led him down a great, empty, glowing corridor and through a valve-door into a small room. "The Garden," he said aloud, and the valve shut; there was no sense of motion but when it opened they stepped out into a garden. It was scarcely out of doors: the translucent walls glimmered with the lights of the City, far below; the moon, near full, shone hazy and distorted through the glassy roof. The place was full of soft moving lights and shadows, crowded with tropical shrubs and vines that twined about trellises and hung from arbors, their masses of cream and crimson flowers sweetening the steamy air, their leafage closing off vision within a few feet on every side. Falk turned suddenly to make sure that the path to the exit still lay clear behind him. The hot, heavy, perfumed silence was uncanny; it seemed to him for a moment that the ambiguous depths of the garden held a hint of something alien and enormously remote, the hues, the mood, the complexity of a lost world, a planet of perfumes and illusions, of swamps and transformations. . . .

On the path among the shadowy flowers Orry paused to take a small white tube from a case and insert it endwise between his lips, sucking on it eagerly. Falk was too absorbed in other impressions to pay much heed, but as if slightly embarrassed the boy explained, "It's pariitha, a tranquillant—the Lords all use it; it has a very stimulating effect on the mind. If you'd care to—"

"No, thanks. There are some more things I want to ask you." He hesitated, however. His new questions could not be entirely direct. Throughout the "Council" and Abundibot's explanations he had felt, recurrently and uncomfortably, that the whole thing was a performance—a *play*, such as he had seen on ancient telescrolls in the library of the Prince of Kansas, the Dreamplay of Hain, the mad old king Lir raving on a stormswept heath. But the curious thing was his distinct impression that the play was not being acted for his benefit, but for Orry's. He did not understand why, but again and again he had felt that all Abundibot said to him was said to prove something to the boy.

And the boy believed it. It was no play to him; or else he was an actor in it.

"One thing puzzles me," Falk said, cautiously. "You told me that Werel is a hundred and thirty or forty light-years from Earth. There cannot be very many stars at just that distance."

"The Lords say there are four stars with planets that might be our system, between a hundred and fifteen and a hundred and fifty light-years away. But they are in four different directions, and if the Shing sent out a ship to search it could spend up to thirteen hundred years real-time going to and among those four to find the right one."

"Though you were a child, it seems a little strange that you didn't know how long the voyage was to take—how old you would be when you got home, as it were."

"It was spoken of as 'two years,' prech Ramarren—that is, roughly a hundred and twenty Earth years—but it was clear to me that that was not the exact figure, and that I was not to ask the exact figure." For a moment, harking back thus to Werel, the boy spoke with a touch of sober resoluteness that he did not show at other times. "I think that perhaps, not knowing who or what they were going to find on Earth, the adults of the Expedition wanted to be sure that we children, with no mindguard technique, could not give away Werel's location to an enemy. It was safest for us to be ignorant, perhaps."

"Do you remember how the stars looked from Werel—the constellations?"

Orry shrugged for no, and smiled. "The Lords asked that too. I was Winter-born, prech Ramarren. Spring was just beginning when we left. I scarcely ever saw a cloudless sky."

If all this was true, then it would seem that in fact only he—his suppressed self, Ramarren—could say where he and Orry came from. Would that then explain what seemed almost the central puzzle, the interest the Shing took in him, their bringing him here under Estrel's tutelage, their offer to restore his memory? There was a world not under their control; it had re-invented light-speed flight; they would want to know where it was. And if they restored his memory, he could tell them. If they could restore his memory. If anything at all of what they had told him was true.

He sighed. He was weary of this turmoil of suspicions, this plethora of un-substantiated marvels. At moments he wondered if he was still under the influence of some drug. He felt wholly inadequate to judge what he should do. He, and probably this boy, were like toys in the hands of strange faithless players.

"Was he—the one called Abundibot—was he in the room just now, or was it a projection, an illusion?"

"I don't know, prech Ramarren," Orry replied. The stuff he was breathing in from the tube seemed to cheer and soothe him; always rather childlike, he spoke now with blithe ease. "I expect he was there. But they never come close. I tell you—this is strange—in this long time I've been here, six years, I have never touched one of them. They keep very much apart, each one alone. I don't mean that they are unkind," he added hastily, looking with his clear eyes at Falk to make sure he had not given the wrong impression. "They are very kind. I am very fond of Lord Abundibot, and Ken Kenyek, and Parla. But they are so far—beyond me— They know so much. They bear so much. They keep knowledge alive, and keep the peace, and bear the burdens, and so they have done for a thousand years, while the rest of the people of Earth take no responsibility and live in brutish freedom. Their fellow men hate them and will not learn the truth they offer. And so they must always hold them-selves apart, stay alone, in order to preserve the peace and the skills and knowledge that would be lost, without them, in a few years, among these warrior tribes and houses and Wanderers and roving cannibals."

"They are not all cannibals," Falk said dryly.

Orry's well-learnt lesson seemed to have run out. "No," he agreed, "I sup-pose not."

"Some of them say that they have sunk so low because the Shing keep them low; that if they seek knowledge the Shing prevent them, if they seek to form a City of their own the Shing destroy it, and them."

There was a pause. Orry finished sucking on his tube of pariitha and carefully buried it around the roots of a shrub with long, hanging, flesh-red flowers. Falk waited for his answer and only gradually realized that there was not going to be one. What he had said simply had not penetrated, had not made sense to the boy.

They walked on a little among the shifting lights and damp fragrances of the garden, the moon blurred above them.

"The one whose image appeared first, just now . . . do you know her?"

"Strella Siobelbel," the boy answered readily. "Yes, I have seen her at Council Meetings before."

"Is she a Shing?"

"No, she's not one of the Lords; I think her people are mountain natives, but she was brought up in Es Toch. Many people bring or send their children here to be brought up in the service of the Lords. And children with subnormal minds are brought here and keyed into the psychocomputers, so that even they can share in the great work. Those are the ones the ignorant call toolmen. You came here with Strella Siobelbel, prech Ramarren?"

"Came with her; walked with her, ate with her, slept with her. She called herself Estrel, a Wanderer."

"You could have known she was not a Shing—" the boy said, then went red, and got out another of his tranquillant-tubes and began sucking on it.

"A Shing would not have slept with me?" Falk inquired. The boy shrugged his Werelian "No," still blushing; the drug finally encouraged him to speak and he said, "They do not touch common men, prech Ramarren—they are like gods, cold and kind and wise—they hold themselves apart—"

He was fluent, incoherent, childish. Did he know his own loneliness, orphaned and alien, living out his childhood and entering adolescence among these people who held themselves apart, who would not touch him, who stuffed him with words but left him so empty of reality that, at fifteen, he sought contentment from a drug? He certainly did not know his isolation as such—he did not seem to have clear ideas on anything much—but it looked from his eyes sometimes, yearning, at Falk. Yearning and feebly hoping, the look of one perishing of thirst in a dry salt desert who looks up at a mirage. There was much more Falk wanted to ask him, but little use in asking. Pitying him, Falk put his hand on Orry's slender shoulder. The boy started at the touch, smiled timidly and vaguely, and sucked again at his tranquillant.

Back in his room, where everything was so luxuriously arranged for his comfort—and to impress Orry?—Falk paced a while like a caged bear, and finally lay down to sleep. In his dreams he was in a house, like the Forest House, but the people in the dream house had eyes the color of agate and amber. He tried to tell them he was one of them, their own kinsman, but they did not understand his speech and watched him strangely while he stammered and sought for the right words, the true words, the true name.

Toolmen waited to serve him when he woke. He dismissed them, and they left. He went out into the hall. No one barred his way; he met no one as he went on. It all seemed deserted, no one stirring in the long misty corridors or on the ramps or inside the half-seen, dim-walled rooms whose doors he could not find. Yet all the time he felt he was being watched, that every move he made was seen.

When he found his way back to his room Orry was waiting for him, wanting to show him about the city. All afternoon they explored, on foot and on a paristolis slider, the streets and terraced gardens, the bridges and palaces and dwellings of Es Toch. Orry was liberally provided with the slips of iridium that served as money, and when Falk remarked that he did not like the fancy-dress his hosts had provided him, Orry insisted they go to a clothier's shop and outfit him as he wished. He stood among racks and tables of gorgeous cloth, woven and plastiformed, dazzling with bright patterned colors; he thought of Parth weaving at her small loom in the sunlight, a pattern of white cranes on gray. "I will weave black cloth to wear," she had said, and remembering that he chose, from all the lovely rainbow of robes and gowns and clothing, black breeches and dark shirt and a short black cloak of wintercloth.

"Those are a little like our clothes at home—on Werel," Orry said, looking doubtfully for a moment at his own flame-red tunic. "Only we had no wintercloth there. Oh, there would be so much we could take back from Earth to Werel, to tell them and teach them, if we could go!"

They went on to an eating-place built out on a transparent shelf over the gorge. As the cold, bright evening of the high mountains darkened the abyss under them, the buildings that sprang up from its edges glowed iridescent and the streets and hanging bridges blazed with lights. Music undulated in the air about them as they ate the spice-disguised foods and watched the crowds of the city come and go.

Some of the people who walked in Es Toch were dressed poorly, some lavishly, many in the transvestite, gaudy apparel that Falk vaguely remembered seeing Estrel wear. There were many physical types, some different from any

Falk had ever seen. One group was whitish-skinned, with blue eyes and hair like straw. Falk thought they had bleached themselves somehow, but Orry explained they were tribesmen from an area on Continent Two, whose culture was being encouraged by the Shing, who brought their leaders and young people here by aircar to see Es Toch and learn its ways. "You see, prech Ramarren, it is not true that the Lords refuse to teach the natives—it is the natives who refuse to learn. These white ones are sharing the Lords' knowledge."

"And what have they forgotten, to earn that prize?" Falk asked, but the question meant nothing to Orry. He knew almost nothing of any of the "natives," how they lived or what they knew. Shopkeepers and waiters he treated with condescension, pleasantly, as a man among inferiors. This arrogance he might have brought from Werel; he described Kelshak society as hierarchic, intensely conscious of each person's place on a scale or in an order, though what established the order, what values it was founded on, Falk did not understand. It was not mere birth-ranking, but Orry's childish memories did not suffice to give a clear picture. However that might be, Falk disliked the tone of the word "natives" in Orry's mouth, and he finally asked with a trace of irony, "How do you know which you should bow to and which should bow to you? I can't tell Lords from natives. The Lords *are* natives—aren't they?"

"Oh, yes. The natives call themselves that, because they insist the Lords are alien conquerors. I can't always tell them apart either," the boy said with his vague, engaging, ingenuous smile.

"Most of these people in the streets are Shing?"

"I suppose so. Of course I only know a few by sight."

"I don't understand what keeps the Lords, the Shing, apart from the natives, if they are all Terran men together."

"Why, knowledge, power—the Lords have been ruling Earth for longer than the achinowao have been ruling Kelshy!"

"But they keep themselves a caste apart? You said the Lords believe in democracy." It was an antique word and had struck him when Orry used it; he was not sure of its meaning but knew it had to do with general participation in government.

"Yes, certainly, prech Ramarren. The Council rules democratically for the good of all, and there is no king or dictator. Shall we go to a pariitha-hall? They have stimulants, if you don't care for pariitha, and dancers and tëanb-players—"

"Do you like music?"

"No," the boy said with apologetic candor. "It makes me want to weep or scream. Of course on Werel only animals and little children sing. It is—it seems wrong to hear grown men do it. But the Lords like to encourage the native arts. And the dancing, sometimes that's very pretty. . . ."

"No." A restlessness was rising strong in Falk, a will to see the thing through and be done with it. "I have a question for that one called Abundibot, if he will see us."

"Surely. He was my teacher for a long time; I can call him with this." Orry raised toward his mouth the gold-link bracelet on his wrist. While he spoke into it Falk sat remembering Estrel's muttered prayers to her amulet and marveling at his own vast obtuseness. Any fool might have guessed the thing was a transmitter; any fool but this one. . . . "Lord Abundibot says to come as soon as we please. He is in the East Palace," Orry announced, and they left, Orry tossing a slip of money to the bowing waiter who saw them out.

Spring thunderclouds had hidden stars and moon, but the streets blazed with light. Falk went through them with a heavy heart. Despite all his fears he had longed to see the city, *elonaae*, the Place of Men; but it only worried and wearied him. It was not the crowds that bothered him, though he had never in his memory seen more than ten houses or a hundred people together. It was not the reality of the city that was overwhelming, but its unreality. This was not a Place of Men. Es Toch gave no sense of history, of reaching back in time and out in space, though it had ruled the world for a millennium. There were none of the libraries, schools, museums which ancient telescrolls in Zove's House had led him to look for; there were no monuments or reminders of the Great Age of Man; there was no flow of learning or of goods. The money used was a mere largesse of the Shing, for there was no economy to give the place a true vitality of its own. Though there were said to be so many of the Lords, yet on Earth they kept only this one city, held apart, as Earth itself was held apart from the other worlds that once had formed the League. Es Toch was self-contained, self-nourished, rootless; all its brilliance and transience of lights and machines and faces, its multiplicity of strangers, its luxurious complexity was built across a chasm in the ground, a hollow place. It was the Place of the Lie. Yet it was wonderful, like a carved jewel fallen in the vast wilderness of the Earth: wonderful, timeless, alien.

Their slider bore them over one of the swooping railless bridges towards a luminous tower. The river far below ran invisible in darkness; the mountains were hidden by night and storm and the city's glare. Toolmen met Falk and Orry at the entrance to the tower, ushered them into a valve-elevator and thence into a room whose walls, windowless and translucent as always, seemed made of bluish, sparkling mist. They were asked to be seated, and were served tall silver cups of some drink. Falk tasted it gingerly and was surprised to find it the same juniper-flavored liquor he had once been given in the Enclave of Kansas. He knew it was a strong intoxicant and drank no more; but Orry swigged his down with relish. Abundibot entered, tall, white-robed, mask-faced, dismissing the toolmen with a slight gesture. He stopped at some distance from Falk and Orry. The toolmen had left a third silver cup on the little stand. He raised it as if in salute, drank it right off, and then said in his dry whispering voice, "You do not drink, Lord Ramarren. There is an old, old saying on Earth: In wine is truth." He smiled and ceased smiling. "But your thirst is for the truth, not for the wine, perhaps."

"There is a question I wish to ask you."

"Only one?" The note of mockery seemed clear to Falk, so clear that he glanced at Orry to see if he had caught it. But the boy, sucking on another tube of pariitha, his gray-gold eyes lowered, had caught nothing.

"I should prefer to speak to you alone, for a moment," Falk said abruptly.

At that Orry looked up, puzzled; the Shing said, "You may, of course. It will make no difference, however, to my answer, if Har Orry is here or not here. There is nothing we keep from him that we might tell you, as there is nothing we might tell him and keep from you. If you prefer that he leave, however, it shall be so."

"Wait for me in the hall, Orry," Falk said; docile, the boy went out. When the vertical lips of the door had closed behind him, Falk said—whispered, rather, because everyone whispered here—"I wished to repeat what I asked you before. I am not sure I understood. You can restore my earlier memory only at the cost of my present memory—is that true?"

"Why do you ask me what is true? Will you believe it?"

"Why—why should I not believe it?" Falk replied, but his heart sank, for he felt the Shing was playing with him, as with a creature totally incompetent and powerless.

"Are we not the Liars? You must not believe anything we say. That is what you were taught in Zove's House, that is what you think. We know what you think."

"Tell me what I ask," Falk said, knowing the futility of his stubbornness.

"I will tell you what I told you before, and as best I can, though it is Ken Kenyek who knows these matters best. He is our most skilled mindhandler. Do you wish me to call him?—no doubt he will be willing to project to us here. No? It does not matter, of course. Crudely expressed, the answer to your question is this: Your mind was, as we say, razed. Mindrazing is an operation, not a surgical one of course, but a paramental one involving psycho-electric equipment, the effects of which are much more absolute than those of any mere hypnotic block. The restoration of a razed mind is possible, but is a much more drastic matter, accordingly, than the removal of a hypnotic block. What is in question, to you, at this moment, is a secondary, super-added, partial memory and personality-structure, which you now call your 'self.' This is, of course, not the case. Looked at impartially, this second-growth self of yours is a mere rudiment, emotionally stunted and intellectually incompetent, compared to the true self which lies so deeply hidden. As we cannot and do not expect you to be able to look at it impartially, however, we wish we could assure you that the restoration of Ramarren will include the continuity of Falk. And we have been tempted to lie to you about this, to spare you fear and doubt and make your decision easy. But it is best that you know the truth; we would not have it otherwise, nor, I think, would you. The truth is this: when we restore to its normal condition and function the synaptic totality of your original mind, if I may so simplify the incredibly complex operation which Ken Kenyek and his psychocomputers are ready to perform, this restoration will entail the total blocking of the secondary synaptic totality which you now consider to be your mind and self. This secondary totality will be irrecoverably suppressed: razed in its turn."

"To revive Ramarren you must kill Falk, then."

"We do not kill," the Shing said in his harsh whisper, then repeated it with blazing intensity in mindspeech—"*We do not kill!*"

There was a pause.

"To gain the great you must give up the less. It is always the rule," the Shing whispered.

"To live one must agree to die," Falk said, and saw the mask-face wince. "Very well. I agree. I consent to let you kill me. My consent does not really matter, does it?—yet you want it."

"We will not kill you." The whisper was louder. "We do not kill. We do not take life. We are restoring you to your true life and being. Only you must forget. That is the price; there is not any choice or doubt: to be Ramarren you must forget Falk. To this you must consent, indeed, but it is all we ask."

"Give me one day more," Falk said, and then rose, ending the conversation. He had lost; he was powerless. And yet he had made the mask wince, he had touched, for a moment, the very quick of the lie; and in that moment he had sensed that, had he the wits or strength to reach it, the truth lay very close at hand.

Falk left the building with Orry, and when they were in the street he said, "Come with me a minute. I want to speak with you outside those walls." They crossed the bright street to the edge of the cliff and stood side by side there in the cold night-wind of spring, the lights of the bridge shooting on out past them, over the black chasm that dropped sheer away from the street's edge.

"When I was Ramarren," Falk said slowly, "had I the right to ask a service of you?"

"Any service," the boy answered with the sober promptness that seemed to hark back to his early training on Werel.

Falk looked straight at him, holding his gaze a moment. He pointed to the bracelet of gold links on Orry's wrist, and with a gesture indicated that he should slip it off and toss it into the gorge.

Orry began to speak: Falk put his finger to his lips.

The boy's gaze flickered; he hesitated, then slipped the chain off and cast it down into the dark. Then he turned again to Falk his face in which fear, confusion, and the longing for approval were clear to see.

For the first time, Falk bespoke him in mindspeech: "Do you wear any other device or ornament, Orry?"

At first the boy did not understand. Falk's sending was inept and weak compared to that of the Shing. When he did at last understand, he replied paraverbally, with great clarity, "No, only the communicator. Why did you bid me throw it away?"

"I wish to speak with no listener but you, Orry."

The boy looked awed and scared. "The Lords can hear," he whispered aloud. "They can hear mindspeech anywhere, prech Ramarren—and I had only begun my training in mindguarding—"

"Then we'll speak aloud," Falk said, though he doubted that the Shing could overhear mindspeech "anywhere," without mechanical aid of some kind. "This is what I wish to ask you. These Lords of Es Toch brought me here, it seems, to restore my memory as Ramarren. But they can do it, or will do it, only at the cost of my memory of myself as I am now, and all I have learned on Earth. This they insist upon. I do not wish it to be so. I do not wish to forget what I know and guess, and be an ignorant tool in their hands. I do not wish to die again before my death! I don't think I can withstand them, but I will try, and the service I ask of you is this—" He stopped, hesitant among choices, for he had not worked out his plan at all.

Orry's face, which had been excited, now dulled with confusion again, and finally he said, "But why . . ."

"Well?" Falk said, seeing the authority he had briefly exerted over the boy evaporate. Still, he had shocked Orry into asking "Why?" and if he was ever to get through to the boy, it would be right now.

"Why do you mistrust the Lords? Why should they want to suppress your memory of Earth?"

"Because Ramarren does not know what I know. Nor do you. And our ignorance may betray the world that sent us here."

"But you . . . you don't even remember our world. . . ."

"No. But I will not serve the Liars who rule this one. Listen to me. This is all I can guess of what they want. They will restore my former mind in order to learn the true name, the location of our home world. If they learn it while they are working on my mind, then I think they'll kill me then and there, and tell you that the operation was fatal; or raze my mind once more and tell you that the operation was a failure. If not, they'll let me live, at least until I tell them what they want to know. And I won't know enough, as Ramarren, not to tell them. Then they'll send us back to Werel—sole survivors of the great journey, returning after centuries to tell Werel how, on dark barbaric Earth, the Shing bravely hold the torch of civilization alight. The Shing who are no man's Enemy, the self-sacrificing Lords, the wise Lords who are really men of Earth, not aliens or conquerors. We will tell Werel all about the friendly Shing. And they'll believe us. They will believe the lies we believe. And so they will fear no attack from the Shing; and they will not send help to the men of Earth, the true men who await deliverance from the Lie."

"But prech Ramarren, those are not lies," Orry said.

Falk looked at him a minute in the diffuse, bright, shifting light. His heart sank, but he said finally, "Will you do the service I asked of you?"

"Yes," the boy whispered.

"Without telling any other living being what it is?"

"Yes."

"It is simply this. When you first see me as Ramarren—if you ever do— then say to me these words: Read the first page of the book."

"'Read the first page of the book,'" Orry repeated, docile.

There was a pause. Falk stood feeling himself encompassed by futility, like a fly bundled in spider-silk.

"Is that all the service, prech Ramarren?"

"That's all."

The boy bowed his head and muttered a sentence in his native tongue, evidently some formula of promising. Then he asked, "What should I tell them about the bracelet communicator, prech Ramarren?"

"The truth—it doesn't matter, if you keep the other secret," Falk said. It seemed, at least, that they had not taught the boy to lie. But they had not taught him to know truth from lies.

Orry took him back across the bridge on his slider, and he reentered the shining, mist-walled palace where Estrel had first brought him. Once alone in his room he gave way to fear and rage, knowing how he was utterly fooled and made helpless; and when he had controlled his anger still he walked the room like a bear in a cage, contending with the fear of death.

If he besought them, might they not let him live on as Falk, who was useless to them, but harmless?

No. They would not. That was clear, and only cowardice made him turn to the notion. There was no hope there.

Could he escape?

Maybe. The seeming emptiness of this great building might be a sham, or a trap, or like so much else here, an illusion. He felt and guessed that he was constantly spied upon, aurally or visually, by hidden presences or devices. All doors were guarded by toolmen or electronic monitors. But if he did escape from Es Toch, what then?

Could he make his way back across the mountains, across the plains, through the forest, and come at last to the Clearing, where Parth . . . No! He stopped himself in anger. He could not go back. This far he had come following his way, and he must follow on to the end: through death if it must be, to rebirth—the rebirth of a stranger, of an alien soul.

But there was no one here to tell that stranger and alien the truth. There was no one here that Falk could trust, except himself, and therefore not only must Falk die, but his dying must serve the will of the Enemy. That was what he could not bear; that was unendurable. He paced up and down the still, greenish dusk of his room. Blurred inaudible lightning flashed across the ceiling. He would not serve the Liars; he would not tell them what they wanted to know. It was not Werel he cared for—for all he knew, his guesses were all astray and Werel itself was a lie, Orry a more elaborate Estrel; there was no telling. But he loved Earth, though he was alien upon it. And Earth to him meant the house in the forest, the sunlight on the Clearing, Parth. These he would not betray. He must believe that there was a way to keep himself, against all force and trickery, from betraying them.

Again and again he tried to imagine some way in which he as Falk could leave a message for himself as Ramarren: a problem in itself so grotesque it beggared his imagination, and beyond that, insoluble. If the Shing did not watch him write such a message, certainly they would find it when it was written. He had thought at first to use Orry as the go-between, ordering him to tell Ramarren, "Do not answer the Shing's questions," but he had not been able to trust Orry to obey, or to keep the order secret. The Shing had so mindhandled the boy that he was by now, essentially, their instrument; and even the meaningless message that Falk had given him might already be known to his Lords.

There was no device or trick, no means or way to get around or get out. There was only one hope, and that very small: that he could hold on; that through whatever they did to him he could keep hold of himself and refuse to forget, refuse to die. The only thing that gave him grounds for hoping that this might be possible was that the Shing had said it was impossible.

They wanted him to believe that it was impossible.

The delusions and apparitions and hallucinations of his first hours or days in Es Toch had been worked on him, then, only to confuse him and weaken his self-trust: for that was what they were after. They wanted him to distrust himself, his beliefs, his knowledge, his strength. All the explanations about mindrazing were then equally a scare, a bogey, to convince him that he could not possibly withstand their parahypnotic operations.

Ramarren had not withstood them. . . .

But Ramarren had had no suspicion or warning of their powers or what they would try to do to him, whereas Falk did. That might make a difference. Even so, Ramarren's memory had not been destroyed beyond recall, as they insisted Falk's would be: the proof of that was that they intended to recall it.

A hope; a very small hope. All he could do was say *I will survive* in the hope it might be true; and with luck, it would be. And without luck . . . ?

Hope is a slighter, tougher thing even than trust, he thought, pacing his room as the soundless, vague lightning flashed overhead. In a good season one trusts life; in a bad season one only hopes. But they are of the same essence: they are the mind's indispensable relationship with other minds, with the world, and with time. Without trust, a man lives, but not a human life; without hope, he dies. When there is no relationship, where hands do not touch, emotion atrophies in void and intelligence goes sterile and obsessed. Between men the only link left is that of owner to slave, or murderer to victim.

Laws are made against the impulse a people most fears in itself. *Do not kill* was the Shing's vaunted single Law. All else was permitted: which meant, perhaps, there was little else they really wanted to do. . . . Fearing their own profound attraction towards death, they preached Reverence for Life, fooling themselves at last with their own lie.

Against them he could never prevail except, perhaps, through the one quality no liar can cope with, integrity. Perhaps it would not occur to them that a man could so will to be himself, to live his life, that he might resist them even when helpless in their hands.

Perhaps, perhaps.

Deliberately stilling his thoughts at last, he took up the book that the Prince of Kansas had given him and which, belying the Prince's prediction, he had not yet lost again, and read in it for a while, very intently, before he slept.

Next morning—his last, perhaps, of this life—Orry suggested that they sightsee by aircar, and Falk assented, saying that he wished to see the Western Ocean. With elaborate courtesy two of the Shing, Abundibot and Ken Kenyek, asked if they might accompany their honored guest, and answer any further questions he might wish to ask about the Dominion of Earth, or about the operation planned for tomorrow. Falk had had some vague hopes in fact of learning more details of what they planned to do to his mind, so as to be able to put up a stronger resistance to it. It was no good. Ken Kenyek poured out endless verbiage concerning neurons and synapses, salvaging, blocking, releasing, drugs, hypnosis, parahypnosis, brain-linked computers . . . none of which was meaningful, all of which was frightening. Falk soon ceased to try to understand.

The aircar, piloted by a speechless toolman who seemed little more than an extension of the controls, cleared the mountains and shot west over the deserts, bright with the brief flower of their spring. Within a few minutes they were nearing the granite face of the Western Range. Still sheered and smashed and raw from the cataclysms of two thousand years ago, the Sierras stood, jagged pinnacles upthrust from chasms of snow. Over the crests lay the ocean, bright in the sunlight; dark beneath the waves lay the drowned lands.

There were cities there, obliterated—as there were in his own mind forgotten cities, lost places, lost names. As the aircar circled to return eastward he said, "Tomorrow the earthquake; and Falk goes under. . . ."

"A pity it must be so, Lord Ramarren," Abundibot said with satisfaction. Or it seemed to Falk that he spoke with satisfaction. Whenever Abundibot expressed any emotion in words, the expression rang so false that it seemed to imply an opposite emotion; but perhaps what it implied actually was a total lack of any affect or feeling whatsoever. Ken Kenyek, white-faced and pale-eyed, with regular, ageless features, neither showed nor pretended any emotion when he spoke or when, as now, he sat motionless and expressionless, neither serene nor stolid but utterly closed, self-sufficient, remote.

The aircar flashed back across the desert miles between Es Toch and the sea; there was no sign of human habitation in all that great expanse. They landed on the roof of the building in which Falk's room was. After a couple of hours spent in the cold, heavy presence of the Shing he craved even that illusory solitude. They permitted him to have it; the rest of the afternoon and the evening he spent alone in the mist-walled room. He had feared the Shing might drug him again or send illusions to distract and weaken him, but apparently they felt they need take no more precautions with him. He was left undisturbed, to pace the translucent floor, to sit still, and to read in his book. What, after all, could he do against their will?

Again and again through the long hours he returned to the book, the Old Canon. He did not dare mark it even with his fingernail; he only read it, well as he knew it, with total absorption, page after page, yielding himself to the words, repeating them to himself as he paced or sat or lay, and returning again and again and yet again to the beginning, the first words of the first page:

> *The way that can be gone*
> *is not the eternal Way.*
> *The name that can be named*
> *is not the eternal Name.*

And far into the night, under the pressure of weariness and of hunger, of the thoughts he would not allow himself to think and the terror of death that he would not allow himself to feel, his mind entered at last the state he had sought. The walls fell away; his self fell away from him, and he was nothing. He was the words: he was the word, the word spoken in darkness with none to hear at the beginning, the first page of time. His self had fallen from him and he was utterly, everlastingly himself: nameless, single, one.

Gradually the moment returned, and things had names, and the walls arose. He read the first page of the book once again, and then lay down and slept.

The east wall of his room was emerald-bright with early sunlight when a couple of toolmen came for him and took him down through the misty hall and levels of the building to the street, and by slider through the shadowy streets and across the chasm to another tower. These two were not the servants who had waited on him, but a pair of big, speechless guards. Remembering the methodical brutality of the beating he had got when he had first entered Es Toch, the first lesson in self-distrust the Shing had given him, he guessed that they had been afraid he might try to escape at this last minute, and had provided these guards to discourage any such impulse.

He was taken into a maze of rooms that ended in brightly lit, underground cubicles all walled in by and dominated by the screens and banks of an immense computer complex. In one of these Ken Kenyek came forward to meet him, alone. It was curious how he had seen the Shing only one or two at a time, and very few of them in all. But there was no time to puzzle over that now, though on the fringes of his mind a vague memory, an explanation, danced for a moment, until Ken Kenyek spoke.

"You did not try to commit suicide last night," the Shing said in his toneless whisper.

That was in fact the one way out that had never occurred to Falk.

"I thought I would let you handle that," he said.

Ken Kenyek paid no heed to his words, though he had an air of listening closely. "Everything is set up," he said. "These are the same banks and precisely the same connections which were used to block your primary mental-paramental structure six years ago. The removal of the block should be without difficulty or trauma, given your consent. Consent is essential to restoration, though not to repression. Are you ready now?" Almost simultaneously with his spoken words he bespoke Falk in that dazzlingly clear mind-speech: "Are you ready?"

He listened closely as Falk answered in kind, "I am."

As if satisfied by the answer or its emphatic overtones, the Shing nodded once and said in his monotonous whisper, "I shall start out then without drugs. Drugs befog the clarity of the parahypnotic processes; it is easier to work without them. Sit down there."

Falk obeyed, silent, trying to keep his mind silent as well.

An assistant entered at some unspoken signal, and came over to Falk while Ken Kenyek sat down in front of one of the computer-banks, as a musician sits down to an instrument. For a moment Falk remembered the great patterning frame in the Throneroom of Kansas, the swift dark hands that had hovered over it, forming and unforming the certain, changeful patterns of stones, stars, thoughts. . . . A blackness came down like a curtain over his eyes and over his mind. He was aware that something was being fitted over his head, a hood or cap; then he was aware of nothing, only blackness, infinite blackness, the dark. In the dark a voice was speaking a word in his mind, a word he almost understood. Over and over the same word, the word, the word, the name . . . Like the flaring up of a light his will to survive flared up, and he declared it with terrible effort, against all odds, in silence: *I am Falk!*

Then darkness.

9

This was a quiet place, and dim, like a deep forest. Weak, he lay a long time between sleep and waking. Often he dreamed or remembered fragments of a dream from earlier, deeper sleep. Then again he slept, and woke again to the dim verdant light and the quietness.

There was a movement near him. Turning his head, he saw a young man, a stranger.

"Who are you?"

"Har Orry."

The name dropped like a stone into the dreamy tranquillity of his mind and vanished. Only the circles from it widened out and widened out softly, slowly, until at last the outermost circle touched shore, and broke. Orry, Har Weden's son, one of the Voyagers . . . a boy, a child, Winterborn.

The still surface of the pool of sleep was crisscrossed with a little disturbance. He closed his eyes again and willed to go under.

"I dreamed," he murmured with his eyes closed. "I had a lot of dreams. . . ."

But he was awake again, and looking into that frightened, irresolute, boyish face. It was Orry, Weden's son: Orry as he would look five or six moonphases from now, if they survived the Voyage.

What was it he had forgotten?

"What is this place?"

"Please lie still, prech Ramarren—don't talk yet; please lie still."

"What happened to me?" Dizziness forced him to obey the boy and lie back. His body, even the muscles of his lips and tongue as he spoke, did not obey him properly. It was not weakness but a queer lack of control. To raise his hand he had to use conscious volition, as if it were someone else's hand he was picking up.

Someone else's hand. . . . He stared at his arm and hand for a good while. The skin was curiously darkened to the color of tanned hann-hide. Down the forearm to the wrist ran a series of parallel bluish scars, slightly stippled, as if made by repeated jabs of a needle. Even the skin of the palm was toughened and weathered as if he had been out in the open for a long time, instead of in the laboratories and computer-rooms of Voyage Center and the Halls of Council and Places of Silence in Wegest. . . .

He looked around suddenly. The room he was in was windowless; but, weirdly, he could see the sunlight in and through its greenish walls.

"There was an accident," he said at last. "In the launching, or when . . . But we made the Voyage. We made it. Did I dream it?"

"No, prech Ramarren. We made the Voyage."

Silence again. He said after a while, "I can only remember the Voyage as if it were one night, one long night, last night. . . . But it aged you from a child almost to a man. We were wrong about that, then."

"No—the Voyage did not age me—" Orry stopped.

"Where are the others?"

"Lost."

"Dead? Speak entirely, vesprech Orry."

"Probably dead, prech Ramarren."

"What is this place?"

"Please, rest now—"

"Answer."

"This is a room in a city called Es Toch on the planet Earth," the boy answered with due entirety, and then broke out in a kind of wail, "You don't know it?—you don't remember it, any of it? This is worse than before—"

"How should I remember Earth?" Ramarren whispered.

"I—I was to say to you, *Read the first page of the book.*"

Ramarren paid no heed to the boy's stammering. He knew now that all had gone amiss, and that a time had passed that he knew nothing of. But until he could master this strange weakness of his body he could do nothing, and so he was quiet until all dizziness had passed. Then with closed mind he told over certain of the Fifth Level Soliloquies; and when they had quieted his mind as well, he summoned sleep.

The dreams rose up about him once more, complex and frightening yet shot through with sweetness like the sunlight breaking through the dark of an old forest. With deeper sleep these fantasies dispersed, and his dream became a simple, vivid memory: He was waiting beside the airfoil to accompany his father to the city. Up on the foothills of Charn the forests were half leafless in their long dying, but the air was warm and clear and still. His father Agad Karsen, a lithe spare old man in his ceremonial garb and helmet, holding his office-stone, came leisurely across the lawn with his daughter, and both were laughing as he teased her about her first suitor, "Look out for that lad, Parth, he'll woo without mercy if you let him." Words lightly spoken long ago, in the sunlight of the long, golden autumn of his youth, he heard them again now, and the girl's laugh in response. Sister, little sister, beloved Arnan . . . What had his father called her?—not by her right name but something else, another name—

Ramarren woke. He sat up, with a definite effort taking command of his body—yes, his, still hesitant and shaky but certainly his own. For a moment in waking he had felt he was a ghost in alien flesh, displaced, lost.

He was all right. He was Agad Ramarren, born in the silver-stone house among broad lawns under the white peak of Charn, the Single Mountain; Agad's heir, fallborn, so that all his life had been lived in autumn and winter. Spring he had never seen, might never see, for the ship *Alterra* had begun her Voyage to Earth on the first day of spring. But the long winter and the fall, the length of his manhood, boyhood, childhood stretched back behind him vivid and unbroken, remembered, the river reaching upward to the source.

The boy Orry was no longer in the room. "Orry!" he said aloud; for he was able and determined now to learn what had happened to him, to his companions, to the *Alterra* and its mission. There was no reply or signal. The room seemed to be not only windowless but doorless. He checked his impulse to mindcall the boy; he did not know whether Orry was still tuned with him, and also since his own mind had evidently suffered either damage or interference, he had better go carefully and keep out of phase with any other mind, until he learned if he was threatened by volitional control or antichrony.

He stood up, dismissing vertigo and a brief, sharp occipital pain, and walked back and forth across the room a few times, getting himself into muscular harmony while he studied the outlandish clothes he was wearing and the queer room he was in. There was a lot of furniture, bed, tables, and sitting-places, all set up on long thin legs. The translucent, murky green walls were covered with explicitly deceptive and disjunctive patterns, one of which disguised an iris-door, another a half-length mirror. He stopped and looked at himself a moment. He looked thin, and weatherbeaten, and perhaps older; he hardly knew. He felt curiously self-conscious, looking at himself. What was this uneasiness, this lack of concentration? What had happened, what had been lost? He turned away and set himself to study the room again. There were various enigmatic objects about, and two of familiar type though foreign in detail: a drinking-cup on one table, and a leafed book beside it. He picked up the book. Something Orry had said flickered in his mind and went out again. The title was meaningless, though the characters were clearly related to the alphabet of the Tongue of the Books. He opened the thing and glanced through it. The left-hand pages were written—handwritten, it appeared—with columns of marvelously complicated patterns that might be holistic symbols, ideographs, technological shorthand. The right-hand pages were also handwritten, but in the letters that resembled the letters of the Books, Galaktika. A code-book? But he had not yet puzzled out more than a word or two when the doorslit silently irised open and a person entered the room: a woman.

Ramarren looked at her with intense curiosity, unguardedly and without fear; only perhaps, feeling himself vulnerable, he intensified a little the straight, authoritative gaze to which his birth, earned Level and arlesh entitled him. Unabashed, she returned his gaze. They stood there a moment in silence.

She was handsome and delicate, fantastically dressed, her hair bleached or reddish-pigmented. Her eyes were a dark circle set in a white oval. Eyes like the eyes of painted faces in the Lighall of the Old City, frescoes of dark-skinned, tall people building a town, warring with the Migrators, watching the stars: the Colonists, the Terrans of Alterra. . . .

Now Ramarren knew past doubt that he was indeed on Earth, that he had made his Voyage. He set pride and self-defense aside, and knelt down to her. To him, to all the people who had sent him on the mission across eight hundred and twenty-five trillion miles of nothingness, she was of a race that time and memory and forgetting had imbued with the quality of the divine. Single, individual as she stood before him, yet she was of the Race of Man and looked at him with the eyes of that Race, and he did honor to history and myth and the long exile of his ancestors, bowing his head to her as he knelt.

He rose and held out his open hands in the Kelshak gesture of reception, and she began to speak to him. Her speaking was strange, very strange, for though he had never seen her before her voice was infinitely familiar to his ear, and though he did not know the tongue she spoke he understood a word of it, then another. For a second this frightened him by its uncanniness and made him fear she was using some form of mindspeech that could penetrate even his outphase barrier; in the next second, he realized that he understood her because she was speaking the Tongue of the Books, Galaktika. Only her accent and her fluency in speaking it had kept him from recognizing it at once.

She had already said several sentences to him, speaking in a curiously cold, quick, lifeless way; ". . . not know I am here," she was saying. "Now tell me which of us is the liar, the faithless one. I walked with you all that endless way, I lay with you a hundred nights, and now you don't even know my name. Do you, Falk? Do you know my name? Do you know your own?"

"I am Agad Ramarren," he said, and his own name in his own voice sounded strange to him.

"Who told you so? You're Falk. Don't you know a man named Falk?—he used to wear your flesh. Ken Kenyek and Kradgy forbade me to say his name to you, but I'm sick of playing their games and never my own. I like to play my own games. Don't you remember your name, Falk?—Falk—Falk—don't you remember your name? Ah, you're still as stupid as you ever were, staring like a stranded fish!"

At once he dropped his gaze. The matter of looking directly into another person's eyes was a sensitive one among Werelians, and was strictly controlled by tabu and manners. That was his only response at first to her words, though his inward reactions were immediate and various. For one thing, she was lightly drugged, with something on the stimulant-hallucinogenic order: his trained perceptions reported this to him as a certainty, whether he liked its implications concerning the Race of Man or not. For another thing, he was not sure he had understood all she'd said and certainly had no idea what she was talking about, but her intent was aggressive, destructive. And the aggression was effective. For all his lack of comprehension, her weird jeers and the name she kept repeating moved and distressed him, shook him, shocked him.

He turned away a little to signify he would not cross her gaze again unless she wished, and said at last, softly, in the archaic tongue his people knew only from the ancient books of the Colony, "Are you of the Race of Man, or of the Enemy?"

She laughed in a forced, gibing way. "Both, Falk. There is no Enemy, and I work for them. Listen, tell Abundibot your name is Falk. Tell Ken Kenyek. Tell all the Lords your name is Falk—that'll give them something to worry about! Falk—"

"Enough."

His voice was as soft as before, but he had spoken with his full authority: she stopped with her mouth open, gaping. When she spoke again it was only to repeat that name she called him by, in a voice gone shaky and almost supplicating. She was pitiful, but he made no reply. She was in a temporary or permanent psychotic state, and he felt himself too vulnerable and too unsure, in these circumstances, to allow her further communication. He felt pretty shaky himself, and moving away from her he indrew, becoming only secondarily aware of her presence and voice. He needed to collect himself; there was something very strange the matter with him, not drugs, at least no drug he knew, but a profound displacement and imbalance, worse than any of the induced insanities of Seventh Level mental discipline. But he was given little time. The voice behind him rose in shrill rancor, and then he caught the shift to violence and along with it the sense of a second presence. He turned very quickly: she had begun to draw from her bizarre clothing what was obviously a weapon, but was standing frozen staring not at him but at a tall man in the doorway.

No word was spoken, but the newcomer directed at the woman a telepathic command of such shattering coercive force that it made Ramarren wince. The weapon dropped to the floor and the woman, making a thin keening sound, ran stooped from the room, trying to escape the destroying insistence of that mental order. Her blurred shadow wavered a moment in the wall, vanished.

The tall man turned his white-rimmed eyes to Ramarren and bespoke him with normal power: "Who are you?"

Ramarren answered in kind, "Agad Ramarren," but no more, nor did he bow. Things had gone even more wrong than he had first imagined. Who were these people? In the confrontation he had just witnessed there had been insanity, cruelty and terror, and nothing else; certainly nothing that disposed him either to reverence or trust.

But the tall man came forward a little, a smile on his heavy, rigid face, and spoke aloud courteously in the Tongue of the Books. "I am Pelleu Abundibot, and I welcome you heartily to Earth, kinsman, son of the long exile, messenger of the Lost Colony!"

Ramarren, at that, made a very brief bow and stood a moment in silence. "It appears," he said, "that I have been on Earth some while, and made an enemy of that woman, and earned certain scars. Will you tell me how this was, and how my shipmates perished? Bespeak me if you will: I do not speak Galaktika so well as you."

"Prech Ramarren," the other said—he had evidently picked that up from Orry as if it were a mere honorific, and had no notion of what constituted the relationship of prechnoye—"forgive me first that I speak aloud. It is not our custom to use mindspeech except in urgent need, or to our inferiors. And forgive next the intrusion of that creature, a servant whose madness has driven her outside the Law. We will attend to her mind. She will not trouble you again. As for your questions, all will be answered. In brief, however, here is the unhappy tale which now at last draws to a happy ending. Your ship *Alterra* was attacked as it entered Earthspace by our enemies, rebels outside the Law. They took two or more of you off the *Alterra* into their small planetary cars before our guardship came. When it came, they destroyed the *Alterra* with all left aboard her, and scattered in their small ships. We caught the one on which Har Orry was prisoner, but you were carried off—I do not know for what purpose. They did not kill you, but erased your memory back to the pre-lingual stage, and then turned you loose in a wild forest to find your death. You survived, and were given shelter by barbarians of the forest; finally our searchers found you, brought you here, and by parahypnotic techniques we have succeeded in restoring your memory. It was all we could do—little indeed, but all."

Ramarren listened intently. The story shook him, and he made no effort to hide his feelings; but he felt also a certain uneasiness or suspicion, which he did conceal. The tall man had addressed him, though very briefly, in mind-speech, and thus given him a degree of attunement. Then Abundibot had ceased all telepathic sending and had put up an empathic guard, but not a perfect one; Ramarren, highly sensitive and finely trained, received vague empathic impressions so much at discrepancy with what the man said as to hint at dementia, or at lying. Or was he himself so out of tune with himself—as he might well be after parahypnosis—that his empathic receptions were simply not reliable?

"How long . . . ?" he asked at last, looking up for a moment into those alien eyes.

"Six years ago Terran style, prech Ramarren."

The Terran year was nearly the length of a moonphase. "So long," he said. He could not take it in. His friends, his fellow-Voyagers had been dead then for a long time, and he had been alone on Earth. . . . "Six years?"

"You remember nothing of those years?"

"Nothing."

"We were forced to wipe out what rudimentary memory you may have had of that time, in order to restore your true memory and personality. We very much regret that loss of six years of your life. But they would not have been sane or pleasant memories. The outlaw brutes had made of you a creature more brutish than themselves. I am glad you do not remember it, prech Ramarren."

Not only glad, but gleeful. This man must have very little empathic ability or training, or he would be putting up a better guard; his telepathic guard was flawless. More and more distracted by these mindheard overtones that implied falsity or unclarity in what Abundibot said, and by the continuing lack of coherence in his own mind, even in his physical reactions, which remained slow and uncertain, Ramarren had to pull himself together to make any response at all. Memories—how could six years have passed without his remembering one moment of them? But a hundred and forty years had passed while his lightspeed ship had crossed from Werel to Earth and of that he remembered only a moment, indeed, one terrible, eternal moment. . . . What had the madwoman called him, screaming a name at him with crazy, grieving rancor?

"What was I called, these past six years?"

"Called? Among the natives, do you mean, prech Ramarren? I am not sure what name they gave you, if they bothered to give you any. . . ."

Falk, she had called him, Falk. "Fellowman," he said abruptly, translating the Kelshak form of address into Galaktika, "I will learn more of you later, if you will. What you tell me troubles me. Let me be alone with it a while."

"Surely, surely, prech Ramarren. Your young friend Orry is eager to be with you—shall I send him to you?" But Ramarren, having made his request and heard it accepted, had in the way of one of his Level dismissed the other, tuned him out, hearing whatever else he said simply as noise.

"We too have much to learn of you, and are eager to learn it, once you feel quite recovered." Silence. Then the noise again: "Our servants wait to serve you; if you desire refreshment or company you have only to go to the door and speak." Silence again, and at last the unmannerly presence withdrew.

Ramarren sent no speculations after it. He was too preoccupied with himself to worry about these strange hosts of his. The turmoil within his mind was increasing sharply, coming to some kind of crisis. He felt as if he were being dragged to face something that he could not endure to face, and at the same time craved to face, to find. The bitterest days of his Seventh Level training had only been a hint of this disintegration of his emotions and identity, for that had been an induced psychosis, carefully controlled, and this was not under his control. Or was it?—was he leading himself into this, compelling himself towards the crisis? But who was "he" who compelled and was compelled? He had been killed, and brought back to life. What was death, then, the death he could not remember?

To escape the utter panic welling up in him he looked around for any object to fix on, reverting to early trance-discipline, the Outcome technique of fixing on one concrete thing to build up the world from once more. But everything about him was alien, deceptive, unfamiliar; the very floor under him was a dull sheet of mist. There was the book he had been looking at when the woman entered calling him by that name he would not remember. He would not remember it. The book: he had held it in his hands, it was real, it was there. He picked it up very carefully and stared at the page that it opened to. Columns of beautiful meaningless patterns, lines of half-comprehensible script, changed from the letters he had learned long ago in the First Analect, deviant, bewildering. He stared at them and could not read them, and a word of which he did not know the meaning rose up from them, the first word:

> The way . . .

He looked from the book to his own hand that held it. Whose hand, darkened and scarred beneath an alien sun? Whose hand?

> The way that can be gone
> is not the eternal Way.
> The name . . .

He could not remember the name; he would not read it. In a dream he had read these words, in a long sleep, a death, a dream.

> The name that can be named
> is not the eternal Name.

And with that the dream rose up overwhelming him like a wave rising, and broke.

He was Falk, and he was Ramarren. He was the fool and the wise man: one man twice born.

In those first fearful hours, he begged and prayed to be delivered sometimes from one self, sometimes from the other. Once when he cried out in anguish in his own native tongue, he did not understand the words he had spoken, and this was so terrible that in utter misery he wept; it was Falk who did not understand, but Ramarren who wept.

In that same moment of misery he touched for the first time, for a moment only, the balance-pole, the center, and for a moment was *himself*: then lost again, but with just enough strength to hope for the next moment of harmony.

Harmony: when he was Ramarren he clung to that idea and discipline, and it was perhaps his mastery of that central Kelshak doctrine that kept him from going right over the edge into madness. But there was no integrating or balancing the two minds and personalities that shared his skull, not yet; he must swing between them, blanking one out for the other's sake, then drawn at once back the other way. He was scarcely able to move, being plagued by the hallucination of having two bodies, of being actually physically two different men. He did not dare sleep, though he was worn out: he feared the waking too much.

It was night, and he was left to himself. *To myselves,* Falk commented. Falk was at first the stronger, having had some preparation for this ordeal. It was Falk who got the first dialogue going: *I have got to get some sleep, Ramarren,* he said, and Ramarren received the words as if in mindspeech and without premeditation replied in kind: *I'm afraid to sleep.* Then he kept watch for a little while, and knew Falk's dreams like shadows and echoes in his mind.

He got through this first, worst time, and by the time morning shone dim through the green veilwalls of his room, he had lost his fear and was beginning to gain real control over both thought and action.

There was of course no actual overlap of his two sets of memories. Falk had come to conscious being in the vast number of neurons that in a highly intelligent brain remain unused—the fallow fields of Ramarren's mind. The basic motor and sensory paths had never been blocked off and so in a sense had been shared all along, though difficulties arose there caused by the doubling of the sets of motor habits and modes of perception. An object looked different to him depending on whether he looked at it as Falk or as Ramarren, and though in the long run this reduplication might prove an augmentation of his intelligence and perceptive power, at the moment it was confusing to the point of vertigo. There was considerable emotional intershading, so that his feelings on some points quite literally conflicted. And, since Falk's memories covered his "lifetime" just as did Ramarren's, the two series tended to appear simultaneously instead of in proper sequence. It was hard for Ramarren to allow for the gap of time during which he had not consciously existed. Ten days ago where had he been? He had been on muleback among the snowy mountains of Earth; Falk knew that; but Ramarren knew that he had been taking leave of his wife in a house on the high green plains of Werel. . . . Also, what Ramarren guessed about Terra was often contradicted by what Falk knew, while Falk's ignorance of Werel cast a strange glamor of legend over Ramarren's own past. Yet even in his bewilderment there was the germ of interaction, of the coherence toward which he strove. For the fact remained, he was, bodily and chronologically, one man: his problem was not really that of creating a unity, only of comprehending it.

Coherence was far from being gained. One or the other of the two memory-structures still had to dominate, if he was to think and act with any competence. Most often, now, it was Ramarren who took over, for the Navigator of the *Alterra* was a decisive and potent person. Falk, in comparison, felt himself childish, tentative; he could offer what knowledge he had, but relied upon Ramarren's strength and experience. Both were needed, for the two-minded man was in a very obscure and hazardous situation.

One question was basic to all the others. It was simply put: whether or not the Shing could be trusted. For if Falk had merely been inculcated with a groundless fear of the Lords of Earth, then the hazards and obscurities would themselves prove groundless. At first Ramarren thought this might well be the case; but he did not think it for long.

There were open lies and discrepancies which already his double memory had caught. Abundibot had refused to mindspeak to Ramarren, saying the Shing avoided paraverbal communication: that Falk knew to be a lie. Why had Abundibot told it? Evidently because he wanted to tell a lie—the Shing story of what had happened to the *Alterra* and its crew—and could not or dared not tell it to Ramarren in mindspeech.

But he had told Falk very much the same story, in mindspeech.

If it was a false story, then, the Shing could and did mind-lie. Was it false?

Ramarren called upon Falk's memory. At first that effort of combination was beyond him, but it became easier as he struggled, pacing up and down the silent room, and suddenly it came clear; he could recall the brilliant silence of Abundibot's words: "We whom you know as Shing are men. . . ." And hearing it even in memory, Ramarren knew it for a lie. It was incredible, and indubitable. The Shing could lie telepathically—that guess and dread of subjected humanity was right. The Shing were, in truth, the Enemy.

They were not men but aliens, gifted with an alien power; and no doubt they had broken the League and gained power over Earth by the use of that power. And it was they who had attacked the *Alterra* as she had come into Earthspace; all the talk of rebels was mere fiction. They had killed or brain-razed all the crew but the child Orry. Ramarren could guess why: because they had discovered, testing him or one of the other highly trained paraverbalists of the crew, that a Werelian could tell when they were mind-lying. That had frightened the Shing, and they had done away with the adults, saving out only the harmless child as an informant.

To Ramarren it was only yesterday that his fellow-Voyagers had perished, and, struggling against that blow, he tried to think that like him they might have survived somewhere on Earth. But if they had—and he had been very lucky—where were they now? The Shing had had a hard time locating even one, it appeared, when they had discovered that they needed him.

What did they need him for? Why had they sought him, brought him here, restored the memory that they had destroyed?

No explanation could be got from the facts at his disposal except the one he had arrived at as Falk: The Shing needed him to tell them where he came from.

That gave Falk-Ramarren his first amount of amusement. If it really was that simple, it was funny. They had saved out Orry because he was so young; untrained, unformed, vulnerable, amenable, a perfect instrument and informant. He certainly had been all of that. But did not know where he came from. . . . And by the time they discovered that, they had wiped the information they wanted clean out of the minds that knew it, and scattered their victims over the wild, ruined Earth to die of accident or starvation or the attack of wild beasts or men.

He could assume that Ken Kenyek, while manipulating his mind through the psychocomputer yesterday, had tried to get him to divulge the Galaktika name of Werel's sun. And he could assume that if he had divulged it, he would be dead or mindless now. They did not want him, Ramarren; they wanted only his knowledge. And they had not got it.

That in itself must have them worried, and well it might. The Kelshak code of secrecy concerning the Books of the Lost Colony had evolved along with a whole technique of mindguarding. That mystique of secrecy—or more precisely of restraint—had grown over the long years from the rigorous control of scientific-technical knowledge exercised by the original Colonists, itself an outgrowth from the League's Law of Cultural Embargo, which forbade cultural importation to colonial planets. The whole concept of restraint was fundamental in Werelian culture by now, and the stratification of Werelian society was directed by the conviction that knowledge and technique must remain under intelligent control. Such details as the True Name of the Sun were formal and symbolical, but the formalism was taken seriously—with ultimate seriousness, for in Kelshy knowledge was religion, religion knowledge. To guard the intangible holy places in the minds of men, intangible and invulnerable defenses had been devised. Unless he was in one of the Places of Silence, and addressed in a certain form by an associate of his own Level,

Ramarren was absolutely unable to communicate, in words or writing or mindspeech, the True Name of his world's sun.

He possessed, of course, equivalent knowledge: the complex of astronomical facts that had enabled him to plot the *Alterra*'s coordinates from Werel to Earth; his knowledge of the exact distance between the two planets' suns; his clear, astronomer's memory of the stars as seen from Werel. They had not got this information from him yet, probably because his mind had been in too chaotic a state when first restored by Ken Kenyek's manipulations, or because even then his parahypnotically strengthened mindguards and specific barriers had been functioning. Knowing there might still be an Enemy on Earth, the crewmen of the *Alterra* had not set off unprepared. Unless Shing mindscience was much stronger than Werelian, they would not now be able to force him to tell them anything. They hoped to induce him, to persuade him. Therefore, for the present, he was at least physically safe.

—So long as they did not know that he remembered his existence as Falk.

That came over him with a chill. It had not occurred to him before. As Falk he had been useless to them, but harmless. As Ramarren he was useful to them, and harmless. But as Falk-Ramarren, he was a threat. And they did not tolerate threats: they could not afford to.

And there was the answer to the last question: Why did they want so badly to know where Werel was—what did Werel matter to them?

Again Falk's memory spoke to Ramarren's intelligence, this time recalling a calm, blithe, ironic voice. The old Listener in the deep forest spoke, the old man lonelier on Earth than even Falk had been: "There are not very many of the Shing...."

A great piece of news and wisdom and advice, he had called it; and it must be the literal truth. The old histories Falk had learned in Zove's House held the Shing to be aliens from a very distant region of the galaxy, out beyond the Hyades, a matter perhaps of thousands of light-years. If that was so, probably no vast numbers of them had crossed so immense a length of spacetime. There had been enough to infiltrate the League and break it, given their powers of mind-lying and other skills or weapons they might possess or have possessed; but had there been enough of them to rule over all the worlds they had divided and conquered? Planets were very large places, on any scale but that of the spaces in between them. The Shing must have had to spread themselves thin, and take much care to keep the subject planets from re-allying and joining to rebel. Orry had told Falk that the Shing did not seem to travel or trade much by lightspeed; he had never even seen a lightspeed ship of theirs. Was that because they feared their own kin on other worlds, grown away from them over the centuries of their dominion? Or conceivably was Earth the only planet they still ruled, defending it from all explorations from other worlds? No telling; but it did seem likely that on Earth there were indeed not very many of them.

They had refused to believe Orry's tale of how the Terrans on Werel had mutated toward the local biological norm and so finally blended stocks with the native hominids. They had said that was impossible: which meant that it had not happened to them; they were unable to mate with Terrans. They were still alien, then, after twelve hundred years; still isolated on Earth. And did they in fact rule mankind, from this single City? Once again Ramarren turned to Falk for the answer, and saw it as No. They controlled men by habit, ruse, fear, and weaponry, by being quick to prevent the rise of any strong tribe or the pooling of knowledge that might threaten them. They prevented men from doing anything. But they did nothing themselves. They did not rule, they only blighted.

It was clear, then, why Werel posed a deadly threat to them. They had so far kept up their tenuous, ruinous hold on the culture which long ago they had wrecked and redirected; but a strong, numerous, technologically advanced race, with a mythos of blood-kinship with the Terrans, and a mind-science and weaponry equal to their own, might crush them at a blow. And deliver men from them.

If they learned from him where Werel was, would they send out a light-speed bomb-ship, like a long fuse burning across the light-years, to destroy the dangerous world before it ever learned of their existence?

That seemed only too possible. Yet two things told against it: their careful preparation of young Orry, as if they wanted him to act as a messenger; and their singular Law.

Falk-Ramarren was unable to decide whether that rule of Reverence for Life was the Shing's one genuine belief, their one plank across the abyss of self-destruction that underlay their behavior as the black canyon gaped beneath their city, or instead was simply the biggest lie of all their lies. They did in fact seem to avoid killing sentient beings. They had left him alive, and perhaps the others; their elaborately disguised foods were all vegetable; in order to control populations they evidently pitted tribe against tribe, starting the war but letting humans do the killing; and the histories told that in the early days of their rule, they had used eugenics and resettlement to consolidate their empire, rather than genocide. It might be true, then, that they obeyed their Law, in their own fashion.

In that case, their grooming of young Orry indicated that he was to be their messenger. Sole survivor of the Voyage, he was to return across the gulfs of time and space to Werel and tell them all the Shing had told him about Earth—quack, quack, like the birds that quacked *It is wrong to take life*, the moral boar, the squeaking mice in the foundations of the house of Man. . . . Mindless, honest, disastrous, Orry would carry the Lie to Werel.

Honor and the memory of the Colony were strong forces on Werel, and a call for help from Earth might bring help from them; but if they were told there was not and never had been an Enemy, that Earth was an ancient happy garden-spot, they were not likely to make that long journey just to see it. And if they did they would come unarmed, as Ramarren and his companions had come.

Another voice spoke in his memory, longer ago yet, deeper in the forest: "We cannot go on like this forever. There must be a hope, a sign. . . ."

He had not been sent with a message to mankind, as Zove had dreamed. The hope was a stranger one even than that, the sign more obscure. He was to carry mankind's message, to utter their cry for help, for deliverance.

I must go home; I must tell them the truth, he thought, knowing that the Shing would at all costs prevent this, that Orry would be sent, and he would be kept here or killed.

In the great weariness of his long effort to think coherently, his will relaxed all at once, his chancy control over his racked and worried double mind broke. He dropped down exhausted on the couch and put his head in his hands. *If I could only go home,* he thought; *if I could walk once more with Parth down in the Long Field. . . .*

That was the dream-self grieving, the dreamer Falk. Ramarren tried to evade that hopeless yearning by thinking of his wife, dark-haired, golden-eyed, in a gown sewn with a thousand tiny chains of silver, his wife Adrise. But his wedding-ring was gone. And Adrise was dead. She had been dead a long, long time. She had married Ramarren knowing that they would have little more than a moonphase together, for he was going on the Voyage to Terra. And during that one, terrible moment of his Voyage, she had lived out her life, grown old, died; she had been dead for a hundred of Earth's years, perhaps. Across the years between the stars, which now was the dreamer, which the dream?

"You should have died a century ago," the Prince of Kansas had told un-comprehending Falk, seeing or sensing or knowing of the man that lay lost within him, the man born so long ago. And now if Ramarren were to return to Werel it would be yet farther into his own future. Nearly three centuries, nearly five of Werel's great Years would then have elapsed since he had left; all would be changed; he would be as strange on Werel as he had been on Earth.

There was only one place to which he could truly go home, to the welcome of those who had loved him: Zove's House. And he would never see it again. If his way led anywhere, it was out, away from Earth. He was on his own, and had only one job to do: to try to follow that way through to the end.

10

It was broad daylight now, and realizing that he was very hungry Ramarren went to the concealed door and asked aloud, in Galaktika, for food. There was no reply, but presently a toolman brought and served him food; and as he was finishing it a little signal sounded outside the door. "Come in!" Ramarren said in Kelshak, and Har Orry entered, then the tall Shing Abundibot, and two others whom Ramarren had never seen. Yet their names were in his mind: Ken Kenyek and Kradgy. They were introduced to him; politenesses were uttered. Ramarren found that he could handle himself pretty well; the necessity of keeping Falk completely hidden and suppressed was actually a convenience, freeing him to behave spontaneously. He was aware that the mentalist Ken Kenyek was trying to mindprobe, and with considerable skill and force, but that did not worry him. If his barriers had held good even under the parahypnotic hood, they certainly would not falter now.

None of the Shing bespoke him. They stood about in their strange stiff fashion as if afraid of being touched, and whispered all they said. Ramarren managed to ask some of the questions which as Ramarren he might be expected to ask concerning Earth, mankind, the Shing, and listened gravely to the answers. Once he tried to get into phase with young Orry, but failed. The boy had no real guard up, but perhaps had been subjected to some mental treatment which nullified the little skill in phase-catching he had learned as a child, and also was under the influence of the drug he had been habituated to. Even as Ramarren sent him the slight, familiar signal of their relationship in prechnoye, Orry began sucking on a tube of pariitha. In the vivid distracting world of semihallucination it provided him, his perceptions were dulled, and he received nothing.

"You have seen nothing of Earth as yet but this one room," the one dressed as a woman, Kradgy, said to Ramarren in a harsh whisper. Ramarren was wary of them all, but Kradgy roused an instinctive fear or aversion in him; there was a hint of nightmare in the bulky body under flowing robes, the long purplish-black hair, the harsh, precise whisper.

"I should like to see more."

"We shall show you whatever you wish to see. The Earth is open to its honored visitor."

"I do not remember seeing Earth from the *Alterra* when we came into orbit," Ramarren said in stiff, Werelian-accented Galaktika. "Nor do I remember the attack on the ship. Can you tell me why this is so?"

The question might be risky, but he was genuinely curious for the answer; it was the one blank still left in his double memory.

"You were in the condition we term achronia," Ken Kenyek replied. "You came out of lightspeed all at once at the Barrier, since your ship had no retemporalizer. You were at that moment, and for some minutes or hours after, either unconscious or insane."

"We had not run into the problem in our short runs at lightspeed."

"The longer the flight, the stronger the Barrier."

"It was a gallant thing," Abundibot said in his creaky whisper and with his usual floridity, "a journey of a hundred and twenty-five light-years in a scarcely tested ship!"

Ramarren accepted the compliment without correcting the number.

"Come, my Lords, let us show our guest the City of Earth." Simultaneously with Abundibot's words, Ramarren caught the passage of mindspeech between Kradgy and Ken Kenyek, but did not get the sense of it; he was too intent on maintaining his own guard to be able to mindhear or even to receive much empathic impression.

"The ship in which you return to Werel," Ken Kenyek said, "will of course be furnished with a retemporalizer, and you will suffer no derangement at reentering planetary space."

Ramarren had risen, rather awkwardly—Falk was used to chairs but Ramarren was not, and had felt most uncomfortable perched up in mid-air—but he stood still now and after a moment asked, "The ship in which we return—?"

Orry looked up with blurry hopefulness. Kradgy yawned, showing strong yellow teeth. Abundibot said, "When you have seen all you wish to see of Earth and have learned all you wish to learn, we have a lightspeed ship ready for you to go home to Werel in—you, Lord Agad, and Har Orry. We ourselves travel little. There are no more wars; we have no need to trade with other worlds; and we do not wish to bankrupt poor Earth again with the immense cost of lightspeed ships merely to assuage our curiosity. We Men of Earth are an old race now; we stay home, tend our garden, and do not meddle and explore abroad. But your Voyage must be completed, your mission fulfilled.

The *New Alterra* awaits you at our spaceport, and Werel awaits your return. It is a great pity that your civilization had not rediscovered the ansible principle, so that we could be in communication with them now. By now, of course, they may have the instantaneous transmitter; but we cannot signal them, having no coordinates."

"Indeed," Ramarren said politely.

There was a slight, tense pause.

"I do not think I understand," he said.

"The ansible—"

"I understand what the ansible transmitter did, though not how it did it. As you say, sir, we had not when I left Werel rediscovered the principles of instantaneous transmission. But I do not understand what prevented you from attempting to signal Werel."

Dangerous ground. He was all alert now, in control, a player in the game, not a piece to be moved: and he sensed the electric tension behind the three rigid faces.

"Prech Ramarren," Abundibot said, "as Har Orry was too young to have learned the precise distances involved, we have never had the honor of knowing exactly where Werel is located, though of course we have a general idea. As he had learned very little Galaktika, Har Orry was unable to tell us the Galaktika name for Werel's sun, which of course would be meaningful to us, who share the language with you as a heritage from the days of the League. Therefore we have been forced to wait for your assistance, before we could attempt ansible contact with Werel, or prepare the coordinates on the ship we have ready for you."

"You do not know the name of the star Werel circles?"

"That unfortunately is the case. If you care to tell us—"

"I cannot tell you."

The Shing could not be surprised; they were too self-absorbed, too egocentric. Abundibot and Ken Kenyek registered nothing at all. Kradgy said in his strange, dreary, precise whisper, "You mean you don't know either?"

"I cannot tell you the True Name of the Sun," Ramarren said serenely.

This time he caught the flicker of mindspeech, Ken Kenyek to Abundibot: *I told you so.*

"I apologize, prech Ramarren for my ignorance in inquiring after a forbidden matter. Will you forgive me? We do not know your ways, and though ignorance is a poor excuse it is all I can plead." Abundibot was creaking on when all at once the boy Orry interrupted him, scared into wakefulness:

"Prech Ramarren, you—you will be able to set the ship's coordinates? You do remember what—what you knew as Navigator?"

Ramarren turned to him and asked quietly, "Do you want to go home, ves-prechna?"

"Yes!"

"In twenty or thirty days, if it pleases these Lords who offer us so great a gift, we shall return in their ship to Werel. I am sorry," he went on, turning back to the Shing, "that my mouth and mind are closed to your question. My silence is a mean return for your generous frankness." Had they been using mindspeech, he thought, the exchange would have been a great deal less polite; for he, unlike the Shing, was unable to mind-lie, and therefore probably could not have said one word of his last speech.

"No matter, Lord Agad! It is your safe return, not our questions, that is important! So long as you can program the ship—and all our records and course-computers are at your service when you may require them—then the question is as good as answered." And indeed it was, for if they wanted to know where Werel was they would only have to examine the course he programmed into their ship. After that, if they still distrusted him, they could re-erase his mind, explaining to Orry that the restoration of his memory had caused him finally to break down. They would then send Orry off to deliver their message to Werel. They did still distrust him, because they knew he could detect their mind-lying. If there was any way out of the trap he had not found it yet.

They all went together through the misty halls, down the ramps and elevators, out of the palace into daylight. Falk's element of the double mind was almost entirely repressed now, and Ramarren moved and thought and spoke quite freely as Ramarren. He sensed the constant, sharp readiness of the Shing minds, particularly that of Ken Kenyek, waiting to penetrate the least flaw or catch the slightest slip. The very pressure kept him doubly alert. So it was as Ramarren, the alien, that he looked up into the sky of late morning and saw Earth's yellow sun.

He stopped, caught by sudden joy. For it was something, no matter what had gone before and what might follow after—it was something to have seen the light, in one lifetime, of two suns. The orange gold of Werel's sun, the white gold of Earth's: he could hold them now side by side as a man might hold two jewels, comparing their beauty for the sake of heightening their praise.

The boy was standing beside him; and Ramarren murmured aloud the greeting that Kelshak babies and little children were taught to say to the sun seen at dawn or after the long storms of winter, "Welcome the star of life, the center of the year . . ." Orry picked it up midway and spoke it with him. It was the first harmony between them, and Ramarren was glad of it, for he would need Orry before this game was done.

A slider was summoned and they went about the city, Ramarren asking appropriate questions and the Shing replying as they saw fit. Abundibot described elaborately how all of Es Toch, towers, bridges, streets and palaces, had been built overnight a thousand years ago, on a river-isle on the other side of the planet, and how from century to century whenever they felt inclined the Lords of Earth summoned their wondrous machines and instruments to move the whole city to a new site suiting their whim. It was a pretty tale; and Orry was too benumbed with drugs and persuasions to disbelieve anything, while if Ramarren believed or not was little matter. Abundibot evidently told lies for the mere pleasure of it. Perhaps it was the only pleasure he knew. There were elaborate descriptions also of how Earth was governed, how most of the Shing spent their lives among common men, disguised as mere "natives" but working for the master plan emanating from Es Toch, how carefree and content most of humanity was in their knowledge that the Shing would keep the peace and bear the burdens, how arts and learning were gently encouraged and rebellious and destructive elements as gently repressed. A planet of humble people, in their humble little cottages and peaceful tribes and townlets; no warring, no killing, no crowding; the old achievements and ambitions forgotten; almost a race of children, protected by the firm kindly guidance and the invulnerable technological strength of the Shing caste. . . .

The story went on and on, always the same with variations, soothing and reassuring. It was no wonder the poor waif Orry believed it; Ramarren would have believed most of it, if he had not had Falk's memories of the forest and the plains to show the rather subtle but total falseness of it. Falk had not lived on Earth among children, but among men, brutalized, suffering, and impassioned.

That day they showed Ramarren all over Es Toch, which seemed to him who had lived among the old streets of Wegest and in the great Winterhouses of Kaspool a sham city, vapid and artificial, impressive only by its fantastic natural setting. Then they began to take him and Orry about the world by aircar and planetary car, all-day tours under the guidance of Abundibot or Ken Kenyek, jaunts to each of Earth's continents and even out to the desolate and long-abandoned Moon. The days went on; they went on playing the play for Orry's benefit, wooing Ramarren till they got from him what they wanted to know. Though he was directly or electronically watched at every moment, visually and telepathically, he was in no way restrained; evidently they felt they had nothing to fear from him now.

Perhaps they would let him go home with Orry, then. Perhaps they thought him harmless enough, in his ignorance, to be allowed to leave Earth with his readjusted mind intact.

But he could buy his escape from Earth only with the information they wanted, the location of Werel. So far he had told them nothing and they had asked nothing more.

Did it so much matter, after all, if the Shing knew where Werel was?

It did. Though they might not be planning any immediate attack on this potential enemy, they might well be planning to send a robot monitor out after the *New Alterra*, with an ansible transmitter aboard to make instantaneous report to them of any preparation for interstellar flight on Werel. The ansible would give them a hundred-and-forty-year start on the Werelians; they could stop an expedition to Terra before it started. The one advantage that Werel possessed tactically over the Shing was the fact that the Shing did not know where it was and might have to spend several centuries looking for it. Ramarren could buy a chance of escape only at the price of certain peril for the world to which he was responsible.

So he played for time, trying to devise a way out of his dilemma, flying with Orry and one or another of the Shing here and there over the Earth, which stretched out under their flight like a great lovely garden gone all to weeds and wilderness. He sought with all his trained intelligence some way in which he could turn his situation about and become the controller instead of the one controlled: for so his Kelshak mentality presented his case to him. Seen rightly, any situation, even a chaos or a trap, would come clear and lead of itself to its one proper outcome; for there is in the long run no disharmony, only misunderstanding, no chance or mischance but only the ignorant eye. So Ramarren thought, and the second soul within him, Falk, took no issue with this view, but spent no time trying to think it all out, either. For Falk had seen the dull and bright stones slip across the wires of the patterning frame, and had lived with men in their fallen estate, kings in exile on their own domain the Earth, and to him it seemed that no man could make his fate or control the game, but only wait for the bright jewel luck to slip by on the wire of time. Harmony exists, but there is no understanding it; the Way cannot be gone. So while Ramarren racked his mind, Falk lay low and waited. And when the chance came he caught it.

Or rather, as it turned out, he was caught by it.

There was nothing special about the moment. They were with Ken Kenyek in a fleet little auto-pilot aircar, one of the beautiful, clever machines that allowed the Shing to control and police the world so effectively. They were returning toward Es Toch from a long flight out over the islands of the Western Ocean, on one of which they had made a stop of several hours at a human settlement. The natives of the island-chain they had visited were handsome, contented people entirely absorbed in sailing, swimming, and sex—afloat in the azure amniotic sea: perfect specimens of human happiness and backwardness to show the Werelians. Nothing to worry about there, nothing to fear.

Orry was dozing, with a pariitha-tube between his fingers. Ken Kenyek had put the ship on automatic, and with Ramarren—three or four feet away from him, as always, for the Shing never got physically close to anyone—was looking out the glass side of the aircar at the five-hundred-mile circle of fair weather and blue sea that surrounded them. Ramarren was tired, and let himself relax a little in this pleasant moment of suspension, aloft in a glass bubble in the center of the great blue and golden sphere.

"It is a lovely world," the Shing said.

"It is."

"The jewel of all worlds . . . Is Werel as beautiful?"

"No. It is harsher."

"Yes, the long year would make it so. How long?—Sixty Earth-years?"

"Yes."

"You were born in the fall, you said. That would mean you had never seen your world in summer when you left it."

"Once, when I flew to the Southern hemisphere. But their summers are cooler, as their winters are warmer, than in Kelshy. I have not seen the Great Summer of the north."

"You may yet. If you return within a few months, what will the season be on Werel?"

Ramarren computed for a couple of seconds and replied, "Late summer; about the twentieth moonphase of summer, perhaps."

"I made it to be fall—how long does the journey take?"

"A hundred and forty-two Earth-years," Ramarren said, and as he said it a little gust of panic blew across his mind and died away. He sensed the presence of the Shing's mind in his own; while talking, Ken Kenyek had reached out mentally, found his defenses down, and taken whole-phase control of his mind. That was all right. It showed incredible patience and telepathic skill on the Shing's part. He had been afraid of it, but now that it had happened it was perfectly all right.

Ken Kenyek was bespeaking him now, not in the creaky oral whisper of the Shing but in clear, comfortable mindspeech: "Now, that's all right, that's right, that's good. Isn't it pleasant that we're attuned at last?"

"Very pleasant," Ramarren agreed.

"Yes indeed. Now we can remain attuned and all our worries are over. Well then, a hundred and forty-two light-years distant—that means that your sun must be the one in the Dragon constellation. What is its name in Galaktika? No, that's right, you can't say it or bespeak it here. Eltanin, is that it, the name of your sun?"

Ramarren made no response of any kind.

"Eltanin, the Dragon's Eye, yes, that's very nice. The others we had picked as possibilities are somewhat closer in. Now this saves a great deal of time. We had almost—"

The quick, clear, mocking, soothing mindspeech stopped abruptly and Ken Kenyek gave a convulsive start; so did Ramarren at the identical moment. The Shing turned jerkily toward the controls of the aircar, then away. He leaned over in a strange fashion, too far over, like a puppet on strings carelessly managed, then all at once slid to the floor of the car and lay there with his white, handsome face upturned, rigid.

Orry, shaken from his euphoric drowse, was staring. "What's wrong? What happened?"

He got no answer. Ramarren was standing as rigidly as the Shing lay, and his eyes were locked with the Shing's in a double unseeing stare. When at last he moved, he spoke in a language Orry did not know. Then, laboriously, he spoke in Galaktika. "Put the ship in hover," he said.

The boy gaped. "What's wrong with Lord Ken, prech Ramarren?"

"Get up. Put the ship in hover!"

He was speaking Galaktika now not with his Werelian accent but in the debased form used by Earth natives. But though the language was wrong the urgency and authority were powerful. Orry obeyed him. The little glass bubble hung motionless in the center of the bowl of ocean, eastward of the sun.

"Prechna, is the—"

"Be still!"

Silence. Ken Kenyek lay still. Very gradually Ramarren's visible tension and intensity relaxed.

What had happened on the mental plane between him and Ken Kenyek was a matter of ambush and re-ambush. In physical terms, the Shing had jumped Ramarren, thinking he was capturing one man, and had in turn been surprised by a second man—the mind in ambush, Falk. Only for a second had Falk been able to take control and only by sheer force of surprise, but that had been long enough to free Ramarren from the Shing's phase-control. The instant he was free, while Ken Kenyek's mind was still in phase with his and vulnerable, Ramarren had taken control. It took all his skill and all his strength to keep Ken Kenyek's mind phased with his, helpless and assenting, as his own had been a moment before. But his advantage still remained: he was still double-minded, and while Ramarren held the Shing helpless, Falk was free to think and act.

This was the chance, the moment; there would be no other.

Falk asked aloud, "Where is there a lightspeed ship ready for flight?"

It was curious to hear the Shing answer in his whispering voice and know, for once to know certainly and absolutely, that he was not lying. "In the desert northwest of Es Toch."

"Is it guarded?"

"Yes."

"By live guards?"

"No."

"You will guide us there."

"I will guide you there."

"Take the car where he tells you, Orry."

"I don't understand, prech Ramarren; are we—"

"We are going to leave Earth. Now. Take the controls."

"Take the controls," Ken Kenyek repeated softly.

Orry obeyed, following the Shing's instructions as to course. At full speed the aircar shot eastward, yet seemed still to hang in the changeless center of the sea-sphere, towards the circumference of which the sun, behind them, dropped visibly. Then the Western Isles appeared, seeming to float towards them over the wrinkled glittering curve of the sea; then behind these the sharp white peaks of the coast appeared, and approached, and ran by beneath the aircar. Now they were over the dun desert broken by arid, fluted ranges casting long shadows to the east. Still following Ken Kenyek's murmured instructions, Orry slowed the ship, circled one of these ranges, set the controls to catch the landing-beacon and let the car be homed in. The high lifeless mountains rose up about them, walling them in, as the aircar settled down on a pale, shadowy plain.

No spaceport or airfield was visible, no roads, no buildings, but certain vague, very large shapes trembled mirage-like over the sand and sagebrush under the dark slopes of the mountains. Falk stared at them and could not focus his eyes on them, and it was Orry who said with a catch of his breath, "Starships."

They were the interstellar ships of the Shing, their fleet or part of it, camouflaged with light-dispeller nets. Those Falk had first seen were smaller ones; there were others, which he had taken for foothills. . . .

The aircar had intangibly settled itself down beside a tiny, ruined, roofless shack, its boards bleached and split by the desert wind.

"What is that shack?"

"The entrance to the underground rooms is to one side of it."

"Are there ground-computers down there?"

"Yes."

"Are any of the small ships ready to go?"

"They are all ready to go. They are mostly robot-controlled defense ships."

"Is there one with pilot-control?"

"Yes. The one intended for Har Orry."

Ramarren kept close telepathic hold on the Shing's mind while Falk ordered him to take them to the ship and show them the onboard computers. Ken Kenyek at once obeyed. Falk-Ramarren had not entirely expected him to: there were limits to mind-control just as there were to normal hypnotic suggestion. The drive to self-preservation often resisted even the strongest control, and sometimes shattered the whole attunement when infringed upon. But the treason he was being forced to commit apparently aroused no instinctive resistance in Ken Kenyek; he took them into the starship and replied obediently to all Falk-Ramarren's questions, then led them back to the decrepit hut and at command unlocked, with physical and mental signals, the trapdoor in the sand near the door. They entered the tunnel that was revealed. At each of the underground doors and defenses and shields Ken Kenyek gave the proper signal or response, and so brought them at last to attack-proof, cataclysm-proof, thief-proof rooms far underground, where the automatic control guides and the course computers were.

Over an hour had now passed since the moment in the aircar. Ken Kenyek, assenting and submissive, reminding Falk at moments of poor Estrel, stood harmlessly by—harmless so long as Ramarren kept total control over his brain. The instant that control was relaxed, Ken Kenyek would send a mind-call to Es Toch if he had the power, or trip some alarm, and the other Shing and their toolmen would be here within a couple of minutes. But Ramarren must relax that control: for he needed his mind to think with. Falk did not know how to program a computer for the lightspeed course to Werel, satellite of the sun Eltanin. Only Ramarren could do that.

Falk had his own resources, however. "Give me your gun."

Ken Kenyek at once handed over a little weapon kept concealed under his elaborate robes. At this Orry stared in horror. Falk did not try to allay the boy's shock; in fact, he rubbed it in. "Reverence for Life?" he inquired coldly, examining the weapon. Actually, as he had expected, it was not a gun or laser but a lowlevel stunner without kill capacity. He turned it on Ken Kenyek, pitiful in his utter lack of resistance, and fired. At that Orry screamed and lunged forward, and Falk turned the stunner on him. Then he turned away from the two sprawled, paralyzed figures, his hands shaking, and let Ramarren take over as he pleased. He had done his share for the time being.

Ramarren had no time to spend on compunction or anxiety. He went straight to the computers and set to work. He already knew from his examination of the onboard controls that the mathematics involved in some of the ship's operations was not the familiar Cetian-based mathematics which Terrans still used and from which Werel's mathematics, via the Colony, also derived. Some of the processes the Shing used and built into their computers were entirely alien to Cetian mathematical process and logic; and nothing else could have so firmly persuaded Ramarren that the Shing were, indeed, alien to Earth, alien to all the old League worlds, conquerors from some very distant world. He had never been quite sure that Earth's old histories and tales were correct on that point, but now he was convinced. He was, after all, essentially a mathematician.

It was just as well that he was, or certain of those processes would have stopped him cold in his effort to set up the coordinates for Werel on the Shing computers. As it was, the job took him five hours. All this time he had to keep, literally, half his mind on Ken Kenyek and Orry. It was simpler to keep Orry unconscious than to explain to him or order him about; it was absolutely vital that Ken Kenyek stay completely unconscious. Fortunately the stunner was an effective little device, and once he discovered the proper setting Falk only had to use it once more. Then he was free to coexist, as it were, while Ramarren plugged away at his computations.

Falk looked at nothing while Ramarren worked, but listened for any noise, and was conscious always of the two motionless, senseless figures sprawled out nearby. And he thought; he thought about Estrel, wondering where she was now and what she was now. Had they retrained her, razed her mind, killed her? No, they did not kill. They were afraid to kill and afraid to die, and called their fear Reverence for Life. The Shing, the Enemy, the Liars. . . . Did they in truth lie? Perhaps that was not quite the way of it; perhaps the essence of their lying was a profound, irremediable lack of understanding. They could not get into touch with men. They had used that and profited by it, making it into a great weapon, the mind-lie; but had it been worth their while, after all? Twelve centuries of lying, ever since they had first come here, exiles or pirates or empire-builders from some distant star, determined to rule over these races whose minds made no sense to them and whose flesh was to them forever sterile. Alone, isolated, deaf-mutes ruling deaf-mutes in a world of delusions. *Oh desolation. . . .*

Ramarren was done. After his five hours of driving labor, and eight seconds of work for the computer, the little iridium output slip was in his hand, ready to program into the ship's course-control.

He turned and stared foggily at Orry and Ken Kenyek. What to do with them? They had to come along, evidently. *Erase the records on the computers,* said a voice inside his mind, a familiar voice, his own—Falk's. Ramarren was dizzy with fatigue, but gradually he saw the point of this request, and obeyed. Then he could not think what to do next. And so, finally, for the first time, he gave up, made no effort to dominate, let himself fuse into . . . himself.

Falk-Ramarren got to work at once. He dragged Ken Kenyek laboriously up to ground level and across the starlit sand to the ship that trembled half-visible, opalescent in the desert night; he loaded the inert body into a contour seat, gave it an extra dose of the stunner, and then came back for Orry.

Orry began to revive partway, and managed to climb feebly into the ship himself. "Prech Ramarren," he said hoarsely, clutching at Falk-Ramarren's arm, "where are we going?"

"To Werel."

"He's coming too—Ken Kenyek?"

"Yes. He can tell Werel his tale about Earth, and you can tell yours, and I mine. . . . There's always more than one way towards the truth. Strap yourself in. That's it."

Falk-Ramarren fed the little metal strip into the course-controller. It was accepted, and he set the ship to act within three minutes. With a last glance at the desert and the stars, he shut the ports and came hurriedly, shaky with fatigue and strain, to strap himself in beside Orry and the Shing.

Lift-off was fusion-powered: the lightspeed drive would go into effect only at the outer edge of Earthspace. They took off very softly and were out of the atmosphere in a few seconds. The visual screens opened automatically, and Falk-Ramarren saw the Earth falling away, a great dusky bluish curve, bright-rimmed. Then the ship came out into the unending sunlight.

Was he leaving home, or going home?

On the screen dawn coming over the Eastern Ocean shone in a golden crescent for a moment against the dust of stars, like a jewel on a great patterning frame. Then frame and pattern shattered, the Barrier was passed, and the little ship broke free of time and took them out across the darkness.